STEVEN PILBEAM

THE HERON RING

ARGIVE GREECE 1200 BC

Image courtesy: Alexikoua. User: Panthera tigris tigris. TL User:Reedside.

HISTORICAL NOTE

Mystery shrouds the Late Bronze Age period in Greece (1600 – 1100 BC) because so little documentation and artefacts survive. There is debate about whether many figures of Greek myth lived or were based on real people. In legend, Iphigenia was the daughter of King Agamemnon, who led the Greek coalition of kingdoms in 1200 BC. In history, Iphigenia appears in literature, such as the plays of Euripides, writing hundreds of years later in the fifth century BC. In his works alone, there are two outcomes for Iphigenia. In *Iphigenia in Aulis*, Iphigenia is ordered to death by her father after he offends the goddess of the hunt, Artemis. His all-seeing seer predicts that without Iphigenia's sacrifice, his fleet would never sail to Troy. In contrast, in Euripides' play, *Iphigenia in Tauris,* she escapes. In mosaics and pottery from antiquity, Iphigenia is often portrayed during the moment of her death on the sacrificial altar and this remains her most widely depicted fate. Academics, historians and archaeologists remain divided in their views of whether Iphigenia's sacrificial death is truth or fiction.

PROLOGUE

I am Iphigenia. Daughter of King Agamemnon. Twice married to dead kings.

Promised to Achilles, greatest warrior who ever lived.

I defied the most ruthless king to set foot in history.

I betrayed my father.

The order was given to drain my blood on the sacrificial altar; the ill omen foretold the Greek fleet, bound for Troy, would fall to the bottom of the sea if I did not die. The war with Troy would be lost.

History says I died.

Men write history.

I lived.

1

Mount Oeta, Northwest Argolis
First summer of the Trojan War
1200 BC

'Stand firm, Argives, stand firm! They'll break on our bronze!'

The son of King Agamemnon thrust his blade into the deafening air, the roar behind him strangled by the grotesque thunder of ten thousand Trojans, Lydians, Phrygians and single-breasted Amazons charging the plain ahead; rolling down the fickle-forested lower peaks of Mount Oeta. The horde swept across the dun land of the mountain at alarming pace, banners eagled, horns calling, the earth convulsing beneath their feet. Hades, it seemed, had hawked the savages from the underworld in disgust when the Amazons, naked and painted, had burst from behind their allied Trojan polemarchs, impatient to begin the bloodbath. The main flank of the Trojan spearmen followed, irked to have been pre-empted, their metal bodies clanging in time like an army of bronzesmiths, leather creaking rhythmically on leather, arrows thrumming ahead in fragmentary accompaniment, the hideous piping of Amazon war cries: voiced into a swarm of sickening sound. Below, beaten to the high ground, the Argive shield wall buckled.

In the shadow of the prince, Aletes, son of no one, was holding the rapidly assembled five-deep Argive line. Men were starting to break away from the phalanx, unlocking their orbed bronze-plated shields. They were outnumbered, three to one; just time to retreat.

'Go if you can live with the shame!' Aletes yelled, his grey eyes flashing silver as he tried to maintain control of the line. If he followed Heracles, son of Zeus, and died here on the mountain, so be it.

'Great Ares, a swarm of harpies is upon us,' a warrior close to Aletes said, too loudly. He shuffled back, forcing those behind him to do the same. Panic was infecting; brave men were falling away like the grain this war was truly being fought over. The Amazons stormed nearer, feet pounding earth like hooves of stampeding centaurs; the formation threatening to disintegrate.

First Spear Melampus ploughed past Aletes, scratching a deep line in the dirt with the bronze point of his weapon, his short, bandy legs braced, swarthy face set like that of a cornered boar.

'This is as far as I go, lads. I'll die here if necessary, but I won't retreat another step.'

'Why did he have to do that?' rasped a spearman further along the phalanx.

'Because he's a sad old relic tired of living,' Aletes said with a grin that defied the fear clawing at his legs and the nausea filling his mouth with saliva. 'And I stand with him!'

Aletes stepped forward.

His friend and mentor shot him a knowing glance, and through locked teeth, growled: 'What took you so long, Ratshit?'

'I had a stone in my sandal,' Aletes said wryly, his attention fixed on the advancing thousands. He could see faces now. Hate-contorted faces. He lifted the pouch that hung around his neck and kissed it; praying the silver heron ring inside would keep him safe, and as a battle axe thumped the bronze outer of his shield, braced himself for the slaughter to begin.

2

Four Moons Earlier
Plains of Zygouris
Argive Greece

The hum of a mosquito. Then nothing. Just the gentlest susurration of breeze in the electrum-hued reeds. Aletes could feel the mosquito crawling up his arm. He was still. It would bite him. Yet that was life. What you want least will come to you when you least want it, his mother Danaea would say. He was still.

He focused his eyes; mist-grey, on the tall reeds ahead. They looked like bronze-tipped ash wood spears guarding the rim of the long-dry riverbed, he thought, not for the first time today. The sun rose high and hot now, making the air bend and hiss like snakes. Hours since one of his fellow herdsmen had knelt beside the dwindling embers of their campfire, and, wild-eyed, spoken of the black-maned lion. He had tracked it to a thicket the other side of the baron river, where he was hidden, while his companion ran to the country estate of Zygouris to inform the young master who would return with his hunting party.

The sun was throttling, but he was used to it. He was only 19 summers but toiling in the heat, and long winters of outdoor living, had weathered his oak-bark skin and a menial diet had deprived his limbs of the ripe muscle his tall build would naturally afford. The fly had found a supple part. His arm started to itch. He was still. Lions were rare in this part of Argolis. When one did stray onto these crowded pastures it was quickly killed or driven away before it could develop an expensive taste for the master's cattle, sheep, or goats. This one, a gnarled old male too slow to catch game in the mountains of Nemea, was enjoying his last meal.

What in Artemis' name? There was something—

He narrowed his eyes to focus; the heat had made them lazy. A girl. Barefoot. Stumbling down the parched throat of the river.

Aletes sprang to his feet. If the lion had not sensed her already, it would at any moment. He half-leapt, half-slid down the steep dirt of the bank into the dust and stones of the riverbed, his hound Argus, panting at his side. Too late to be still, too late to be quiet; the lion would know they were there. Keep facing the lion, he reminded himself. Stay big, don't run. Only his sling. Only the sharpened staff. He reached into the kidskin pouch on his hip and took a heavy oval stone from it, and as he pounded the earth, the narrow muscles in his thighs tearing at his skin, loaded it into his sling.

Argus dropped back and Aletes knew. A blur of snarling fury burst from the thicket. Ears flat. Yellow fangs. Black tail swiping the scabbed earth. Glottal snarls and tearing gusts of hot breath blasted from its bloodstained maw, so that for an instant Aletes stood rigid, betrayed by fear. So was the girl. Silent except for breathing in triple-time. A roar like bronze being sawn resurrected Aletes. The stone fired through the air with an accuracy honed by seasons of practice. Swift as an arrow. The lion had already punctured the girl's thigh. Too late. The stone struck the predator's eye as beast and human cried out in ugly song. A second stone. A second hit. The lion swiped furiously at air, the girl clawing the ground to get away. It spun and came at Aletes.

Aletes scrabbled in his pouch; did not see Argus hurtling forward. No. The hound rammed into the lion's flank, yet it pinned Argus down, ripped open his belly and tore out the dog's throat. Rage. Aletes sprinted over the stony ground and drove the fire-hardened point of the stave up under the beast's ribcage. The lion let out a bowel-loosening roar, and with the deeply embedded stave protruding from its flank, fled the riverbed.

Breathing hard, Aletes ran to the girl. Thank Hera, the wound was of the flesh, not below. There were two deep pyramids in her thigh. He needed to stop the blood; he ripped a piece of thin chiton from her dress and tugged it tight above the wound. Just in case. Another tight below and a thicker piece across the body of the wound. She was barely conscious, thrashing her head back and forth. She had other injuries too – her hand and wrist were misshapen and the colour of plum. Broken. He took a deep, ragged breath, looking around for any sign or sound of the lion returning, and placed both big, calloused hands on her wrist. Twist.

The girl's eyes shot open; huge near-black anthracite.

'Filthy Hillman!' she shrieked, recoiling in agony.

She lashed at him with her other hand, hitting, slapping. 'Keep your hands off me!'

'You are safe. There are no Hillmen here,' Aletes managed, silently wounded to be mistaken for a Hillman.

'Aegisthus,' she slurred.

Her eyes focused for a wingbeat and she seemed to calm.

'Aegisthus,' she repeated, her eyes rolling.

'Sleep now,' Aletes said. 'Sleep now.'

Aletes sat back, exhausted, his thigh-length tunic heavy with sweat. He went to bandage her wrist in case she awoke manically again. A silver ring on her finger stole the light and gleamed like a mocking spirit; he jolted backwards as if stung by a scorpion. What in Hera—

The symbol of the Spartan royal house. The heron. She was either a thief or the rich blood of old King Atreus flowed in her veins. He carefully peeled a rope of hair that had wrapped across her moist face, moonless midnight hair as raven as her eyes. Beneath the dirt, hers was an expensive beauty. She was Aphrodite in mortal guise; her face sculped into high bones on her cheeks, the full, firm lines of her slightly parted lips, and he could see her skin would ordinarily be honey-hued, soft, and flawless. Someone who

13

is cared for. Though ruined, her chiton was intricately embroidered with gold and red threads in geometric patterns and valuable stones, a silver band encircled the top of one arm. A serpent of mistrust was uncoiling in his belly: the ring was an ill omen. The shade of his beloved long-dead mother, Danaea, spoke.

'Do not scurry like a startled lizard my son. You know the man of whom she speaks. You must take her to him.'

'Mother, the high lord? I will be punished if I take her there. What if the spirit made me kill the lion? It was meant for the hunt and now I must be punished. The master's son is on his way here. He will think his prowess as a hunter is being questioned. A low born is not allowed the honour. It is law.'

'Look how brave you are, my son. You have fought a lion with a sling and stave. The people of Argolis will be incredulous. Have courage again. If you leave now you may reach the warden of Zygouris before his son arrives.'

Aletes ran to his earlier place of concealment. He picked up the goatskin gourd of water and worsted cloak and returned to the girl who was in a shaking, feverish sleep. He needed to clean the wounds, but it was wiser to leave here. He crouched down and lifted her; in her loose-limbed state she was heavier than she looked.

He glanced over at Argus.

'Be patient, friend. I will return with a honeycake to pay Cerberus at the gates of the Underworld. I'm told the rabbits are as big as badgers there.'

Tears fell from his grey eyes as he dragged his throat into a swallow.

'Why does the young master dislike you?' Danaea asked to distract Aletes from his torment.

Aletes gave a wry smile. 'Because I let the cattle foul in his swimming water,' he said.

'Perhaps he has cause to dislike you then, son,' Danaea said, smiling.

'It was a particularly large bull who slipped past me. I should not have been daydreaming. When I got to the pool, I found the bull chest deep in the water, long strings of mucus dangling from its mouth. Glaukos prowled the pool naked as the day he was born, and he got his henchmen to drain the sap out of me. Euthemus is a red bearded giant with broken front teeth and flat, fist fighter's nose. Alcinous is a lank haired cyclops. Their fists were heavy as war hammers and by the time Glaukos came to me, I was flat on my back.'

'I know. You expected to die that afternoon,' Danaea said. 'You came to me at the shrine. It was three days before you could stand. Three days with nothing more to sustain you than the cool, clear spring water I made sure ran pure. I held healing hands over you, my son.'

Aletes rubbed the kink in the bridge of his nose.

'You did mother, as always.'

Pausing under the shade of bowing cypress trees, Aletes carefully laid the girl on the needle-carpeted ground and sat back exhausted; what had he heard? She had called him a Hillman, one of that savage race that filled the nightmares of Argive children. A primitive tribe, they had been driven from the fertile plains of Argolis generations ago; now their menfolk slunk from their mountain hideouts on moonless nights to kill, burn and reive the Argive usurpers' cattle. Few men encountered a Hillman war band and lived.

Aletes coaxed a few drops of water past the girl's cracked lips and drank sparingly from the gourd himself, silently scolding his eyes for looking too eagerly upon her. Whatever she turned out to be, he knew with unshakable certainty that she was, even in her wretched condition; quite beautiful. Her proximity filled him with a tumult of exquisite feelings. While not handsome in the way that mature, heavily set heroes were deemed to be, Aletes had always received attention from the rustic girls. But this girl could be royal, and he should not be gaping at her with eyes stretched by stalks of barley as they followed the contours of her lightly clad, nut brown body; her once-ivory, soaked chiton, allowing his eyes to see more than he should. He forced himself to turn away; ashamed.

Too late. He saw a blur of movement as fast as a hawk catching prey, something was around his neck. Thick, suffocating, his eyes flashing gold. He was dragged backwards, kicking, trying to get a foothold in the dirt. Losing breath, head plugging with blood, sight failing him as red veins burst and he fell limp to the floor, the world darkening.

The girl. Eyes open: black as death. Her mouth hung open

in a silent scream. A sorceress after all. She was Medusa, he had looked on her too long, and she had turned him to stone.

3

Two Days Earlier
Harbour town of Aulis
Boeotia, central Greece

'Did he think I would go to the altar like an obedient deer?'

Iphigenia was pacing the chamber of her father's palace in the sea-eyeing port of Aulis. She had been summoned to marry godlike Achilles, prince of the Myrmidons in the north, yet she had stepped into a trap like easy game. The howling thunder of the storm mocked her idiocy; there was to be no wedding. Lightning was Artemis' rage: King Agamemnon had insulted the goddess of the hunt, claiming to be a better marksman than her. The king's all-seeing seer, Calchas, had warned the only way to make amends was to sacrifice his daughter. Else, his one thousand ships, crammed into the harbour and bound for Troy to invade, would never leave the coast of Aulis. Artemis was the protector of young women; Iphigenia did not believe the goddess would demand her death. This was Calchas' work.

'He knew you would come to marry Achilles. He fooled us both', Clytemnestra said to her daughter, her face obscenely shadowed.

Too easy to fool, Iphigenia cursed herself. She had always known he was king before father. Agamemnon had gulled her by reminding his youngest daughter that despite only eighteen summers old, she was already twice widowed. Were it not for Agamemnon's great friendship with Achilles' father, King Peleus, the prince would have refused her, believing it inauspicious to take so unfortunate a bride.

Her first husband, Liodes, the youngest son of King Diomedes of Argos, had been killed by a corrupted jawbone. Betrothed at seven, to cement an old political alliance, the wedding had not taken place until Iphigenia flowered during her thirteenth summer. On the day of the bedding feast, Liodes had stumbled into the great hall at Argos with the side of his pock-scarred face swollen like a pomegranate. He was very drunk, having consumed a copious amount of undiluted wine to dull the pain. He was hallucinating; the fever building inside him. Rather than following tradition and leaving the feast to bed his virgin bride, he had begged the presiding seer to drain the virulent infection.

The learned seer had cautioned against doing anything until the fever broke and swelling subsided, but the tormented groom insisted he go ahead. A plump, grain-fed dove was sacrificed to Apollo, god of healing, and with raw cries reverberating from the hall's rafters, the shaman went to work with the point of a fire-cleansed dagger. The procedure did not go well. When a third rotting tooth had been removed, and the last fragments of diseased jawbone were scraped out, Liodes had fainted due to the searing pain and loss of blood, never to regain consciousness. Four days later, he crossed into the Underworld, the infection in his jaw, spread to the rest of his body and seized his heart.

Quietly relieved, Iphigenia had remained at Argos long enough to attend lavish funeral games in honour of the dead prince—games at which his possessions, including she as his wife in ages not long past, were offered as prizes. Then, she took her leave of Liodes' grieving family, and swathed in the flowing black pharos and veil of widowhood, journeyed back to the city of Mycenae. The following spring, she was escorted to Pylos to marry King Nestor's favoured son, Neleus. Barely a full turn of the seasons after the ceremony, Neleus drowned during a storm at sea, giving rise to suspicion among Iphigenia's many suitors that the gods intended her for something other than marriage. Talk turned to her joining the Daughters of Artemis at the goddess' temple in Tauris. She had enrolled as a priestess and was looking forward to her ceremonial induction to the order when war was declared against Troy. To seal his union with the Myrmidons, Agamemnon announced his daughter's betrothal to Achilles.

The bronze doors boomed. It was the king. He had come for her. Pounding. A voice like the king's.

'The shaman and his pack of wolves are on their way!'

'Brother!' Iphigenia unbolted the chamber doors, Prince Orestes pulling at them in the statue-lined feasting hall outside to get inside as fast as he could.

'Why do you wait?' he insisted, securing the doors behind him.

A swan feather plumed bronze helmet obscured most of Prince Orestes' young, handsome face, and in the cheating light he resembled his raven-haired titan of a father. He was fully armoured in a muscle breastplate adorned with medallions of bravery and trophies from the gods to protect the Argive heir to the throne, the mounds rising from his upper arms encircled by silver armlets. He embraced his sister while leading her to the postern in the corner of the room with a strong hand on her shoulder.

Coruscating lightning lit the antechamber, the thunder was so loud it belched and rumbled like a cave filled with flatulent titans gorging on human flesh, while overhead the wind clawed at the clerestory with invisible talons, the driving hail a plague of rats scurrying across the tiled roof.

'They are coming to seize you,' Orestes continued. 'Mother, unless you want to see my sister butchered on the sacred horns, you must order her to flee at once. My charioteer, Perimedes, is waiting in the court behind the palace. Reach him along the same passage used by servants to bring food.'

Orestes pointed to the small, oak postern at the back of the chamber; the concealed opening to a narrow passageway that lay under the skin of the palace and led down and out to the sky.

'Perimedes is loyal. Listen, sister, he has vowed to serve me until his last breath. He will take you wherever we order. Ride all night. Stop for no one.'

Where, merciful Hera, and to whom? Clytemnestra silently implored her ravaged mind, seeking divine help for a destination more palatable than the one she had reluctantly decided. The gods had taken her mind's sight because she defied them now; she was sure of it. Where, in all Argolis, could she send her fugitive daughter? Think. Other than a man she had long reviled, who could be persuaded to succour Iphigenia until her ruthless father found another way to placate the angry gods and forgot, or ceased to care, he had been defied?

As the queen strode the chamber, more flickering lightning pierced the leaden heavens with the sound of rocks being crushed. It deepened the shadows lurking like faceless wraiths in corners and recesses, and transformed the flute playing nymphs in pastoral scenes upon the frescoed walls into slavering, feral-eyed spirits.

'Mother, for Zeus' sake, there is no time,' Orestes appealed.

Clytemnestra halted, clasping her hands to stop them shaking. She was about to respond, when Iphigenia did so for her, speaking with conviction neither of them felt.

'I shall go to Achilles. His camp is barely an hour from here.'

'If you can reach him,' Orestes questioned; barks and the hard slap of footsteps coming from beyond the chamber's heavy doors. 'Achilles' pavilion is close to our father's. I fear you will blunder into the shaman's clutches.'

'Then I shall ride north to Electra.'

'Our sister cannot protect you in Phocis without her husband's word. King Pylades should not be trusted.'

'Which leaves one other person,' Clytemnestra said, stealing her focus back from the gods. 'You must go to Mycenae, to the city warden, Aegisthus.'

'To Aegisthus! Lady, are you mad?' Orestes demanded.

'The warden will help us, I promise you.'

'He is the king's chief minister,' snorted Orestes. 'He curries favour in my father's presence like boarhounds beg for scraps. Apart from his smirking son, Glaukos—'

'He is the last person we should turn to,' Clytemnestra finished for him. 'Precisely why we will.'

Spears. Pounding the chamber doors. Orestes unsheathed his sword, the aptly named Cleaver of Limbs.

'The warden it is,' he said. 'If you are wrong, may the gods forgive you.'

'Trust me,' said Clytemnestra, taking a silver ring inscribed with the heron sigil of her childhood home, Sparta, from her finger and pressing it into Iphigenia's unsteady hand. 'This ring will show Aegisthus you speak for me. Tell him I have sent you to seek his protection, that I trust him to know what needs to be done. I will follow you to Mycenae.'

'Mother, these doors will not hold!' bellowed Orestes.

Iphigenia opened her mouth to speak, but a war hammer smashed through one of the door's splintered panels like a mailed fist. The hammer withdrew, and through the ragged hole it left, a pitted amber eye impaled her momentarily, blinked once, and ducked out of sight. Tightly clutching the heron ring, she turned to Orestes with proud tears in her swollen eyes.

'Do not do anything reckless,' she said, managing humour.

He answered her in the silent language of those joined by blood. He nodded and adjusted his grip on the Cleaver of Limbs. 'Go!'

A stub-fingered hand reached through the splintered wood of one door to lift its bronze latch. Orestes' blade scythed downward, severing flesh and bone at the wrist. Blood spurted from the maimed limb, and as a shriek of agony rang out, the arm jerked backwards like a decapitated snake. Iphigenia looked back at her brother by the chamber doors, and her mother, beside her at the postern, ready to conceal the entrance to buy them time.

'Go,' Clytemnestra repeated.

The doors were about to give way. Iphigenia threw the hood of her cloak over her head and slipped into the narrow, lamplit passage beyond the postern.

Orestes stepped back.

'They will not touch us. They would not dare.' Clytemnestra shouted from the rehidden entrance, hearing the clapping of Iphigenia's leather sandals on the stone as she ran down the concealed passage.

'Calchas will take any excuse to be rid of us!' Orestes hurled through the bulging door. This is your work, Calchas! You put this

24

sacrifice into the king's head!'

Calchas, preceded by his armed acolytes, stalked imperiously into the room. Gaunt and spectral in his flowing robe, Calchas' rabid gaze fell first upon Clytemnestra, standing in front of the oak postern like a resolute sentinel, and then the prince and his blade.

'Swat them both aside,' he rasped, his wizened face a rictus of fury. The heavily drugged, prayer chanting acolytes swarmed eagerly forward. Orestes responded instantly, bringing the Cleaver of Limbs through a leather helmet and the skull it was worn to protect. Blood and brain dribbled over the youthful acolyte's face, and as he died at Orestes' feet, the agile prince swivelled left and right with predatory skill, fending off a succession of spear and sword thrusts.

Bronze clanged and scraped on bronze, the cries of stricken acolytes filling the air like a frenzy of feeding gulls as a second and third enemy fell across the first, and another span away with bright arterial blood spurting from his slashed neck. It splattered Orestes' face and made the ivory hilt of his sword slippery, yet he fought like a demented titan until groaning, writhing acolytes littered the floor like apples in a harvest-ready orchard. For every acolyte who fell, it seemed as if two more replaced him. Breathless, drenched in sweat and leaden-limbed, Orestes retreated until his back was pressed against the oak postern. There, snarling oaths of defiance, he slowly fell beneath an onslaught of hacking, stabbing blades.

'Mother pay the ferryman for me,' Orestes cried out. Pinned

to a nearby wall, a spearpoint pricking the soft skin of her throat, Clytemnestra turned her head toward her stricken son. To honour him by watching his last moments with unflinching eyes.

4

The Lair of the River God

The outpost at Megara was one of many strongholds that guarded and maintained the Argives' extensive network of highways. These were arteries through the body of Argive Greece, the sea-kings finding strength by linking their sword hands and combining as one giant, patient, power. Its heart drummed in Agamemnon's city of gold, Mycenae. He was king of kings in a coalition stretching up to Thessaly in the north where his impetuous champion Achilles was steadied by his father King Peleus, down through the mountains of Phocis, where Agamemnon had united his eldest daughter Electra in marriage with King Pylades. In the south-west stood Agamemnon's brother King Menelaus of mighty Sparta, with the ancient warrior lords of Argos and Tiryns to the east, and the sophisticated force of the city of Knossos on the southern isle of Crete.

Approaching the outpost, Iphigenia was curled into the concave hollow of the four-horsed chariot. Her cloaked arms were wrapped around the trunk-rooted legs of her brother's charioteer, Perimedes, her body vibrating as they shuddered along. She had slept only for wretched moments as they rode, rattling south from Aulis through the sharp spring night. Now, as dawn painted a grey and lemon sky, Perimedes swung off the gravel road into the fort at Megara. The garrison stationed there provided shelter, sustenance and fresh horses to the chariot-borne couriers who routinely traversed the empire. Thirsty merchants, pilgrims and peasant farmers were welcomed, travelling to and from the bustling markets in the city of Corinth, buying and selling their oil, textiles, gold, silver, electrum, carved ivories, or wheat, barley, lentils, olives, and wine. A convenient median stop on the journey from Athens to Sparta.

They entered the fortification through the unguarded open gateway, slowing now they were off the main road from Aulis. Orchards, vineyards, gardens, embroidered the landscape as the chariot shuddered up to the turf-roofed blocks enclosing three sides of the courtyard.

Perimedes had not reached his position as the prince's charioteer by missing that the yawning gates were unmanned. His military gut was aware. The more forceful occupant of his stomach, however, urged him on. Hunger.

Iphigenia felt a chaos of emotion. She had been so sure Calchas was plotting against them with his prophesy that the goddess Artemis demanded her death. What if she was wrong? Artemis could hunt them down, draw her marked arrow. Iphigenia had betrayed her father. The king. The people. The men on the boats. Though the storm had ceased wherever they were now—a night's ride from Aulis—who was to know if it had claimed her father's warships in the harbour? How many good men had fallen to Poseidon's palace at the bottom of the sea for her defiance? How many more would die when Troy inevitably invaded, seizing the upper hand? How many would starve without the grain and reopened trade routes this war promised? All for her ego. Or was it her fear? She had felt fury for her father at first, but if the omen was true, he was acting as a king, where she had failed as the daughter of one.

'Why are we slowing?' she asked, using Perimedes' leg to draw herself up to stand. 'Have we reached Mycenae? We must keep going. I gave my word we would not stop.'

'I agree, Iphigenia,' Perimedes responded respectfully, a reassuring smile lightening his youthful face. 'But the horses are exhausted and a short halt to change them and reenergise with bread and cheese won't endanger us. If the shaman's dogs are still giving chase, which I doubt, they'll be far behind, these are the swiftest horses in the...'

He tailed off. 'Wings of Icarus!'

The body of the garrison's polemarch hung by his ankles on the porch of the barrack block. Naked and mutilated, Perimedes saw it in one blink of his eyes before the second disfigured corpse lying beside the well in the middle of the compound.

'Ass,' he admonished himself. 'You rode into a trap.'

Heaving. Perimedes' whole, huge mass behind the reins, trying to swing the four tired horses around the well.

'Hold on!' he shouted like the sounding of a horn.

Iphigenia gripped the drawbar of the chariot with one arm, the other on the side of the vehicle's guard to spread her weight, breathing like a wild dog. A filthy one-eyed Hillman in a wolf headdress charged from a ransacked storeroom and leapt on the drawbar. His rancid breath through black teeth made her jerk away as fast as the ibex thigh bone club he was about to bring down on her skull. Perimedes' dagger was in the Hillman's good eye before Iphigenia breathed again, the blinded savage devoured by the wheels of the chariot.

'Keep down! Pray we outrun these godless vultures!'

Arrows. Thumping the frame of the chariot, others cracking bone as they stuck in the horses' shoulders, thuds as they hit the hollows and punctured their organs. Panic and Perimedes' whip driving them on. Swarming like hornets from a disturbed nest, whooping Hillmen sprang from hiding to converge on the chariot or race ahead to help close the serrated perimeter gates.

'Get down!' Perimedes demanded this time, nodding his head to the hollow at the front of the chariot. He slashed left and right with his dagger, and Iphigenia scrabbled at her belt where she had stored the jewelled dagger he had given her. She could not get to it, the force of the carriage too strong. More arrows hit the chariot, two of the four horses were lung-impaled but galloped on, bloody froth flying from their muzzles, trampling cursing Hillmen as they plunged through the fast-narrowing aperture between the gates.

Back on the clear road, Iphigenia watched the outpost recede into the distance with the dagger clasped in her hands like a prayer.

'Hera be thanked,' she muttered, setting the dagger on the floor of the chariot and rising to her knees as she gripped the bar. 'Oh, merciful Fates, no!'

Perimedes was already falling backwards. The shaft of an arrow protruded from his chest, buried almost as deep as its crow feather fletching.

'The bridge,' choking on arterial blood erupting from his throat. 'Too fast.' The reins slipped through his fingers. Iphigenia grabbed at him with her free arm, trying to pull him in. 'No', he pushed her hand away, falling like a pillar, out of the open back of the chariot, onto the road.

No. The bridge ahead. A stone and timber structure that spanned a deep ravine and the storm-swollen river that swirled beneath. It grew to fill her vision like a clenched fist, and when the moment of impact came, she was flung across the necks of the whinnying horses, plunging over the wooden parapet of the bridge. She hit the water stunningly hard. The river god seized her. It was Alpheus, still so in love with Artemis, avenging Iphigenia's wrongdoing to the goddess, she was certain of it in her panic. He dragged her down into his icy, murky domain, sweeping her along with careless brutality, keeping her submerged until every part of her screamed for air and light. Iphigenia passed out for an instant and an age — she had no idea which — until awareness returned in a moment of breathless hysteria, and as foaming water invaded her lungs, she was carried upward by the current and hurled against jagged hardness.

Rocks.

The rocks were close to the torrent's edge and, miraculously, stood in weed-clogged water no deeper than her waist. Retching violently, searing pain in her arm and wrist, she hauled herself up the overgrown riverbank into a deep crevice amongst a pile of moss-covered rocks. Trembling with shock, her laboured breathing shallow in her throat, she huddled there until fear of something more terrible than an angry river god gave her new strength.

'I saw her, Drago, not a stone's throw from here.'

'You're talking dogpuke, Naxos. You've been chewing the magic bark again.'

Footsteps rustled in the undergrowth. The voice again.

'I doubt a strong young buck, much less a bone bag of a girl, could survive in there.'

'I saw her, I tell you. Stop moaning and help me find her.'

A fearsome, hirsute creature loomed over the crevice, muttering curses as he probed the knotted undergrowth with the head of a stone axe. He was hunchbacked and blade-thin, the smell of him a stench of unwashed flesh and poorly cured animal skins. Overpoweringly foul. He parted a screen of coarse grass and reached into the crevice, lips peeling across black stumps that were once teeth, as his dirt encrusted fingers curled around Iphigenia's ankle.

5

Waking

Zygouris, Argolis

'Filthy Hillman, keep your hands off me!' Iphigenia cried out.

She swiped her unhurt arm with unexpected force, sending the shaven-headed novice priestess who had been wiping her face with a cool sponge, stumbling backwards to avoid the blows. An expensive, boldly pigmented earthenware bowl shattered as the novice priestess flew back, echoing the waking recognition of the loud throbbing in Iphigenia's thigh and wrist. Wounds that writhed and cried like monstrous living creatures.

'Where is this place?' The words cracked as she woke. Tongue sitting like a toad in her mouth, the organ bloated from dehydration.

'The demesne of Zygouris,' Elissa replied, gathering shards of broken bowl. 'Forgive me Iphigenia of Mycenae. If my clumsiness has added to your discomfort, I will carry out a penance. I will empty the holy mother's stinking chamber pot every morning before prayers—'

The Fates had placed Iphigenia in the hands of a highly skilled healer. Semele, the holy mother, had drawn upon her considerable lore of herbaceous remedies to treat Iphigenia's injuries. An application of salve from crushed roots to each of the deep lacerations had ensured that while they were badly inflamed, the tell-tale odour of the rotting sickness was not present. The holy mother had rebandaged Iphigenia's broken wrist, satisfying herself the herdsman had correctly realigned the bones.

'How did I get here?' Iphigenia asked, interrupting Elissa's well-versed grovelling.

'You were brought here yesterday by the young master.'

She hesitated. Iphigenia's intense eyes bid her continue.

'It was not the young master who saved you from the lion. That was Aletes. My brother, Kleonike, told me. He said it was the fiercest beast to wander out of the hills of Nemea since the days of old King Atreus, and but for Aletes' bravery you would not be alive. Do you not remember?'

'Aletes?' Iphigenia repeated slowly.

Without waiting for invitation, her plump cheeks flushed, Elissa settled her equally generous buttocks upon the soft sheepskins on the bed. Glancing towards the closed door, she listened to ensure they were not about to be interrupted.

'Aletes is a herdsman on the estate…the lion stood as tall

as my shoulder, with eyes of smoky amber and teeth the size of my thumb…'

Elissa held her thumb aloft. It blurred as Iphigenia's eyes rolled, her head drumming. Frenzies of heat shook her as she shivered from cold.

'…Glaukos is punishing Aletes by forcing him to run against the hounds. He says he must take the place of the lion as the hunt is now ruined—'

'Glaukos?'

'Yes, you are at the Lord Aegisthus' country estate. His son Glaukos—'

'The estate of Lord Aegisthus?'

'Yes Iphigenia, yet the warden is away on official services in the city. If he were here this would nev—'

Too slow. Iphigenia cursed silently, her fever intensifying her irritation with the novice priestess. Faster. She needed to explain faster. An injustice would happen if she did not stop it.

'Where is this lion slayer?'

'Iphigenia, please. Lay back down. Have some lemon and honey. Here—'

'Where are they?' Iphigenia spoke now with the power of Agamemnon.

'The courtyard—but you'll never get past the holy mother.'

Iphigenia left the chamber wearing Elissa's linen robe. The novice priestess had been ordered to take her place in the bed. Sweat fingered down Iphigenia's forehead and temples like hot oil.

The oakwood door from the bed chamber opened onto a narrow, pillared, ornamental balcony overlooking the shadow-shrouded rectangular central hall of the villa. A shallow crackling circular hearth and the brilliant oranges, reds and golds of the colossal lions, warriors, and gods in the walled frescoes, were the only occupants of the main space of the house. Four rotund wooden columns sheathed in gold and bronze surrounded the hearth, worshipping up to the high opening leading out to the sky and only source of light. Iphigenia saw another chamber door along the walkway, and at each end, steep steps down to the hall.

Upon the vibrantly tiled floor, painted in broad sweeping lines of ebony, saffron and azure, a youthful likeness of the lord of the manor in full armour hunting wild boar from the back of a chariot alongside the goddess Artemis. As Iphigenia tried to focus her eyes, the goddess pounced from the fresco, drawing her silver bow. Iphigenia fell back into the shadows, breathing hard.

Just as she concealed herself, the holy mother appeared at the far side of the hall. Iphigenia limped through the second door into what, judging by the wall hangings and odour of cleaning oil and leather, was the bedchamber belonging to the master of the house. There, she waited with the door slightly open, holding her heavy breath as the holy mother shuffled by, muttering the words: 'Terrible, terrible business. Are the gods all asleep?' Moments later, her voice rang out like the braying of a war horn as she remonstrated with the unfortunate novice priestess. Iphigenia struggled to the bottom of the stairs, unbalanced, with warm blood seeping from her thigh. Outside, blunt shouts and frenzied barking, urged her on.

Iphigenia blinked against the brightness of the sunlight. The courtyard was forty paces long and bordered on three sides by busy storerooms, stables, and workshops. At its far end stood the fortified stone entrance gates to the villa in the outer wall of the estate. In the median between the gates and where Iphigenia stood, was a large well.

'Come on,' she muttered to herself. 'Focus.'

Her eyes were blurring now, her vision swirling like coloured marble. That must be him? The boy who killed the lion. More a man than a boy. He was kneeling in front of the well, wrists and ankles lashed together behind his back. Stripped to his loincloth and leather sandals, his torso, lithely sculpted with muscle, had been smeared with the lion's congealed blood and fat. A crude wooden sign hung around his neck, scrawled with a single word: sorcerer. A large crowd of house slaves, field slaves, and freedmen had been ordered to assemble in front of the villa's imposing portico entrance where two towering stone columns in vivid red pigment stood guard.

Glaukos, the young master of Zygouris, kept watch over his captive in the courtyard. Two summers older than Aletes, he was a head shorter. A head that sat neckless and large on an overdeveloped upper body. Hours on the training field rather than the battlefield: running in full armour in the highest sun, launching

38

spears, lifting stones, had crafted rampart shoulders and arms fortified with stone boulders rising from his upper arms. He had always quietly held Achilles' physique as a vision to emulate, yet he could not replicate his symmetry. Glaukos' left hand was gloved. Knuckles broken. Bones bent. Only the two fingers by his thumb retained dexterity, but it was not his sword hand. From the same chariot fall, a scar now pulled upwards on his left eye and dissected his eyebrow, forming a constant expression of surprise ironic on a man more familiar with cynicism than amazement.

An uneasy muttering went among the mouths of the watchers. The stench of putrefying offal had driven the pack of hunting dogs into a baying, snarling frenzy. Yellow eyes bulged. Spittle-jaws. Straining on leashes. It took all the strength of one-eyed Alcinous, among the men in Glaukos' circle of trust, and the smaller handlers, to keep the pack under control. Alcinous had let his dogs reach Aletes. Iphigenia could see the ripped, blood-wet skin on Aletes' arm and elbow where the dogs had sunk their teeth.

Grunts and gusts of steadying breath were all Aletes would allow to leave his mouth. Defiance. His eyes dug at the ground, jaw set, fists gripped against the pain. A performance that incensed Glaukos. The maddened boarhounds surged forward again, ridges of powerful muscle bunching and rippling beneath their short brindle coats. They hit the defenceless herdsman with a force that knocked him flat. His cheekbone cracked as it made impact with the stone slabs of the courtyard.

'In the name of my father, King Agamemnon, halt these

hounds!' Iphigenia demanded, her head swimming, hot bile coating the back of her throat. 'This unjust punishment is an affront to the gods. Release this boy from his bindings.'

The daughter of King Agamemnon? Aletes' eyes rose at last, staring incredulously at the girl.

What was this? Glaukos almost laughed. He took his time before ordering the dogs back and walked towards his cousin, Iphigenia, at his leisure. Close, less than a finger away, he sniffed.

'You don't look very *well*.' He sniffed again. 'This is *my* estate. This manhunt is going ahead. That worm has broken the law and will be punished for it.'

'Your *father's* estate,' Iphigenia corrected.

Glaukos snorted air from his nose and looked into her eyes. Same arrogant black spheres as her father. Irrationally, he almost struck her, his face twitching as it often did when he tried to control his temper. He had not seen Iphigenia in the last year and the talk was true. She had something of the beauty of her aunt, that whore Helen of Troy. Darker looks of course, the same abundant black curls as that dog of a father. Like Agamemnon, she was rash and rude. He turned, saying nothing, moving back towards Aletes.

'He saved my life,' Iphigenia said, trying to appeal to Glaukos.

He turned back. Irritated. 'He broke the law. As I am sure you are aware, only high-born men have the honour of hunting lion.'

'The lion attacked me! I would not be alive without him.'

'You got in the way, that changes nothing. He ruined my

hunt, tried to ridicule me, and furthermore there is evidence he used sorcery to make the kill. I have every right to punish him.'

'Under the authority—'

'The authority of who?' Glaukos cut her off. 'You hold no authority here. And why exactly are you here? Wandering Zygouris alone? Look at the state of you. Shouldn't you be at Aulis, warming the bed of your new husband, Achilles?'

'Release the boy or I will say nothing.'

'Alcinous, set the hounds on him. Let us see if fresh blood loosens her tongue.'

'Hold!' Iphigenia's eyes were filling with darkness. Head orbiting. Nausea rising to her throat. She cursed a world that forced her to walk into battle without a blade. A woman was a swordless, wordless warrior with tied hands. She blamed herself for not being shrewd enough to learn to handle a sword. For without a sword no one heard you and you were no one.

'Young master, let me take the king's daughter,' the holy mother said, stepping across the courtyard, face lined with concern.

'Why not find the ignoramus who's supposed to be looking after her? After she's flogged she might be more vigilant.'

'No doubt she would. Yet as you know, it's not your place to mete out punishment to the daughters of this or any holy order. Your authority is confined to earthly matters. This is of little comfort to the blameless herdsman you are punishing.'

'Zeus will shortly be the judge of that.'

'Agamemnon will be the judge of you if his daughter comes to harm here. Let me return Iphigenia to her chamber.'

The holy mother was holding Iphigenia up now. Aletes' fellow herdsman Kleonike hurried across to take the load of the princess, who was fast passing into a fevered sleep. A bronzesmith eased the holy mother's arm away so he could take the other side.

'Take her,' Glaukos said, dismissively.

He squinted up at the cloudless sky with his uneven eyes to check the position of the sun.

'Alcinous, get the insect on his feet. If we delay, we'll need torches to end the manhunt.'

Alcinous drew his dagger from his belt. He forced Aletes onto his face, his booted foot between the herdsman's shoulders, half-suffocating him on the stone as he cut the ropes binding his wrists and ankles, slashing his forearm as he did.

'Careful, I want him to make a chase of it.'

Alcinous sheathed his dagger. He hauled the mute herdsman to his feet. For a wingbeat Aletes stood with his head bowed, his thick oak hair falling over skin like a dropped pear: cut and misshapen, circular shadows of red and violet ruptures around his right eye and cheek. His wrists stung as sorely as when he fell in the stable as a boy, the hand that broke his fall cracking into a hornets' nest. The dog bites on his shoulder and arms felt as if they were rising and bubbling like lava. He clenched his jaw, asking Apollo to take his pain and whispered again to his mother. He met Glaukos in the eye. Fury. It was the reaction Glaukos wanted to see.

'Well, insect, are you ready to answer to the gods?'

Glaukos wanted all in the courtyard to hear. He pointed to the dazzling sun, fast approaching its zenith.

'You have until golden Helios journeys the width of my palm, then I release the hounds. If, as decreed, you reach where the road to Tegea meets the road from Mycenae, you will be adjudged innocent of the crime of sorcery. If, on the other hand, you fail to get that far or fail to provide me with good sport, these short-tailed bitches will tear you apart. Do you understand?'

Glaukos waited for Aletes to respond. He was a gambler who had made a winning throw in a game of flip the marked stones. The place he had chosen to end the hunt was devoid of trees or high rocks. In the unlikely event of Aletes getting that far there was nothing for him to climb to escape the scent-crazed dogs. He was already condemned. Glaukos was enjoying the sport, despite his victim's refusal to prostrate himself and beg for mercy.

'Do you comprehend what I have said?' he repeated.

Aletes turned and drove his knee into Alcinous' crotch beside him. Alcinous' legs buckled, and as he crumpled in a heap with an agonised grunt, Aletes' bolder friends in the crowd cried encouragement.

'The next man who speaks will run with the insect', Glaukos spat. He turned back to Alcinous with his gloved hand raised to stop the retching henchman drawing his dagger for a second time.

'No, Alcinous, we will allow him this small gesture of

defiance. It will be his last in this world after all. Have my hunting chariot brought from the stables. Game this spirited—

'Riders approaching, Lord… your father… and a sizeable escort of palace guards.'

'The king?'

The warning had come from the lookout in the watchtower above the main gate. Glaukos set off in that direction, cursing his lack of foresight. The now animated group of freedmen and slaves followed a safe distance behind him. He had not expected to see his father until the following morning, until after the royal judges finished sitting and his old score with Aletes was settled. He had sent word to Lord Aegisthus at the Palace of Mycenae to inform him after discovering Iphigenia on the plain.

'The Argive queen. It's the queen's escort,' the lookout clarified.

The queen? It had not occurred to him Clytemnestra might be in Mycenae with his father. Why was she not still in Aulis, where the Argive host is mustered, with her daughter's new husband, the strutting Myrmidon peacock, Achilles? It was clear the old nag had nibbled his father's ear until he left as rapidly as possible. They must have set out as soon as his man Euthemus arrived with news of Iphigenia.

Glaukos climbed the wooden steps to the perimeter wall's narrow parapet and assessed the view over the fertile land cloaked by dusty mountainous terrain. A long column of royal guards marched along the rutted track that led to Zygouris, a sand-like plume of dust rising into the unblemished azure behind them. Bronze bossed shields and spear points glittered in the sun like nuggets of gold, the distinctive black plume on each guard's helmet mimicked the mane of the galloping horses. His father's chariot trundled behind that of Clytemnestra; between him and the phalanx of guards, rode red-haired Euthemus.

Cursing, Glaukos cuffed aside the lookout and descended from the narrow parapet two steps at a time.

'Alcinous, get him out of sight.'

He aimed a frustrated kick at the hissing gander that refused to move out of his path.

'You two, flay the hide off that pile of carrion and lay it out in the hall for the master to inspect. You, Codros, return to your kitchen and prepare a feast to celebrate the rescue of the king's daughter. Spit roast a hog and bring a portion of its liver and a twist of hair to me in the shrine.'

The family shrine was a modest, wooden pillared temple standing next to the columned entrance of the villa. With a roof of tiles, the structure housed a simple stone altar upon which libations were poured or offerings burned to honour the gods. Saffron incense sweetened the cool air inside. Glaukos hoped the sight of him at prayer, entreating the goddess Demeter to restore Iphigenia to full vigour, would soften his father's inevitable criticism of his decision to punish the herdsman. The prospect of being rebuked in the presence of the haughty queen, Clytemnestra, curdled the juices in his stomach. He considered mounting his chariot, heading for the taverns and brothels of Mycenae, yet he knew avoiding his father for a few days would only exacerbate the situation. He would face the old goat, accept whatever penalty he bleated.

Now he spoke to Zeus. All powerful, father of the gods. Before the shades of his illustrious ancestors, he vowed Aletes would go to the crows. By Zeus, who was he to ridicule a lord? A cousin of King Agamemnon no less. A herdsman. It was laughable. He remembered training with his first bronze. How his father, without sword or shield, had ordered him to thrust for his heart. Glaukos, only ten summers old, hesitated. His father, fast and strong then, kicked the blade from his son's hand, kicked again at his chest. On the floor, bloodied back of his head, his father made clear his lesson. Men take advantage of weakness. Hesitate and they will strike.

A fly tried to enter his ear. He jolted, flapped it away. But it came again. He could not see it, but it was there. Forcing him to consider an argument. Balanced Zeus. Weighing truths on his golden scales. A question. Did he enjoy tormenting the herdsman too much to be rid of him?

6

Harbour of Aulis
The same morning

The water was cold, icy cold, and with an angry grunt Agamemnon awoke and sat bolt upright. He blinked water out of his bloodshot eyes and swore at Menelaus, the warlord who had doused him. The only one who could get away with it. His brother. King of Sparta. Ugly memories crowded back into Agamemnon's mind. The lightning. The thunder. The haunting echo of the shaman's voice.

'Your daughter must die, spawn of Atreus. In all my seasons with the gift of vision I have never seen a clearer set of portents. Her life must be offered up tonight on the sacred horns of Zeus, or your heroes will be vanquished in this ill-omened war.'

'It is the only way to appease them, Calchas? My precious daughter, Iphigenia? Before the shades of my ancestors I will not consent to this.'

'Then you are doomed, Agamemnon, you and all who sail with you. Poseidon will scatter this mighty fleet far and wide across the ocean. Many thousands of heroes will perish, and when the remnants of the Argive host finally muster for battle, the horse lords of Troy will hurl them back into the sea.'

'Because I skewered a flea-bitten deer?'

'Because you are an insolent heretic and believe you stand above the laws of the gods. You were warned the ground you trod was sacred, yet instead of abandoning the hunt and offering proper recompense, you insulted the goddess Artemis. You claimed to be the better marksman and said she was vexed because of it.'

'I spoke in jest. I had drunk a deal of wine and forgot myself. I did not mean to give offence.'

'Yet offence was given and now you must make amends. Give up your daughter, or the storm will continue to rage. One by one your faint-hearted warlords will desert you, and alone you will stand before this long night ends, and a cheerless dawn casts light on this scene of desolation.'

'Ye gods, what have I done?' Agamemnon said, almost weeping as he returned to the present. His dripping face was drained of colour against the potent black of his wet hair, dusted by time only at the temples. He was confused, badly hungover; the result of drinking himself into a guilt-numbing stupor the previous evening.

'What choice did I have, brother? The wind was howling, battering our ships into firewood. If I had not agreed to the seer's

48

demand—'

He paused, tipping an ear to the roof of the pavilion perched in the dunes on the higher ground of the sea-facing port of Aulis, which watched like a falcon over the ships on the beach. The harbour lay in the heart of Argive lands, a launch point to a strategic finger of water pointing towards the open Aegean Sea and, over the waves: Troy. The harbour held fifty huge sails; the rest of the Greek fleet so large it crawled like a thousand-legged millipede along the Attica coast. Menelaus' Sparta matched his elder brother's fifty galleys, the sea-lords of thirty Greek city states in all sending ships: Corinth, Boeotia, Attica from the centre, Achilles' Myrmidon cruisers sailing from Pharsalos in the north; their golden sea nymphs on their sterns. Gathered to move in unison across the sea to rout out those horse-loving cowards hiding behind their titan walls at Troy.

'Apollo's bow, it has stopped raining. Does this mean he took my precious daughter's life?'

'It does not,' said Menelaus, firmly. He was shorter, stockier, less hirsute, and fairer than his elder brother, with a fire of flame hair. 'Your daughter escaped during the night.'

'Escaped?' Agamemnon's eyes were like black blood.

'The shaman was adamant—'

'The shaman was…' Menelaus searched for the word.

'*Mistaken*,' he went on. 'No royal blood was spilt, yet the tempest blew itself out. Long into the night the storm tormented the ships in the harbour, shrieking like a flock of ravenous harpies.

Shortly before dawn, the wind vanished and the waves on the ocean became ripples on a pond.'

Menelaus cleared his throat and looked around as if for support before continuing. 'There is worse to tell you, brother, and you must gird yourself. I fear your son, Orestes, has been severely wounded.'

'Orestes, wounded?'

'Speared more times than a cornered boar. He rode to the palace to warn his sister. The seer invaded with his pack of rabid jackals. Orestes refused to let them pass. He lives, brother.'

'They attacked the heir to the throne?' Agamemnon rose to his feet like an enraged bear. He clubbed the empty water jug from Menelaus' hands.

'Calchas, you treacherous maggot, I'll pluck out your eyes!' he roared furiously, and with powerful muscles bunching, tendons braced like hawsers beneath dusky leather skin, he hoisted the heavy couch he had been sleeping upon above his head and cast it across the pavilion with the strength of Heracles. The couch narrowly missed an ivory statue of Zeus seated on a cedarwood throne, adorned with ebony, gold, and gemstones. It landed instead on the shins of an unfortunate scribe, snapping them, and scattering the cluster of watching warlords standing beside. A low table stoned through the air as if from a siege catapult, raining breads, cheeses, olives, grapes, figs, plums, and berries onto the trampled shingle ground a short pace from the pavilion's crowded entrance. Everyone but Menelaus jolted back out of reach, for

50

Menelaus had never lived in awe of his brother's legendary rages. Agamemnon cast about for something, or someone, to break.

'Find him for me, Menelaus,' he demanded. 'Arrest the ranting zealot and drag him here on his knees!'

'He is outside, brother. I anticipated you would want a word.'

Menelaus gave a prearranged signal to the sentries at the larger of the two entrances to the pavilion. A servant from the smaller one at the rear was disappearing to replace the spoiled food now decorating the floor, aware the king required a constant accompaniment of delicacies whatever mood he was in. The sentries ducked under the hide-draped main entrance, and after a brief commotion during which Agamemnon hollered at the nearest attendant demanding to know where his food had disappeared, the sentries returned carrying a pole from which the seer hung suspended like the carcass of a skinned goat. Naked and savagely beaten, Calchas looked as if he had been dragged behind a chariot all the way from the palace at Aulis. His wizened body was a bloody patchwork of livid cuts and violet bruises, yet despite his many injuries, his spirit had not been broken. As he writhed and twisted beneath the stout pole, he spat a stream of virulent threats and curses.

'Put him at my feet,' Agamemnon growled.

With deliberate brutality the guards dropped one end of the pole, landing Calchas awkwardly on the nape of his neck. The impact stunned him, but he reared up onto bony knees. With amber eyes blazing, he shook his tightly bound hands.

51

'Call off these whore-suckled churls! I am the high priest of the temple. How dare they abuse me. Remove these bonds, or I will curse every spineless cur here!'

Unmoved, Agamemnon's pitiless black eyes bored into Calchas like a hunting raptor.

'Silence his bleating,' he said tersely.

In response, one of the guards drove a hobnailed sandal into Calchas' battered face. The dazed shaman rocked back on his heels, his bottom lip dangling like a cockerel's wattle. Instead of curling into a protective ball, he suddenly lunged forward like a wild dog, sinking his exposed teeth into the prominent ridge of muscle above his assailant's knee. Crying out in half-humiliation, half-pain, and helped by the other guard, Agamemnon's man set about beating Calchas senseless, only halting when the impatient king intervened.

'That will do. I don't want him crossing the River Styx just yet. Too swift an end would be more merciful than he deserves.'

Darkness. A shadow swallowed the pavilion. Day turned to night. The two guards stepped back. More dead than alive, a gleeful Calchas forced himself upright, jerked back his head and spat a glob of bloody phlegm onto the strips of studded leather protecting the groin of one of his tormentors. It was an act of defiance that made Agamemnon cock an eyebrow in amused disbelief.

'A sign! A sign of Zeus' displeasure!' Calchas exclaimed.

All except Agamemnon turned to stone.

'He is incensed!' Calchas cackled on. 'Unless you release me at once he will hurl down a thunderbolt and burn this pigsty to a crisp. Release me! Remove these bonds and prostrate yoursel—

His voice cracked as the sun reappeared in a blaze of dazzling golden splendour.

'Just a cloud,' said Agamemnon, relief rising from the throats of those around him. All but Calchas. The seer shrunk back like a leper hiding in the shadows.

'You are a fool, Atreides. An arrogant, blaspheming fool. Zeus will exact a terrible price for inflicting these injuries upon me. He will stain the shores of Asia red with Argive blood. The slaughter will go on. Season after season. Before you return home, defeated, there will be more widows in Argolis than cattle in the royal herds.'

'Blind and castrate him,' Agamemnon responded, dismissively.

'No! Hold! You cannot do this. I need my own purified seed to conduct the ritual of the earth mother's rebirth.'

'You have conducted your last ritual.'

'Please, I beg you, heed me a moment!'

'I am done heeding you, Calchas. For two days I have sat in this infernal mire while the tempest raged, and you probed the entrails of every grain fed beast brought before you. Oh, I have listened. Like a fool I heeded your vengeful council. Though it cost me a treasure more precious than I can describe.'

Sorrow like Daedalus felt watching his son Icarus fall to his death from the sky, wax wings melted by the sun, fell upon

Agamemnon's face with its labyrinth of lines and battle-earned scars. There for only a breath, it was just Menelaus who caught sight of it. Agamemnon's expression hardening, he spoke again to the impassive guards.

'You heard the order. Blind and castrate him. Boil the rest alive. I want all trace of his existence erased from this camp.'

'Have mercy!' shrieked Calchas, and now at last there was terror in his scratching voice. He tried to throw himself at Agamemnon's feet, but one of the guards pinned him on his back while the other sawed off his penis, scrotum, and testicles. Calchas writhed and screamed like a pig, and with bright blood pumping from the gaping wound, slumped unconscious. He was thus spared more excruciating pain when his eyeballs were gouged out by a spatulate thumb and permanent darkness engulfed his world.

'By the stars, my throat is as dry as an old hag's crotch,' Agamemnon said, sniffing. 'What does a king have to do to get some wine?'

Agamemnon had already dismissed the mutilated seer from his mind. He gulped mouthfuls of wine from the twin handled gold cup passed to him by an attendant. He drained the cup, belched appreciatively, and holding it out to be refilled, ordered two other attendants—his appointed dressers—to fetch him a clean tunic and his panoply of armour.

'I have an army to command,' he said.

His great girth was being strapped into a cuirass of finely wrought bronze when a swarthy, furtive warlord from the distant

54

Isle of Ithaca stepped forward.

'Great Lion, might I have a word. I have devised a ruse to get us inside the ramparts of Troy. It involves dismantling a few ships and building a large wooden horse. I have discussed the idea with Menelaus, Nestor of Pylos, and other learned members of your council. We are convinced it will work.'

'A wooden horse, Odysseus?'

'Yes, sire, a horse on wheels with room inside its hollow belly to hide a handpicked war band. When the Trojans find it in our abandoned camp they will assume we have sailed home and left it to honour their victorious gods. They will not resist hauling it into the city.'

'What if they decide to burn it?' asked Agamemnon, doubting the Ithacan's sanity. 'No, don't bother answering that. I have neither the time nor inclination to listen to more of this implausible fantasy.'

Menelaus smiled inwardly at the barb of derision in his brother's voice. It told him Agamemnon's self-confidence had returned in full measure. The irascible titan before him was the same warlord who had held together a fractious alliance of Argive kingdoms for forty summers. So, we will fight and win this ill-fated war, Menelaus assured himself, doubts taking flight as he watched Calchas dragged from the pavilion by his calloused feet. His empty eye sockets were oozing wine-red mucus, and the mushroom cap of his shrivelled penis protruded from his toothless, blood-brimmed mouth.

'When do we sail, son of Atreus?' asked Diomedes of Argos; a square-jawed chieftain with shoulders as broad as a stable door and a chest as deep as the rump of an ox.

'The next tide,' said Agamemnon, brusquely. 'Assuming enough of our hulls have survived the storm, and my faint-hearted host is still camped on the plain outside.'

'They are, lord of men,' said Diomedes, visibly stung by the note of scorn in the king's voice for his own army. 'None who threatened to desert have done so. Now that Helios has ridden forth to warm their backs, they are eager to depart these shores.'

'I am relieved to hear it. And you, Ajax of the Hammer, how bright burns your ardour? Are you ready to crush Trojan skulls with that great mallet of yours, to raze their halls and enslave their women and children?'

Ajax grinned at the prospect and kissed the smooth bronze head of his war hammer.

'I am, king. When we set foot on Trojan soil my loyal hammer will be guarding your left flank.'

'And my Spartans to your right,' said Menelaus, confidently.

Menelaus was relieved to have his brother back to his senses. The King of Sparta had been prowling the pavilion like a caged panther. His wife Helen had been gone a long time now; the Trojan prince who abducted her too long left breathing. He would slit Paris' throat slowly, cut off his head and feed it in pieces to Helen as she returned as his queen.

One by one, Agamemnon addressed members of his war

council, issuing fresh orders and occasional rebukes, offering words of encouragement and advice, or sharing a ribald joke. It was a vintage performance from the now single-minded Argive king, a born leader of men who had, for the time being, put aside the apparent crushing burden of his grief. Dressed at last in full armour, he stood splay-legged and imperious. His bronze breastplate caged his barrel chest, a gift from King Cinyras of Cyprus. A slippery eel of a king, Agamemnon had decided long ago. Yet he would take the magnificent armour. The bronze breastplate was decorated with bands of blue enamel, gold, and beaten tin. In between the shoulder plates, the throat guard embellished with intricate rainbow serpents, while on his stone pillar legs bronze greaves fastened at the heels with silver clasps.

Agamemnon called for a haunch of mutton to dull the cramps in his belly.

A horn. Chariots in the Mycenaean quarter of the camp.

Menelaus answered his brother's questioning glance with a single word of explanation: 'Antmen.' The name the formidable Myrmidons were widely called. It was their proud boast that long ago, on their original island home, Zeus had seen a line of black ants on the branch of a tree and turned them into men. Ever since, they had worn distinctive black armour into battle and adorned their banners and oval shields with a menacing depiction of a giant black ant. The creak and shake of axel and harness, snorting of exhausted horses, indicated the chariots were lining up across the open dirt outside the pavilion.

'I wondered when he was going to show up,' Agamemnon said, sourly.

Achilles.

The previous night, while the storm still swiped and slashed, the gold-maned warrior had refused to relinquish his search for Iphigenia. Declaring his immortal love, he led his escort into the howling maw of the tempest, vowing to find Iphigenia and deliver her to a place of sanctuary. Already very drunk, Agamemnon had a hazy recollection of dismissing this as nothing more than a cynical ploy. Achilles loved everyone. He was renowned for it. He was currently embroiled in a passionate affair with his cousin and charioteer, Patroklos, and his actions were clearly intended to antagonise the Argive king and endear him to the many who knew and adored Iphigenia.

Now Agamemnon was not sure. Perhaps he had been too quick to judge Achilles. Perhaps the Myrmidon prince, rumoured the son of a goddess, was genuinely fond of his daughter and had kept his promise not to rest until he found her. She might even be with him now.

'Out of the way!' Agamemnon pushed aside those blocking his path.

It was unusually hot for late spring, let alone in full armour, and Agamemnon's body had already begun to weep. From where he clanked to a halt, the encampment was laid out before him. General order. Clusters of chaos. Interspersed intense activity. War bands mustered from the four corners of Mycenae's empire were busy dismantling shelters, filling sodden fire pits and latrines, loading equipment onto ox-drawn carts or onto pack animals. Polemarchs beaked orders and strutted to and fro like truculent peacocks, while nearer the walled town of Aulis, warrior centipedes wound their way down to the brilliant azure ocean, bedrolls, cooking tripods and shields slung upon their backs. Closer to hand, all activity had come to a temporary halt as curious warriors gathered to watch the unfolding drama. An expectant hush settled over the Mycenaean camp as Achilles leapt from his chariot and carefully laid a cloak-swathed body at his booted feet.

Agamemnon's throat closed and his heart pounded like a shipwright's mallet. For the flick of a serpent's tongue his worst fears were confirmed. Iphigenia. Achilles drew back the bloodstained cloak to reveal the mutilated body of Perimedes. Heads craned. An uneasy murmur rippled the serried ranks of warriors like the sound of the sea in the distance. Agamemnon licked desert-lips and breathed a slow, barely perceptible sigh of relief.

'We found him on the road to Corinth, near the staging post at Megara,' said Achilles, omitting to bow or offer Agamemnon any form of deferential greeting. 'The godless vermin who did this were still there, defiling his corpse. There was no sign of the lovely Iphigenia.'

'No sign?' echoed Agamemnon, his swart brows knotting.

'There was a bridge ahead and a scatter of debris that indicated a collision at speed. What was left of Perimedes' chariot lay on its side, two of the horses, dead in their traces, forelegs and necks broken, a coat of arrows like a porcupine. Yet of Iphigenia there was no sign. If she fell in the river she could not have survived. The water was deep and swift flowing. The river god would have taken her.'

'You searched the area thoroughly?'

'Before we could do anything we were set upon by a horde of shrieking Furies. Four of my boldest warriors were felled by their flint tipped arrows. We had no choice but to retire.'

'You abandoned her? Left her at their mercy?'

'We were caught in the open, outnumbered ten to one.'

'The champion of all the Argives, routed by a band of bone wielding primitives?'

Agamemnon's voice was a barbed lash of derision, yet far from deterring Achilles, it inflamed him. He lifted his beardless, beautiful jaw defiantly, aquiline nostrils flared, shards of ire glowing in his garnet eyes.

'Your memory is conveniently short this morning, Agamemnon. It was your pride that spawned the tempest. Your pact with the shaman that cost Orestes his life and forced my bride to flee in the night.'

'Orestes is still alive.'

'Barely, thanks to you,' Achilles said, and with one hand, he deftly caught and adjusted his grip on the spear tossed to him by his charioteer, Patroklos.

'You are a fortunate man Agamemnon. But for my father,

60

King Peleus, who loves you like a brother, I would make you answer for your betrayal before all gathered here. It would be no more than you deserve to skewer you on this spear like a squealing hog.'

Sharp intakes of breath from the onlookers. Achilles rooted his feet, arched his spine; hurled the heavy spear through the air. Agamemnon saw no more than a glint of bronze as it arrowed towards him. Buried. In the grass a stride in front of the king. Aimed to miss. Menelaus and eight royal guards drew their blades. Only Agamemnon's raised hand prevented them charging the Myrmidon chariots. Silence. A lone vulture circled overhead, drawn to the sickly stench of carrion. The threat of violence clung to the sky with the monotonous ringing of cicadas.

Agamemnon stepped forward and pulled the spear from the ground. He tossed it disdainfully aside.

'You are right to speak of deceit, but wrong where you point the finger,' Agamemnon began. 'Your bride was my daughter. Precious beyond words. In surrendering to her sacrifice, I thought to save the lives of thousands of Argives camped along this storm-battered coast. Thousands more, starving in Argive towns and villages, while horse worshippers stuff their bellies with grain in Troy and prevent the passing of our ships. Their lives depend upon us prevailing in this war. Know now, son of Peleus, the shaman has paid for his mendacity. Know also that when this war is won and the granaries of Krimea are in our hands, I will compensate you for your loss with the pick of King Priam's concubines. Now return to your ship and gird yourself, for we sail on this morning's tide.'

Some in that bristling throng cheered, yet Achilles appeared unmoved, standing with his hands braced upon his athletic hips. His godlike face lifted like the head of a stag in rut, tasting the air for females.

'It will take more than a single Trojan concubine to dim the memory of Iphigenia's flawless beauty,' he said, theatrically.

'Three of Priam's playthings then.'

'And a cart laden with palace treasure?'

'One cart, and not a bronze trinket more. You are a bigger brigand than your father, King Peleus.'

Achilles swept his bellicose gaze over the press of watching Argives. Then he turned slowly, confidently, on his heels and mounted his chariot beside the tall figure of Patroklos.

'Before all here, I shall see you honour your pledge,' said Achilles in his singing, low voice, and with his clenched fist raised in the air, a black ant banner snapping in the breeze above his head, he rode away down the teaming hillside. One by one his depleted command followed him.

'I will one day teach you a lesson in manners,' said Agamemnon; grinding his tightly clenched teeth as he strode across a bloom-dappled meadow to where Perimedes' body lay on the flattened grass.

Close behind him, Diomedes of Argos asked: 'Why wait? In challenging you, Achilles flouts the authority of this whole council. Let us ride down this hillside together and drive him and his Antmen rabble into the sea.'

'And forget why we are here?'

Agamemnon halted abruptly. The nose and ears had been hacked off Perimedes' head and his eyes hooked out on the point of a horn dagger.

'We can sack Troy without him,' said Ajax of the Hammer, but Agamemnon shook his head dismissively.

'You and I know that but try convincing the men we lead. Achilles is their talisman, and without him in the field we may find the Trojan host, which outnumbers ours anyway, is too tough a nut to crack. Now be gone, all of you, and make ready to sail. Tonight, we will eat a frugal supper on board ship, with a briny spray in our faces.'

The Argive warlords dispersed, some of them to parts of the vast camp nearly an hour distant. They left Agamemnon in pensive mood, gazing at the remains of a young hero whose handsome face and infectious laugh had been so familiar. For a long while he said nothing, and when at last he glanced up, his red-veined eyes were submerged in tears of regret.

'Gutted like a fish,' he said to Menelaus, one of only two warriors who had remained in attendance. 'If they did this to my daughter her shade will never find peace. I cannot bear the thought.'

Menelaus clapped a consoling hand on his brother's shoulder.

'Do not torment yourself,' he replied. 'You heard what

Achilles said. The river was in full spate. It would have carried her far beyond their clutches.'

Agamemnon switched his attention to the second man standing there.

'Build a pyre for your son,' he said to Terpander, the wedge bearded polemarch of the royal guard. 'Then find my daughter. I have to know what became of her.'

'I will find her, great lion,' said Terpander, stooping to pick up his butchered son's corpse without a word more. He carried the huge body effortlessly, it seemed, in his mighty arms, refusing the help of those who stepped forward. He had reached a nearby grassy knoll, and along with a growing band of fellow mourners, had begun to gather timber for a funeral pyre, when Agamemnon's mind returned from the dark place into which it had crawled.

'The queen is with Orestes?' he asked grimly.

'Tending his injuries herself,' confirmed Menelaus.

'He will make a full recovery?'

'Given time. He will be strong enough to follow us when the moon of the dog star wanes.'

'Best I keep out of the way then,' said Agamemnon, with a rueful grimace, and with Menelaus at his side, he set off towards the harbour where his war fleet now sat in calm waters. Like all Argives, Agamemnon was a born seafarer. It was not long before the sharp tang of brine in his nostrils and the sight of riggers, caulkers, and carpenters, hard at work, quickened his blood. He stripped to his loincloth and sandals, and with all thought of his estranged family put aside, toiled under the hot sun until the tide turned. Then he summoned a herald and gave the order to put to sea.

7

Marked by the Gods

Aletes filled his lungs with night air to calm his nerves as he limped past the columns of the villa entrance at Zygouris into the vestibule within. Heavy fatigue and a building fever from his wounds contorted the oil torches mounted on the walls into exotic dancers, rippling and bending their flame limbs to show him the way into the central hall under one of the two square stonework arches. Terpander, head of Agamemnon's royal protection, followed two strides behind, nodding to the guards to let Aletes through.

Terpander had ordered his search party to fall in behind the queen's escort when they crossed by chance near the road from Corinth to Mycenae earlier in the height of the sun. The queen had news of her daughter and communicated a look of silent contempt when the polemarch stated he had been sent from the camp at Aulis by the king. Clytemnestra's hunting chariot and escort were trailed by the king's cousin, Lord Aegisthus. Like the days of old, Terpander thought. The grey wolf sniffing around the queen, stalking, lurking. All saw it. Except the king. No matter, he was the king's eyes. He watched the watcher. He had not seen them in each other's company for many summers now, but the queen had clearly sought the lord's help to find her daughter and he had given it.

Instructed by the queen to return the herdsman who had helped her daughter, Terpander had found Aletes crouched beside a mound of earth and rocks placed over a small clay pot containing the ashes of his dog, the pyre erected from dead wood and undergrowth. As the story went, the herdsman had escaped from his tormentors after they punished him for slaying the lion. An unfortunate business. The herdsman had gulled the useless cyclops guarding him, leaving his so-called guard bound, a mouth stuffed full of horseshit-soiled hay, and a sign dangling around his neck saying sorcerer.

Terpander's broad mouth wormed into a smile. By all accounts, this unknown herdsman's actions were as valiant protecting the king's daughter as those of his strong son, Perimedes. The smile vanished. The polemarch swallowed hard and raised his head.

Aletes strained into the room, the sandals taken from one-eyed Alcinous' stinking feet after he had distracted him on his blind side and stuffed his mouth with stinking hay, loose on his feet. The sandals had caused him to turn his ankle on his escape. His ankle and foot now sat as one oblong slab of raw pig's meat. On the same leg, the worst of the dog bites just above his knee had grown fat and juicy, making the joint stiffen. The pain was a sickness that bled sweat down his temples. The limb was rigid as he moved, splayed outwards, like the leg on the small eating table from where Lord Aegisthus had risen and was approaching from across the blazing ornate central circular fire.

Aletes tried to focus his eyes. His vision blended on the two other seated figures, each at their own small table by the fire. He thought one might be the girl—the daughter of the king, he corrected himself—but he could now see amber hair and the woman was older. He hoped the girl's absence meant she was resting and not something worse.

Lord Aegisthus was close enough for Aletes to count the wiry pewter hairs sprouting from his pinched nostrils. His receding hair was the colour of iron, and Aletes knew his temperament was usually as unbending. His lips were hidden in his feathery beard; mouthless, like an owl. Until he spoke.

'You found him in this condition?'

'We did, my lord,' replied Terpander, a stride behind. 'He returned here of his free will and suffered no ill-treatment at my hands.'

'Come. Sit,' Aegisthus said. He gestured Aletes to one of the individual tables nobly born Argives dined upon. Aletes caged his breath to hold in the pain as he fell rather than sat on the fleece laid on top of the oak stool, clamping his eyes shut to suppress the need to cry out from the ulcerous soreness. He refused to give Glaukos the satisfaction, who he now recognised as the other diner. A slave poured Aletes a cup of chilled and diluted red wine. He drained it, holding out the cup gratefully to be refilled. In the better light, Aegisthus could see one side of the normally symmetrical angles of the herdsman's fine face now bulged like an overripe fig.

'These wounds are your work?' said Aegisthus, rounding on his son.

Glaukos lobbed a piece of hog meat into the tangle of boarhounds beside the circular hearth.

'Minor injuries, father. The herdsman was interrogated as you would expect. Given the gravity of the charge, his treatment was lenient.'

'Lenient?' Aegisthus countered, looking again upon Aletes. 'Beaten with fists and half crippled by these hounds? What chance would he have stood in the trial of strength had we not arrived?'

'More chance than he earned. The lion's hide lies there, father. Look again and tell me a peasant with a sling, a sling unlawful for a lowborn to own, could vanquish such a beast? Consider, father, its prodigious size. You believe he plucked out that eye with a *sling*?'

Glaukos held aloft the sling and leather pouch of shot he had taken from Aletes. Although unlawful, many Argive herdsmen carried the simple but effective weapon to ward off hungry wolves and hunt an occasional rabbit for their cooking pot. Glaukos knew this alone was not justification to punish Aletes, so he had taken the precaution of scoring potent symbols on the smooth stones with the point of his dagger.

The queen rose. A master of handling the quarrels of men. She had spoken with her daughter upon arrival, rushing to her bedside. Iphigenia had relayed the bravery of the herdsman and the unjust punishment in the courtyard. Yet, the queen knew the word of two women would hold no credence. They would be dismissed as hysterical.

Instead, she asked strategically: 'Perhaps we should hear from the herdsman?'

Hush enveloped the hall. Tension crackled like the flames of the shallow fire burning in the hearth, while even the boarhounds seemed to stop snuffling and farting and pricked up their ears. Aletes struggled to swallow. Though it had been an unusually hot day for spring, the nights bore a chill, and he shivered, yet his tunic was wet with sweat. The room was a lake he was swimming through. Deep and cold.

'You see how the spider hesitates, afraid of snaring himself in his shameful web of lies?'

'Let him speak,' snapped Aegisthus.

Aletes' modest manner provoked Glaukos more than if he had shamelessly boasted. Aletes gave most of the credit for slaying the lion to poor loyal Argus. Before he fell silent, Glaukos had interrupted him several times, pouring scorn on his truthful, understated account.

'The gods have spoken,' said the holy mother, emerging unexpectedly into the hall.

Her eyes were feral, having taken a hallucinatory draught. Her hands were gloved with blood and the earthenware bowl she held contained the quartered liver and gizzard of Zygouris' resident gander, the same gander at which Glaukos had earlier aimed a petulant kick.

'The gods speak of my daughter?' Clytemnestra asked urgently, fearing another ill omen.

'The gods speak of the lionslayer. I hear the roar of destiny. He is marked by the gods for greatness. To stand shoulder to shoulder with the heroes of Argolis. A hero in the guise of a herdsman who will one day save the dynasty of Atreus.'

Glaukos nearly choked on his mouthful of octopus.

'A hero?' he mocked; mouth full, words slurring from too much wine. 'Horns of the Minotaur! Why not the son of Zeus! Perhaps he is Heracles' long-lost brother!'

'Glaukos, hold your tongue.'

'I will not be silenced father. Whatever noxious draught the old bat has taken, it has not helped her grasp of the facts. This herdsman has nothing better than sow's piss in his veins.'

'He is of noble birth,' said the holy mother, unperturbed.

'You're scraping the depths of Tartarus now, by the gods!'

'He was born to nothing, yet he has the blood of a mighty dynasty flowing through his veins. He is sprung from noble loins and has the right to bear the arms and panoply of a hero.'

'Who sired the bastard?' Glaukos asked, knowing the answer.

'I am told a band of Dorian led Hillmen have been raiding the outlying regions of Elis,' Aegisthus interjected, addressing Glaukos. 'They have burned farms, butchered the inhabitants, and eluded the host sent to eradicate them. I had planned to leave this matter with the Elians, but you will go to their aid instead.'

'You're sending me to Elis?'

'You and your heavy-handed oafs, Alcinous and Euthemus.'

'I am convalescing.'

'Your hand is sufficiently healed. You will go to Elis, expunge this Hillman filth, and reflect upon your handling of the situation here.'

'And conclude what, father? That whatever I say or do where your pet...'

He searched for the word. '...where your pet', he repeated, 'is concerned, is wrong.'

'You exaggerate as usual,' Aegisthus replied, unmoved.

'Then send Aletes to Elis with me. If he's destined to save us all as this fat goose says, he needs all the training he can get.'

'Aletes goes to Mycenae with Terpander. His training will take place more appropriately there; he will train with the latest levy of recruits.'

'While I am exiled to the wilds of Elis, to spend the summer riding after a band of reiving Hillmen?'

Aegisthus' mouth disappeared again into his beard. He

peered at his son owl-eyed and mute.

Glaukos rose to his feet, wine-legged. As he drained the contents of his gold cup, the nearest boarhound instinctively turned its head to avoid the young master's temper. The heavy cup bounced off the back of its skull.

'Glaukos, be seated. I have not given you permission to depart this hall.'

'I am preparing for Elis, father, as you command.'

Before Aegisthus could speak again, Glaukos strode up to Aletes. Terpander reacted. A step forward. Instinctive.

Glaukos smirked. 'Acquired a royal bodyguard no less. You are welcome to him, Terpander.'

He looked straight at Aletes' ruined face and silently entreated Artemis, hunting from her chariot on the tiles under his feet, to make the herdsman's injuries scar.

'Come back to me when you've held a sword in your hands', he said. 'Then we'll settle this. We'll see if you're protected by the gods when I gut you like a fish.'

Glaukos left, sniffing, snorting, from the hall, body bull-like with the Olympus-swell of his shoulders and stumpy, shapeless legs. Euthemus followed behind as always. Aletes watched him go, disbelieving. He had always believed his father was Admetus. The summer after his birth Admetus had been killed during the annual bull leaping festival. He was gored to death when the wrong bull was released into the enclosure where he waited nervously to vault over its sharpened, flower-garlanded horns. It was rumoured at the time Aegisthus had ordered Admetus' placid bull be switched with a particularly vicious behemoth, yet nobody was fool enough to openly voice their suspicions. All Aletes knew for certain was that his mother, Danaea, had never been allowed to remarry. There was no shortage of willing suitors, but as warden of Zygouris, Aegisthus had always found fault in them and refused to give his permission.

Only one night ago, Aletes had sat under the stars at Zygouris with Argus licking his hand for another piece of rabbit, talking simple pleasures with Kleonike or one of the other herdsmen. Was that life at an end? Worse, it may be many moons before he could revisit his mother's shrine.

'Terpander, Aletes will join your palace guards. Let us test the holy mother's prophecy and see for ourselves. Favoured by the gods or not, you will need all the help you can get to prove your worth on the field of battle and earn the rank of hero.'

Aegisthus paused, as if considering something of importance.

'You have until first light to say your farewells. This audience is at an end. Terpander's Senior First Spear is waiting for you in the vestibule. He will introduce you to your new comrades from Terpander's escort.'

'Not just yet. I have been asked to say a few words before he departs.'

Clytemnestra moved serenely from her place as honoured guest beside Aegisthus' table. She was dressed in a loose-fitting ivory pleated pharos with ornamental red and gold meander symbol design, that swept the mural painted tiles as she approached Aletes. Her hair was a mesmerising mixture of red and brown pigments, neither one, yet both at once. Touched with frost at the temples, she wore her hair in an elegant chignon framed by ringlets on the nape of her neck. Her gold pendant earrings were inlaid with cornelian and she smelt of fragrant oils, reminding Aletes that beneath the ill-fitting tunic he had stolen from Alcinous, he stunk of lion entrails.

'I am in your debt, Aletes of Zygouris.'

The words were strange to Aletes. The queen speaking his name as if he were someone to be spoken of.

'It is a debt so great it may never be repaid. Yet I hope you will find me an ally if you should ever believe yourself in need of my help.'

Aletes wanted to ask after the princess. Yet he did not know how to speak to a queen, let alone if he was permitted. He was ashamed of how he looked. How he reeked.

Clytemnestra stepped back so she could gauge Aletes' full measure before continuing.

'We will ask Zeus to hold his hands over you and await the day you return to Argolis with the lion emblazoned shield, top knot and armbands of a hero. Before then, perhaps one reward we could provide would be a bath.'

Not trusting himself to speak, he nodded courteously to the queen and an inscrutable Aegisthus, before turning to leave. With every step, Terpander thumped a table as Argive warriors pounded the backs of their shields saluting bravery on the battlefield. A considerable honour from the phlegmatic commander. Aletes' bruised chest swelled beyond his injuries as he struggled out of the hall into the darkness.

8

The Heron Ring

'Right then, you sorry looking piece of gristle, my name for the record is Melampus. I am Senior First Spear in the palace guard, and it is my thankless task to turn you into something resembling a fighting man. I've had harder tasks, but for the moment, I can't recall one.'

Melampus was a short, bald headed veteran with a voice that grated like bronze tyres on gravel. He could have been carved out of a mountain, a man of living rock; rugged face, muscle-ridged legs, broad expansive peaks for shoulders. He stopped speaking mid-sentence, leaned closer to Aletes and sniffed his tunic like a hog rooting for acorns.

'Is that rat shit I can smell?' he asked, feigning abhorrence.

'Lion fat, First Spear. I was daubed with it so the young master's hounds could follow my scent more easily.'

'Smells like rat shit to me,' said Melampus, his curled lip

revealing the gaps in his stained teeth. 'From now, until you earn a better one, that will be your name. Do you agree, Ratshit?'

'It's a fine name, First Spear.'

'Good, then let's get started. We don't want the king to need saving before you've learned how to properly hold your cock, do we. That wouldn't do at all. Stop limping like a lame mule and follow me. I've a few friends I'd like you to meet.'

Aletes followed the bandy legged First Spear out into the moonlit courtyard. It was an Argive custom to provide sustenance to passing travellers, so in keeping with this tradition, victuals and rush mattresses had been set out in the torch-lit columned vestibule. The palace guards were a stoical bunch and having availed themselves of the food and jars of sweet red Zygourian wine, most had chosen to sleep outside wrapped in their thick military cloaks in the cool night.

Melampus picked out a trio of warriors playing a game of flip the marked stones on the steps of the open sided temple, and with Aletes hobbling behind him, strode towards them.

'Is it true, First Spear?' a voice called out of the shadows. 'The bearded heifer you met earlier this evening managed to rouse the greasy serpent between your legs?'

Bawdy laughter and hoots of derision. Melampus chuckled in good humour.

'She did, Maron, I'm pleased to say.'

'What potion or magic did she use to achieve that?'

'No potion or magic, Maron. Just lips as soft as your big

sister's. She wasn't as experienced as your sibling, I'll admit, but I enjoyed her all the same. We're meeting again later in the same tack store, after she's shaved her back and polished her horns, of course.'

'I heard she tried everything to wake the shrivelled serpent, but nothing had the desired effect?'

'If you say so, Maron. Believe what you like, but while you're lying there showing Sirius, the dog star, how to wring the neck of a capon, I'll be in the tack store enjoying sweaty seconds.'

This time the laughter was directed at Maron and satisfied he had given as good as he got in the exchange, Melampus switched his attention to Aletes.

'Here we are, Ratshit. These three unsavoury looking stallions are Pytho, Echetus and Chersicrates. They are brother and mentor to you now, so listen to what they tell you, do what they say, and you might yet earn your ration of oil and porridge. You got that?'

'Yes, First Spear,' said Aletes, concealing an overwhelming desire to be somewhere else.

'Good. You're clearly a quick learner, which will stand you in good stead. One other point, before I leave you to sort out your affairs. You're a royal guard now, so from the moment the first cock crows you're mine to command. Mine, you understand? From the first cock crow, you won't so much as fart without getting my permission first.'

'Does that include silent farts, Spear?'

'Another comedian, eh?' Melampus' hot breath reeked of tooth rot, garlic sauce and olives. 'Careful, Ratshit, you have to earn the right to poke fun at me. Until you do I suggest you keep quiet and do as you are told, otherwise you'll upset me. You'll also upset me if you don't clean up that wound, Ratshit. Don't want your leg falling off on the road to Mycenae, do we. Good night and sweet dreams.'

Melampus winked at the three relaxing guards and without another word, set off to keep his appointment in the tack store.

'I think he likes you,' said a grinning Echetus, the youngest of the three companions. Feeling less than convinced, Aletes managed an amused smile in reply.

Chersicrates, a lean framed warrior with oily hair and crooked teeth too big for his mouth, picked up a half-full wine jar and tossed it to Aletes.

'Help yourself. And don't let First Spear rattle you. His bark is much worse than his bite.'

'Much worse,' confirmed Pytho, the oldest and hence most senior of the three. He was a lead-limbed man with a face like a gnarled tree stump. His splayed nose had been broken more times than he could remember, part of his right ear bitten off during a drunken tavern brawl many seasons ago.

'The way he sounds off you'd think he wanted to throttle you,' Pytho continued. 'But the truth is, he loves us all like sons. We're the kids he never had, and when you're in a tight corner there's no one better to have watching your back.'

'No one better,' agreed Echetus, gathering up the crudely scored pebbles they had been playing with and shaking them in his cupped hands. 'He's also an expert at flipping these stones, as most of us know to our cost. He'll take the snot out of your nose if you're foolish enough to bet against him. I uh, don't suppose you're interested in a small wager?'

'Not just now,' said Aletes, as anxious to avoid being fleeced by Echetus as he was about the lateness of the hour. 'There's something I must do before sunrise.'

'Might want to use some of that wine on that scratch on your knee Ratshit,' Pytho said, using a twig to rake the wax and other debris out of his mutilated ear and eyeing Aletes' nasty inflammation. He rummaged in a sack beside him and threw Aletes a square of linen. 'Then you'd best get along. If Spear says he wants you here at dawn, he means dawn.'

'Yes, get going,' said Echetus. 'I hope the wench you're meeting is kinder on the eye than Spear's cross-eyed heifer.'

The distance to the cave holding his mother's shrine was an hour's effort on good legs. If he left now, in his slowed state, he could make it back in time for four hours of sleep before Eos' rosy fingers opened the gates of dawn. Aletes had no intention of leaving Zygouris without the precious terracotta figurine of Danaea. He handed the wine jar back to Chersicrates, thanking him, having soaked the linen from Pytho in wine. He would wait until he was alone to clean the wound; the sting would bring tears to his eyes he did not want them to see.

Aletes left the amiable guards to resume their game of chance, making his way along a pillared pergola weaved with vines and blooms, which formed an enclosed walkway into the beautiful, stretching gardens of the villa. There, he took a familiar route through the orchard to the vast rows of olive trees, where much of the work of the slaves at Zygouris took place to produce the oil and fruits for which the prosperous estate was famous. He felt in the dark in the place the rope was always hidden for scaling the spiked perimeter wall. Cicadas sang to the night.

He was deliberating what he would say to his mother's shade when the birdlike figure of Aegisthus flew out of the trees holding a small oil lamp. The warden was alone, with his free hand raised in a conciliatory gesture.

'I apologise if I startled you.'

'What do you want with me?' asked Aletes, warily.

'The chance to redeem myself.'

The Lord's familiar tone was as disconcerting as the words. It was unusual for the warden to acknowledge the existence of a servant, much less engage one in meaningful conversation.

'I first met your mother, Danaea, three summers before I earned the top knot of a hero,' he said, launching into something of a prepared oration. 'We would meet in this very grove, the bond between us stronger than the arms of Heracles. But for the tragedy of her humble birth, I would gladly have taken her for my wife.'

Was he hallucinating? Aletes touched his moist forehead

with the skin of the back of his hand.

'She was the love of my life,' Aegisthus continued, the tremor in his voice threatening to betray him. 'And you Aletes, despite my many shameful denials, are the fruit of our sweet, doomed liaison. You were born during the first winter of her marriage to Admetus, and while your wrinkled face was still wet from your mother's womb, and the dutiful Admetus paraded you as his own, I swore an oath before Zeus to protect you. It is a vow I have endeavoured to keep, although at times it may not have appeared so. It is the reason I sent you to join the brotherhood of herdsmen, thus you would spend as little time here on the estate under the scrutiny of Glaukos. We all make decisions we regret, Aletes, and my failure to claim you after Danaea perished will haunt me until we are reunited in Elysium and I beg her forgiveness.'

Aletes had no words. Poseidon had struck the ground of his world and he was losing his foothold, falling through the cracked earth. Day was night. Lies truth. He had dismissed the holy mother's words in the villa, convincing himself it was a way for the priestess to show him kindness. Now this?

'Why did you not adopt me into your house?'

Aegisthus' face betrayed an emotion, one so raw, that Aletes knew in his stomach he was telling the truth. And he knew what the answer would be.

'Glaukos. Had I made you his rival you would not be alive today.'

'You could have made me his brother.' Aletes said.

83

Aegisthus sighed. 'Oh, you have your mother's heart, Aletes. Glaukos would always have eyed you as a rival. As my father murdered his half-brother Chrysippus to take the throne, we descendants of Atreus are cursed. Glaukos would not have been able to help himself, I am sure of it. Look how he persecutes you with only rumour to move him.'

No wonder Glaukos despised him, Aletes realised. For a moment, he felt a soul-breaking grief for what could have been.

Someone was approaching. The rustling loud; not attempting to conceal themselves. They too had a lamp, their movement deliberate.

'Warden'. A woman's voice. She held up the oil lamp and Aletes saw her cloaked face.

Like every young man in Argive Greece, he had heard stories about the unrivalled beauty of Helen of Troy. Yet he would sail a thousand ships to certain death for the face he saw now in the golden light of the lamp.

'Iphigenia, what are you doing here?' Aegisthus said, irritated. 'This is no place for you.'

'Warden, I apologise for interrupting your conversation. I assure you I heard nothing. I am here to thank the herdsman and to pass a gift. I saw you follow the herdsman here and I concede I then followed you, hoping you would facilitate our meeting.'

The warden did not like the brazen behaviour of Agamemnon's youngest born. The king and men of war spent too long away; the women of the Palace of Mycenae taking liberties with their freedoms like the women of Sparta who ran wild because their men were always off picking a fight. Look what had happened to Iphigenia's aunt, Helen. Yet Aegisthus was a man who looked for opportunity in a situation. He would return Iphigenia to the queen after she had spoken with Aletes. Clytemnestra would be further in his debt. They could continue the conversation they were having in Mycenae a day earlier when she had come to the city to seek his help.

'You heard nothing that was said?'

'Nothing, Lord Aegisthus.'

She was probably lying, Aegisthus weighed up. Sly, like that father of hers. However, she was not in a position to reveal his secrets now that he knew hers.

'Continue,' Aegisthus said.

Iphigenia gave a small cough. He understood her meaning. Riled at being ordered about like a donkey by a woman, he suppressed his temper only by reflecting on the queen. He could still remember the first time he had set eyes upon Clytemnestra, he mused, as he stepped away into the darkness far enough to give them the space insinuated by Iphigenia. All those years ago, Clytemnestra rode in her Spartan father's gold sheathed, garlanded chariot through the streets of Mycenae's congested lower city, a vision of auburn-haired loveliness in a shimmering, open fronted saffron bridal gown. Upon her head sat a crown of fragrant garnet-hued roses, while a necklace of delicate white lilies and purple chaste tree blooms hung across the deep cleft between her full, firm breasts. Aegisthus had been smitten since that morning – the morning of her betrothal to his cousin King Agamemnon.

Iphigenia spoke when Aegisthus was three or four strides down the row of olive trees.

She held the oil lamp high in an awkward-angled arm. The light allowed her to see Aletes' striking grey eyes—she had never seen eyes like it. She lifted the oil lamp; Aletes was a head and shoulders taller than her.

'Would you like me to hold that for you?' he said nervously. He did not know how to refer to the daughter of a king.

'Yes, thank you. You are taller than me, you can light us better.'

Aletes took the lamp and she lowered the hood of her cloak. The girl had been bathed and cared for again. Her freshly washed hair lay in a trove of ringlets and plaits darker than the sky around them, curling down her neck and the front of her cloak like silk. Her eyes were calm now, the fear in the riverbed gone, and they were black diamonds, prisms of beauty. He thanked Apollo, his patron god, that they were outside, and she might not notice his humiliating stench.

'I came here to give you this as a token of gratitude from my family.'

In her palm, she held the ring he had seen in the riverbed: the silver heron ring.

'It belonged to my mother, her mother, and hers before. By

all accounts it was forged by the Ephors of Knossos in a time before our conquering forefathers sailed here. It is said it protects all who wear it. From what I have heard of your destiny, you may need it.'

'You do not need to give me anything,' Aletes said. 'Your kind gratitude is more than I deserve.'

'You saved my life', she said.

'As you saved mine in the courtyard,' Aletes replied. 'We are even.'

'I should like you to have it.'

It was an order. Like a queen.

He held out his large hand and for the briefest of moments, he felt the soft skin of the tips of her fingers against his palm. The warm silver of the ring heated by her hand.

Silence. Neither knowing what to say. Strangers. Bound. Aletes wanted to ask why she had been in the riverbed. What had led her there? What had happened? Yet it was not his place.

It was Iphigenia who broke the uneasy quiet. Pausing. Looking over her shoulder. Finding the words in a whisper.

'I too know what it is to have a father betray you.'

Aletes met her eyes, wounded and broken as his own. He opened his mouth to sound the questions she had given him silent permission to ask.

9

The Equal of Achilles

The journey to the city of Mycenae was long and arduous. Aletes had heard many a starlit story about the fortress fit for a god: the defensive walls encircling the city built by giant cyclopes who piled them higher than four warriors tall, each stone on stone the weight of a whale. The citadel perched like a crown on its soaring acropolis like the warrior lord who ruled high over Argive Greece. Lord of lords. Agamemnon. Mycenae was the foremost city of Greece, a state populous thirty thousand strong, at the centre of the Argives' sprawling power and wealth.

The stones below Aletes' feet started as little more than a rutted track. Helios, the sun god, had ridden his chariot halfway across the sky by the time the column of guards, tramping in the stinging heat behind commander Terpander's own earthbound, creaking chariot, finally reached a paved highway. Aletes was limping heavily and struggling to keep up, burdened as he was by

Melampus' supplies bag, his rolled-up cloak, and his own meagre bundle of possessions.

Sweat gathered in his hair causing it to stick to the skin on his neck. Itching. As he had been ordered to march at the rear of the column, his parched throat and nostrils were clogged with thick dust. Every step had become a torment. His injured leg and ankle were almost too sore to bear down upon, and only because his enraptured mind was oblivious to his physical suffering, was he able to continue. Aletes touched the small pouch hanging around his neck. The heron ring was safe there with the terracotta figurine of his mother he had collected from her shrine.

'I could have dealt with that lion cub myself of course,' Iphigenia had joked, causing Aletes' lips to wriggle into a smile at the memory, just as they had done in the moonlight last night.

'The heron ring will protect you and bring you good fortune.'

Good fortune, had she said? By all the snow on soaring Olympus, he had thought of nothing else since being summoned to First Spear Melampus by a rudely braying ibex horn. Since he had limped through the gate at Zygouris like a heavily burdened mule, the early morning sun stabbing his eyes after only three hours of sleep following the events of the orchard, his pilgrimage to his mother's shrine, and scrubbing himself clean of the vile smell and tending to his wounds in the pool of the cave. Good fortune? Yes. He had met her.

'You'll be in our prayers, Aletes!' The track ahead was lined with friends and well-wishers shouting support.

'May the gods hold their hands over you!'

'Danaea would be so proud today!'

'Take this stone… bring down a Trojan for me!'

Aletes had placed the nicely weighted stone in the pouch of shot on his belt. Terpander had restored it to him, along with his sling. The stone had been chucked by his fellow herdsman Kleonike, the one who had first spotted the lion.

'You call this marching, Ratshit?'

Aletes snapped out of his reverie to find Melampus striding along beside him, glowering like an enraged minotaur. He realised he had fallen even further behind the rest of the dust-swathed column.

'This isn't a gentle stroll in the country. We're not a bunch of idle herdsmen with nothing better to do than plant our arses in a shady spot and wile away the day. Now move along, or I'll have you chopping firewood and digging shitholes until your hair turns grey.'

Aletes shifted the heavy load he carried from one screaming shoulder to the other. He blinked the sweat out of his eyes. Lengthening his lopsided gait, he managed to close the gap between him and Pytho, the warrior he was supposed to be marching behind.

'That's better,' growled Melampus. 'Make sure you keep up, or next time I drop by for a chat I'll bring another sack for you to carry.'

He grinned, slapped Aletes on the back of the head and set

off back to his usual place behind Terpander's chariot.

'You must be deaf as well as stupid,' Pytho said over his shoulder. 'I tried to rouse you more times than Spear has teeth left in his mouth, but you stared right through me.'

'I was daydreaming,' Aletes admitted, sheepishly.

'She must be some girl, judging by your moonstruck gape,' said Echetus, tramping along beside Pytho.

'I wish she was mine,' muttered Aletes, scolding himself when he realised he had spoken the words. Iphigenia was the daughter of King Agamemnon no less. Articulating such disrespect would find him shackled by the ankles, chiselling rock in a silver or copper mine.

Above that, she would no more think of him than she would a snail in the palace garden. He tried to focus on placing one unstable leg in front of the other. Yet his thoughts returned to Iphigenia's words in the orchard.

'By all accounts, the shaman Calchas suffered greatly for his deception,' Iphigenia finished summarising the events at Aulis.

'Do you forgive your father?' Aletes had asked, wincing at his clumsy question.

'He is the king,' Iphigenia answered like the daughter of one.

Aletes had nodded in understanding.

'No doubt I will return to the palace at Mycenae. I hope you excel in your training and you prove the words of the holy mother true.'

Before Aegisthus had stretched his talons and told Iphigenia she had to return to the villa with him, she spoke again. As if she wanted the lord to hear.

'Men say destiny decides all. I believe the gods show us the way, but we can change our paths. Herdsman or hero, I saw how brave you were in the riverbed. I saw you slay the lion. Remember that.'

And she was gone.

Yes. Destiny was one thing, but if he could prove himself on the battlefield as the holy mother had said, and become a great warrior, perhaps he could impress Iphigenia.

By all the gods of Olympus.

Aletes had stopped marching. His eyes and movement stolen by the vision of what was surely Zeus' golden palace. They had reached the giant silver-blue stone defensive walls of Mycenae. Within them, the citadel sat on an acropolis between two mountain peaks, a city in the sky tiering upwards as if growing up from the rock itself. The peaks protected the palace like a jewel; it gleamed and blinded like the sun. A broad paved highway cut through the congested suburbs, branching in two directions before it joined the steep circuitous ramp leading to the famous Gateway of Lions. The first of these arteries continued to wind around the lower city until it arrowed west towards Arcadia, the Nemean hills and eventually Elis. The second curved south across the Argive plain to Argos, Tiryns, and the productive slaving port of Nauplia.

Aletes found himself marching along the former of these

arteries. He had expected the column of guards to be greeted by an enthusiastic crowd as at Zygouris. He was soon to learn that at the bustling heart of empire the comings and goings of a contingent of guards was a common event. The only people to take interest in them as they negotiated a path through the ebb and flow of carts, caravans and pedestrians was a gaggle of sharp-tongued harlots. These tawdrily dressed ladies of the night were haggling for fresh fish and vegetables at a roadside market, and as the column went by, they reminded the dust-shrouded warriors where best to spend their hard-earned coin. Echetus was quick to point out they needed no reminding.

The guards' barracks were situated a bowshot beyond the western ramparts of the citadel. The pediment above its main entrance was adorned with a couchant bronze lion and plaque inscribed with the words: we who watch and serve. It was laid out in the style of a fortified provincial outpost, and comprised of a complex for the commanders, guard accommodation, storerooms, and a gymnasium. Adjacent to this structure was a vast rectangle of well trampled land, the rather grandly named Field of War. Here, new recruits and veterans alike were put through their paces, and, for three seasons out of four, they slept under the stars.

That evening the barracks complex was a hive of fevered activity. Recruits were rounded up by units of guards and herded in from the inhabitants of the city. After being issued with a spear, shield and long worsted cloak, the new arrivals were organised into groups of seven, each group under the watchful eye of a veteran.

They were provided with a bronze tripod and cauldron and would receive a generous ration of long-stored flatbread, porridge, cheese, and pork, goat or lamb stew. Aletes was relieved to be placed under the tutelage of Pytho. After getting to know his new companions, he settled down to the grinding routine and drudgery of military life.

During the moons that followed, he learned martial strategy, guile and how to move like a seasoned veteran. He was taught to drill with instinctive precision and self-discipline, wielding a spear twice as tall as him with one hand and a shield nearly half his weight, without clattering into or sticking the man in front or to one side of him. He mastered offensive and defensive manoeuvres, how to wheel left or right, to retreat in an orderly fashion, how to lock his shield into the armoured wall of a close order phalanx. Speed and dexterity followed. When a day's training was done, Melampus would usually reward him with a menial task. Late into the night he cleaned, sewed, or polished for the veteran polemarchs, and when they feasted, he served wine with bread to dip on their table, with roasted and chopped lamb, pork or beef, olives, figs, and grapes.

'I can see Terpander now,' Pytho once teased when the subject came up, 'sitting in his favourite chair beside a blazing winter hearth, boasting to his grandchildren about how he was served at table by none other than Aletes of Zygouris.'

The days were gruelling, and by the time Aletes joined his companions around the campfire he was often too exhausted to listen to the yarns being told or join in a game of flipping the marked stones. He would curl up on the ground in his regulation cloak and slip into a sleep that danced with dreams. A past life. A life never lived. A life that could have been.

Above all, he dreamed of Iphigenia. He applied himself to his duties the morning after these visions with a zeal no one could match. This intensity of effort soon marked him out as the ablest recruit in the heaving camp.

Three moons passed. The summer reached its highest heat, and Athena lent her artfully precise hands to sculpt Aletes into an efficient killer. More than the equal, Melampus suspected, of even the toughest veteran under his command.

'If I were a Trojan confronted by him,' Melampus was once heard to mutter. 'I'd turn tail and run. No, I'm not jesting. There's no shame in running from the likes of him. He's fast, quick-witted and uses a sword as if he was born with one in his hand. He can hurl a spear with greater accuracy than any man I know, and I've seen him take the head off a crow in flight with that infernal sling of his. I don't believe we've seen his like since Achilles visited Mycenae with his father, King Peleus, and came here to train.'

Such unstinting praise, coming as it did from a seasoned warrior like Melampus; not quick to impress, was guaranteed to set the hearts of ordinary men racing. Gods-fearing men, who believed in divine intervention and the predefined nature of a mortal man's destiny. It could not fail to add to their already healthy respect for the formidable former herdsman. As they tramped out of camp to the rhythmical sounds of drum, horn, and hobnailed sandal, it left them in no doubt that Zeus himself held his hands over them.

10

Present Day: 1200 BC

Mount Oeta, Northwest Argolis

First summer of the Trojan War

The order to march. Unexpected. The Argive contingent snaked northeast from Mycenae; more than two thousand spear points gleaming like golden leaves in the late summer sunshine. They were bound for Boeotia and the grass-rich plains of Thessaly beyond, and as they moved the already cosmopolitan force was swollen by contingents from the allied cities it collected on the way. Men from Corinth, Athens and Thebes strode boldly out to join them, supply bags, helmets and shields slung upon their backs. By the time the host made camp in the shadow of Mount Oeta, six days' march from Mycenae, it had almost doubled in size and the ardour of its warriors was tempered somewhat by the prospect of imminent battle.

The daunting challenge they faced had been spelt out to

them by Prince Orestes. He had spent much of the summer in Athens, recuperating from the wounds inflicted by Calchas' acolytes, and upon joining the expedition on the road to Thebes, he had assumed command.

A large host of invading Trojans, he explained, had landed unopposed in southern Macedonia. They had sacked the city of Phlegria, then marched south into Thessaly. A force from the garrison town of Iolcus had been sent to check its progress. It had not been heard from since. It was therefore assumed destroyed, Iolcus sacked or under siege, and the Trojans predicted to have poured into the south. The whole of Argolis now lay at the Trojans' mercy.

'Which means it's up to us to stop them,' said Aletes, squinting up at Oeta's blunt bald peak.

He was standing knee-deep in the shallows of a bracing, fast-flowing stream, scrubbing bronze cauldrons and clay bowls, and filling leather gourds. He was stripped to his loincloth, and above the ridged stone slabs of his bark brown belly, the ripe muscles of his shoulders and chest bulged, his armoured limbs moving broadly from his body. His biceps were round, plump cuts of meat sitting against his forearms, rising against cords and veins, and his massed thighs and calves completed the symmetry of a hero carved in marble. There was a resolute gleam in his grey eyes, while the thick pelt of russet beard sat like a battle shield on his strengthened jawline and thickened neck. The appearance of a mighty Argive warrior.

'If we reach the high ground north of here, we can hold them until the king sends reinforcements.'

'And if he doesn't send reinforcements?' asked Echetus.

'We'll probably die here.' Aletes rammed the wooden plug into the neck of another dripping waterskin. 'The road to Thebes will lay open and the whole of Argolis will go up in flames.'

Later that morning, when Aletes was sent to scout the road ahead with Pytho and Chersicrates, he was first to spot they had been beaten to the high ground.

Ten thousand Trojans, Lydians, Phrygians and single-breasted Amazons swept across the mountain plain in the hissing heat, a dense pall of dust swirling around them like an infinite swarm of hornets. Chariot-borne heroes raced across the advancing line, javelins aloft, war cries shooting like arrows through a sky of invisible gods who watched and waited to be entertained.

'How many would you say?' asked Pytho, crouching down beside Aletes in a shallow rocky defile.

'Six, maybe seven thousand,' Aletes estimated.

'More like ten,' said an anxious Chersicrates, his eyes darting along the shallow gully for a way to retreat unseen. 'Come on, let's go. I've heard what these Amazon harpies do to their captives. I don't want my balls turned into a pair of fetching earrings.'

From the exposed low ground looking up at the hulking body of Mount Oeta, Aletes wondered if the stories of Mount Olympus, home of the gods, could be true. For how could a mountain be more mammoth than what stood ahead of them now? Aletes watched a single Trojan chariot ride out from the uncomfortably close enemy line. The chariot moved at speed, drawn by a pair of powerful, grey-dappled white stallions. It dragged the blackened body of a hero in its wake. The long-dead corpse jerked and twisted on the end of a length of rope, and as the chariot sped between the opposing forces, dust spiralled upward from sharpened hooves and spoked wheels. With the Trojans baying encouragement, gesturing contemptuously at the less animated Argives, the chariot halted. A warlord in brazen panoply stepped confidently onto the ground, well within range of Prince Orestes' archers.

The man was a colossus. His blade was broad, rune etched, the hilt in his huge hand encrusted in the gold that was piled high in the treasuries of Troy. In the other, brilliant, giant like the sun above, a spherical shield emblazoned with the front facing head of a horse. Unhurried, he turned to salute his people. A roar erupted, as if the mountain exploded from within. A pounding of shields like a stampede of stallions from Troy. Finally, he addressed the Argives; scorn stamped upon his battle-scarred face.

'Men of Argolis!' he bellowed. 'I am Hector, son of Priam. This bronze in my hand is the Reaper of Shades. Note you well my face, for it is the sight of the only Trojan prince you will see before you are despatched to the dark abyss of Tartarus. While your king hesitates before the walls of Troy, I am here to burn your homes, reive your livestock and avail myself of your wives and daughters.

Your fates are sealed, men of Argolis, so those who can pay a ransom, step forth and declare yourselves. The rest prepare for slavery or death.'

The mountain shook again with approval from the Trojan host. Hector held the leash of the war beast with its ten thousand heads; it paced forward, eager for its hunt to begin, slavering, yapping. Hector heeled the monster with his lofted sword. With a bellowed order half lost in sound, he had his charioteer drag the ruined body forward and arrange it at his sandaled feet. A thin silence covered the battlefield like a mask of death.

'Behold you the work of the Reaper!' Hector proclaimed. 'This lump of raw meat is Halitherses, commander of your garrison at Iolcus! He was idiotic enough to challenge me to a test of arms. He hoped to save his city but was feeble and deserved to die ignominiously. After I slit his throat, I plucked out his eyes on the point of my dagger so his shade would roam the underworld sightless and ashamed. I cut off his manhood and fed it in tiny pieces to the crows. The shade of Halitherses cries out for vengeance, men of Argolis! So, I ask you, is there one among you bold enough to meet me in single combat? To restore the honour of your people and decide this day in a bloody fight to the death?'

Hector lifted the front of his tunic, and in a gesture of contempt for all it was to be Argive, urinated in the corpse's obscene, gaping mouth.

'Well? Men of Argolis, will one of you step forward or are you all cowards?'

Hector's goading had the desired effect. As he fell silent, a groundswell of indignation rippled through the bristling ranks of the Argives like flames of a scrub fire in high summer. There was much gesturing, nodding of plumed bronze helmets and boar's ivory heads, while in front of the agitated host, Orestes, Terpander, and a hand's count of other leaders, knotted together in an exchange on which the destiny of four thousand Argives hung. Orestes, not yet returned to full vigour after his mauling at Aulis, strode purposefully towards the Trojans and had to be restrained.

Terpander mounted his chariot while the heroes were distracted. The low ground rumbled. Rapping of spear hafts on shields.

'I don't like the look of this.' Pytho muttered. 'Terpander's bold and strong as a bear, but he's old and won't get the better of Hector. Unless you want to die needlessly, or get buggered by a cross-eyed Lydian, I suggest you be ready to take to your heels.'

Terpander's chariot came to a violent stop a spear's throw from Hector. He dismounted and armed with spear, sword, and lion-emblazoned shield, clanked in bronze towards his grinning adversary. Terpander was a big man, almost as tall and broad at the shoulder as Hector, yet his stature seemed diminished next to the supreme confidence of the Trojan. The two heroes engaged in speech. Then Hector threw back his head and laughed deridingly, and as the older Argive bridled and hefted his spear, cries of encouragement grew from both hosts.

Hurled with venom, Terpander's spear came within a

thumb's width of felling the Trojan prince. It sliced through the rim of Hector's shield and gouged a groove in the bronze of his breastplate. It took all the Trojan's guile and massive strength to resist the attack, but from the moment he parried Terpander's follow up sword thrust, the outcome of the contest was decided. In a single fluid movement, Hector hurled his spliced shield at Terpander and leapt into the air towards him, climbing the sky, the Reaper of Shades aloft. The sound of bronze striking bronze resounded across the plain as Terpander struggled desperately to defend himself. He struck out with his shield, but it crumpled like a woven reed basket under the wheel of a lumbering cart, and when the black plume on his helmet was cut off by another scything downward blow, he was left dazed, disorientated. Again, and again, the Reaper bit into muscle and flesh, until at last a blood shrouded Terpander slumped to his knees and implored Hector for mercy.

The foremost prince of Troy showed him no more than he had to Halitherses. Urged on by the frenzied Trojan host, he drove his sword through Terpander's open mouth, snapping his teeth at the gums and splintering the back of his skull. Terpander fell backwards all but dead, and while his body twitched and jerked, Hector cut off his bearded head, ensuring the Argive's shade would be denied entry to Elysium. Unless Terpander's body was buried or cremated intact, his shade was doomed to roam the twilight world of the undead. The worst fate of a warrior on the battlefield.

Terpander's charioteer decided to vacate the field. He

turned the chariot's skittish geldings in a tight arc, almost out of range when a Mysian arrow drilled into the back of his neck, through the small gap between the top of his leather cuirass and the rim of his helmet. He collapsed over the front of the chariot, and as the hurtling carriage bounced over his dying body, crushing bone and bursting flesh, the Trojan horde howled its approval. Moments later, a section of the Trojan centre suddenly broke formation. Defying the orders of their Trojan officers, they charged the Argive line.

The female warriors of the Amazon tribe fought naked and painted and placed little store on a quaint custom of deciding battle in a fight to the death between champions. Most had one of their breasts sliced off to enable them to wield axe and spear more lethally, teeth filed into points to rip and tear the living flesh of their victims. As Hector held aloft Terpander's severed head, bloodlust had gained the better of them. They ploughed past their Trojan commanders and charged the plain.

'Go if you can live with the shame!' Aletes was crying out as the Argive line threatened to fall apart.

The Amazons were coming. The Trojans. The entire enemy. The battle axe hurtled at him. Behind his shield Aletes touched the pouch around his neck, Iphigenia's words shaped on his lips.

'Herdsman or hero, I saw how brave you were in the riverbed.'

He tried to be brave again. His mother's words now. You cannot live well unless you die well. He would try. The gods

105

seemed to speak to him now, their voices in his ears repeating three words.

Fear... Courage... Destiny...

11

The King Returns to Argolis
Southern Greece

Agamemnon stood shading his eyes from the prow of the black hulled war ship. The sea breeze ruffled the waves in his hair, death dark with silver strands woven by the hands of time. Salt had stiffened his beard into clumps of tangled spiders. A sharp tang of brine filled his splayed nostrils, gulls cried like hungry newborn babies in his ears. He watched one of the scavenging birds swoop down near a fishing boat draped with nets, to snatch a fish from the spume-flecked, sapphire ocean laying like a drape of lightly ruffled silk. Then, as the ship's crew furled the billowing, eye-adorned canvas sail, he scanned the crowded shoreline to see who waited to greet him with his sour-faced wife and daughter.

The king's temper was as sore as piss on an open wound. Now he had been given time to pick over it, he was starkly aware his daughter's defiance made him look weak. If a daughter could defy a father, a princess betray a king; what could others do? Had the Fates spun him a different yarn on their loom of fortune, he would be considering his options where his daughter and wife were concerned. As it was, his daughter had been handed another opportunity to help the Argives win this war.

Soon the deck polemarch yelled out. 'Raise oars and stand to!'

With a bump and grind of timbers, the creaking vessel settled against the harbour wall of Nauplia. Crewmen swarmed ashore to secure thick hempen ropes to the warship's moorings. Flanked fore and aft by heavily armed royal guards, Agamemnon stepped onto solid ground.

'Poseidon be thanked,' he muttered, a relieved smile creasing his sun-bronzed skin.

'Have you brought us Priam's head?' a voice from the crowd shouted.

The substantial collection of local fishermen and downtrodden people in the harbour had begun to voice their discontent at the surprising lack of progress by the Argives in four moons of war with the city of Troy.

'Or better still one of his precious stallions,' said another. 'At least then we could eat it!'

'Where are the grain ships you promised? What are we meant to eat?'

A young mother tried to approach the king, a wailing infant clutched in her malnourished arms. One of the Nauplian guards shoved her backwards, and when she stumbled and nearly dropped the baby, the crowd's mood blew hostile like a changed sea wind. A fisherman punched the guard, knocking him senseless. The incident threatened to spark a minor riot. More guards clanked forward to contain the violence, using their locked shields to drive back the crowd.

'Welcome to Nauplia, great lion,' said the leader of Nauplia's council of elders once a semblance of order had been restored. 'I trust your voyage from Troy was swift and uneventful?'

'It was until now, Nausithous.'

Agamemnon switched his attention to Iphigenia.

'My little heron chick. Place a kiss on your father's cheek.'

It was the public display of unity Iphigenia and her mother had chanced on. Calchas had been punished, his deception made wide knowledge. At length, Iphigenia and her mother had discussed how the king would react. The queen knew her husband. Practical. If it served his purpose to keep them alive, he would.

With the eyes of the crowd on her, Iphigenia stepped towards her swarthy father, reached up and placed an obedient kiss on his cheek.

'Good,' said Agamemnon, his reaction that of someone who has swallowed an instantly efficacious potion. 'On pain of death, let no one mention this unfortunate episode again, or use it to drive a wedge of bitterness between us.'

He clamped a heavy arm around Iphigenia's shoulders and pulled her closer to him. His hirsute armpit stank of brine and sweat.

'What of you, good wife?' he continued.

Clytemnestra's smile was as warm as an ice-covered crag in midwinter. It slipped from her pallid face almost as soon as it appeared.

'I bid you welcome, husband.'

'As do I,' Lord Aegisthus said, deflecting the king's attention from the taciturn queen. 'Might I suggest we proceed with all haste to the palace? A light repast has been prepared, and while we eat I would like to discuss the situation in Boeotia. What is left of Orestes' beleaguered host at Mount Oeta is in urgent need of reinforcement.'

'Where are the Spartan and Pylian support?'

'They have arrived here in Argolis, Lord. Two hundred fully trained spears are camped nearby with the rest of the relief force, ready for you to inspect. Both wardens have had difficulty filling their quotas and claim if there is a repeat of last winter's food riots they may struggle to restore order.'

'How many does the entire relief force number?'

'Enough to lift the siege of Trachis, where Orestes is presently holed up, and drive Hector's army from Boeotia.'

'The precise figure, warden?'

'Less than two thousand, but hopefully Achilles can be persuaded to swell that number with his black-armoured Myrmidons.'

Agamemnon snorted air out through his beetle leg nostril

hairs.

'Achilles has returned to Pharsalos.'

'Achilles has sailed home?' Aegisthus tried to look surprised. The king and his golden champion had fallen out more times than he could count. He was shrewd enough not to ask what this quarrel was about.

'The reinforcements are ready to mobilise to Boeotia?'

'They are.'

'Then leave Achilles to me. I have an offer he will not refuse.'

'Oh, and tell the wardens that food riots are the least of their concerns,' Agamemnon added. 'If Hector breaks through into Laconia they'll be wearing slave collars and eating boiled leaves for the rest of their lives. Point that out on the next clay tablet you send them.'

'Ah Glaukos', the king said. Glaukos had been hanging back a distance from his father after their disagreement at Zygouris.

'Walk with your king,' Agamemnon said. 'I asked you to join us here as I have something to discuss with you and your father. I trust you have fully recovered from your recent injuries?'

'I have, Lord of Men,' Glaukos said eagerly, inclining his head in a cursory gesture of respect.

Like his father, he looked for the opportunity in every situation. One had presented itself today. Achilles abandoned the fighting? Achilles was as good as a god to the Argive warriors; without him on their side, Hector would drive the Argives back to the sea. The Trojans would never seek terms now. There would be no heavily laden grain ships sailing unmolested through Trojan waters from the grainfields of Krimea. The promise of the warrior king worthless. In every Argive city, thousands would starve and there would be more bloody food riots on the streets of Mycenae.

Agamemnon was looking sceptically at Glaukos' crushed hand and the studded black glove that concealed it.

'Tell me again what happened Glaukos. Chariot racing in Athens were you not? I believe Orestes was also present?'

'He was, Lord of Men,' said Glaukos, the king's unusually cordial manner making him wary. 'He was leading the last race of the festival when the reckless fool in the lane next to him lost control on a bend, flipped over and landed on top of me.'

'Your sword hand is undamaged?'

'It is, thanks to the good fortune of the goddess Tyche.'

'And your injured hand? Can you still heft a shield and take your place in a defensive wall, should the need arise?'

'I can. As I proved during my recent expedition to Elis. My father sent me to wipe out a raiding band of Hillmen. We tracked them to their lair, slew sixty of the vermin and several of their Dorian masters. We drove spears into the bellies of the breeding females and buried the clan shaman alive. Nothing living was spared. Their lice-infested infants provided good sport for our archers when hung naked by the ankles from trees.'

'I'll wager they did,' said a delighted Agamemnon, scanning the once grand courtyard they had entered. On its far side stood a small palace, built in the days before the King of Nauplia was slain by Agamemnon's conquering forefathers. More recently, it had been used to house a slave market.

'You have proved yourself worthy of my trust,' Agamemnon continued. 'I have a mission of greater importance than butchering a few dozen Hillmen. But first I need to eat. Horns of the minotaur, that spit roast sheep smells good.'

The situation in Asia was little short of disastrous. The fighting had begun with an unexpected night attack by the Trojans. Argive losses numbered in the thousands. Most of the fleet burned to ashes where it was beached. Agamemnon responded by launching a simultaneous assault upon the four great gates of Troy. Siege towers, scaling ladders, giant catapults and armour-plated battering rams deployed, yet each attack was repulsed with the loss of hundreds more warriors. Badly mauled and demoralised, the Argives retreated behind their hastily erected barricades to lick their wounds. Several more desperate attempts were made to seize the initiative; each attack beaten back with more heavy losses.

The exception was Achilles' raid into the heartland of Lydia in the Troad, the peninsula of cities allied with Troy along the West of Anatolia. The expedition resulted in the sack or capture of eleven provincial towns. Fighting under their feared black ant banners, the ferocious Myrmidons seized vast herds of livestock from the fertile land, slaves, and piled their carts high with tribute. The Lydian host was recalled too late to intercept Achilles, and for a full cycle of the moon thereafter the Lydians withdrew from the fighting to mourn their dead, rebuild homes and farms, and their damaged city defences. This provided the Argives with welcome respite, a chance to regroup and strike hard at the depleted defenders of Troy. Yet instead of seizing this opportunity to launch a concerted push for victory, Achilles' exploits drove a wedge of acrimony between he and Agamemnon.

One of the towns Achilles besieged was Lyrnessus. Its stubborn occupants held out until the Myrmidons cut off their underground water supply and they were forced to seek terms. Achilles had exacted a high price for their defiance, and to ensure they remained neutral and did not threaten his lines of supply, he seized the king's two daughters as hostages. He kept the fairest for himself, and upon his return to Troy he presented the elder sister, Chryseis, to a grateful Agamemnon, as part of his share of the spoils.

In return, Agamemnon ordered feasts and trials of athletic prowess in Achilles' honour. A mood of renewed optimism surged through the Argive camp. A mood quickly shattered when proud Chryseis stabbed herself in the throat with a blade of glass from a bronze mirror rather than share her captor's bed. At once, Agamemnon demanded Achilles hand over the younger hostage, Briseis, as compensation. Achilles refused, and when compelled by Agamemnon's council of war, Achilles stormed to his pavilion and refused to rejoin the fighting. There he remained until late summer when news of the Trojan invasion of Thessaly and Boeotia stirred him into action. Mustering half the Myrmidon host, he seized what ships he needed and sailed to defend the Myrmidon capital of Pharsalos. A clutch of sympathetic lesser warlords followed suit, and it had taken all of Agamemnon's powers of persuasion to prevent a complete abandonment of the war. He had succeeded on condition he returned from Mycenae with Achilles at his side and conclusive proof, in the form of Hector's severed head, that the Trojan threat to Argolis had been removed.

'You see, good wife, I am left with little choice,' Agamemnon said with a mouth full of spit roast sheep, flicking his fingers in the air for his bowl to be refilled. 'Without Achilles and his Myrmidons, the Argive alliance will fragment. I must therefore return Briseis to him along with another once-coveted gift.'

'You have this Briseis with you?'

'Trussed up in the hold of my ship. She's a comely enough creature, yet hardly worthy of all this fuss.'

'What is this gift you refer to?'

'Iphigenia. I am sending her to Pharsalos to marry Achilles, assuming he still wants her. She will leave at first light, escorted by Glaukos and a contingent of palace guard. I will send a herald ahead to give Achilles the good news and urge him to march on Trachis without delay.'

'At first light?' Clytemnestra retorted. 'Iphigenia is not yet recovered from her ordeal. You will send her on a hazardous journey of three days?'

'I thought she wanted to marry Achilles?'

'Indeed', Clytemnestra said, picking each word precisely.

115

'We travelled to Aulis for our daughter to marry Achilles if you recall.'

Agamemnon sucked in a long breath through his nostrils.

'Iphigenia is reluctant to travel anywhere without me at her side,' the queen added.

'Then she must be persuaded, or forced if necessary,' said Agamemnon, pursing his lips as if he had a painful sore on the tip of his tongue. 'Have you not listened to a single word I have said? I do not like this any more than you, but Achilles has left me no choice.'

'Could you not travel to Pharsalos?'

'I am King of all the Argives. I will not go olive bough in hand to anyone, even my old friend, King Peleus. Besides which, there are the minuscule matters for me to attend to at Mycenae such as, ah yes... how to feed a murderous, ravenous mob, and prevent them burning the city.'

'Then permit me to travel with my daughter, at least until we reach Phocis and the protection of Electra?'

'Out of the question. I need you at my side to help placate the people. They have always favoured you, and knowing you share their hardship will assuage their anger.'

Agamemnon tossed a clean-picked bone into the empty clay bowl from which he had already mopped up the last traces of richly seasoned stew with another crust of white bread. Belching contentedly, he rose to his feet.

'If you are ready, warden. You too, Glaukos. Let us see if

the force you brought with you is up to the task.'

He half-turned, glanced back at Clytemnestra, and spoke in a conciliatory tone. 'The runner we send to Achilles will halt at Phocis for rest and victuals. Prepare a despatch for him to carry to Electra so she knows where on the road to meet her sister.'

He strode off, flanked on one side by Aegisthus and on the other by an attentive Glaukos.

Iphigenia had watched from the table as she was spoken for and acted for as if she had no more life in her than a shadow wandering voiceless and purposeless in the Meadows of Asphodel. She pushed away the heaped platter of stew she had picked over and gripped her fists so hard they creaked like the leather of a saddle on a wind-brushed horse, galloping free and far.

12

The Lyre Strumming Boxer

The port of Sicyon offered a swifter sea route to the northern provinces of Agamemnon's Mycenaean empire and the capital of Achilles' homeland in Thessaly: Pharsalos. The journey came with increased risk. Located on a rocky headland, Sicyon was little more than a heavily fortified fishing village; the small fleet of warships patrolled the Sea of Corinth for Dorian led pirates. Officials, merchants, and private travellers used the route in a game of chance. The village was also a place of rest, refreshment and modest entertainment, and Iphigenia's escort arrived weary in the evening after a day's travel from Nauplia.

The escort crept into the port like a lizard, Glaukos' chariot at the twitching head, riding solo: the thick body made up of two other chariots and a mule-drawn chariot laden with a belly of tribute for Achilles, supplies and chests of belongings, while the king's palace guards tailed at the back. In the second chariot, beside Alcinous, Iphigenia travelled holding a parasol to keep off the flaming sun. In the third chariot, the hostage Briseis, another prize to be returned to Achilles, blistered in the sun, lashed by the wrists to the ash wood bar of the chariot, chaffing like dry meat being cut with a blunt knife. The giant Euthemus, Glaukos' second man, guarded her.

It was only when Glaukos had punched Briseis with full, hideous force, the bone in her beautifully freckled nose cracking in two, and later dragged her into the bushes, that Iphigenia had seen, in horrifying clarity, that she had underestimated her cousin. Until then, she had reasoned his trouble with Aletes was a focused ulcer of bitterness. She could understand their rivalry now she had spoken with Aletes in the orchard. Glaukos was brutal, as were all Argive men. Yet those men rarely enjoyed inflicting pain in the way she now saw Glaukos did. His torture of the hostage was not to inflict suffering on an overt enemy, it was to punish one at home: Iphigenia.

Glaukos had tormented the golden-haired hostage from the moment they departed Nauplia. The escort had halted under the highest sun to shade and water the horses. Glaukos left Briseis roasting in the fire of the sun as if venison on a grate. Iphigenia waited until he was distracted and took Briseis her goatskin gourd of water. Her wrists were raw, her face stinging. Drawing on her mother's direction, Iphigenia tried to speak tactically.

'Achilles will be angry if Briseis is mistreated. She is a prized gift to show Achilles my father sincerely wishes to put aside their differences.'

Glaukos breathed out sharply. 'Achilles no longer cares for this mewling Lydian. She's been ravished by your father, she's soiled goods. Providing she can still breathe when I hand her over, he will not mind if she's been repeatedly beaten and ridden like a gutter-born prostitute.'

'I do not believe you,' Iphigenia said, shaking her head in disgust. 'I have met Achilles. I know him to have honour, loyalty, compassion.'

'He did until Deidameia perished,' agreed Glaukos. 'Then grief warped his mind and he turned to his boyhood friend, Patroklos. Try ousting him from your new husband's bed and you'll find that out to your cost.'

Like her father so often, Iphigenia allowed impulse to move her before she considered the consequences. She began picking at the ropes coiled around Briseis' wrists.

'Either you release Briseis or I will,' she was saying.

It was then Glaukos had shoved Iphigenia away and drew back his arm like an archer stretching his bow. He released his hand into Briseis' delicate features with a sickening crack. Briseis let out an awful gasp like a deer thumped by an arrow and she slipped into darkness.

As evening approached and Briseis regained lucidity, Glaukos had cut her bonds and dragged her sobbing into the trees and dark undergrowth that bordered their camp for the night. When he proceeded to viciously beat and rape her, he knew that he did so with impunity.

Iphigenia's palace guards were still.

'How can you just sit there?' Iphigenia had raged at them. To a man, they averted their eyes. Their responsibility was to protect the daughter of the king. They were not going to risk their lives for one unfortunate enemy Lydian, even if they felt uneasy about her treatment.

All the time, a corrupting guilt that she had caused Briseis' torture, punished Iphigenia without Glaukos needing to lay a hand on her. She gripped her fists so hard her knuckles turned white. So many times in her now nineteen summers she had wished she had been born a man. Not because she hated her gender, but because this world was made for men. She would have lethal, trained arms, and stick her sword into Glaukos' throat. She would show no mercy. She blinked away hot, unsummoned tears, refusing to let them fall, denying Glaukos the satisfaction.

Now, the low, setting rays of the sun on the second day of their journey stabbed at the eyes of the travellers and arrowed off the bronze armour of the military men. Barefoot children playing on the sides the well-worn road into Sicyon ran shrieking at the sight of them, alerting the half-asleep lookout to their arrival. A horn blared. Curious onlookers gathered.

A storm threatened above. Iphigenia was grateful for the refreshing, cool breeze that wafted off the sea and dried the sweat on her forehead. As well as tormenting herself with visions of

Briseis' suffering, she was trying to piece together what she had seen in the darkness of the camp when all were sleeping last night.

In the thin light of the fire in the dead of night, she had made out Glaukos disappearing into the trees and the silhouette of a second figure standing taller by a horse's muzzle. A glint of a spear grabbed the light of the fire, and a star-shaped broach dazzled in the shard of flame, as did matching star buckles on his cross-strapped sandals. Euthemus was kneeling with his back to Iphigenia, ready to move to Glaukos' defence if needed. Sharp voices slicing the point between a whisper and a voice. Anger.

Shaking away the visions of the previous night, Iphigenia gazed across the spume bearded waves to where three of her father's warships waited at anchor, ready to take her on the next stage of her journey. Braziers had already been lit on each vessel's upraised stern deck to mark its position in the gathering darkness. They were beacons of hope, Iphigenia told herself. One more day and she would be reunited with her sister. With Electra's assistance, she would put a stop to Briseis' shameful mistreatment and she would persuade Achilles to help lift the siege of Trachis.

Glaukos halted his chariot before the mixed band of part-time local militia and battle-hardened Mycenaean veterans who waited to receive him outside Sicyon's ornamental octopus gates.

'Greetings, my lord,' said the brothel keeper with cropped, grey-flecked hair and a pointed beard, who doubled as Master of the Watch. 'On behalf of the people of Sicyon, I bid you welcome again to our humble home.'

Glaukos pointed up at the billowing purple-bellied storm rolling ominously nearer, blotting out the westering sun and deepening the gloaming.

'A tempest is coming, Orthagoras,' he said, a first distant rumble of thunder confirming his words and echoing the groaning in his stomach. 'I suggest we skip the formalities and head inside. I'll inspect our transports in the morning, after we've honoured the Dioscuri. The storm will be long gone by then, and with the twins' blessing we can safely put to sea.'

'As you wish, my lord.'

The Dioscuri were the twin sons of Zeus, traditional protectors of seafarers. Although indifferent himself, Glaukos knew there was not an Argive under his command nor on board the king's warships who would attempt to cross the Sea of Corinth without offering generous tribute to the twins. He pulled hard on the chariot's reins to steady the nervous pair of roan stallions in the traces.

'We dined on succulent venison last night, Orthagoras. A speckle-coated doe I rode down and spliced myself. I trust your elders are serving an equally pleasing meal this evening?'

'Swordfish, my lord. I watched it carried ashore this morning.'

'That will do nicely. Iphigenia of Mycenae will not be joining us, I'm afraid. She's unwell and wishes to retire to a bedchamber. Convey this news to our hosts and arrange for victuals to be served to her and the Lydian in her quarters.'

Orthagoras focused his discerning eyes on Iphigenia and the bloodied hostage. He kept his thoughts to himself.

'The elders will be disappointed,' he said. 'Electra sojourned here on her way to marry King Pylades. They were looking forward to spending some time with her younger sister.'

'Break it to them gently then. I assume the Dorian I placed in your care has been constantly guarded? No more attempts to escape?'

'None, my lord. Your threat to remove her son has done its work.'

'All the same, Orthagoras, stay vigilant. Her husband may go back on his word. He doesn't know I've moved the runt. If he strikes, it will be against this shit sack of a port. You have the seasoned fighters I left behind when I first brought the Dorian she-wolf here. King Pylades will despatch a contingent of Phocians to supplement the numbers. They'll arrive any day. You'll have more than enough spears to defend these ramparts against the Ironmen, no matter how many clans come against you. I expect you to prevail, Orthagoras, and the hostage to still be here when I return for her.'

'She will be my lord. You have my word.'

'You gave me your word once before, which turned out to be worthless. Just make sure she's here for the sake of your family and every other miserable peasant in Sicyon.'

Glaukos paused to let his message sink in. As the creaking octopus gates were heaved open, his expression suddenly lightened as if the prior conversation had been a figment of Orthagoras' imagination.

'And how is your younger brother, the boastful Philocletes? Has he recovered from the hiding Euthemus gave him last time we were here? Hera's tits, I bet he wishes he hadn't bragged about never losing a boxing match!'

'He is still convalescing,' said the master, grinding his teeth to resist an urge to add an ill-advised comment he would later be made to regret.

'That's a shame. If he were fit, and the terms favourable, we might be tempted into a rematch.'

A squall hurled grit into the horses' eyes and muzzles, causing them to snort and toss their heads. Ponderous drops of rain began to fall, dappling the parched ground like the freckles on Briseis' ruined, fair-skinned face.

'You had best lead on.' Glaukos flicked the reins in his hand and clucked encouragement to the prancing stallions. 'The skies are about to open, and I would prefer to rinse the dust from my mouth before I take a bath.'

The elders of Sicyon greeted the news of Iphigenia's poor health as Glaukos expected. Effusive platitudes of sympathy and concern were extended to the popular daughter of the king, yet like Orthagoras before them they were careful to keep their true thoughts to themselves.

Glaukos had visited their humble hall once before, detouring on his way home from Elis earlier that summer. The memory of his behaviour was still fresh, not least the savage beating Philocletes had suffered for his imprudent boast.

'Our shaman will prepare a potion to help you sleep,' said Hermione, the shrew-faced wife of Sicyon's leading elder. She was standing beside her partially deaf husband, Megapenthes, in the port's drab yet spacious feasting hall. Though she spoke directly to Iphigenia she kept a wary eye on Glaukos.

'When you are host to a malign spirit, the best remedy is prayer and a good night's rest.'

'Yes, a nice pair of breasts,' agreed Megapenthes, struggling to follow the conversation despite holding a large spiral conch to his least deaf ear. 'Achilles will be pleased with those.'

'I said rest, husband, not breasts.'

'I don't want to rest. I had a nap earlier and now I am ravenous. I want to eat swordfish with our guests and hear the latest from Troy and Mycenae.'

'No, you senile old goat, it is Iphigenia of Mycenae who – oh, never mind!'

She clapped her small hands sharply.

A previously unnoticed female stepped out of the shadows at the back of the hall. She was closely followed by Orthagoras' so-called boastful brother, Philocletes. He wore the wounds of that ill-fated fight of which Glaukos spoke, with a deep limp and fist-flattened nose.

'Take Iphigenia of Mycenae to the guest chamber and see she and the Lydian are made comfortable for the night,' said

Hermione. 'Bring nourishment to them in the room.'

The woman bowed grudgingly. She had striking slanted feline eyes and Iphigenia saw she wore a star shaped pendant around her neck. On each of her bare, shapely shoulders, was a matching star, scarred into her skin.

She was the Dorian that Glaukos had spoken of. Iphigenia was sure of it. She knew he had been sent to Elis, perhaps she was captured there. Why was he holding her hostage? From what she knew, Dorians were not a wealthy people, so holding her for ransom was unlikely to bring much of a reward.

Hermione clapped her hands again. Iphigenia was escorted from the hall, the Dorian helping to support Briseis. The kitchen master and his assistants filed the other way, holding platters of wonderfully scented grilled swordfish that roused Iphigenia's appetite for the first time in days. More assistants passed, with simply engraved craters for diluting wine, serving boards, knives, and the small, individual tables necessary for the elders and their unwelcome guests to dine upon.

'What have we here, Orthagoras? The fellow with the lyre looks like he can handle himself?'

Glaukos' close-set eyes had fixed on a tower of a man of perhaps thirty summers, who had slipped into the hall at the end of the long line of servants. He moved with lion-like power and economy, an athletic body clad in a short linen tunic and sandals. His leather-skinned face was handsome yet unmistakably that of a man who lived by his fists. He wore a neatly trimmed beard and thick cap of tight hazel curls and under the bulging muscles of an arm, he carried a lyre. Seating himself on a stool at the back of the hall, he started to strum a melodious tune. His baritone voice had the texture of slow poured honey and soon held the attention of everyone in the torch-lit hall. Everyone except Glaukos. He was looking at the minstrel's excellent physical condition.

'He is nephew to Hermione and hails from nearby Corinth,' Orthagoras explained, looking pleased with himself. 'I am told he fights with the fist as a leisure pursuit and has won the odd crown of laurel.'

'The odd crown, you say?' Glaukos replied, amused that Orthagoras, with a little help from Hermione, had the temerity to try to fleece him and avenge his pummelled brother with such a brazen deception. The minstrel was clearly a seasoned fighter.

'What terms do you propose, Orthagoras? They will have to be tempting to persuade Euthemus to accept the challenge?'

'Four seasons' profit from my harbour brothel against the tavern Euthemus won from my brother.'

'The minstrel must be good!'

'It's a fair offer.'

'I have a better one.' Glaukos looked at the shrew face of the elder's wife. 'The minstrel is nephew to Hermione, so let him fight for his aunt's virtue. If he wins, your brother gets back his tavern. If he loses, Euthemus wins the brothel's proceeds for the stipulated period and gets to bed the old crone.'

'For a stone?' blurted deaf Megapenthes, misunderstanding

again. 'Not much of a prize, is it? Why would they want to fight for a stone?'

Mutterings of disbelief rippled around the hall from those who had heard clearly. Hermione blanched and gripped her husband's arm as if fearing she was about faint. The three warship masters, who had joined the gathering shortly after Glaukos' arrival, glanced at each other and shook top knotted heads with barely concealed disgust on weathered faces. Even Euthemus looked taken aback by the effrontery of the proposal.

'She's older than my grandmother,' he said dismally.

'She is, though she doesn't have horns or eat grass like most of your conquests,' teased Glaukos, enjoying the look on Hermione's squashed face. Whatever the outcome of the fight, he intended to seize the profits from Orthagoras' brothel for at least a full turn of the seasons. The scheming Watch Master deserved to be punished for his audacity. Hermione had played her part and was no less deserving of a reprimand, yet tempted though he was, Glaukos did not intend to prolong her discomfort after the last punch was thrown.

Contrary to appearances, the bearded she-goat standing before him was one of the few people in Sicyon with a backbone. Pushed too far, she would stand up to him. She would ignore his threat to gut Megapenthes like the swordfish they were about to devour, and after he departed at dawn, when unseen by one of the Mycenaean veterans, she would send a clay tablet of complaint to Glaukos' father at Mycenae. Aegisthus had not been made aware of the hostage Dorian's existence. When he found out, he would demand answers, and unable to recall his son from Pharsalos, he would despatch an armed delegation to question Hermione, Orthagoras and every loose tongue in Sicyon. Given what Glaukos and his allies had planned, an inquisitive father was the last thing he needed.

'That's settled,' he quickly concluded. 'The terms of the wager are agreed. Now I suggest we eat this delicious food while it's still hot. Grilled swordfish is a favourite of mine, and I'm so hungry I could eat Alcinous' loincloth! Steady with the wine, Euthemus. This minstrel will be no pushover.'

As it happened, the minstrel came within a single good punch of winning the contest. Euthemus, red-bearded and unusually tall, was bigger, younger, and heavier, yet the nimble-footed minstrel more than compensated with speed and guile. Time and again, the minstrel's war hammer fists penetrated Euthemus' lumbering defence. They struck him with the force of stones dropped from battlements, winding him, rocking him back on his heels. Blood flowed from Euthemus' thick lips and clotted in his nostrils. Both eyes had begun to close from damage when he heeded the advice Glaukos had given him during the previous fight in this place.

'Dogshit to time honoured rules, Euthemus. Gouge out his eyes or bite off his nose. Just make sure you beat the crap out of that dancing cockerel.'

Lunging forward, Euthemus grabbed the startled minstrel in

130

a rib-cracking grip. He butted his now helpless opponent in the head. Again. Again. Again. Cheekbone split open, already-flat nose obliterated. The minstrel was unconscious before Euthemus released him, unaware his testicles had ruptured from a vicious stamp. Savage kicks broke two ribs, another downward impact perforated his eardrum and left one side of his face like raw pork. Euthemus straddled him, landing more punches before Glaukos ordered Alcinous to 'pull the feral cur off'.

'A spirited scrapper, Megapenthes. He might have won had the Fates been kinder. As it is, he won't be crooning any melodies for a while, will he?'

Before Megapenthes could mumble a reply, Orthagoras spoke for the elder.

'My lord, this wager is between the two of us. Hermione wanted nothing to do with it and only agreed to summon her nephew because I pressed her. She doesn't deserve to have her honour injured on my account. The profit from my harbour brothel is yours for as long as we agreed. I pray you settle for that.'

'What say you, Euthemus? You want to bed the elder's wife, or are you prepared to settle for the proceeds of the brothel?'

'I would prefer to bed the Dorian, my lord,' said Euthemus, emboldened by his triumph.

'I don't recall mentioning her. You've done well, Euthemus, so if our host has no objection, I'm prepared to overlook your presumption. After I have finished with the Dorian, you may grease your stunted weapon.'

Later that evening, Iphigenia was first to hear the rap of hobnailed sandals approaching along the dimly lit corridor. She was sitting on a couch in the guest bedchamber and had not long finished eating the frugal fish supper the star-marked Dorian had brought to them, sipping a cup of honey-sweetened lime cordial. Briseis was sitting on the narrow bed opposite, picking over her food, breathing through her mouth. The priestess' nose sat ruined and fat, her eyes plump as the pillows around her, so swollen she could barely see from them, the sockets underneath corrupted purple, grey, yellow.

The footsteps halted abruptly, and the blink of an eye later the chamber door was thrown open. The huge figure of Euthemus stood splay legged in the threshold, framed by flickering lamplight.

'Come with me,' he barked.

He faced the dark-skinned Dorian marked by the stars rather than Briseis.

'Don't make me come in there to fetch you. It will go badly for your boy if I do.'

Iphigenia rose to her feet. 'Where are you taking her?'

Euthemus behaved as if he heard nothing. He stared through her.

The Dorian was already moving towards the door, head bowed in the manner of one who has learned the hard way to do what she is told, when she is told.

'You can't stop this. If I don't go quietly, they will punish or kill my boy. Look to yourself and Briseis.'

Euthemus grabbed the Dorian around the top of her arm, and with his other hand thrust into the deep crease at the base of her buttocks, propelled her along the corridor. He grinned at Iphigenia, and with a lecherous laugh rolling up his throat, slammed the door shut behind him. As soon as she heard him moving back along the corridor, past where the dutiful Philocletes was standing guard, Iphigenia, pulsating with fury, started to push the heavy couch across the tiled floor.

'Help me lift this,' she said to Briseis.

Together, quietly as they could so not to alert Philocletes outside, they wedged the couch under the bronze latch of the door. Briseis stepped back and squeezed her eyes shut in pain, the stooping movement causing blood to rush to her bloated face.

'This won't stop Glaukos,' she said, breathing raggedly out of her mouth.

'Perhaps,' admitted Iphigenia. 'But it's better than sitting here doing nothing. Come on, let us move the bed and the chest.'

Slumped with their backs against the barricade, breathing hard, they began speaking as two women in any place but here, strolling in a market for delicious fruits and sweetmeats, or at one of the festivals exclusive to adult women, chatting with the freedom of a world without men.

Iphigenia fetched a damp cloth. She dabbed it softly as she could under one of Briseis' eyes as they spoke. The Lydian princess winced.

'You are to marry Achilles?' Briseis said.

'Yes,' Iphigenia replied, expecting the question. She had heard rumours that Briseis had fallen in love with Achilles during her time with him. She hoped she did not do her further harm now.

'Achilles will be kind to you,' Briseis said, looking into Iphigenia's big black eyes. 'And it helps that he looks like a god.'

Both young women laughed, becoming less nervous since Philocletes down the corridor had not seemed to hear their rearrangement of the room.

'Though it appears there is a hero to rival Achilles,' Briseis said, with a hint of good-hearted mischief. 'The guards in the camp spoke of a warrior. They said he saved your life when he was just a herdsman. That he slayed a lion with only a sling before becoming one of the greatest fighters in the army. Will you tell me the story? Take my mind from this place.'

Iphigenia pulled a fleece off one of the couches and wrapped it around their shoulders as she recounted the events of the riverbed, of Zygouris, and the orchard. She kept the words of the prophesy to herself, after all, Briseis was still an enemy.

'And is he as handsome as Achilles?'

Iphigenia laughed. 'Well... Achilles has hair of gold, Aletes has eyes of silver... his face is different to Achilles, how can I say... more earthly than divine, yet somehow just as beautiful.'

'And is he as great a warrior as Achilles?'

'I saw him in the city of Mycenae only twice since he began his military training. He was double the size I remembered him! In fact, I saw him in only his loincloth, cleaning chariots and grooming

134

horses! I heard rumours he has become a skilful warrior with spear and sword. One of the greatest in the camp. He was one of the two recruits awarded the honour of protecting the battle standard when he left Mycenae, I know a modest achievement in heroic terms, but he is fighting in Boeotia now, with my brother Orestes.'

Briseis smiled. The daughter of the king who had shown her so much misery had been kind to her. She did not want to insult Iphigenia by saying too much, yet she believed that much like herself, the enemy princess' heart had been won by a great warrior favoured by the gods.

13

Raiders

Knocking. Diamond sunlight filled the room with prisms of light. Iphigenia watched fingers of red, orange, yellow, green, blue, violet, in the air, as if Apollo's hands pointed her to the day and willed her awake.

Louder. Her eyes caught up with her ears. It was morning.

'Mistress, let me in. You have been summoned to the harbour. Unless you soon appear, Glaukos will be very angry. Open the door, I beseech you.'

It was the Dorian captive. Briseis was stirring now too, in a coil beside her on the floor. Iphigenia began dismantling the barricade.

The wine-purple bruising on the Dorian's face and arms told Iphigenia that Briseis' temporary reprieve had been a victory at the expense of the Dorian. Sanctuary with her sister Electra at Phocis was still a day's journey. The threat of further violence had not diminished. Iphigenia splashed water on her face from the jug on the bedside table, freshening her breath with a mouthful of lukewarm lime cordial. She passed what was left to Briseis, swept her cloak around her shoulders, and looked into the Dorian's slanted eyes.

'I would know your name before we go, and that of the son who has been taken from you?'

The Dorian looked anxiously at the chamber door, her ear tuned to the impatient muttering of Philocletes and the two Mycenaean veterans who were waiting in the corridor beyond.

'I am Melissa, daughter of Neoman, King of the Ironmen. My son is named for his grandfather. Why do you ask?'

'So that when I reach my sister, Electra, at Phocis, I can tell her exactly who her heroes should hasten here to rescue.'

Melissa forced a smile and lifted her head in defiance.

'Do not concern yourself. My husband, Teucer, will come for us before then,' she said, feigning confidence.

She turned to Briseis and switched to her native tongue. Briseis listened carefully, her expression clouding, and with a nod of the head, replied in fluent Dorian.

'What did she say to you?' Iphigenia asked, as they followed Philocletes along the short corridor. The two Mycenaeans clanked along in single file behind them. Briseis hesitated before replying in a whisper.

'She said your sister's husband, the King of Phocis, is in league with Glaukos. She fears your sister cannot help you and your life is in danger until you reach Achilles.'

Iphigenia studied the pattern on the tiled floor, trying to hide the panic in her eyes.

'Ah! Achilles' addled bride has deigned to join us!' Glaukos said sarcastically, as the women reached the beach.

He was standing beside a blazing driftwood fire upon which a rattle shaking shaman had dedicated the head and fins of last night's swordfish to the Dioscuri. Behind him, the last of three warships to be loaded with men, horses, a mule, intricately carved wooden chests of clothes and belongings, geometric patterned amphorae of wine, olives, and oil, was moored against the barnacle crust of the jetty wall.

Megapenthes, Orthagoras, and an odd crowd of forcibly summoned locals waited nearby, impatient to see the last of their troublesome guests. Hermione stood at her husband's side, a strained smile fixed upon her puckered face.

Megapenthes took the conch from his ear. With tears blistering his piglet eyes, wet bottom lip quivering, he blew away non-existent grains of sand.

'What upsets you, husband?' Hermione asked him. 'Are you not as pleased as the rest of us to see the back of this black hearted monster?'

'I wanted to show Iphigenia of Mycenae my peacocks,' Megapenthes said, sulkily. 'One of them is called Achilles, and he, too, is looking for a wife. She would have enjoyed meeting him.'

Not for the first time, Hermione found herself struggling to suppress a desire to scold her husband for being so childish. It was not his fault, she reminded herself. Past illness had deprived him of his wits. Perhaps by turning him into an imbecile the gods were punishing her, for not providing her husband with the sons he had so diligently prayed for.

The final warship rowed out to sea, and Hermione smiled. As oars lifted and dipped to the beat of the deck master's drum, she took Megapenthes by the arm.

Come, husband. I should like to meet this peacock, Achilles. Let me see if he is as handsome as you say he is.'

By the time the sun passed its highest point, the three Argive warships had long left Siconian waters. Glaukos' forty oared galley took its place at the front of the strung-out line in the turquoise waters of the Sea of Corinth. Above, the sun drummed heat from a brilliant sky, seeing Iphigenia seek refuge under a canvas awning stretched across the warship's stern. Briseis was beside her, Glaukos unwilling to cause a scene in front of the crowd at Sicyon when Iphigenia insisted they travel together.

They watched the rugged coastline of Phocis slowly merge out of the shimmering distance. Glaukos had not troubled the women again since the voyage began, so for that small mercy Iphigenia was grateful. Yet the longer she was alone, the more questions plagued her like the mosquitos that had feasted on her feet and calves in the night at Sicyon.

Was the Dorian telling the truth? Was it a trick? What was

the purpose of Glaukos' alliance with her sister's husband, King Pylades of Phocis? Without doubt, the tall stranger speaking sharply with Glaukos in the camp had been Melissa's husband, Teucer. Why meet in the darkness? If he had been there to negotiate the release of his wife and son, what had happened?

'Raiders, my lord! Approaching from the west! May the twins preserve us!'

The lookout's voice was loud, shrill, cracked.

Five black sailed ships. A course parallel to the Argives. Ironmen and Illyrians. The pirates kept just out of arrow range, patched canvas sails billowing in the stiffening breeze like the bellies of pregnant sows. A rocky islet loomed ahead, and as it drew nearer Iphigenia saw that three more pirate ships were waiting in line off its seaward side. They wanted to shepherd the outnumbered Argives through the narrow channel between islet and mainland, yet the reason for doing this did not become apparent until the panic-stricken lookout announced the channel was blocked.

'Whirlpool!' The lookout shrieked again.

The lookout yelled down again, informing Glaukos the pirates shadowing them were changing course and were about to launch an attack. Iphigenia watched in horror as they converged upon the second and third Argive warships, lit arrows nocked and loosened from their decks, setting fire to the sky, arcing towards the Argive ships holding the royal guards like flocks of flame-winged herons. Dense black smoke coiled up into the cloudless azure as sails and rigging burned. The sound of splitting timbers, like bones cracking, as both vessels were rammed. Grappling hooks and ladders were quickly secured, and with a roar, a host of war-blooded Ironmen and dark-skinned Illyrian fighters swarmed over the Argive vessels like locusts over a field of barley.

All of Iphigenia's palace guards were on the second and third warships. She had only just realised. They had been so unmoved regarding Briseis she had not noticed their absence, like a fool. Again, a fool. The outnumbered guards were being slaughtered by the pirates.

'We have to help them!' she cried out.

The deck fell from Iphigenia's feet. The ship slewed sideways. Briseis screamed and grabbed at the warship's gunwale. Iphigenia clawed at the planking, managing to find a grip.

The whirlpool.

As if Poseidon had unleashed one his sea monsters, talons dragged the warship towards its gaping maw with awesome power and speed.

'We'll beach in that cove!' yelled Glaukos, struggling to make himself heard above the cries of men, creak of straining timbers, the terrified whinnying of the roan stallion on board. 'Row! Row for all you're worth!'

He grabbed at the smaller arms of a rower, yanking him away from his oar and heaving the oar back as he took over. 'Row! Row!'

Banks of oars churned the violently rotating water. Iphigenia had never been so glad to have Glaukos on board.

'Row!' He boomed again, his huge shoulders exploding with effort. It was working. The warship started to level. Pulling clear of the whirlpool.

'Hera be thanked,' Iphigenia muttered.

The ship suddenly lurched. An ear-punching groan of splintering timber, the stomach of the ship ripping open on a submerged reef. The terrible cries of drowning men carried to Iphigenia from the rapidly flooding rowing deck. Water boiled over the ship's stern, knocking her into the water. The last thing she saw as she was swept over the vessel's steeply angled side was Glaukos clinging to its broken mast, his legs wrapped in tangled rigging.

'Teucer, you mindless dog! If the tribute is lost, I'll boil your son alive!' he was yelling, the rest of his tirade lost as the current dragged her down.

Iphigenia was kicking upwards, but her chiton twisted and imprisoned her limbs. Her arms were stretched ahead of her, yanking from their joints. Up. Up.

A hammer leg. Almost in the head. The stallion. The horse's hooves were like heavy bronze chariot wheels rotating at full speed as Iphigenia managed to push at the water above her head to stall her ascent. Just enough time for the stallion to pass. Spluttering upwards she grappled for the horse's tail, floating across the surface. She was gasping for breath. Lungs burning.

'Briseis!' Iphigenia called out, before a wave choked

sickening saltwater down her throat.

'I'm here! Iphigenia!' gasped Briseis, coughing up a lungful of murky water. She had manged to clamber over the back of the stallion.

'The stallion's legs!' Briseis shouted, purging mouthfuls of water. 'Don't get —

Water filled Briseis' mouth. She coughed again, Iphigenia struggling to stay above the waves.

'— too close! Grab my hand!'

Briseis threw out one arm, the other gripping the stallion's mane, her lean muscles tearing at the effort. Iphigenia grappled for Briseis' fingers.

She managed to link hold of Briseis' wet hand, slipping, digging her fingers in, finally getting a grip around her wrist.

Pirates in the water. Glinting blades gripped between their teeth, swimming after the Argive survivors. How far were they from land? More raiders. Pouring out of the woods in the cove. Spears and axes ready. At the water's edge.

'What are we going to do?' Briseis shouted. 'Iphigenia!'

A wounded Argive crawled from the surf and raised one hand in a futile appeal for mercy. The tall, spear-hefting Dorian who strode forward showed him none. Wordless, he jerked back the Argive's head by his hair, thrusting the iron-bladed spear into the soft flesh at the bottom of his throat and out the back of his neck. Bright blood ran, crying, down the Dorian's spear and his greave protected legs and sandals.

Cross-strapped sandals. Star shaped buckles.

14

Realm of the Ironmen

Horror-eyed, Iphigenia staggered coughing, gasping, from the sea, into the grabbing hands of five raiders. They dragged her off the beach, beyond a screen of wave-sculpted boulders, into the shade of broad trees that covered the steep ridge and broken ground up to the white sand of the cove. They pinned her on her back, and while one of them held a dagger to her throat the others tore off her clothing with rough hands.

They were wolves. She pushed and hit out; she could not stop them, and as one of her whooping assailants forced open her legs, she braced herself to endure the pain and degradation with the same courage as Briseis when Glaukos raped her. Courage that Briseis was drawing upon again, judging by the bestial grunts and defiant cries that emanated from somewhere close by. Iphigenia spat at the dark-skinned face looming over her. Her attacker merely grinned, licked the phlegm from his lips and bearded chin and reached under his tunic.

The iron blade of a spear burst through his chest, slicing his heart in two. The violator's grin became a hideous realisation of death. His bulging eyes, astonished, then full of fear. With a sound like a foot being pulled from wet mud, the iron blade withdrew. Drenched in the dead raider's arterial blood, Iphigenia mustered the dregs of her strength and heaved his wet, dying body aside before it smothered her.

'Get away from her!' a voice was booming to the other raiders. 'She is the daughter of Agamemnon I ordered you not to harm! Stand back! I will end you all!'

Authority. Power. The voice alone was enough to know the tall Dorian meant it. The attackers fell away.

'My companion! Please!' Iphigenia panted. 'She's the daughter of a king. She's valuable!'

The Dorian watched Iphigenia rearrange her torn chiton. Her breasts were full and pert, he observed, beautifully in proportion with the rest of her shapely young body.

'Release the priestess of Apollo,' he called out, using a title Iphigenia had not heard before. In addition to being the King of Lyrnessus, Briseis' father was high priest of the city's ancient cult of Apollo, his wife and daughters, honorary priestesses.

'Release her! Or I'll gut each of you and strangle you with your entrails!'

The spear in the Dorian's hand dripped with blood as he

surveyed the carnage. As many as twenty Argives made it ashore. The warships burned like funeral pyres upon the waves. Two guards were still putting up a brave, hopeless fight. Bodiless staring heads in the sand, arms chopped off at shoulders, hands severed at wrists still gripping shortswords. The remaining trunks of bodies were being stripped of valuable armour and weapons, and grotesquely mutilated.

Three Argives managed up the beach unchallenged.

Glaukos shouldered his way through the raiders, clutching a sword sheathed in leather. Euthemus and Alcinous followed behind.

'Achilles' tribute.' Glaukos thrust the sheathed sword horizontally into the Ironman's hands. 'A chest of gold and jewels went with it. Thanks to your incompetence it's at the bottom of the sea.'

The pirates edged forward, eager to silence the rude Argive. Teucer stopped them with a raised hand. He drew the ancient weapon from its rosette decorated scabbard and examined it appreciatively. The words, Atreus, and, Drinker of Blood, were inscribed upon its bronze leaf shape twin-edged blade with ornate lions of gold, the hilt inlaid with gold and the mesmerising blue of lapis lazuli.

'I didn't know the reef was there,' he shrugged.

'You should have sent divers to check the seabed,' countered Glaukos. 'No wonder the Dorians are a meagre people if they're all led by dullards.'

Teucer's back stiffened and his intelligent brown eyes narrowed. Quick as a striking asp he pressed the point of the sword against Glaukos' throat.

'I don't have to listen to your insults, Argive. One word from me and your gutted corpse will be a feast for the crabs.'

'You'll never see your wife or son again.'

'Careful, Teucer,' he went on. 'I haven't ventured into a scorpions' nest without securing my return. My agents at Sicyon have orders to wait until the new moon rises. Three days. Without word by then, they'll bugger, blind and slowly spit-roast your pretty wife. They'll send orders to the stronghold where your son is held to do the same to him. Their deaths will be slow, painful, and undignified. Understand me?'

Teucer plunged the point of old Atreus' sword into the sand. He grabbed Glaukos by the front of his cuirass. Weapons bristling, the watching raiders ready to butcher the two hulking Argives they guarded the moment the order was given. Euthemus and Alcinous swallowed hard.

'Are they already dead? Tell me! Are they?'

'They're alive', Glaukos croaked.

'Prove it, damn you! Prove they're alive.'

'Ask Agamemnon's daughter. Your wife served her and her Lydian mongrel food last night.'

'Is it true?'

Iphigenia was still on her knees, struggling to grasp what was happening to her. Even his treatment of Briseis had not

148

prepared Iphigenia for this. *This* is what Glaukos was capable of? What else? She knew in that moment the war with Troy was lost. Her father's head would roll like those on this beach. Her brother would be next. Her mother…

'Speak!' the Dorian demanded.

Arrows. One stuck in the throat of a raider two strides from Iphigenia. Voiceless, he grabbed at the arrow, gasping, desperate to live. Another arrow licked the air and thumped into the spine of a raider further off, his legs buckling as he sunk into the sand. More arrows rained.

'Phocians!' shouted Alcinous. 'Black raven banners!'

'Electra?' Glaukos wrenched Teucer's hand away and squinted through the trees in the direction Alcinous was indicating.

Sure enough. One hundred or more Phocians racing off the wooded ridge beyond the cove and forming a shield wall at the far end of the beach. The auburn-haired woman who led them had dismounted from her chariot where the trail ended at the top of the steep, rock strewn ridge. Sword in hand she now stood beside her senior polemarch, a short distance behind the shield wall. Archers and slingers were using the fringe of dense brush along the perimeter of the beach for cover, stepping into the open to shoot bronze-tipped shafts or hurl smooth round stones.

Another raider's head cracked, spilling open like an egg, an arrow sliced through his ribs and out the other side.

'We need to leave,' Glaukos yelled, running for cover. 'Electra has to believe her sister has drowned.'

'Why are they here?' Teucer demanded.

'We don't have time for this! Give me Achilles' sword.'

A roar erupted from along the beach as the Phocian shield wall made impact with the disorganised, but larger, swarm of pirates.

Teucer turned to the raiders holding Iphigenia and ordered them to bind her hands and prepare to leave. He did not like what Glaukos was forcing him to do, but if he wanted to see his wife and son in this life, he had no choice. Distasteful as it was, he had to continue playing a reluctant part in Iphigenia's abduction. He pulled the Drinker of Blood from the ground, swept off the sand, and sheathed it before holding it a hand away from Glaukos' reach.

'Our agreement stands? You'll bring my family to Tricca three days after the next full moon?'

'A horse,' Glaukos demanded, deliberately stalling. He jerked his head to summon Euthemus and Alcinous. 'Yes,' he continued. 'As long as my bride comes to no harm.'

Bride? Never. Iphigenia was disgusted. She would cut her own throat first, just as Briseis' proud sister had.

A horn blared three times. More and more raiders waded ashore from their rock-anchored ships, eager to join the struggle on the beach. The already outnumbered Phocians had to choose between retreating or standing their ground with a high likelihood of being surrounded and slaughtered. Electra scrambled back to her chariot.

Glaukos slung the old king's sword across his shoulders and

scanned the wooded ridge again, checking in case a party of Phocians had been sent there to guard the main force's flank.

'Do with the Lydian as you see fit. I never intended to give her back to Achilles. If she's of no interest to you, leave her to amuse your raider friends.'

Without waiting for Teucer to answer he set off through the trees, head bent forward, his two faithful men running full pace behind.

'My sister can help you,' Iphigenia said, trying to strategise. 'I can speak to her. She will help you return your wife and son.'

'How will she do that?' grated Teucer, raising his hand to prevent Iphigenia being yanked backwards off her feet by the ropes.

She desperately considered tactics. What would her mother do? Her father?

'Electra will send a runner to the queen at Mycenae. When she learns how you have been wronged, the queen will order every Argive villa and hovel searched until your son is found and returned to you with his mother.'

'For a Dorian?' Teucer scoffed.

'I can write and tell her so.'

'Why would I trust an Argive?'

'This Argive helped me,' Briseis said. 'She can be trusted.'

Teucer considered it, his experienced eyes looking left and right. They settled on Briseis.

'I hear you, Priestess of Apollo, and I beg you not to judge me too harshly.'

Teucer's depleted war band travelled fast, north across Phocis and then deep into the rugged wilderness of Epirus. They halted just once that afternoon to slake their thirsts from the gurgling water of a meandering stream. Teucer gave the order to move out again, setting a relentless pace until long after the gilded sunset came and went. Iphigenia struggled along in the middle of the column, her legs heavy with fatigue, the rope around her neck chaffing in the darkness. For a long while, she clung to the hope the Phocians had seen her, that Electra was giving chase and her force would fight for her. Yet with the onset of a starless night illuminated by only a pale segment of moon, she was forced to accept that was not going to happen. Electra had been gulled into thinking she was dead, and when news of the ambush reached Mycenae, her mother would believe so too.

It was three days before Teucer's returning war band approached the serrated gates of Tricca. The town stood on a broad plateau at the head of a steep sided valley. Its high perimeter wall was made of dressed stone blocks hewn from quarries in the surrounding forest. A single paved road dissected the town from north to south, leading to the central marketplace. The tight dwellings around it were timber, tile, and humble mud brick. The exception was the royal palace of stone, in the style of an Argive country villa.

Smoke danced into the chill dawn air from smouldering

cooking fires. Most of the population was still asleep, but several blasts on the lookout's horn and the barking of countless dogs, soon had everyone awake. The huge gates creaked open, and as Teucer's weary party made their way along the offal littered street, an animated throng gathered to shout greetings to their returning men. By the time they reached the arched gateway that led into the royal compound, most had risen from their beds.

Many cursed or spat at Iphigenia, calling her Argive scum, suggesting various ways her life might end. A few hurled stones, human faeces or in the case of one toothless crone, her worn out footwear. Tightly bound, Iphigenia bowed her head and tried to avoid the more painful or disgusting projectiles. She kicked out at a scrawny cur that snapped persistently at her ankle, noticing as she did, that groups of fur clad Hillmen were interspersed among the baying crowd.

'Bleed you stinking pile of bat dung!' snarled a blade-thin scarecrow with lips peeled over rotten teeth. 'How does it feel to be on the receiving end?'

'Be thankful Naxos can't get at you with his skinning knife. He'd make you suffer the torment of a thousand lingering deaths.'

'Too right I would, Drago. Snot from a hog's nostril is worth more than her scrawny Argive hide.'

The Dorian king's name was Neoman. He waited to receive Teucer outside the vestibule of the palace, which was decorated with bright frescoes of warriors in battle, their famous iron swords and spears at the fore of every huge work of art. The king was tall, bull-chested, his cropped hair and beard the same shade as the iron for which they were known. His wife was much younger. Laodamia's eyes were brilliant blue against the heavy kohl lining them, aflame with hatred for all Argives as she watched Iphigenia.

Neoman held up a hand, palm outwards.

'Greetings, Teucer. My heart is lifted to see you back among us. The ambush was a success?'

'It was. Except for the untimely appearance of a large party of Phocians, all went to plan.'

'Yet my daughter is not with you?'

'The Argive will bring her with him when he collects his future queen, who we keep as hostage.'

'The Butcher of Calydon venturing here?' asked Laodamia, stunned by Glaukos' brazenness.

Calydon was the small town south of Tricca that Glaukos had boasted to Agamemnon about sacking earlier that summer. Instead of turning back at the border of Epirus as Argive war bands usually did, he had continued to track the party of Hillman raiders returning there after burning and pillaging farms in Elis. He had slaughtered most of its Dorian and Hillman inhabitants and by chance captured Melissa and her son, who were there visiting her husband's dying grandmother.

'That is his intention.'

'Then I shall cut out his cruel heart the instant we have him at our mercy. I will personally avenge the slaying of Calydon's women and children.'

'He won't be at our mercy,' said Teucer, irritated by Laodamia's irrational outburst. 'Glaukos isn't dull witted. He won't come within hours of these stout walls without ensuring his safety. He'll be well guarded, and at the first hint of trouble, Melissa and little Neoman will be killed.'

'Who is to say they're not already dead?' Laodamia snarled.

'If I thought that for a moment I would strike the first blow.'

'You have proof they are alive?'

Teucer beckoned Briseis forward. 'King, you should recognise this woman. Briseis, daughter of your good friend, King Chryses of Lynassos. She too was a hostage of the Argives. Bound for Pharsalos as a wedding gift for Achilles. Glaukos decided to leave her with me. She was with Melissa at Sicyon.'

'Welcome, Priestess of Apollo,' said the king. 'Well?'

'I saw and spoke with your daughter, Melissa.' She dared say no more.

'She is hale of mind and body?'

'She… In truth, she has suffered at Glaukos' hands.'

'You mean he has beaten and violated her?'

'Yes.'

'Bestial swine,' hissed Laodamia, her eyes stabbing at Iphigenia like iron spears. 'So be it. For every cut and bruise he has inflicted, his bride will suffer threefold. Guards! Chain the witch with the field slaves.'

'She is not to blame,' Briseis tried to appeal. The two impassive, hard-faced Dorian guards who stepped forward paid no attention. One of them grabbed the halter around Iphigenia's neck, the other her tightly bound arms. Together they half dragged, half carried her out of the royal compound. Briseis tried to stop them until Laodamia placed a restraining arm on her shoulder and steered her firmly aside.

'Come, Priestess of Apollo,' she said, reassuringly. 'Do not concern yourself with the Argive any longer. You are too kind.'

'She tried to help me. She does not deserve to be treated so badly.'

'You are tired and confused,' said Laodamia, guiding Briseis towards the warm, smoke-thickened confines of the vestibule. Teucer and Neoman were already inside, both men keeping their own council for different reasons. Teucer was struggling to banish reawakened images of Melissa's suffering from his mind, while Neoman knew better than to interfere while his hot-blooded wife was incensed.

'You will see matters differently after food and rest. If there is good in the Argive's heart, her gods will hold their hands over her.'

The field slaves' barracks were located near the settlement's north gate. It was a large, cold building with no central hearth or other fitments, no windows and an all-pervading stench of human sweat and excrement. Stout rails ran the length of its interior on either side of a narrow central aisle, each one securely bolted to the floor. Heaving rows of men, women and children were chained by the ankle to these rails, with nothing more to sleep on than a thin layer of straw. Most had been awakened by the commotion and watched with lifeless eyes as Iphigenia was dragged along the aisle and chained to an upright post used regularly for floggings.

'That should keep you out of trouble,' said the senior guard. 'Don't look so high and mighty now, does she?'

The second, younger Dorian stepped up and drove the toe of his sandal hard into Iphigenia's ribs.

'I had an uncle living in Calydon,' he growled, clenching his teeth. 'He died rescuing his family from the flames that engulfed his home.'

The senior guard glanced warily over his shoulder. 'Let's go, before you get us both flogged. Teucer said she wasn't to be harmed.'

The Dorian guards left Iphigenia curled in a ball, wheezing and coughing. She kept her head covered by her hands and stifled her sobs, not wanting her captors to know how close her spirit was to being broken. She was still huddled on the soiled floor when a pair of Hillman overseers arrived to escort the slaves to their scattered places of work.

The harsh guttural voice and familiar gait of one of these shaggy haired savages turned Iphigenia's blood to ice. He was small and hunchbacked, with a long, crooked snout, tiny bird-sharp eyes, and a mouth of decay. He held a stone axe and the smell of him – a fetid stench of unwashed flesh and poorly cured animal hides – was overpoweringly foul. He shuffled the length of the

157

overcrowded barrack, releasing slaves from iron manacles as he went, and bending over Iphigenia, stroked the soft, smooth flesh of her thigh.

'It's her alright,' he drooled. 'I'd recognise that shapely ankle anywhere. This time she can't escape from us.'

Iphigenia reared up against the flogging post and struck out with her feet, knocking the stone axe from the startled Hillman's grasp.

'Filthy Hillman,' she cried out. 'Keep your hands off me!'

'Why, you fiery little she-goat!'

The Hillman snatched up his axe with a snarl and raised it above his lice infested head. He was about to bring it crashing down on Iphigenia's skull when his hirsute companion grabbed him.

'Steady, Naxos. Lord Teucer will scoop out your pea-sized brain with a spoon and boil it into glue if you spill a drop of her tainted Argive blood. If you must fondle the wench, wait until she has toiled in the fields or royal kitchens for a few days and learned a little… servility. Hard work and the lash will drain the sap out of her.'

'Not from her it won't.'

'Patience, Naxos. Wait until our Dorian masters are all drunk or feasting. Then you can creep in here and do whatever you want to her.'

Naxos grunted and lowered his club. 'You're right, Drago. Patience will bring its reward. I'll make her wish the river god had ended her worthless life.'

'Don't leave marks that can be traced back to you.'

'Don't worry, the weapon I'll be using has a blunt tip,' said Naxos, chuckling lustily as he knelt and released his intended victim from the chains binding her to the post.

The instant she was free Iphigenia scrambled away backwards on her hands and knees like a scorpion, just as she had from the rocky crevice. This time Naxos followed her however, cackling gleefully as he poked her in the ribs or between the legs with his stone axe. He tugged spitefully at the lead around her neck, and keeping one eye on her high kicking feet, pranced around her like a demented satyr.

15

A Prince in Mourning

The blue-pink dusk had almost darkened to a night crowned with stars, yet not a single torch or lamp illuminated the taverns, stalls, and shuttered homes of Pharsalos. Riding his winded mule, the only horse restrained on the shore after the shipwreck, Glaukos looked up at the towering citadel gates emblazoned with a giant ant ornament. The whole city was under a mantle of gloom as if its sacred black ants had massed and covered it in darkness. Pharsalos, it transpired, was a city in mourning.

'It's been like this for three days,' said the Master of the Watch at the gates. 'Since his ashes turned up in a sealed jar.'

'Whose ashes?'

'Lover boy's, of course.'

'Patroklos?'

'The Queen of the Amazons cut his throat.'

'How? I thought Achilles had withdrawn from the fighting?'

'He has,' replied the Myrmidon. 'But Patroklos got bored sitting on his pampered arse and decided to find himself something "useful" to do. He ignored Achilles' order not to leave camp and took himself on a scouting trip to Trachis. When Queen Penthesilea took her usual morning stroll around the citadel walls and enquired if there was anyone inside with courage enough to challenge her, the hot-headed fool stepped forward.'

'What in the name of the gods possessed him?'

'Who knows. But whether it was courage or folly, the whole thing was over faster than you could pluck a goose. Queen Penny stabbed him in the throat with her spear, then hacked off his balls while he bled out on the ground. I'm told she had them made into an attractive pair of earrings. The bits she didn't want were cremated and sent back here. Since then Achilles has been inconsolable. He's ordered a period of mourning to last until Patroklos' death is avenged.'

Glaukos jerked up the mule's head with a heated curse. A violent twitch contorted his sweat-glazed face. He did not need a shaman's insight to work out who was responsible for thwarting his plan. The brutal death of Patroklos had been arranged by Zeus, the principle supporter of the Argive cause, to persuade Achilles to rejoin the fighting. Zeus knew that once the raw pain of Achilles' grief subsided, he would go looking for Penthesilea. He would invite the posturing Amazon to fight him to the death, a challenge Queen Penny would hurl straight back in his face. It was one thing to trade blows with the likes of Patroklos, another to do battle with the boldest champion in Argolis. She would resort to calling him names from a distance and enraged by these insults Achilles would unleash his fearsome Antmen. A bloody, decisive battle would ensue. By the time Achilles rode from the field, an earring wearing head would be bouncing behind his chariot, and Agamemnon would be celebrating a resounding victory.

Worst of all, he would be there to witness it. Glaukos had no choice but to offer Achilles his help.

'When is the funeral? No doubt games will be held to honour Patroklos' shade? I intend to take part once I have eaten and rested.'

'I'm afraid you're too late,' said the Watch Master, much to Glaukos' relief. 'The funeral games were held yesterday on the field of war. There was feasting, dancing and a rousing eulogy from old King Peleus. Achilles himself won the chariot race and all but one of the contests. He would have won the wrestling as well if he wasn't too drunk to stand up. Later he donned the regalia of a shaman and took up the sacrificial knife. By the time he'd finished butchering rams there was more blood in the collecting jars than horse piss in a stable midden.'

'Where's Achilles now?'

'In the great hall, last I heard, making final preparations for tomorrow's muster. His son, Neoptolemus, is with him.'

'He has ordered a muster?'

'He marches for Trachis at first light.'

'Does Achilles know I'm here?'

'He does. I sent word as soon as you were seen approaching the city.'

'Then you'd better take me to him. He'll be eager to hear the news I bring from Mycenae. Have one of your men take care of this mule. I'll proceed on foot.'

Glaukos headed towards the brooding bulk of the palace, the Master of the Watch close behind. He was halfway across the stone slabbed courtyard when he saw the vestibule entrance was unguarded. There were warriors in the vicinity, but instead of standing at their posts, they were crouching behind the short, decorative columns of the courtyard peristyle. Odd to say the least, and Glaukos was about to say as much to the Watch Master when a sharp retort split the air.

The sound was a tightly cranked catapult arm being released. It came from above and behind. Before Glaukos could react, a burning ball of oil-soaked grass and reeds arrowed low overhead with a stomach-churning whoosh. Smoke and tiny fragments of debris followed in its wake like the tail of a comet. The size of a bull's head, when it hit the slabs in front of Glaukos, it exploded into a hundred flaming fragments.

Glaukos spun round. Defensive crouch. Hand closing around the hilt of the Drinker of Blood as he searched for his assailants. It was nearly dark and the brightness of the fireball had temporarily blinded him, eyes flashing white and red. His eyes adjusted and he picked out the cumbersome war machine positioned on the rampart above the main gate. Two naked figures.

Working furiously to reload the catapult. One of them a youth, the other the most symmetrically athletic man in Greece.

'I wouldn't waste your breath,' said King Peleus from under the palace entrance columns. 'He's far too drunk to listen to you. I wouldn't stand out there either. Achilles means you no harm, but in his state he might just kill you by mistake.'

'Have the Keres stolen his wits?'

'You could be forgiven for thinking so. As it happens this latest prank was Neoptolemus' idea. He thought it would be amusing to watch you bolt for cover like a startled hare.'

'I hope I haven't disappointed,' Glaukos said, a second howling fireball arcing down from the battlements. It landed on a cracked flagstone a short distance behind the Watch Master, and as he sprinted towards the vestibule behind Glaukos, it showered him with viscid globs. His cloak burst into flames, and with a frantic yelp he threw off the garment. Peleus stamped on it like he would a scorpion. He followed up on the small puddles of magma-like fire scattered across the vestibule floor. Acrid black smoke coiled up towards the high ceiling. Demented laughter rang out around the courtyard.

'Welcome to Pharsalos, son of Aegisthus,' said Peleus, dousing the last of the flames with the contents of a wine jar. He was a tall, broad-shouldered man with eagle eyes the colour of dark honey. He had the same features as Achilles, as if chiselled by the gods, and despite his advanced age, wore the scalp lock of a hero in his thinning silver hair.

164

'This is hardly how I would have chosen to receive you, but nobody listens to me anymore. How fares my old friend Agamemnon?'

'He is hard pressed, Lord.'

Glaukos chose his words carefully. Peleus was no fool. A lifelong friend of Agamemnon's. He did not want to say anything to arouse the old king's suspicion, or to prompt a detailed examination of the ambush.

'He marches north to Trachis as we speak, and remains undaunted as you would expect, but he bids me urge you to persuade—'

'Glaukos, you brigand, you pilfering worm! Don't think you can hide behind my father. Explain yourself!'

All eyes turned towards the vestibule doors as Achilles burst across the threshold in the guise of a demon risen from the bowels of the Underworld. His godlike naked body was daubed from head to foot in a grey hued mixture of ash and mud he had first applied when told the news of Patroklos' death. It had been plastered on him so long the sweat of his exertions had turned it into a foul-smelling slime. His unkempt hair was clogged with the same filth, tangled into cords as thick as forest vines. His dilated eyes were piercing orbs of polished yellow ivory, while his impressively large penis swung between his legs like the neck and head of a strangled dove. Without warning, he threw Glaukos on the floor and straddled him.

A similarly disguised Neoptolemus followed his father.

Neoptolemus prized the Drinker of Blood from Glaukos' undamaged hand, drew it from its leather scabbard, and pressed the point to the helpless Argive's windpipe.

'What have you done with it, you deceitful maggot?' demanded Achilles. 'The missive from your king promised me three things: a bride, the return of a hostage and a wagon laden with gifts. You have brought me none of them. I'll not ask again, where have you hidden my tribute?'

'I have hidden nothing,' Glaukos protested. 'We were ambushed by pirates off the coast of Phocis. The treasure you speak of now lies at the bottom of the sea.'

'Poseidon has it? He seized the lot?'

'All save the sword at my throat.'

'Briseis? Iphigenia?'

'Drowned,' gulped Glaukos, suspecting this was more than horseplay. The blade at his throat had drawn blood, Achilles foaming at the mouth like a rabid wolf.

'I did everything I could to save them, but the current was too swift. Briseis was hurled onto rocks as sharp as an eagle's talons and killed instantly. She did not suffer. Iphigenia was already unconscious and face down in the water when swept far out to sea. I swam after her, but she slipped below the waves before I could reach her. That was the last I saw of my beloved cousin.'

Achilles sat back. Glaukos wondered if he had been struck dead with grief. Still as a god in marble. Was it Briseis or Iphigenia who had wounded him?

'What do you think, Neo. Is he telling the truth?' His voice was numb, indifferent.

'He'th lying through hith teeth,' said Neoptolemus, his pronounced lisp further accentuated by his intoxicated condition. He belched resonantly and swayed back and forth, the point of the sword slipping dangerously close to Glaukos' jugular vein.

'Let me teach him a lethon, fattther. Let me chop oth that shrivelled claw on the end of his arm.'

'I think not,' asserted King Peleus, knocking the rune-marked sword aside as it started to rise in Neoptolemus' unsteady grasp. He pushed the wine sotted youth backwards over his outstretched foot, so he landed awkwardly on his rump and dropped the gleaming bronze.

'Glaukos comes as a friend to speak on his king's behalf. I will not have it said we ignored the time-honoured tradition of providing hospitality to travellers and mutilated his envoy in a drunken prank.'

Peleus turned to Glaukos. 'Iphigenia dead? A cursed bride. I am sorry for her loss. Agamemnon's favourite daughter.'

'Why should we care what is said?' asked Achilles.

'Because the Argives are our friends and allies, and we will need their help.'

'We Antmen settle our own scores, father.'

'We do when we can,' agreed Peleus. 'On this occasion that will not be so easy. It will take many more warriors than we can gather to besiege Trachis and prize the Amazon queen out of her comfortable new bolt hole.'

'Has Trachis fallen?' asked Glaukos, curiosity overcoming his reluctance to speak. Out of the corner of one eye he watched Neoptolemus untangle his arms and legs and start to crawl towards him. The youth's malevolent chuckle was punctuated by a series of violent hiccups.

'It was taken by treachery,' explained Peleus, using his foot to pin Neoptolemus to the tiled floor like a squirming bug. 'Hector bribed a local goatherd to show him the hidden entrance to a cave that led to the Trachians' underground water supply. From there, a narrow passage gave access to a storeroom beneath the feasting hall. Hector waited in the storeroom with a small band of warriors. In the dead of night, he took Orestes and the Argive garrison by surprise.'

'The war is all but lost then? Agamemnon will have to recall the host from Troy to defend – Arrgghh! Let go of my balls!'

'I will when you stop interrupting.'

Achilles' hand was clamped around Glaukos' testicles. 'I was about to say I have no intention of laying siege to Trachis, father. Assuming the hidden entrance has been sealed, and there's no other easy way in, I'm going to challenge the Amazon queen to settle our differences honourably in single combat. I'm confident she will accept.'

'She will not.'

'She will when I start hurling insults at her and her ancestors. She won't want to lose face in front of her people. She will come after me like a wounded boar flushed out of the undergrowth.'

'The Amazon will not fight you,' said Peleus, adamantly. 'For all her warlike bluster, she lacks the courage to confront you. She'll feign indifference and laugh off your insults from the safety of Trachis' lofty ramparts. Unless you come to your senses and make peace with Agamemnon, she'll still be taunting you long after this season's grapes have been harvested from the vine.'

'Please, my balls...' Glaukos appealed.

Achilles' brow folded into a haunted frown. The red mist of drunken madness slowly lifted from his eyes. His wise father had confirmed what he suspected. Penthesilea was a coward and would use any ruse to avoid facing him. He needed a better plan, and the Argives' help to execute it.

Achilles released Glaukos' testicles and hauled him groaning to his feet.

'I am told the Amazon queen likes to feast on the flesh of stillborn infants and fornicate with beasts of the forest. It was a mistake to think such an abomination would feel compelled by honour to accept my challenge.'

'You agree with me at last? You will put aside your differences with Agamemnon and fight at his side?'

'I will, father. My quarrel with Agamemnon is over, at least until the next time he fleeces me. But know that I do this for Prince Orestes and not for Agamemnon. On the night Trachis was sacked, Orestes was preparing to attack the Amazon stockade and avenge Patroklos on my behalf. I can do nothing less than help him in

169

return. If my friend is still alive, I will deliver him from captivity.'

'You will sail back to Troy with Agamemnon?' asked Glaukos, bracing himself for the answer. He was standing doubled over, hands on knees, nauseous pain cramping his lower belly.

'I will, with Queen Penny's painted head spiked on the prow of my warship.'

Achilles wrapped an arm around Glaukos' hunched shoulders and led him towards the dimly lit hall.

'You will accompany me, of course. I want you to take Patroklos' place as my charioteer. I can think of none more worthy than the Argive's esteemed envoy. You can handle my highly-strung stallions with a crushed hand?'

'As well as any man,' said Glaukos, morosely, distracted by the scene of carnage that greeted him as he entered the great audience hall. There were very few lamps or torches burning, so the main source of light was the fire that blazed in the upraised central hearth like Hephaestus' forge. Tongues of flame licked up towards the oculus. They cast menacing, wraithlike shadows upon the walls and ceiling and picked out a tangled pile of naked, mutilated corpses. A dark slick of blood had spread across the boldly patterned floor, indicating how long the butchered captives had been there. A naked man hung upside down from a rope looped over a roof joist at the far end of the hall. His hands were tied behind his back and three arrows protruded at angles from his blood-drenched torso. At first Glaukos thought the unfortunate Trojan was dead, but when Achilles took up his nearby bow and nocked an arrow, the enemy's eyes opened round and white. Muffled pleading escaped from his gagged mouth as he writhed and twisted on the end of the rope like a hooked fish.

Achilles hesitated, turned to Glaukos, and thrust the bow into his gloved hand.

'Show me what you can do,' he said, stepping aside.

As Glaukos sighted along the arrow, he channelled his frustration into the bronze head of the smooth, feather fletched shaft. His mouth twisted into a grin as the bowstring thrummed and the arrow drove through the Trojan's eye. Deep into his brain, killing him.

'Excellent shot,' exclaimed Achilles, delighted, slapping Glaukos roundly on the back. 'Neo, stop taking trophies from those damned corpses and fetch me and this peerless marksman a horn of wine. When our thirsts are quenched we'll pour a libation to the gods and ask them to hold their hands over us during the fighting to come.'

Two days later, Glaukos stood alone on the footplate of Achilles' chariot waiting for the signal to attack. Despite the early hour, it was stagnantly hot, the still air moved only by the rhythmic vibrating of cicadas that seemed to emanate from every bush and clump of tall grass.

On the far side of the low, crumbling ridge that concealed him and the Myrmidon host from the defenders of Trachis, a solitary stooped, hooded figure drove a small herd of goats towards the posturing queen of the Amazons. A short distance to the west, Agamemnon's two thousand hard-pressed relief force and the much larger Trojan host surrounding it, watched the unusual tableau unfold.

The ruse had been suggested by Achilles himself. Glaukos grudgingly conceded it might just work. Audacious and simple, the key to its success relied on Penthesilea having no idea who the hooded figure was.

The recently arrived Myrmidons had moved into position under cover of darkness, and by the time the fearsome, single-breasted Amazon rode out of Trachis with her escort to taunt the hard-pressed Argives, the trap was ready. Penthesilea was no fool and sensed mischief. Yet she was inherently curious and lulled into a false sense of security by the numerous single combats she had fought and won. She made the fateful decision to stand her ground and see what transpired.

'You see,' she declared to the Amazons crowding the ramparts of Trachis and the encircling Trojan host. 'The Argives no longer have the courage to venture forth and challenge me. Instead, they send a goatherd with his scrawny flock to assuage my thirst for blood!'

Leaning indolently against her spear, Penthesilea basked in the derisive laughter that reverberated along the congested ramparts and across the Trojan-held plain.

The laughter stopped.

The goatherd had thrown off his cloak. Golden hair. Golden

eyes. Son of a goddess. Achilles wore no armour; he closed the gap to his prey with startling speed, divine muscles driving and rippling at the helm of his undefeated skin. Before Penthesilea could react, the vengeful Myrmidon was upon her, the Drinker of Blood driving up under her bony ribcage and cut her arched spine in two.

A horn blared. A deafening roar. The Myrmidon host poured over the crest of the ridge. Glaukos found himself well to the fore of the hurtling formation, a bronze shod wheel behind the chariot carrying Neoptolemus, and with a few discrete tugs on the reins he slowed Achilles' galloping stallions to a more cautious pace. Archers' bows were drawn on the ramparts of Trachis, gleaming spear points protruded from the encircling Trojans' hastily formed shield wall. Dying heroically might appeal to Neoptolemus and one or two other battle-drunk Myrmidons, but it was not the outcome Glaukos had planned.

Head low, Glaukos swept by Achilles, who straddled the disembowelled body of Penthesilea and was hacking off her testicle adorned ears screaming: 'Patroklos! Patroklos!'

One of the wing-hoofed stallions stumbled, a bright crimson froth spraying from its distended nostrils. Glaukos realised at once what was happening, and a heartbeat before the lung-shot animal collapsed, upending the speeding chariot, he dived clear. His helmeted head struck a rock, and while he lay there unconscious, the savage fighting danced its death around him.

'He lives, Athena be praised!' said Agamemnon, a knot of

weary, battle-grimed heroes pressing in around him, Euthemus and Alcinous among them.

The battle was all but decided when Glaukos finally recovered his senses, his eyes blinking open to find a jubilant, gore-splattered Agamemnon peering down at him. To Glaukos' astonishment the king lifted him in a rib crushing embrace and kissed him on each cheek.

'I owe you a great deal, son of Aegisthus. Achilles has tipped the scales of fortune in our favour. Today we have won a famous victory. Trachis is ours again and Hector is scurrying north with his tail between his legs. It's only a matter of time before we drive him back across the sea to Troy.'

'Thank the gods,' Glaukos lied, before passing out again.

16

Dungeons of Troy

Two days horseback to the north, outside the Trojan held town of Iolcus, Hector rallied his force for one last defiant stand. The battle was bloody, one thousand Trojans claimed by Argive earth, their bodies to become the dirt of the land of their enemy. No longer armed with the weapon of surprise, Hector faced a stark choice. Lock horns with Agamemnon again and find a secure, well-provisioned base before winter, or abandon the campaign as lost. Hector chose the latter. He declared he would face Agamemnon and his Myrmidon fighting peacock beneath the ramparts of Troy. The prince marched his hungry, depleted, exhausted host back into Macedonia, the victorious Argives at their heels all the way to the sea. Hector reached the strand where his ships were beached and embarked for the towers of Troy.

Much of the booty they had taken was abandoned. Prisoners were put to death or incapacitated by chopping off their hands. The rest were put to death. Only Prince Orestes and a handful of heroes who could prove they came from a family who could pay their ransom were loaded onto the Trojan ships. Some would indeed be ransomed. Others would be butchered in the funeral games of eminent Trojan warlords.

Aletes was one of a hundred warriors herded into the small-stoned marketplace of Pydna to await his fate. He had been captured with Orestes in Trachis, part of a night raiding party hand-selected by the Argive prince. He was naked and chained, the skin on his muscle-ridged torso diseased with raw bruises, fairly sure two of his ribs were broken.

Some men were crying. Brave men. Others cursing. The odd hysterical scream for mercy.

'Pay me a visit when you get to Elysium and I'll treat you to a slice of my old ma's special recipe game pie,' Pytho said.

'I'll do that,' said Aletes, feeling it would be an honour to die beside a good friend like Pytho.

Aletes was looking forward to being reunited with his mother. He would see Argus too and they would chase rabbits with his sling. He tried to keep that vision in his sight, yet regret tortured him. He knew the daughter of a king would never be his. He had heard the rumours that she was marrying Achilles. Yet, he would fight every one of these Trojans in single combat here in this square for the chance to see those eyes again. Oh, those eyes, like a star-filled night. To have the chance to speak with her again, the words that spoke right to his bones. Words that seemed fated to be spoken. Surely his destiny had been to meet her, for how else could he have killed the lion and discovered his path.

Aletes reached into the pouch and managed to take out the silver ring. He kissed it. Eyes closed. The ring would help him meet his fate with dignity and courage.

'Show me the trinket, Argive.'

Aletes opened his silver eyes to see a warrior in richly decorated armour. His breastplate was covered in gold scales, with black horse heads encrusted in what looked like black sapphires or opals. Rubies, emeralds, diamonds, dazzled. His face was once handsome, blighted by war; a fresh-scabbed gash dissected his black bearded chin and ran up across his lips into his cheek. The blade of his sword dripped with the blood of Aletes' comrades.

'Try my patience, Argive, and you will squander your chance to live.'

Aletes held out the silver heron ring. He gazed out at the wonderful blue of the sky. A short distance off, a Pylian noble with a lock of flaxen hair twisted into a ceremonial braid was being marched towards the much smaller group of prisoners that included Prince Orestes. Outraged, the Argive prince was demanding to die with his men or fight Hector in single combat to win their release. A Trojan guard rammed a spear into Orestes' ribs, temporarily silencing him.

'Don't worry, prince,' gloated the guard. 'If your father doesn't cough up enough gold or silver bars, your turn will come.'

'Move along, Paris,' one of his comrades remarked,

stepping up to Pytho. 'Hector doesn't want this to take all day.'

'My brother may want this one. He bears the Spartan royal seal. Who *are* you?'

Aletes said nothing. Like Orestes, he saw no honour in surviving a cull with so many valiant warriors maimed and slaughtered.

'Speak. Are you royal?'

Paris lifted his dripping sword.

'He's royal,' Pytho interjected. 'I've served him all my life. His father is King Agamemnon's cousin. He will pay handsomely to keep his favourite son alive. If he says different, he's lying.'

Aletes shook his head and scowled at Pytho.

'And you're the King of Sparta I suppose?' said the Trojan guarding Pytho.

'Nothing quite so grand, I'm afraid. My mother was a whore from Tiryns, my father a stonemason's labourer exiled for stealing and eating a goat. They were both worth ten of you.'

The Trojan drove his sword through Pytho's ribcage, piercing his heart.

'Live for me, Aletes,' the gnarled old veteran managed to gasp. His eyes betrayed him for a moment: Aletes saw fear, regret. Then defiance. A grin fixed on his face as he crumpled to the floor.

Aletes' eyes flashed like a blade in sunlight. He wanted to scream until the hate left his body. He gripped his fists so hard he nearly cracked his own bones.

Paris curled his fingers around the ring, then shoved Aletes towards the group with Orestes.

'Don't think you're saved, Argive.' He prodded Aletes with the point of his sword.

Aletes did not see the guards grab him. He was still looking back at Pytho. They were not guards. Argive men? Orestes was in front of him, snarling like a wolf. His eyes were as black as his sister's, the rest of his face belonged to his father. His hand closed around Aletes' neck.

'What are you doing with that ring?'

His upturned mouth was convulsing as he growled. His grip tight. Aletes tried not to struggle, it would make it harder to breathe. The Trojan guards let them get on with it, amused by the fickle Argives turning on each other.

'I'll kill you with my bare hands if you've touched her.'

'It was given to me, Prince,' Aletes managed.

Aletes did not want to dishonour Iphigenia by saying in front of these men that she gave the ring to him.

'The last time I saw that ring it was being pressed into my sister's hand. Tell me. Why do you have it?'

'I killed a lion. It was a reward. I would kill the lion again to serve your sister. To serve you. To serve the king. If you don't believe me kill me. I join my ancestors with a clear conscience. Kill me now.'

He was struggling to breathe now. The Prince was boring into his silver eyes. The same silver eyes his sister spoke of when she wrote to him while he was recovering from his injuries in

Athens.

Orestes released his grip.

'You are Aletes the Lionslayer?' Orestes said.

'Some call me that,' Aletes said, rubbing his throat.

'I know your name. Now I know your face.'

The killing was over. Only a dozen Argives survived. They were marched onto the shingle beach, split into two groups; herded onto warships. The airless space below the rowing deck was an oven.

'Is it true?' Orestes asked, as they were chained to the creaking hull of the warship. 'Are you Aegisthus' bastard?'

A commotion. Two Trojan guards started to beat the braided Pylian. Orestes' body instinctively moved.

'Don't.' Aletes said, blocking the prince with his body.

The bound Pylian was kicked in the head and stamped on, his face cracking, pulped, blood slipping from his mouth. Unconscious, he was dragged on deck to be flogged.

The six captives were silent until the lash stopped.

The deck hatch flew open and Paris descended into the thick heat. He held the Pylian's severed head by its flaxen braid. He lobbed it towards the chained Argives. It hit Aletes' leg, hot and wet.

'A lesson to you all. Without his head the insolent Pylian will be denied entry to Elysium. His sightless shade will roam Tartarus in perpetual torment. Any man who speaks out of turn will suffer the same fate.'

For a dip and sweep of the warship's oars, Paris glowered at Orestes. Prince to prince. He was willing him to move. Looking for an excuse. He took a step and grasped a fist of Orestes' sweat-soaked hair.

'It may interest you to know I've bedded your sister, Electra,' he said in a gloating hiss. 'I rode her like a whore the last time I visited your court as Troy's ambassador. She begged me to take her with me when I returned to Troy, but I opted instead for the more mature charms of your Spartan aunt.'

Orestes reacted like a panther prodded with a stick. Metal chains clanged as he strained against them, launching at Paris to bite his scarred cheek. Paris stepped back, easy. He reached for his dagger. It was halfway from its enamelled scabbard when the deck master bellowed an order and struck up a booming, pulse-like drumbeat. Banks of oars churned the ocean as the sleek vessel lurched into motion.

'You are fortunate, Argive.' He rammed the dagger back into its decorative scabbard.

As he climbed up into the sunlight, Orestes hawked his disgust and rasped through clenched teeth.

'I'll finish that lying Trojan dog. Men watch your backs. Trojans aren't used to the taste of defeat. They'll try to vent their frustration on you.'

Aletes stared at the Pylian's severed head. The deck master's persistent beat throbbed between Aletes' ears as the undulating warship moved swiftly out to sea. To Troy.

Four days later the vanquished Trojan host reached its destination, an isolated Mysian cove south of Mount Ida. After ensuring there were no Argives in the vicinity, the warriors beached their wedge-prowed ships and dispersed far and wide to their cities of origin. Hector was last to set off home, marching northwest across the foothills of soaring Ida with the band of emaciated captives and a depleted host strung out behind him. That night, he crossed the swift flowing River Scamander and in the raw grey light of the following dawn, gazed upon Troy's impregnable walls and towers.

Entering the city was not a problem, as it was the Argive camp on the far side of the plain presently under siege. All that would change of course once Agamemnon returned with Achilles at his side, yet for now Hector was able to approach one of Troy's four eternal gates, built by Poseidon and Apollo, without fear of being molested. This was a blow to the morale of the captives who had clung to hope they might be rescued before Hector could fight his way into the city. Instead, they endured the taunts and physical abuse of the mob as Hector strode towards the palace complex like a conquering hero.

Aletes looked on Troy as if he saw his own tomb. No Argive was getting out of there. No Argive was getting in. Troy's walls must have been constructed by the gods, Aletes told himself. Their defences were on a scale he had never seen. Invincible. Melampus had often told him Troy was a city with few rivals in the ancient world, but now he saw how the First Spear's flattering comments did Troy scant justice. The cyclopean walls were dressed limestone slabs that made the largest Argive citadel look like pygmies lived within its walls. Troy was a city for giants. Its teaming streets were so broad they allowed a two-way flow of carts and chariots. There were white stone fountains, huge marble statues and triumphal arches at all the main intersections, while the citadel itself was dominated by the towering marble columns and pediment of the Temple of Poseidon, Troy's chief benefactor and guardian.

For all its wealth and splendour, Troy was a city struggling to cope with the demands of a protracted, hard fought war. The decisive battles of the old order had become two seasons of this strange war, through spring and into autumn. Too many of her sons had been killed, and despite the venom hurled at the Argives, the people were uncertain. The plenty of the past was running dry as the dust beneath their feet. Side streets were clogged with the rat-infested shelters of the homeless, while in every temple precinct and many public gardens, the remains of a funeral pyre smouldered.

'Look in their eyes, my friends,' Orestes muttered, 'I have never seen a people so close to despair. One more concerted push and my father will have them beaten.'

A sharp lump of masonry struck Orestes hard on the temple from the mob. His lost his legs beneath him and his palm burned through the dirt as he tried to break his fall.

There were no dungeons as such in Troy. They had never needed them, preferring to ransom or sacrifice wealthy and influential enemies. Several storerooms deep beneath the palace had been adapted for the purpose. A narrow stairway led down into a gloomy subterranean world. The Argives descended in single file, shuffling along a short passage where half-men of bone, with red-rimmed eyes and wild beards, crowded at the barred hatches on their cell doors for news of the war.

'Take heart,' Orestes urged them. 'My father is at the gates with Achilles by his side. We will all be home soon.'

With his club, a guard imposed the strict rule of silence Orestes had chosen to ignore. The impetuous prince slumped to his knees under brutal blows. Aletes threw himself over the prince's back, the club smashing into his spine as he wrapped his arms around Orestes' head and his own. The guard stopped short of causing more damage; these prisoners needed to live. For now. Aletes dragged his prince towards the relative safety of an open cell. He propped him against the wall, as far as possible from the bloated, fly-infested corpse and leather bucket of waste that occupied the opposite end. Ordering the present incumbents to move aside, he cradled the prince's bloodied head until he recovered his senses.

'Help me get up,' Orestes grunted. 'By the gods, they dare to strike me again! I'll eat the crust off that bucket rather than obey their silence!'

'Don't be a fool,' Aletes hissed, holding him down. 'You'll end up like him.'

They both looked at the maggot-ridden corpse.

'They won't kill me. I'm worth too much alive.'

'I wouldn't bank on that,' came a voice in the darkness.

'You might be the son of the Argive king, but that is no guarantee you will feel sunlight on your face again.'

'Idomeneus?' Orested realised. 'I thought you perished in the first attack, when the Trojans burned half our fleet?'

'I often wish I had,' said the skeletal King of Crete. 'I would trade this stinking shithole for the fragrant meadows of Elysium in the blink of an eye.'

'Why have you not been ransomed?'

'My sons tried to buy my freedom. I am told the Trojans refused to negotiate. Holding out until they captured enough Argives to force Agamemnon to lift the siege. They may have reached that goal now you have taken up residence. I suggest you heed your friend's advice and remain silent until we know for sure.'

'My father will not negotiate, not now Achilles has returned to the fray.'

'Then you'll be squatting over that bucket for many a moon. Agamemnon's only other option is to starve the Trojans, sealing our fates in the process. When the food runs out, we'll be first to suffer. Without the scraps, we'll end up eating our own dead and licking the slime off this floor. Our only chance is a negotiated peace with a full exchange of prisoners. Until that happens you should keep quiet and conserve your strength.'

'I can't abide this festering squalor.'

'That's what our friend over there said. He was headstrong

and proud like you, and resolved to seek a swift, honourable death. The guards cut out his tongue to stop him taunting them, then broke both his legs. He died slowly in agony.'

Orestes looked at the corpse's broken legs, blackened by corruption, then at Aletes. The only sound was the grotesque buzz of flies crawling in and out of the corpse's gaping mouth.

'My father once told me I couldn't sit still or stop fidgeting long enough for his horse to piss,' he laughed darkly. He looked at Aletes. 'With your help, my friend, I will prove him wrong.'

'I'll be right here,' Aletes assured him. 'I'm not going anywhere, am I.'

So time passed, dragging its immortal heels as it went. Their only contact with the outside world an occasional visit from baton-fisted guards, the only clue to the length of their confinement their increasingly hirsute appearance and shrinking bodies. At first, Aletes tried to keep track of each passing day, scratching lines on the cell wall with a rat bone whenever the dawn watch changed. But as days turned into seasons, he became disorientated, and with constant hunger gnawing at his shrivelled belly, he languished in a silent, sunless world where violence, physical debasement and suffering were his ever-present companions.

The meagre scraps of stale bread and spoiled fruit they existed upon often failed to materialise, while their strictly rationed water looked as if it had been used to wash the guards' sandals and loincloths before being brought to them. Ailments of all kinds flourished, an outbreak of fever, suspected to be plague, killing five prisoners the same night on one bleak occasion.

Aletes became gravely ill, and a frantic Orestes feared for his friend's survival.

'You must not die. You are my brother. I cannot go on without you,' he implored.

Idomeneus was struck down too. One of the five who perished, his wise council and pithy humour was sorely missed. Orestes consoled himself by reminiscing for long periods about his privileged royal childhood. He would tell Aletes stories, Orestes still sharp enough to notice how his friend strengthened when the words fell onto his sister. He told more stories about Iphigenia, how she would escape from her weaving lessons as a child and come to find him in the courtyards after he had finished military training as a boy. She would ask her big brother to play the warriors game, where they cut off the nine heads of the Hydra with his wooden training sword, or she would pretend she was Jason searching for the golden fleece, while he would be the monsters she had to slay.

Slowly, Aletes regained speech, and started to tell his own stories. His life at Zygouris. The friction between he and Glaukos. The regrets of a brother he was never given the chance to love. Could Glaukos have been how Orestes was to him now? Could there be a chance they could resolve their differences and unite as brothers?

Orestes feared not. He believed Glaukos to be a dark man. Yet he did not want to dampen any drop of hope in a place like this.

One day, Aletes' story was interrupted by the sound of the

heavy doors swinging open. New arrivals. They were Spartan. Captured during an epic battle. Two of them were mortally wounded and died a short while later. The remaining four were unscathed and told a tale that shook their news-starved audience to their protruding bones.

17

The Queen's Ring

Achilles was dead.

Killed after slaying Hector in a ferocious single combat. He was struck down by a poisoned arrow to the heel, one of the few parts of his body not protected by brazen armour. In the battle that followed, Ajax of the Warhammer, boyhood friend and staunch ally of Agamemnon, was slain, the Argive host routed. A fractured Agamemnon had retired to his pavilion, and for several days thereafter sought solace from the contents of looted Mysian wine jars.

'Some say Achilles was punished by the gods for treating Hector's body disrespectfully,' said the Spartan spokesman, his armour still covered in bits of flesh, smeared blood, and the dents of spear and sword that had nearly taken his life.

'Whether true or not,' the Spartan continued, 'the Trojans didn't take kindly to watching Achilles drag their prince's corpse around the city walls behind his chariot. King Priam sent emissaries to plead for his son's return for a proper funeral, but Achilles was so consumed with bloodlust he slew them too. It was while taking Hector on a final lap of honour that Paris, a renowned marksman, avenged his brother and took a shot at him from the battlements.'

'When?' asked Orestes. 'How many times has autumn come and gone since I was incarcerated?'

'Three times, by my reckoning. This is the tenth season of the war. Some are saying it could be ten *years* before this war ends.'

Orestes was stunned. Two and a half years they had rotted in the darkness. With a slow shake of his head, he slumped against the cell wall. They could not win this war without Achilles. The war would not last ten years. It was over. The Argives would be driven back into the sea. His father would lose his throne and his head. His mother, Iphigenia...

'Then we are without hope,' he said. 'After what Achilles has done, Priam will never agree to our release. We'll either be butchered at Hector's funeral or left here rotting to torment our kin.'

Aletes could not find the words to console him. He had sunk into the same despair.

'I am ashamed of you,' said a stern Danaea late into the night as Aletes stared at the stone walls. 'You have done nothing to help your ailing prince. He has lost the will to live, and while you sit here moping, his strength ebbs away. If he dies, his sister will never forgive you.'

From the moment Orestes woke, Aletes set about restoring the prince. He gave up half his meagre food ration, lying to the distant prince that they had been given extra. When that had little effect, he took a share from the other prisoners. He talked incessantly about boar hunting, bull leaping and the lavish feasts the old master held at Zygouris, feasts the servants had described to him when he raided the kitchen for leftovers.

Orestes had finally begun to take an interest when Paris appeared at the cell doors.

Flanked by torch-bearing guards, the Trojan prince scanned the pathetic huddling captives. So long in the dark, the prisoners flung their hands out to shield their eyes, blinking against the brilliance of the torches. Blinding.

'Look at me,' he demanded. 'Move your hands. Let me see your eyes.'

'This one,' Paris said at last. 'The one with the grey eyes.'

It was not until Orestes gripped his arm that Aletes realised he had been singled out.

'Don't let them see your fear,' Orestes was saying through his broken teeth. 'Remember who you are, and if the worst happens we shall meet again in Elysium.'

'I will remember,' Aletes said, fearing that even he did not know the answer to who he was.

Rough hands hauled him to his feet and dragged him from the cell. The bronze plated doors clanged shut behind him. Paris was different. As he led the way, he didn't spit venom or provoke the Argive. Up. Up. Aletes was stumbling, being held up on each side.

White. White light. He could not open his eyes. He was moving sightless, being heaved along. Was he blind? He tried to open his eyes. Blurs of golds, yellows, oranges, reds. He frantically covered his eyes with his hands.

Darker now. The pressure off his arms. The guards had set him down. A sweet smell.

The room was coming into focus. A bath chamber? Was he in Elysium? Had Paris thumped his sword into his heart?

'Bring him to me as soon as he is ready,' Paris instructed.

After relieving Aletes of his filthy rags, six muscular court eunuchs, who were mute after being deprived of their tongues, gestured him into the grand chamber. A bronze bathtub of scented rose-petalled water awaited him. He was scrubbed, mint and honey oils applied to his skin and matted hair, which was shorn with his beard, and he was given a short linen tunic that rested on his wasted thighs.

He was led to a wing of the palace holding the private royal apartments. Head bowed submissively, he tried to remember his surroundings as he shuffled along behind the senior eunuch, his sight returned. He had already noticed the relaxed demeanour of the three eunuchs who escorted him. No doubt they assumed a captive who was so emaciated posed little threat to them. He observed it was dark outside, and through the partly open shutters of the same window, he established that the ground floor annex they had entered was surrounded by luxuriant gardens.

Aletes started to plan. He would need Hermes, the bringer of good fortune, to look kindly upon him. Yet he had nothing to lose, and if the chance to escape presented itself he would not hesitate to take it.

His journey ended in a chamber with vibrant frescoes on the walls; he became transfixed as he was lured into a world where graceful Aphrodite and lyre-plucking Apollo enjoyed the company of dancing nymphs, birds, fawns, and other woodland creatures. The crimson tiled floor was covered with woven rush mats. A large bed was positioned close to twin veranda doors, in the bed a dying woman. Her honey-blonde hair was combed out over a nest of pillows, and she was dressed in a pleated turquoise gown that accentuated the striking aquamarine of her eyes. She was so pale he could almost see through her skin, blue veins meandering like frozen rivers on the surface of gaunt arms. Her windpipe rattled when she breathed; infrequent, heavy, slow breaths. She smiled vacantly at Aletes. Paris beckoned him closer and the silver in her hand glinted in the lamplight.

'Helen has a fever,' Paris whispered. His voice was full of cracks. Aletes saw that love had broken him in a way no man could on the battlefield. Despite the hate and the war and the death, he felt empathy for Paris.

'She has requested to hear from your own lips how you came by the ring she holds. If your answer pleases her you will be rewarded for your trouble.'

Paris indicated the crust of fresh light bread and selection of cheeses on the ornate table. Not for the first time, Aletes had to quell a bestial urge to launch at the table and stuff the food into his mouth. Even now, the smell tormented him.

'If it does not please her, I will drag you outside, cut out your tongue, and behead you with a blunt axe. I take it you know who Helen is?'

'Your queen,' replied Aletes. He had known at once who she was. The aunt of the woman he loved. Every Argive knew of Helen of Troy. He had heard the story many times; it was one of Melampus' favourites. He told it well. About the Spartan queen with the beauty of a goddess, who eloped with her lover, Paris. He had been the Trojan ambassador at the court of King Menelaus. When Paris refused to return Helen, war had threatened between the two ill-matched adversaries. Menelaus eventually backed down, but two summers later, when the food war began, he had been first to set foot on Trojan soil, so great was his desire to slay the lecherous mongrel who had cuckolded him.

Helen tried to hold up the engraved silver ring, but it slipped through her fingers. Paris reached over and gently placed it in her palm, his hand lingering over hers. She was still beautiful, Aletes saw. One of the most beautiful women in the world. Even in death.

'My sister, Clytemnestra,' she managed. 'It is ten long seasons since I heard from her. Tell me how she fairs and why she gave you this precious token?'

Aletes had not expected to see the heron ring again after

194

Paris snatched it. It had saved his life then and now, incredibly, it was holding protective hands over him again. He started to recount the events that had led to him meeting Clytemnestra at Zygouris. As he spoke, he tried to use his peripheral vision to register the veranda doors. The gap-toothed guard in front of them had latched the doors but not bolted them. If he could get past Gap Tooth he could lose himself in the palace gardens before the alarm was raised. He could easily outrun the eunuchs and be long gone by the time dogs were fetched to track him down. Paris had already dropped his guard once. It would be a mistake for him to do so again.

'Half-brother to Glaukos?' Helen managed. 'How unfortunate for you.'

Aletes found himself warming to the failing queen. He knew what she wanted to hear, and as an attentive maid sponged the sweat from Helen's pallid brow and met Aletes with kind brown eyes, he described Clytemnestra's joy at being reunited with her lost daughter. He spoke as modestly as the truth would allow, repeating the words Clytemnestra had spoken that evening at Zygouris. He spoke still when a single tear escaped under Helen's closed eyelid. It trickled towards her grey-hued lips, and with a barely audible sigh, her head rolled to one side. Paris pressed his ear to her stilled chest. He reached, desperately, for the bronze mirror and held it close to Helen's nose and mouth, but no trace of breath misted its polished surface.

'The seers!' he barked madly, barging past the eunuchs

when all three of them failed to react. He threw open the chamber door, stepped into the deserted corridor and screamed for assistance.

Aletes saw his chance. The senior eunuch, nearest to him, was the only one he could see carrying a weapon. The eunuch was still gaping in the direction of Paris when Aletes grabbed the ivory hilt of the dagger in his waistband and stuck it in his jugular vein. His eyes cried out silently as he fumbled for the hilt and lost control of his body. Aletes removed it for him. He would be needing it. He dropped to a defensive crouch, his bones creaking, unbalanced from lack of food, preparing for the offensive from the two unarmed eunuchs. They were already wedged side by side in the doorway, calling for help as they fled.

Gap Tooth drew his sword and flicked his fingers in a beckoning gesture. He was big and eager to claim the praise for killing the spirited Argive. He grinned confidently and roared with a huge open mouth. With a deft flick of the wrist Aletes hurled the eunuch's dagger. It sliced through the ugly hole where Gap Tooth's front teeth once were, severing the base of his skull from his spine. His body collapsed in on itself as he choked on blood.

Aletes grabbed the heron ring from Helen's lifeless hand. She had no further use for it, he told himself, and stepping around Gap Tooth's twitching corpse, swung open the veranda doors.

The scents and sounds of the garden at night swamped his senses like an intoxicating drug. Fresh air. With hollering and curses carrying to him from inside the palace, he set off at a run to find somewhere to scale or get through the garden's high perimeter wall. He passed a bolted gate and had begun to think there was no way out when he spotted the giant fig tree a short distance ahead. Its fruit-laden branches had been carefully trimmed back, but one contorted bough grew close enough to the wall's parapet. Feeling dizzy now in his gaunt state, he had to steady himself before clambering up the tree's vine-swathed trunk.

He was about to lower himself into the street. Dogs barked. Torches flickered along the same path through the gardens he had taken. Guards.

Aletes dropped over the wall. He hit the ground so hard his wasted legs buckled, but he managed to roll, which stopped him breaking his ankles. He scrambled up, running bearlike, half on his hands for a few strides, before pushing his back up straight.

He could lose the guards in the lower city. Then he could work out his next move. Since Hector's death, the strictly enforced curfew had been lifted. Concerned with the plummeting morale of the people, King Priam had decreed any shops, brothels or taverns with food, drink, or services to sell, were free to open. Aletes found himself surrounded by clusters of men and women on street corners and cobbled squares, bright lights, bawdy laughter, infectious music. He slowed to blend in with the revellers, aware the further he got from the palace the less interest anyone took in him. The few who did connect him with the chasing band of guards turned their backs.

Lungs and limbs tried to move like the old Aletes, when he

was big and strong, but they were faltering. He had to pause, squeezing his eyes shut at the pain of wheezing, suffocating from overexertion. He tumbled rather than walked now, crossing a junction and then a maze of identical streets and alleys. A narrow path between high-sided buildings. A courtyard. He gulped water from the decorative fountain in the centre. His vision was smearing, twisting, he was blacking out in patches.

Somewhere to hide. Somewhere. Anywhere. Where?

The low-sided wagon stood inside a spacious temple precinct. It was piled high with grey bodies, pustules and ulcers on their skin, violent red eyes, and bloody, disfigured mouths. Plague. More bodies, bloated and stinking, on the flagstones. Across the enclosure, next to a scroll-topped marble altar, the smouldering remains of a funeral pyre for cremating the bodies.

Was that how Helen had died?

Aletes had no choice. He climbed in amongst the cold bodies, pulling a woman and a young boy on top of him, sticky oozing of mucus and blood from their bodies transferring onto him. The stench made him retch violently. He was maddened, crazed. Only the knowledge his pursuers were close prevented him throwing off the bodies in disgust.

Nailed sandals on stone. Footsteps around the shadowed courtyard. Yet even the yapping dog with them kept its distance from the bodies. No one risked getting plague. Not even soldiers with a score to settle. If you survived the mysterious fever, some went blind and their fingers turned black before falling off.

When the noises subsided, Aletes moved the arm of the woman to gain more air. Hermes, who guided all to the Underworld, tapped his shoulder in the darkness with his serpent staff and Aletes followed him to a place of half living, half death.

'It's too dangerous,' a voice was saying in the morning light. 'There are Argives out there.'

The jingle of a harness. The grunting and clomping of oxen on stone. Daylight.

The smell hit Aletes again as if for the first time. Unnatural. Obscene. He thought he was going to be sick and panic gripped him. He visualised sweet smells. The bath in the palace. Rose oils. Honey. The citrus and sweet spices of Iphigenia's hair.

'That kind of talk will earn you a flogging,' a second voice returned.

'Better that than fall into the hands of Argives,' said a third. 'I don't want to spend the rest of my days labouring in fields or in a sweltering quarry because the smell of burning corpses offends the king's delicate nostrils.'

'Grave pits outside the walls are safer,' one of the voices asserted. 'Priam has been advised that smoke from the pyres is spreading the fever.'

'Smoke from the pyres,' snorted the first temple slave. 'If I had a fattened capon for every new theory I've heard I'd never be hungry again. The king hasn't got a clue, has he? A few days ago, he was blaming midges in the water. Next thing you know he'll ban farting in public.'

'Quiet. The high priest is coming.'

Aletes lay rigid as the corpses around him as more bodies were stacked on the creaking wagon, unbreathing as the dead when a contingent of spearmen and Mysian archers arrived to escort them. He heard someone order the servants to gather up shovels and adzes, then led by a prayer-chanting seer, the gruesome procession got under way. Aletes saw glimpses of blue sky and buildings, and after what seemed an age, the weight of bone and flesh above him crushing his lungs, the shadow of the city walls covered the wagon like a shroud. Huge wooden gates swung open. The oxen lumbered onward.

Aletes was outside the city but still had the Mysian archers to contend with. He had witnessed the lethal accuracy of their short, curved bows. He knew that once the cortege halted and a defensive perimeter was established, they would pick off a fleeing man easy. He waited until the plodding oxen turned off the well-worn track and the seer stopped chanting. Then he began to haul his body up.

The bodies were moving. They were alive. The watching Trojans and Mysians were astonished. Frozen. Then afraid. To a man they saw an evil spirit unleashed from the Underworld to punish them for their words against the king. Aletes could see their fear and realised if he moved slowly they may believe him undead. It went against every instinct of survival, to run as fast as he could, to flee, but he made deliberate, exaggerated movements.

As soon as he was on his feet, standing on the dead, he bolted. Like a stag, running for his life, he leapt from the cart and made for a nearby copse, and the dark fringe of brush that marked the meandering course of the River Scamander. He ran with his head down and emaciated limbs pumping, and he had almost reached the collection of trees before the stunned Mysians recovered their composure.

Bows strained. Arrows nocked. Aim.

The first bronze-tipped shaft narrowly missed its target, thumping into the trunk of the nearest tree. A second arrow grazed Aletes' bicep, and had he not stumbled, the third would have spliced his spine. He rolled head over heels, and as more arrows stung the trees and ground around him, dived into the shady copse. He lay there panting, completely spent, and had still not recovered when a strong hand grabbed him roughly by the arm and flipped him onto his back. A tarnished bronze sword bit into his exposed throat.

Euthemus.

Aletes never thought he would be so pleased to see him.

'Give me one good reason not to kill you,' Euthemus growled.

Aletes was too breathless to speak. Over Euthemus' broad shoulder he saw more Argives crouching behind trees or in the dense undergrowth. Beyond, at least a dozen Trojans were bearing down on them. He heard the distinctive thrum of bowstrings and three of the Trojans sprawled dead in the grass. The remainder halted, slung their large oval shields on their backs for protection, and beat a hasty retreat.

'Well? Speak or die.'

Despite the henchman's threat, Aletes was elated. He knew he would not be harmed in front of so many witnesses. He grinned broadly, heedlessly.

He held up the gleaming heron ring.

'Take me to the king!' he bellowed between rapid breaths. 'I have news of Prince Orestes! The Prince lives!'

18

The Wooden Horse

Glaukos had been looking forward to attending that morning's council of war. The struggle with Troy was lost, and after another long night of discussion with his closest advisors, Agamemnon was expected to announce his decision to return to Argolis. His last slim hope was Odysseus and the eccentric Ithacan's ridiculous wooden horse.

Already Glaukos could hear craftsmen hard at work from his pavilion, which he shared with King Pylades of Phocis and two other warlords. The horse would be ready a day or two hence, yet nobody seriously believed it would fool the victorious Trojans. They would burn it, reduce it to ash along with any heroes unfortunate enough to be concealed in its hollow belly. When the news was brought to Agamemnon, waiting at sea with the remnants of his once mighty fleet, he would have no choice but to sail home in disgrace.

Home to face the wrath of his people. Glaukos smiled. A people with empty bellies mourning the loss of so many loved sons. Once they learned their great sacrifice had been in vain, that the Trojans still controlled the sea route to Krimea, Agamemnon would not live long. Statues of the king and his Atrean forefathers would be torn down, and while the hungry mob rampaged, Glaukos, Pylades and their small but potent band of conspirators, would storm the Mycenaean palace.

Glaukos lifted his leg and farted, absently fondling the buxom, honey-skinned Mysian slave girls who lay each side of him on the hard bed. Both responded by parting their legs, and he was debating which one to penetrate first when an armour clad Euthemus burst uninvited into the pavilion. Glaukos sat up abruptly, making no attempt to cover his obvious state of arousal. On the opposite side of the cluttered pavilion Pylades and two more equally curvaceous females emerged from beneath a rumpled linen sheet. Bleary-eyed and clearly hungover, Pylades demanded to know what was going on.

'My thoughts exactly. Euthemus, this intrusion had better be merited. I thought you were on patrol this morning?'

'I was, my lord,' said Euthemus, watching the Mysian slave girls enviously. 'But something happened you should know about.'

'Spit it out, I'm busy.'

'He's escaped, my lord. Your father's bastard has escaped from Troy with news of Prince Orestes.'

'You're sure it's him?' he demanded, his face pulsating.

'It's him. He's thin enough to squeeze through the neck of a wine jar, but there's no mistaking who it is.'

'He brings news of Orestes?'

'That's what he claims. He's being escorted to the king as we speak.'

'Then we must get over there.' Suddenly galvanised, Glaukos pushed the two Mysians aside, swung off the pallet and scooped his chiton off the mat covered dirt floor.

'Pylades, my good king, I suggest you stop amusing yourself with those two and get dressed. We don't want to miss what's said.'

The massive timber structure rose into the clear blue sky as tall as the mast of an Argive warship. It was mounted on a four-wheel timber platform, and although not yet complete, clearly resembled a stylised horse. It was largely obscured by scaffolding and ladders, and as craftsmen swarmed over it, the abrasive sounds of saw, chisel and hammer filled the air. Glaukos spotted Aletes waiting on the far side of the giant wooden horse. He was escorted by King Menelaus of Sparta, and by his side Amasis, the veteran Spartan hero who had led that morning's scouting party. The wily Ithacan, Odysseus, stood close by, gulping water from a goatskin gourd. All four were surrounded by a growing press of warriors who had heard news of Aletes' escape from Troy.

Glaukos hung back in the crowd. He shuffled sideways to get a better view, halting once the sun was behind him and its gilded rays no longer speared his darting eyes. He ducked when Aletes appeared to glance straight at him, lifting his eyes as an expectant hush settled over the tight-packed gathering. Grunting, thumping, scraping and an occasional curse continued to emanate from inside the horse. After a brief silence, a pair of thick calves, then huge hairy thighs, dropped through the trap door in its rectangular belly.

The legs belonged to Agamemnon. As he descended the wood and rope ladder, all eyes turned in his direction. He was clad in a sweat-stained tunic, felt cap, and judging by the amount of sawdust sprinkled in his wedge beard and clogging his nostrils, he had been hard at work for some time. He handed the heavy mallet he had been using to the master carpenter, and with a nod to Menelaus, focused his discerning gaze upon the emaciated figure standing before him.

'You are Aletes the Lionslayer,' he stated rather than asked.

'Some call me that,' Aletes said, bowing deferentially.

'Then you are the one who saved my daughter from the black maned lion. Before she was tragically drowned, she told me how you charged the beast when it had her under fang and claw. You stood your ground alone, without flinching, and felled it with nothing more than a stave and slingshot. You are worthy of your name, Aletes the Lionslayer. Many an Argive hero would not have had your courage, and for that you are deserving of my thanks.'

'Worthy of the name,' agreed Menelaus, raising a muscular arm in fisted salute.

Aletes' mouth ran dry. Then wet. Nausea welled up from his stomach. He stumbled backwards, his legs dropping away beneath him.

'A stool!' Agamemnon hollered, flipping his hand in the air.

A slave brought a three-legged stool and Aletes sat like a ghost. He had died in that moment, he was sure.

He wanted to shout out. Drowned? How? Where? Are you sure?

But he could not ask the king. He could not reveal an intimacy that could see him lose his tongue.

'Fetch food! Water!' Agamemnon bellowed.

'I was fortunate, King of Men,' Aletes managed, being served cool water. The words were stale and meaningless now, only there only to fill the silence. 'The gods were holding their hands over me, and my dog, Argus, was at my side. I could not have done it without him.'

'Did this Argus hurl the stone that blinded it? Or drive a stake into its feral heart? No, I think not.'

Agamemnon snorted a plug of snot from each of his nostrils and gestured to Odysseus to pass him the kidney shaped gourd. The gristle in his bristled throat plunged noisily up and down, and as Aletes watched him slake his thirst, he remembered the words Iphigenia had said in the orchard.

'I too know what it is to have a father betray you.'

'Do not vex me with talk of dogs, Zygouris.' Agamemnon tossed the gourd back to Odysseus and wiped drips of wine from his grey streaked beard with the back of a hand the size of a spade. 'Tell me news of my son, Orestes. Is he alive and hale?'

'He is alive, lord.'

'But not in rude health?'

'He looks much as I did before the Trojans cleaned me up. Beneath nine long seasons of accumulated filth he has shrunk to a shadow. His eyes still blaze with defiance as you would expect, but his body is a withered husk of skin and bone.'

'You last saw him when?'

'Yesterday evening. We were sitting side by side against the same dungeon wall.'

'Yet now you stand before me bathed and groomed while he rots in a stinking cell?'

The change in the king's demeanour was sudden. The suspicion of a king is unrivalled. Born to suspicion. Yet he was right to be. Aletes was aware he looked like a serpent in the grass. If he could not make the king believe him, they would never save Orestes.

Aletes raised himself from the stool, slowly, legs shaking, head tipping him off balance. Silver eyes proud as they met the king's without fear.

'If I could be there and Orestes here now before you, I would give these arms, these legs—'

He pounded his bony chest. 'This broken body.'

His low, powerful voice was muscled with emotion.

He pounded his chest again. 'This is all I have.' He gestured to his sorry body.

'If you don't believe me, Orestes will not survive. I love him like a brother, king. I will tell you what happened and for the sake of a prince, all will listen.'

The room fell silent. Even the workmen inside the wooden horse seemed to have temporarily stopped, straining to hear.

As the words came, the mention of Helen roused no reaction from Menelaus. The Spartan king was sick of men's eyes turning to him every time her name sounded. A horn of shame. He had long come to terms with the treachery of a wife he had lusted after but never really loved. She was a beautiful, highly desirable woman, yet it was the shame of being cuckolded rather than her loss that he found impossible to live with. A proud and vengeful man, he would not rest until he plunged a dagger into Paris' lecherous heart and watched his life drain out of him.

'The prince's will is strong.' Aletes went on. 'He has survived when others have perished. But he is failing, lord. We don't have weeks. If he's not released in days, I fear—'

Agamemnon held up his hand for silence.

'Can he last a few more days? While I negotiate his freedom?'

Aletes shook his head. His eyes translating what the king feared.

'Then I cannot help him.'

Agamemnon tipped back his shaggy head, and with his face contorted into a mask of pain and impotent rage, shook his huge

209

fists at the unblemished heavens.

'Have I not been punished enough!' he cried to the sky. 'Not my son! First you take my daughter, is that not enough? Vengeful gods. You have denied me victory. Is that not enough? That I must sail home in shame?'

'Lord of Men, do not despair,' Odysseus said, confidently. 'King Priam's downfall is close to hand.'

Agamemnon half turned, burning like one of Zeus' thunderbolts.

'I take it you mean this infernal horse? Forgive me, Odysseus, but I do not share your misplaced optimism. I embraced this project to avoid dwelling upon the futility of our present situation, not because I believe in it. Hard labour is all that prevents me going mad.'

'Troy will fall, king,' the wiry, olive-skinned Ithacan persisted. 'My shaman has seen it written in the entrails of a goat. When Priam's heroes discover the horse in our abandoned camp it will not be hard to persuade him that we have sailed home and left it to honour their gods. Priam will order it hauled inside the city. His people will rejoice, revelling late into the night, and when at last they sleep, the twin spectres of death and destruction will steal from the horse's hollow belly.'

'Your seer has been too long in the sun. The success of your ruse relies on the Trojans being complete fools, which they are not. They will find the heroes concealed in this contraption's belly, and when they do, reduce them and the horse to a pile of cinders and ash while laughing at us.'

'Then send one man,' Aletes said.

The king's eyebrows raised to the sky.

'Fill the horse with tribute instead. Leave enough room in its neck to hide one man. The Trojans will search the horse but find only tribute. Satisfied it's safe, they will bring the horse into the heart of the city, as close to the Temple of Poseidon as they can get it. The more time that passes, the more they'll celebrate, and when they're all drunk or asleep, a rope can be lowered from the West Wall for a waiting warband to climb. One man can go unseen.'

Agamemnon considered Aletes as if for the first time. At last, the king spoke.

'One man could be hidden, but changes will have to be made to the inside of the horse. How long would that take, Odysseus?'

'It can be done in a day.'

'Which leaves one question. Who do we hide in the horse?'

'I would have that honour,' said Menelaus, his tone assertive, defying anyone to challenge his claim. 'I have unfinished business with Paris and long ago vowed to be the first Argive warlord over Troy's ramparts.'

'First you shall be, Menelaus, but at the fore of a handpicked war band, not squeezed into the neck of a horse. You have the girth of a Cretan fighting bull, brother. We would have to completely rebuild the horse to get you in.'

'I know the layout of the city, King of Men,' Aletes said. 'And thanks to the Trojans I'm slender as a blade of grass.'

Agamemnon was unconvinced.

'I do not doubt your courage, Lionslayer. But we will only get one chance at this and you have only just returned to us. Perhaps if you'd had time to rest and build up your strength?'

'I do not need rest, King. Like King Menelaus, I have made a promise I intend to keep. I will get your heroes inside the city, and once the West Gates are open, lead them to Orestes.'

'The gates will be heavily guarded. King Priam is cautious and will not relax now victory is within his grasp. In addition to the regular watchmen, Mysian archers now patrol the ramparts. If you are seen, all is lost.'

Aletes was about to do what went against everything he was. For Orestes' sake. He boasted.

'I am destined to save the dynasty of Atreus.' His voice was louder, stronger. 'The prophesy, witnessed by Lord Aegisthus, foretold I would transform from herdsman to hero, to stand shoulder to shoulder with the best among the Argives. I stood shoulder to shoulder with Orestes at Mount Oeta. I stood with him in the dungeons of Troy. I stand with you now. The prophesy is true. I will open the gates of Troy, my king.'

Agamemnon ran his tongue over the front of his teeth, pushing out his top lip. What if the gods had not abandoned him?

'Bring back my son, Lionslayer,' he said at last, with a slow nod of his head. 'One condition. You eat like a king tonight. Eat like me! You'll need all the strength you can get.'

He turned to his man. 'Amasis, escort Zygouris to my quarters and instruct my head servant to attend his every need. Menelaus and I will join him there this evening, together we will consume my last jar of Lyrnasson wine. You will also join us, Odysseus. I am eager to hear how you intend to persuade King Priam to take the wooden horse into the city, should he prove reluctant.'

'I thought Sinon of Argos had been allotted the task?'

'Sinon has the fever. You said Priam could be easily persuaded, so here's your chance to prove it.'

Agamemnon had started to climb back inside the horse when Aletes lost control of his tongue again, emboldened by the king's decision.

'A word, king, if I may. You said Iphigenia of Mycenae was tragically drowned. When did this happen?'

Agamemnon's ursine frame stiffened. He halted abruptly halfway up the ladder.

'Nine seasons ago,' he said, gruffly. 'Shortly after Orestes was captured. She was lured into a trap off the coast of Phocis, while on her way to marry Achilles. She perished when her ship was sucked into a whirlpool, struck a reef, and Poseidon, allied to these dirty Trojans, snatched her into his watery world.'

'Lured into a trap?'

'Pirates. Led by Dorians.'

Agamemnon lifted his foot onto the next rung of the ladder.

'The sea of Corinth is infested with them, but not usually in

213

such numbers or allied with Ironmen. Ask your half sibling, Glaukos. He was escorting her.'

Amasis clamped a restraining hand on Aletes' shoulder. He shook his head before speaking quietly.

'The king has much on his mind and won't take kindly to more distraction. Come. I will tell you what I can.'

'You know what happened to her?'

'I know as much as the king.'

Amasis led the way down from the yellow grassed mound where the giant horse stood.

'I was with the king at Trachis when he learned what had befallen her. His daughter's body was never found, so for a long time he refused to accept she was dead. He might be indebted to Glaukos for bringing Achilles to Trachis and turning the tide of war in our favour, but the truth is, he has never entirely trusted him.'

Aletes lengthened his stride to keep abreast of Amasis. The dusty track they followed dissected the Mycenaean quarter of the Argive camp. It was located where a sleepy Mysian fishing village once stood, a short ride from Troy's horse emblazoned West Gate. Thatch-roofed hovels had long since been replaced by an untidy, densely packed sprawl of tents, dugouts and pavilions, the boats, nets, and homes of the fishermen consumed by countless Argive cooking fires.

'Glaukos survived? Who else?'

'Just the two men who follow him like trailing dogs. They were sucked into the whirlpool with Iphigenia, but by the time they surfaced she had vanished they said, and the rest of the Argive warships were on fire. A score or more survivors managed to swim ashore, but Dorian hoplites and a swarm of Illyrian pirates were waiting for them there. By the time Electra appeared with the Phocian host, most had been butchered.'

'Electra confirmed Glaukos' version of events?'

'Not at first. She thought she had seen Iphigenia on the beach, but the seasoned trackers Agamemnon despatched to scour the coastline found no sign. They searched inland as far as the boarder with Epirus, but when no trace of her sister was found, Electra reluctantly accepted she had been mistaken.'

'The search could not have been more thorough,' Amasis added, sensing Aletes' unease. 'When the trackers returned empty-handed, Agamemnon sent them back again with a different hero leading them. Still they found noth—'

'By the three sons of Cronus!' exclaimed a familiar guttural voice. 'I'll cut off my right bollock if it isn't. Aletes, you worthless pile of rat shit! I told the boys you'd show up again!'

The voice grated like bronze tyres on gravel, and with a leap of joy Aletes recognised the short, bandy-legged figure leading a file of weary Argives towards him. The figure broke into a jog, and moments later Aletes was enveloped in a suffocating embrace as Melampus' sour breath – a rich blend of tooth rot, garlic sauce and olives – smote his nostrils.

'Throw you out did they, Ratshit? Get tired of you complaining about the lack of meat in your stew or fresh straw on the floor of your lodgings?'

'Not quite, First Spear.'

'Echetus, Chersicrates! Look who's crawled out from under a rock! By the stars it's good to see you again. I had a hunch you and Pytho would return. Where is Half Ear?'

Aletes shook his head solemnly. 'He was killed at Pydna.'

Melampus was silent. Disturbingly silent. Finally, he sucked air through the gap between his bent front teeth. 'He was uglier than a toad and sang like a herd of cows all farting at once. No better man to have watching your back.'

'No better man,' Echetus and Chersicrates echoed.

Melampus chuckled fondly. Lost in his memories for a wingbeat. Then he sucked in more air through his teeth, pinched his nose between his finger and thumb, sniffed, and wrapped a muscular arm around Aletes' shoulders.

'Come on, you look like you could use some hot grub. We're off duty and collecting our ration of fish tripe and stale bread. As a special treat, we'll boil up Echetus' loincloth and make you a bowl of arse crack stew.'

'Sounds delicious,' grinned Aletes. 'Much as I'd like to join you, I'm afraid I can't. I've been ordered to accompany Amasis.'

'What's his business with you?'

'The king's business,' Amasis interjected. 'A matter we cannot discuss.'

'Is that so?' Melampus' curiosity was whetted. He pulled Aletes to one side of the track, away from the inquisitive ears of the

Argives gathered around them. Amasis followed.

'Alright, we're on our own now,' Melampus said in an exaggerated whisper. 'You can tell me all about it.'

'I wish I could.'

'Don't worry about Amasis here. I'm an old friend of his father's, the warden of Sparta, and King Menelaus. Aren't I lad. What does Agamemnon want with you?'

With a resigned shrug from Amasis, Aletes informed Melampus what had been decided during his audience with the Argive king.

'The holy mother was wrong then, all those moons ago in the great hall at Zygouris,' he said, grimly. 'You are not destined for greatness. To stand, as she put it, shoulder to shoulder with the best among the Argives. Climb in that wooden horse and you'll never be seen again. There's no way a fellow in your condition can gain the ramparts of Troy alone.'

'But if she's right, I'm the only one who can do it.'

Melampus examined him. The son he never had. He ran his fingers over his beard.

'You would do the same. I know it.'

'Not on an empty belly I wouldn't,' said Melampus, brown eyes round and concerned.

He grabbed Aletes' arm and set off towards a section of the Mycenaean camp that overlooked a broad shingle strand where a line of beached Argive warships stretched off into the distance as far as the eye could see.

'Don't worry, Amasis,' Melampus called over his shoulder. 'I'll bring Aletes back as soon as he's eaten a horse and told us all his news. The king need never know he went missing. I'd invite you to join us, but there won't be enough fish heads and tails to go around.'

The hide-roofed dugout had been home to Aletes' companions for almost as long as the two and a half years he had languished in the dungeons of Troy. It was cramped and stale, yet pleasantly cool during the heat of summer and warm when the gales of winter scoured the Scamandan plain. Beds lined with dry grass had been cut into its earthen walls, the large flat rock jutting out of the compacted floor served as a convenient table. There was a small shrine to Zeus, adorned with seashells and smooth, unusually coloured pebbles, and in the corner opposite, a smoke-stained tripod and cauldron stood over the ashes of a cooking fire.

Aletes made himself comfortable on a wooden stool. He gulped down a horn of diluted local wine—by far the best wine he had ever tasted—and after recounting his experiences to an enthralled audience, listened with mounting consternation to the catalogue of disasters that had befallen the Argive host. He ate a crust of dark bread and a bowl of thin gruel made from scraps of fish and rotting vegetables, washing it down with yet more of the coarse local vintage. Then he climbed onto one of the pallets cut into the dugout wall, and for the first time in many a long moon, fell into a deep, untroubled sleep.

Some while later Melampus shook him gently awake by the shoulder. It was growing dark outside and a single smoky lamp had been lit in the crowded dugout.

'Time to go,' said a sombre Melampus. 'Echetus and Maron will escort you to the king's compound. I've been summoned to an urgent meeting of First Spears. The wooden horse is finished, barring a final lick of paint, and word is this camp will be abandoned tonight. Judging by the mood, this will be the king's last throw of the marked stones.'

Aletes nodded drowsily and climbed stiffly to his feet.

'Take this sword,' Melampus added, thrusting a sharp-edged blade into Aletes' hand. 'Don't stray off the track we followed to get here. This camp can be a dangerous place after sunset.'

The two men embraced spontaneously. One by one, the rest of the dugout's occupants stepped forward to do the same.

'You will rejoin us before we depart?' asked Chersicrates.

'Sadly not. I have a different role to play,' replied Aletes, and leaving Chersicrates to ponder what he meant, he left the dugout.

Outside, a sharp tang of brine pervaded his senses, masking some of the less pleasant odours of the congested camp. He heard the shouts and singing of men at work, the hiss and rumble of waves on the nearby beach. Glancing that way, he saw preparations were advanced for what remained of the Argive fleet to fake its departure. Gangs of caulkers, riggers and carpenters repaired long-beached hulls, using guttering torches and braziers to hold back the gathering darkness. Out in the bay, silhouettes in a violet-crimson sunset, more high bowed warships rode sedately at anchor, ready to sail on the outgoing tide on the order.

Aletes strode between Echetus and Maron, and not for the first time that day his thoughts turned to Iphigenia. According to Amasis her body had never been found, which was strange given the sea god had returned the bloated remains of all the others. Why then was Iphigenia not among them? And if, as Electra originally suggested, she had reached the beach alive, why was there no ransom demand? The implications of that did not bear thinking about, and with hot bile coating the back of his throat, Aletes struggled to banish a host of bestial images from his mind. This time tomorrow he would be sealed inside the wooden horse. To survive, he would have to abandon Iphigenia just for a short while. First, he must help her brother.

'If it isn't the Lionslayer himself.'

Aletes came to an abrupt halt as if he had been addressed by Nemesis or another equally nefarious creature from the Underworld. With his heart pounding in his mouth, he gazed into the darkened area from whence the spectral voice had come. At the far end of a narrow, well-trodden pathway, in a small open space where spare axles, wheels and other chariot parts were stored behind the canvas walls and roofs of shelters, there he was.

Aletes' hand dropped to the hilt of the borrowed sword.

'No words for your brother, Lionslayer,' the bodiless voice said.

War changes a man, Aletes considered. Two and a half

220

years was a long time. They were older now. Grown men. Was he changed?

'Brother?' Aletes repeated.

Aletes glanced at Echetus and Maron, who were vigorously shaking their heads.

'Remember what Melampus said,' urged Echetus. Yet Aletes was a fly to carrion. He was desperate for news about Iphigenia, whatever dubious source it came from.

'Wait for me here,' he said, drawing the sword from his belt and entering the jaws of darkness.

He was more than halfway towards the open space, and almost completely immersed in shadow, when two more indistinct figures appeared behind him and bundled Echetus and Maron along the pathway. All four men held drawn swords. Blades met in the darkness, scraping, clanging, Maron sweeping his blade instinctively, not needing eyes. The cold of metal in his groin. He grabbed at the wound. Wet. A pulling, draining sensation. He swung out with his sword. He knew it was over. Cold. Hard. Metal through his chest. No air. He slumped, bleeding out on the ground.

Aletes' blade was scraping against another. He couldn't see Echetus but he could hear him grunting, growling. A sick crunch as his sword snapped near the hilt. Echetus tossed his broken weapon.

Two assassins ran him through simultaneously, one sticking his blade down his throat, the other through his gut, then they converged upon Aletes. They pressed him back into the cluttered space at the end of the pathway, and although he fought like a cornered lion, wounding both of his attackers, the outcome was inevitable. Gasping for breath, the sword in his hand too heavy to wield offensively, Aletes braced himself to die as fearlessly as his companions.

Glaukos' laughter cleaved the balmy night air. He had left the fighting to his two loyal men, but now the herdsman's teeth had been drawn, he moved closer and pressed the point of his sword against Aletes' heaving chest. Alcinous' blade was similarly levelled, despite a glancing wound across his shoulder and upper arm. Euthemus was more badly hurt, and sheathing his sword, quickly tied a tourniquet around his thigh.

'How predictable you are,' Glaukos said.

'What have you done with her?' Aletes yelled, saliva stringing from his mouth like a fighting dog.

'You believe she would look on *you*? The daughter of a king?' He let out a derisive laugh. 'You tend goats.'

'We're blood,' Aletes said. 'Surely that means something?'

Glaukos looked at him, breathing heavily. He could see nothing of his father's hawkish looks in him. How did he know he was even his father's son?

'I'd wager she can look after herself. Rather *feisty*. I'd look to yourself. You seem to be in a pickle.'

'Horseshit,' said a guttural voice at the entrance to the pathway.

Glaukos saw the bronze-tipped spear poised above

222

Melampus' shoulder. At least two more similarly armed, capable looking warriors flanking him.

'This is a private matter. You have no business here.'

'You made it my business when you butchered two of my men. Put up your sword or I'll skewer you.'

Glaukos moved before Melampus finished speaking. He grabbed Aletes around the neck, pressed his sword into his armpit and shuffled slowly forward.

'Step aside and I'll let your friend live,' he rasped, Alcinous and the temporarily disabled Euthemus close behind him as he crabbed sideways.

Aletes had no idea if Glaukos would kill him. Only one action left. He stopped dead. Head thrown back. A crack. Bone. A cry of pain.

Melampus' spear split the air fast. Bronze whistled. Glaukos threw himself to the left. The spear smacked into the chest of a horrified Alcinous behind. Alcinous' one eye stretched in horror as he tried to pull the spear from his chest. Another spear narrowly missed Glaukos on the run, Euthemus fleeing after him.

Chersicrates and the other spearman turned to give pursuit. Melampus stopped them with a terse command.

'Let them go, lads. We know who they are. We can pay them a visit later. We need to hide these bodies before the king's marshals come asking awkward questions.'

Melampus planted his foot on Alcinous' panting chest and withdrew his deeply embedded spear. The dying man groaned; his chest stopped moving.

'What were you thinking?' Melampus grunted at Aletes. 'I warned you not to leave the main track, yet here you are, lured into the dark like a mariner onto Sirens' rocks. If I'd taken the direct route to First Spear Machaon's quarters instead of keeping an eye on you, you'd be crossing the River Styx with these two idiots.'

'It wasn't their fault.'

'You're right, it was *yours*. Don't make that mistake again. What did you think, you'd smother him with brotherly love? As you embraced, he'd tell you where he's hidden the king's daughter?'

Aletes met him eye to eye. How did he know about that?

'Where are you going?'

'To find Glaukos and settle this. It's my fault Echetus and Maron were killed.'

Melampus saw the silver glint of caged fury in Aletes' narrowed eyes, the tightly clenched muscles on each side of his jaw, and promptly stepped across his path. He had seen that look before, at the first battle of Trachis. Exhausted, outnumbered, Melampus' section of the line was being overwhelmed when tattooed Amazons surrounded a wounded Argive. The helpless youth's pleas for mercy had cut through the Argives like a lash, but it was not until the blood-crazed Amazons started to slice up and devour the youth's living flesh that Aletes erupted. Ignoring Melampus' repeated order to "lock shields and stand fast", he charged the feasting Amazons, slaying all who had tasted Argive flesh. It was as if no blade or missile could touch him. Still

224

possessed by a terrible lust for battle, Aletes cleaved a bloody path back to his place in the front rank of the Argive line.

'Listen to me,' Melampus said, grabbing Aletes by a bicep. 'Go after him now and you'll be dead within the hour. Glaukos shares his lodgings with King Pylades of Phocis and a couple of other high warlords. He'll be protected by a small army of Phocian royal guards and his own loyal acolytes. You'll be lucky to get in the same room as him, never mind close enough to lunge with your sword. You'll be cut down the moment you try.'

'This is a private matter between me and Glaukos.' Aletes pushed Melampus aside. 'There's no reason for Pylades or anyone else to get involved.'

'Then you're a fool.'

'In which case, tell Amasis I'm sorry for letting him down.'

Head tilted forward, his hand clamped firmly around the hilt of his sword, Aletes strode into the darkness.

He called back. 'He is a virtuous hero and will understand why I have to do this. I did not seek this fight, yet so the shades of our comrades can find peace, I am honour bound to finish it.'

'Amasis might,' Melampus called after him. 'But the king never will. Nor will your beloved girl when she is found alive. She'll never forgive you for throwing away your life and squandering the chance to rescue her brother.'

Melampus had chosen his words well.

Aletes heard shouts, and peering into the dark, saw a trio of torch-bearing marshals approaching along the main track. His mind made up for him, he turned back towards a relieved Melampus.

'Marshals coming,' Aletes warned, tucking his sword under his belt. 'We don't have long.'

'We'll hide our boys behind that stack of chariot wheels and axles,' Melampus asserted. Chersicrates can come back later with help and place them by the Altar of Zeus. The shaman there will conduct the necessary rituals without asking questions. This one-eyed mongrel we'll leave for the rats.'

19

An Unexpected Ally

Several of the warlords present that evening had hunted lion, yet none of them had killed one single-handed. They had cornered their prey in the traditional manner, chasing it to a standstill with a pack of ferocious tribal Molossians, disabling the lion with arrows before dismounting from their chariots to despatch the exhausted beast. When Agamemnon rose to his feet therefore and recounted Aletes' exploits in the arid Zygouran riverbed, the warlords gathered in the makeshift feasting hall had listened in respectful, increasingly incredulous silence. That hush had become a murmur of admiration, accompanied by enthusiastic nodding of heads by the time Agamemnon finished describing the events surrounding Aletes' escape from Priam's dungeons.

The initially sceptical warlords looked upon the bastard son of Aegisthus with respect and, in some instances, embarrassing adulation. When Agamemnon raised his oft-filled gold cup and invited those present to join him in a toast, they did so in the time-honoured fashion. They chanted the name Agamemnon used when addressing the former herdsman, and pounded the tops of their individual, bone-strewn tables.

'Zygouris! Zygouris! Zygouris!'

Agamemnon lifted his hand for silence.

'You see, my lords, the fate of this expedition lies in safe hands. When King Priam orders the gates of Troy thrown open, he will be inviting in the instrument of his destruction. In the dead of night, when he and the Trojan rabble are done celebrating their victory, Aletes will free himself from the secret compartment in which he has been sealed. He will make his way to the city's ramparts, slaying any who cross his path. He will lower a rope to the hand-picked men hiding outside the West Gate. That war band will be led by the lord seated to my left, King Menelaus of Sparta.'

Cheers. Chants. Tables thumped.

Glaukos was seated in his usual place between the tables occupied by his closest allies, King Pylades and King Meleager of Thebes. More than once, the grin on his face curled into a sneer. He touched the painful bruising on his broken nose.

On the opposite side of the timber and canvas walled chamber, an already drunk Neoptolemus rose, swaying, to his feet. Now fifteen summers of age, the son of Achilles had grown taller and stockier since Glaukos saw him. Yet he still cut a comical figure when clad in his late father's gold decorated bronze armour. As he struggled to draw his sword from a scabbard longer than his leg, the warlords stopped cheering and began to snigger.

'This thord is called the Reeper of Thades,' said Neoptolemus, his unfortunate lisp accentuated by his inebriation. 'Most of you saw my father take it oth Hector before he himself woth cowardly slain. I hath vowed to avenge the death oth my father. I mean to kill the archer-assassin, Parith, but to ensure that I reach him thirst, before any other Argive, I must join Menelaoth's war band.'

Agamemnon silenced the mocking with a disapproving glower.

'The son of Achilles is welcome,' he said diplomatically, his true thoughts hidden. Including the wine-sotted youth was a risk, but better that than offend every hero in the Myrmidon host. If he proved a liability, Menelaus would have to take the necessary action: leave him gagged and bound under a thicket somewhere or silence him permanently. By the time the Myrmidons found out what had become of their beloved prince they would be too busy raping and plundering to care.

Smiling, Agamemnon saluted Neoptolemus with his gold cup.

'I would recommend girding yourself with a shorter blade, my lord. If you attempt to scale the walls with the Reaper slung on your back, you are likely to fall and break your neck or poke out the eye of the hero following you. Might I suggest—'

'Forgive me, brother,' Menelaus interrupted. 'Was that a horn I heard, or did a god fart?'

A horn. Distant but sonorous. More urgent now. The warlords rumbled like an earthquake, all up on their feet as one.

The Master of the Watch burst in to confirm what they already knew.

Neoptolemus was one of those who had drawn his sword, arching his spine to free the point of the heavy blade from its long scabbard. He lost balance and toppled backwards over his stool, cracking his head on a wooden post supporting the roof. He lay sprawled on the rush-strewn earth floor, unconscious and unseen amongst overturned tables and stools.

'Lord, the camp is besieged,' the Master of the Watch began. 'The Trojans have launched a mass attack on the Spartan section of the perimeter defence. Several structures ablaze.'

Agamemnon raised his hands to quell the raucous clamour and prevent a headlong rush for the guarded exit.

'Let us not be hasty!' Agamemnon implored, yelling above the stampede. 'The assault may be a ruse. Priam has used diversionary action before to get at our fleet. If he succeeds again, we'll be stranded here till next spring. Menelaus, take ten of our number and return to the Spartan camp. I'll join you there after securing the beach. Athens and Corinth, help Odysseus protect the wooden horse.'

More tables and benches were knocked over as the crowded, torch-lit chamber quickly emptied. Aletes, seated to the right of the king, was one of the first to reach the canvas atrium, but before he could go any further a hand like a grappling hook gripped him by the shoulder.

'Not you, Zygouris,' said Agamemnon. 'You have your part to play on the morrow. Until then we must keep you out of harm's way.'

Aletes looked agitated, a reaction the king took as his eagerness to fight Trojans. If Agamemnon had known what was really troubling him, how hard it had been to sit there impassively all evening staring at Glaukos' smirking face, he would not have fanned the flames of sibling strife.

'Glaukos, this hero is a brother to you, is he not? See that he comes to no harm.'

Agamemnon sensed the tension at once. The king was a brother after all. Only brothers understand brothers.

For a good while, Aletes sat back in the chair by the king's throne, and Glaukos on a stall across the room.

At last, curiosity got the better of the older brother.

'Are you afraid?' Glaukos asked with a sneer.

Aletes levelled his eyes at him, upturning his chin.

'Afraid of what?'

'When Priam finds you in that bloody horse.'

He laughed and Aletes half-laughed back. It was ridiculous, fair enough.

Meleager, big and wide, and goat-faced Pylades, returned to the room. His back-up seemed to remind Glaukos of his plans.

'It's a shame you won't get to see those black eyes again. Rather wonderful aren't they. I can't tell you how sad that makes me.'

'Nor I,' said a grinning Pylades.

'Sad,' agreed Meleager.

The curule chair clattered behind him as Aletes shot up. He had tried not to dwell on Iphigenia or the callous slaying of Echetus and Maron. He had tried instead to focus upon Melampus' good advice, but Glaukos' spite-fuelled words had goaded him beyond endurance.

Each of the high lords confronting him was a hero in his prime, trained from an early age in the deadly art of Argive warfare. Yet none of that mattered. All he wanted was to wipe the gloating smirk off Glaukos' face. As his hand dropped onto the hilt of his sword, he decided which of the three warlords he would engage first. Meleager the strongest and fittest. Then the lighter framed Pylades. Glaukos last. Granting him quarter if he begged. Only after he revealed what he had done with Iphigenia.

A loud and protracted belch distracted him. He turned towards the source of the glottal voidance and propped against a wooden post, rubbing his bloodied head, he saw a dazed Neoptolemus. The young prince's short, bony legs were covered by a jumble of benches and tables, and kicking them aside, he rose shakily to his feet. He held the Drinker of Blood aloft in both hands, waving it erratically from side to side.

Spraying sputum from his lips like mizzle, Neoptolemus stumbled to Aletes' side.

'S-stand aside, my lords, and unhand your thords. Ith you

refuse, I will be forced to make you do s-so!'

'*You?*' snorted Glaukos. 'One skinny runt against the three of us. Exactly how do you intend to do that?'

'I will s-summon my Myrmidon guards, a number oth whom are waiting for me outside this chamber. They are all s-seasoned veterans, s-sworn to defend my life with their own. I'll not answer for the cons-sequences.'

Glaukos eyed his companions. Neoptolemus never went anywhere without a large escort, so the drunk prince was unlikely to be bluffing. Ready as Glaukos was to take advantage of Aletes' lapse of control, he had no desire to tangle with a band of battle-hardened Myrmidons. Even when outnumbered, which on this occasion they were not, the men of the far north had a habit of winning fights they started.

Glaukos held up his hands, palms open. 'Your wine wits have deceived you, young Neo. The goat herder was about to attack *me*.'

'You were t-taunting him, I heard every word. I may hath drunk a horn too much wine, but I am not the f-fool you take me for.'

'On that we must agree to differ.'

Neoptolemus lurched at Glaukos. He caught his two middle toes on an upturned stool and recoiled with the sting, nearly tripping over.

'I recall the night you turned up with empty hands to Pharsalos. Your story about the pirate attack woth plausible enough, but to claim that you and your tame baboons were the only s-survivors woth imbecilic.'

Glaukos couldn't help be amused. He was ridiculous.

'Now that we've cleared that up, what happens next?' Glaukos mocked. 'Are we free to go, or do you intend to carry us out on our shields?'

'You can go,' Aletes interjected. 'I will make my own way to the king's quarters.'

'Until next time then.'

Glaukos turned, Pylades and Meleager close behind him. Neoptolemus sheathed his dead father's sword and looked around for the nearest jug or horn of wine. Finding both, he first drained the half empty horn and gulped undiluted wine from the terracotta jug.

With another belch, he wiped a smear of ruby tinted wine from his hairless top lip.

'I must take my leave oth you, Zygouris. I return with all haste to the Myrmidon camp to supervise the preparations for its def-fence. I will ask Thaos, captain oth my personal guard, to s-stay behind with a couple of trusty spears and escort you to Agamemnon's enclosure. See you on the ramparts oth Troy.'

As was Argive nature, Aletes took what he saw at face value. After what had just happened, he realised how misleading appearances could be. Despite his clumsy manner and a cruel speech impediment inflicted by the pernicious gods, Neoptolemus was not quite the witless provincial he was assumed to be. Beneath

Achilles' bulky armour was an honourable young hero who had inherited his dead father's legendary courage, and an ability to reason that few in the Argive camp would have credited. Given time, he would make a fine king.

'Why did you help me?' Aletes asked, clasping the other's proffered hand. 'I am a stranger to you. A lesser man would have weighed the odds and left me to fight it out.'

'I did not hath a choice. My f-father's shade would hath renounced me ith I had acted in such a cowardly way.'

Neoptolemus averted his eyes, awkward at the round praise.

'Yes, we are s-strangers, Zygouris, yet perhaps we hath more in common than you think. It ith a mistake to believe that you and my f-father were the only ones held in thrall by Iphigenia's f-flawless beauty. My own heart woth enslaved from the f-first day I met her. When others mocked or jeered, she offered f-friendship, s-support and a s-smile to melt the winter snow on Mount Oeta. Once my father ith avenged, I would be honoured to join your quest to f-find her.'

'The honour would be mine,' Aletes said, watching the prince blush as he tucked a jug of wine under his thin arm, calling Thaos as he went.

Agamemnon was squatting on a pinewood commode, surrounded by an exultant press of warlords when Aletes was admitted into his presence. While he noisily evacuated his bowels, a prayer chanting

235

shaman used a dagger to prize a deeply embedded arrowhead from the king's upper thigh. At his feet was the partly crushed head of a dark-skinned Trojan.

'Meet Agapenor,' he said to Aletes, grunting, farting, and shouting to make himself heard. 'Next to Hector, the best of King Priam's sons. At this rate, he'll run out of princely blood to offer up to our thirsty gods.'

'I'll drink to that!' bellowed Menelaus, the long shaft of dead Ajax's bone and blood smeared war hammer that he had won at the funeral games to honour that mighty warrior, resting easily on one of his lintel-like shoulders.

'The Trojan cur never saw what hit him,' Agamemnon continued. 'I cracked his skull so hard his helmet split open like an egg and one of his eyeballs popped out. His head had to go. No peace for him in the Underworld.'

A fresh outburst of raucous cheering filled the stale air as Menelaus lifted his cup in salute to Agamemnon.

'Here's to you, brother!' Menelaus said. 'And the hard-fought victory your quick thinking enabled us to win. After last night's mauling, the Trojans will think twice before launching another mass attack.'

'Let us hope so,' said a wincing Agamemnon, voiding a large malodorous stool the instant the barbed arrowhead was cut from his thigh.

'Truth is, we came within the width of a gnat's cock of defeat last night and being driven from this camp. Our losses were nearly as heavy as the Trojans' and equally unsustainable.'

Agamemnon rose to his feet, frustrating the shaman's attempts to stem the fresh flow of blood from his thigh.

'You should lay down, oh glorious son of Atreus, at least until your wound stops bleeding,' the shaman implored. 'You look fevered, and the royal motion is worryingly flaccid. A clear sign you have lost too much blood.'

Aletes had been summoned to the king earlier than expected. It was still dark outside, and he had only managed a few hours of ravaged sleep. After the night attack, Agamemnon was keen to implement Odysseus' plan before the Trojans regrouped and launched another offensive.

'This is no time to rest,' Agamemnon said, testily. 'Sponge my arse clean, then go sacrifice Agapenor's horse to the gods. Menelaus and I will be inspecting the wooden horse, so you can bring word to me there that the omens are favourable. Favourable, mind you. We do not want to hear any more bad news. The rest of you bold titans, return to your camps and make ready to sail on the next tide. There will be ample opportunity to slake your thirsts after this day's work is done.'

As the pavilion gradually emptied, attendants appeared bearing trays of cold hare, beef, pork, cheese, grapes, and fresh white flatbread from the royal kitchen.

'Come, Zygouris, join us. This may be your last chance to eat a good meal for a while. Try some of the spiced hare before Menelaus consumes the lot. He may be a span shorter than me, but he's twice as wide and as gluttonous as a hog at the trough.'

His hunger sated, and still clad in battle-tarnished armour, Agamemnon made his way to the dusty, sparsely grassed knoll in the centre of the Argive camp where the huge wooden horse stood facing the distant walls of Troy. Menelaus walked beside him, shortening his stride to compensate for the king's increasingly heavy limp. They conversed in guarded tones, Menelaus objecting to the inclusion of Neoptolemus in his otherwise carefully selected scaling party, Agamemnon interrupting their discourse to greet by name all the First Spears and many of the warriors they passed.

Aletes followed close behind, with a shield-bearing escort of royal guards. When they reached the barren knoll, he saw how close they were to the Spartan camp, where the fiercest of the previous night's fighting had taken place. The towering wooden horse was undamaged however, protected by the Argive favouring gods from a storm of Mysian fire arrows. As Aletes looked on, Odysseus' craftsmen applied a coat of black paint to the wheels of the platform it was mounted upon, and a final touch of red ochre to its scalloped mane.

'You have done well,' Agamemnon said to Odysseus, wiping beads of sweat from his leathery forehead. He had just finished inspecting the changes made to the sweltering interior of the wooden horse, paying close attention to the secret space in its arched neck where Aletes was to be concealed.

'I don't doubt the Trojans will be eager to parade this impressive trophy and the riches it contains around their city. Yet there will be those in King Priam's council who will be cautious. If they hold sway, it is up to you to persuade King Priam this equine tribute is no threat to his people. You must convince him it has been built to acknowledge his victory in this great war and to honour the courage of his fallen heroes. If you fail, our last hope will be lost.'

Odysseus pursed his lips and became pensive for a series of heartbeats. Tall and lean, Aletes considered that he looked more oriental than Argive, like the Hittite allies of Troy he had encountered on the battlefield.

'I will not let you down, warrior king,' he said at length, speaking with greater belief than he felt.

'You have a ploy in mind?'

'Not yet, but I will think of something should the need arise. I always do.'

'I wish I shared your confidence.'

'My father said as much when I told him I was going to marry the daughter of Icarius of Sparta. Like all Spartan maidens Penelope was very beautiful and besieged by suitors from all the great cities of Argolis. She told me herself not to waste my time, that she could never wed a man she considered uglier than a drooling satyr.'

The story drew a laugh from the men.

'Yet before the season turned, we were betrothed. If necessary, I will use the same subtle guile on King Priam, lord. I will get this wooden horse into the city.'

'Be sure you do,' said Menelaus, his blunt manner reflecting

239

the antipathy he felt towards anyone who preferred to negotiate with an enemy rather than simply batter him into submission. 'We are all counting on you, Ithacan. Stay focused and try to remember it is the gates of Troy we want open, not Penelope's pretty legs.'

'Thank you for reminding me.'

A procession of chanting, drum-beating shamans came into view, led by the shaven headed grey beard who had tended Agamemnon's wound. The grey's beard's flowing robe was darkly stained with blood, as was the tunic of the young acolyte behind him who carried a bowl containing the dissected heart of Agapenor's horse.

'Well, seer, have you brought me good news?' a scowling Agamemnon said in greeting.

'I have, King of Men. The omens for today are most propitious. The one you call Zygouris, known to the gods as the Lionslayer, will ride the timber stallion into Troy, climb the ramparts while the city sleeps, and lower a rope to the waiting Argives.'

'And afterwards?'

'I have told you all I know. The gods have drawn a veil there. But this a good omen, king.'

Agamemnon waved his hand dismissively and turned to Menelaus whose eyes were already upon him.

'There you have it, brother. As far as this ruse is concerned, the portents are favourable. I have the sweet smell of final victory in my nostrils. Did I not tell you this slayer of lions would bring us a change of fortune?'

'You did, but until I am inside the city, I refuse to believe it.'

Menelaus lifted the war hammer from his shoulder, braced its long shaft against the slabs of muscle piled on his forearm and pointed it at Aletes.

'I'm eager to crack more skulls, Zygouris. Starting with that wife seducing serpent, Paris. Once his shade has departed this world, you and I will fight on side by side. We will cleave a bloody path through the city, all the way to the citadel and Priam's gold decked palace.'

'Shoulder to shoulder, lord.'

Two tribute laden carts jangled. A whip brandishing teamster walked beside the pair of oxen harnessed to each creaking cart.

Aletes' heart soared at the sight of a familiar bald head and bandy legs. Fresh resolve coursed through him, banishing self-doubt and the nagging concern that he had no right to be there, that he was an imposter on the stage of momentous, world-changing events. He was the Argive king's appointed horse rider, and now, like Menelaus, he was impatient to get on with the task entrusted to him.

'The time has come for us to part,' said Agamemnon, casting his eye over the mound of tribute on each cart. Bronze clasped chests and caskets, jars of exotic spices, unguents and precious Phrygian honey, amphorae of wine and olive oil stamped with royal intaglios confirming the contents' exceptional quality. Bundles of bronze rods, cauldrons and cooking tripods, stacks of gold and silver cups, bowls, platters; all worked by the finest craftsmen and gleaming brightly in the fierce morning sun. Jewelled swords, daggers, precious-stoned bronze breastplates, an emerald-inlaid saddle, bolts of rare silk cloth from the Far East and an ivory statue of Poseidon, the Trojans' patron god, the size of two huge warriors standing feet on shoulders, looted from a temple in Lydia almost ten seasons before. Agamemnon was loath to part with so much accumulated wealth, even for one or two days, but he consoled himself with the knowledge he would soon get all of it back and much, much more.

'The tide will shortly turn, Zygouris, so I must board ship and make ready to sail. The next time we meet I will be sitting on Priam's high-backed throne, using his loose head as a footrest.'

'And I'll have introduced Paris to Ajax's fist,' said Menelaus, kissing the hammer's smooth blunt head. He grinned savagely at Aletes, and with the parting words, 'until later', set off with his elder brother.

Aletes watched them walk side by side, gently bickering as they often did, halting after a short distance to tip back their braided, scalp-knotted heads and laugh uproariously at one or the other's ribald quip.

Aletes hawked the dust out of his throat and squinted up at the confined space in the horse's neck where he was soon to be sealed. There were narrow, cunningly located vision slots on the bottom and either side of the steeply curved, dowel-secured base panel that he would release once he was inside the city. None of these three tiny slots were visible to the naked eye, even when close. Aletes had used one of the carpenters' scaffolding platforms to satisfy himself this was the case, checking as carefully as he knew the meticulous Trojans would.

'Second thoughts?' asked Melampus, puffing out his stubbled cheeks and rubbing the small of his back as he placed a jewellery-filled trunk on the horse's sturdy wooden carriage.

'Second, third and tenth thoughts. What brings you here, old friend?'

'I swapped duties with the First Spear assigned to gather up and deliver all this looted treasure.'

'Just so you could see me off? How touching.'

'That and to bring you some news.'

'Oh?'

'Glaukos. Don't look so alarmed. He won't be troubling either of us for a while. He's been sent to guard the Phrygian road at the head of a large Mycenaean war band. I suspect the king is aware of the antagonism between you and decided to get Glaukos out of the way. Meanwhile his ally, Pylades, has been laid low by a wound from last night's fighting. Took an arrow in the shoulder which snapped his collarbone. The tip had to be pushed out through his back. Thought you'd want to know what Glaukos is up to, so you can forget about him and focus on the night's work ahead.'

'Glaukos won't like being stuck out on the Phrygian road while the Argive host is plundering the city. Unless there's a flood of wealthy refugees to rob and ravage or ready to sell in eastern slave markets, he'll find an excuse to abandon his post. You'll need to keep your wits about you. Don't stop looking over your shoulder.'

'Don't worry, I know what to do,' said Melampus, a hint of playful sarcasm in his voice. 'You don't get to be a Senior First Spear without being able to look after yourself.'

'Point taken,' said Aletes, matching the other's wry grin.

Odysseus had finished supervising the unloading of the tribute, exhorting the Ithacans he commanded to greater haste. Now he was striding towards Aletes with a scuffed wooden mallet, wooden bolster, and water-filled leather flask in his hands.

'Leave the carts and get back to the beach,' he ordered Melampus. 'If the tide hasn't already turned, it will do shortly. You risk being left behind.'

'Perhaps I could squeeze in the horse with my friend?'

'You are not the first to seek that privilege, so even if there was room I would have to say no or incur the wrath of at least two warlords I'd prefer not to fall out with.'

Melampus looked back at Aletes, and for once he found himself at a loss for words. He would usually turn to banter during difficult moments in a conversation, but on this occasion any attempt at humour seemed a poor choice. Instead, he gazed in admiration at the reduced warrior he saw in front of him, and prayed he had the physical strength to carry this through. Melampus felt himself welling up, tears of pride stinging his bulging eyes. He turned away abruptly, bending his head forward before Aletes saw anything untoward.

'Stay strong, and may Zeus hold his hands over you,' he said, brusquely. Then he stalked off through the eerily deserted camp, following a worn track that cut through a shifting barrier of dunes, fringed by long yellow grass, before reaching a beach now near empty. The second teamster hurried after him, jogging at times to match the older man's stride.

Odysseus placed the mallet, bolster and freshly filled flask in Aletes' hands. The water felt pleasantly cool through the flask's supple leather skin, but Aletes knew it would not stay like that for long inside the oven-like horse.

'Don't worry,' Odysseus said. 'I'll make sure you are inside the city before nightfall. Drink sparingly and you will have sufficient water to last. Now we need to move fast. We must seal you in the horse's neck before the tribute is loaded, so there is no way to discover you from below.'

20

Duping the Enemy

The one-armed First Spear leading the scouting party was in no mood for lengthy explanations, part truths or what he considered outright lies. He made this clear by stopping Odysseus midsentence, grabbing the lyre he had been playing and smashing it against one of the cart's huge wheels. When he spoke, the First Spear's voice was a jackal-like yap that carried clearly to Aletes inside the horse. Two of the hoplites he commanded dragged Odysseus off the cart and forced him to kneel on the ground. A spear haft jammed into temple, his head instantly pounding, unaware of the fist coming at him, cracking the socket, closing-up his eye.

The First Spear ordered his men to stop. He stepped forward.

'Now start again, Odysseus of wherever in Hades' name you said you are from. Get straight to the point, and if you want to see golden Helios rise again, cut out your devious Argive lies.'

'I'm from the Isle of Ithaca, I'm telling the truth,' said Odysseus, a high pitch ringing in his ears muffling all sound, the sight in his right eye obscured by blood.

'I have not been left behind as a punishment or because I fell asleep drunk. I have met your king before, and because he knows me, and will trust my words, I have been chosen to convey a message of great importance.'

'What message would that be, Ithacan?'

'Agamemnon grows weary of this endless fighting. He wishes to make an honourable peace with the Trojan people, settle our differences and live in harmony as we did before. He has built this horse as a token of his good intentions, and to honour your patron god, Poseidon.'

'Good intentions, my hairy arse,' growled one of the Trojans who had beaten Odysseus. 'It's a ruse, Theano. Let me spill his guts and be done with it.'

'No. Trick or not, his fate is for others to decide. Tecton, you're the fastest runner. Get back to the city and tell Lord Paris what we have found. Go, and be quick.'

Tecton was a youth of no more than fifteen summers. With his large oval shield slung upon his back, the front facing head of a horse crudely painted upon it, he set off at a sprint towards the distant city. First Spear Theano posted a lookout, then settled down with the rest of the scouting party to wait.

So far so good, thought Aletes, barely breathing as he put

the small hide flask to his crusting lips and sipped, desperate not to make the faintest of sounds. A kohl-dark slab of shadow crept from under the horse and spread across the patchy grass like a stain. It became hotter still. The shadow was several paces long and had assumed the shape of an elongated horse when the lookout announced that Tecton was returning.

'Is Paris with him?'

'Paris, Priam and half the city rabble, by the look of it.'

The ululating throng swept across the plain outside the city walls like an inrushing tide. Ahead of them, King Priam rode his gleaming, gold encased royal chariot, his long white hair streaming behind him, while in their wake dust rose into the sky like the smoke of a forest fire. Aletes heard the clamour and rattle of speeding chariots long before he saw them. The sound was almost as unnerving as the Amazon charge at Mount Oeta, and as the animated mob surged and eddied around the giant horse, Aletes touched the heron ring and prayed his luck would hold. He heard Paris' voice cut through the hubbub like a sword, organising a wall of shields around the base of the mound. Order was quickly imposed, and when King Priam dismounted his chariot and approached Odysseus, only the distant whisper of waves and chatter of cicadas penetrated the expectant hush.

The bruised and bloodied Ithacan answered Priam's questions with the same calm assurance he had shown Theano. When he explained Agamemnon had at last accepted defeat and sailed home, a tumultuous cry of unrestrained joy from a thousand people of Troy shook the air. It took some time to restore calm; starved, butchered, besieged for ten long seasons, the Trojans were, as Odysseus had predicted, too willing to accept their once implacable foe had finally given up and scurried back to Argolis.

Paris was not so easily convinced. Aletes heard his hobnailed sandals crunching the rocky ground as he slowly circled the horse. Aletes caught a thin glimpse of the Trojan's once handsome face as he passed below each vision slot.

Paris stopped pacing and stared right at him.

Sweat dripped into Aletes' eyes, stinging, distorting his vision. He held his breath and squeezed his eyes, wincing.

'If you are lying,' Paris said. 'I will make you eat your slippery tongue. Get off your knees. Show me the treasures inside.'

Unsteadily, Odysseus got to his feet and used the U-shaped clasp on the end of a long pole to open the trap door in the horse's rectangular wooden belly. Using the same stout pole, he hooked down the coiled rope ladder within.

'Everything is as I described,' Odysseus said, stepping back so Paris could climb the ladder, a shortsword drawn in the prince's hand. 'You saw me break the Argive king's seal to lower the trap door.'

'I saw,' replied Paris, pushing aside items of tightly packed tribute to make room for himself inside.

It seemed an eternity. Paris rummaged around below Aletes, at one point standing on a chest and reaching up to prod the boards beneath Aletes' feet with the point of his sword.

Satisfied the space did not sound hollow or appear large enough to conceal a hero, he continued his inspection elsewhere. Clutching his fallen brother Hector's black-crested helmet and jewelled dagger, he eventually descended into dazzling sunlight and held the precious spoils aloft. Approval rose from a thousand throats; tears moistened the old king's limpid blue eyes. Although it was several moons since his favourite son had perished, his pain was raw.

'Have the horse brought into the city,' Priam said, taking the helmet and dagger from Paris and remounting his chariot. 'Put this welcome herald in the dungeons with the rest of the Argives. We will decide what to do with them after we have thanked the gods and enjoyed a period of celebration.'

It took a team of eight oxen the rest of the afternoon to haul the wooden horse inside the city walls. Wide though the streets were, there was only just enough room for the lumbering procession to pass. Eventually they halted in a broad, paved, fountain-adorned square. The setting sun was a disc of molten gold on the rugged horizon and celebrations were well under way. Closer, smoke was visible in the darkening sky, rising above the Argive camp. Paris had ordered it burned.

The skin of Aletes' throat stuck together it was so dry, creating the impulse to cough uncontrollably. An impulse Aletes had to concentrate hard to supress. It distracted him at least from the tormenting stiffness, rigid as a corpse from the inability to stretch his limbs.

As night dropped its cloak, revellers filled the streets and square below Aletes. The garland-draped horse became the focus of a wild, spontaneous party. The warriors detailed to guard the horse were soon as drunk as everyone else, plied with food and drink by lascivious tavern wenches or respectable mothers and wives who for one night forgot they had husbands. All night, dancing and drinking, the joyous people of Troy were unaware that Nemesis, the goddess of vengeance, was walking among them. When at last the city slept, and the pale light of dawn bled into the slate sky, the instrument of her retribution stirred like a voracious bear.

His movements made sluggish and clumsy by long inactivity, Aletes used the mallet and bolster to carefully release the wooden dowels holding the base panel in place. When it swung clear on two short retaining straps, the fresh dawn air rushed in, as invigorating as a plunge in a deep pool. For a wingbeat Aletes let the clean air wash over him, stimulating his senses and reactions. Satisfied it was safe, he lowered himself to the ground, the pouch containing his sling and shot gripped between his teeth, a hugely heavy coil of rope slung over his shoulder. One of the warriors guarding the horse stirred as Aletes landed beside the wheeled platform with a soft thud. Aletes killed him with silent efficiency, cutting his voice by opening his throat from ear to ear.

Low. In the shadows. Making his way towards the city wall. He passed a tavern where a few brave revellers were still drinking, a brace of painted harlots doing brisk business in a side alley.

251

Aletes gave them a wide berth.

All now relied on Troy's complacency. There had to be fewer archers on the walls, widespread distraction, and complete belief the Argives had fled.

Light. It was getting lighter. A wave of panic leapt upon Aletes as Dawn crept her fingers around the gates, making it hard to breathe for a fraction of a moment. He snatched back his senses. Bury the fear he told himself. Come on. For Orestes. Come on.

Up. Climbing the stone steps to the ramparts. A Mysian archer stood ahead, looking out towards the winding River Scamander. Torches illuminated the walkway but Aletes could not see far enough to identify where the next archer was positioned. The archer wore a helmet. Back of the head was not an option.

'For you, Kleonike,' Aletes said silently. The stone he loaded into his sling came from his herdsman friend. 'Your stone. Your kill.'

Aletes scuffed his sandal across the stone step. Deliberate. The sling already wheeling around his head. The archer turned on cue. Neck exposed. The stone smashed into his windpipe, shocking him, silencing him. His instinctive archer's arms momentarily slow. Aletes cut the archer's throat as he grappled for his shortsword, holding him as they sunk to the cold ground of the battlements, dying in his arms. Not kindness. Necessity. Must not alert the other sentries.

Aletes uncoiled the rope. An eternity. Unrolling and unrolling. He swung the looped end around the rampart, the estimations of preparation correct, tugged it tight, looped it again, and hurled the rope down. Down. Down. Down.

It hit the ground and the rope was pulled taut.

Climber.

Aletes dragged the body into the corner in front of the steps. Took the Mysian's helmet and placed it on his head. Still no other sentry across this section of wall. Flickers of time passed. Agonising. Two archers came walking leisurely around the corner in conversation. Recognition was slow. Their arrows not drawn. Confusion bought Aletes' time. The figures stretched their bows. Shouting. Demanding to know who he was.

A horn blared from another part of the ramparts. An instant before the nearest archer loosed his arrow Aletes hurled a second stone from his sling. The Mysian went down, stunned or dead, and reloading as he moved, aimed at the second archer. Too late. The Mysian had already dropped to one knee to take better aim.

Bowstring thrummed.

Aletes felt his whole body reverberate. The thud was heavy. No pain. That meant it was bad.

'What kept you?' King Menelaus growled. His shield had taken the arrow, his spear hurtling through the air, ramming through the archer's breastbone and out of his spine.

Another warrior over the wall. Menelaus used his huge shield to ram the Trojans racing up the rampart steps, sending them flying, breaking each other's limbs, the King of Sparta crushing skulls as he stamped on them, pressing towards the West Gates to throw them open. Neoptolemus now one stride behind him, burying his sword in chests, slicing off hands still gripping swords.

Aletes grabbed a look at the sea. Billowing sails filling the bay from horizon to horizon. The leading warships were already disgorging warriors into the waist deep surf, but who did the gods favour, and would Agamemnon reach the city in time?

The stone was slippery with mucus and blood and Aletes nearly fell as he hurled himself into the fighting crying 'For Orestes!'

The West Gates were open. Troy was a warrior without armour. Vulnerable. Bleeding. But the city fought on. They were beginning to drive the Argives out.

Agamemnon's last great gamble was about to fail.

Until a freak accident tipped the scales of destiny in his favour.

Paris, moving backwards, tripped over the scraped and dented shield of one of his fallen warriors. He sprawled on his back like an upturned tortoise. Exposed. Helpless.

'I have him,' cried a jubilant Menelaus, and brushing Neoptolemus aside, sprang forward with Ajax's gore-splattered warhammer poised aloft. The Spartan king's reactions were hampered by fatigue, the fearsome hammer a fraction slow to scythe downwards. Paris rolled aside, and in the same fluid movement thrust his sword up between the Spartan's splayed legs. Menelaus died on his feet with his eyes bulging, desperately clutching his groin to stem the flow of bright arterial blood, excruciating, knowing it was a mortal wound.

'A fitting end for a cuckold, clutching his spurned manhood,' leered Paris.

Shrieking like a blood-crazed Amazon, Neoptolemus burst through a press of transfixed Argives with the Reaper of Shades raised above his shoulder. The dripping blade slashed diagonally through Paris' neck, from one ear to his breastbone, practically decapitating the stupefied Trojan.

'For the s-seducer likewise,' stammered Neoptolemus. 'S-speared like the c-countless wives and maidens you've ravaged!'

Neoptolemus lifted his blood-spattered face to the sky, his spindly legs spread, arms of blood stretched upwards, so that for a curious interlude he seemed to grow taller, broader, filling Achilles' gleaming bronze armour.

'I hath avenged you, f-father. May your shade at last f-find peace,' he cried out.

He strode towards the nearest Trojans, heedless of the carnage and chaos. The Trojans scattered. As if the ghost of Achilles had risen from the underworld.

The first phase of the battle was over, and Aletes could see it would soon become a rout. The city's fate was sealed, for although the sack would take three days to complete, many of the Trojans fighting valiantly to the last, the outcome was now inevitable.

Aletes now had to reach the palace dungeons before the Argive captives were used as hostages. Or worse. He climbed back up to the ramparts and retrieved the rope he had lowered to

Menelaus' warband. He slung the enormous coil over his head and one shoulder, and he had started to retrace his footsteps when confronted by a familiar bandy-legged figure.

'Thought I might tag along,' grinned Melampus, his rheumy eyes orbs of yellow ivory in a face dappled with blood, sweat and specks of brain. 'Make sure you don't lose the sword I lent you.'

'This blunt edged pruning knife you mean?'

'That's the one. Belonged to my pappou, that sword. He used it to geld pigs. Where are we going?'

'To find Orestes. We'll need a spear, and you'd best strip off your armour. They won't be handing out garlands to the first Argives to reach the palace.'

The streets were crammed with people now: men, women and children of all ranks and ages fleeing in every direction, some carrying bundles of possessions, others as naked as the moment they had leapt terrified from their beds. Sounds of bedlam filled the smoke tainted air, the panic-stricken citizens of Troy too preoccupied with saving their own precious skins to notice the two inconspicuous figures moving purposefully among them. There were exceptions to this, but whenever Aletes was challenged or stumbled upon a large band of warriors preparing to defend a temple complex, administrative building, or major junction of streets, he and Melampus changed direction and moved on, fast. In this way, they reached the place where he had scaled the palace's soaring perimeter wall.

Breathing hard, Aletes squinted at the contorted, fruit-laden branches of the fig tree on the far side of the palace wall. Just visible was a fork in its gnarled trunk and a bough that grew close enough to the wall for them to jump from one to the other.

'Let me do this,' Melampus said, panting from exertion, taking the rope from Aletes and tying one end around the middle of his spear's smooth ash wood shaft.

'You may be lethal with that harlot's thong you call a sling, but I was hurling spears before you learned to crawl.'

'Make it quick then. They look like they mean business,' Aletes said, indicating the hundred-strong body of Trojans that appeared at the far end of the crowded street.

Marching five abreast, in close order, they were making rapid progress towards the palace, the clank of armour and rhythmical tramp of hobnailed sandals rising above the cacophony around them.

Spear and rope sailed through the air. Third attempt. The spear wedged sideways across a fork in the nearest bough and held firm. By now the Trojan phalanx was halfway along the street and starting to take an interest in the two apparent thieves. The hero in command pointed at them and barked an order to the harelipped First Spear beside him. In response, Hare Lip and four warriors peeled off the column and sprinted forward. Aletes tugged on the rope to check it would support him before starting to climb. Melampus followed, grunting like an irascible boar. He pulled up the rope behind him barely a sword thrust before Hare Lip reached out to grasp it.

Cursing, Hare Lip stepped back.

'Let them go. I got a good look at the older ugly one. When we take back the city we'll cut off their hands for stealing figs and whatever they find in there.'

Aletes and Melampus kept low. The manicured bushes, shrubs, trees, were adequate cover. Aletes raced towards the ground floor annex, hoping his memory was right.

The opulent chamber where Helen died was occupied by three people. A small boy sat on the bed looking up at two very different adult males. One was old, wispy-haired and frail, his long linen robe hanging off protuberant shoulders.

The other was a hero in his prime: tall, broad of shoulder and deep-chested, clad in scarred and dented armour clearly worn for functional as well as ceremonial purposes. His black hair was gathered into a plaited scalp lock on the crown of his head, the red-crested helmet tucked under his arm and decorative gorget around his neck denoting the polemarch of the elite palace guard. A warlord best avoided under the circumstances.

Aletes was about to move on, find another way into the palace, when snatches of conversation carried to him from inside. He stopped at once, realising that despite the big Trojan's presence, this was too good an opportunity to pass up.

'You must be brave, my son,' the Trojan was saying. 'I won't be long and pappou is here to look after you. We have to give your aunt, Polyxena, and her children the chance to leave with us.'

'I'm frightened, father,' the child blurted.

'So is pappou. But he isn't weeping like a little girl. He doesn't want to shame your mother's shade with his tears. You must be strong for me, my son. I will return as fast as I can, then we will leave together. The passage to the royal stables isn't far from here.'

The Trojan ruffled the boy's thick, straw hair. With a nod to the older man, he strode from the room.

'I don't want them harmed,' Aletes said in a terse whisper. Without further explanation he burst into the chamber and made straight for the boy's ancient grandfather. Before the old man knew what was happening, he was pressed against the chamber's muraled wall with a sword point pricking his wattled throat. Melampus seized the terrified boy. He pinned him squirming to the bed, a bear paw of a hand clamped over his mouth to prevent him crying out.

'Hurt my grandson and you won't leave this room alive,' the old man said defiantly, his cloudy eyes searching the unfamiliar outline of the youthful face before him.

'What is your name?' Aletes asked.

'I am Anchises, father of Aeneas, the boy's sire.'

'Who is Aeneas?'

'He is son-in-law to King Priam, and the man who will kill you if you harm so much as a hair on his son's head.'

Melampus winced at the mention of Aeneas. It was a name he had heard many times before while Aletes was imprisoned, uttered in wary, respectful terms by Argives licking their wounds after facing the powerful Trojan on the battlefield. His young friend had a herd bull by the horns, and unless he was careful, they would get badly gored.

'Do not be concerned,' Aletes said. 'If we meant you harm your blood would already be staining the rugs on this chamber floor. Do as I say, and no harm will come to either of you. What is the boy's name?'

'He is Ascanius.'

'Well, kindly tell Ascanius to stop biting my companion and sit quietly until his father returns.'

They sat, absurdly, in the comfortable, pleasantly cool bed chamber, as if a city were not dying around them. Figures or small clusters of people passed one way or the other in the corridor beyond.

After what seemed an eternity, Aeneas' heavy, ground-devouring footsteps approached. Aeneas entered the chamber and halted abruptly, his hand instinctively gripping the hilt of his sword. In seconds, he calculated it was not possible to kill either intruder before his son or father were slain. His hand released his sword.

'Who are you?' he said, deliberately keeping his voice low, controlled. 'Whatever you want you can have it. Just let them go.'

'I want your help,' Aletes countered, matching the Trojan's brevity. 'There is someone held captive in the palace dungeons who means as much to me as Ascanius means to you. Help me rescue him and your loved ones will be released unharmed.'

'Who is this someone?'

'An Argive warlord, captured many seasons ago.'

Aeneas considered, the ridge of muscle on each side of his bearded jaw clenching and unclenching as he evaluated what the Argive had said. Aletes saw the glint of impotent fury in his narrowed tawny eyes and knew the powerfully built Trojan would lash out with lethal effect if he sensed a hint of indecision or weakness in either of his son's captors.

Beads of sweat trickled down the bottom of Aletes' back beneath his tunic. The old man's shallow, sour breath vibrated softly in his pinched nostrils before fanning Aletes' hand. The tense hiatus went on, until strident voices and a drumbeat of yet more footsteps hurrying along the corridor, finally brought it to an end.

'You are the one who escaped,' said Aeneas, with a slow nod of the head. 'The one who hid among the plague-infected corpses. How can I trust the word of someone so careless with his own life to spare the life of others?'

'There is no need for anyone here to get hurt. When the warlord I seek is released we will go our separate ways. I swear it before the shade of my long dead mother, whose memory is as precious to me as your son's departed mother is to him.'

Aeneas hesitated again, glancing first at his tightly held son and then his near-sightless father. The Argive's words were well chosen, he grudgingly conceded. He still intended to kill him the first chance he got.

He resolved to bide his time, wait until the Argive curs dropped their guard.

'The warlord you seek will be in the palace courtyard with the rest of the hostages. If he's to be saved there's no time to lose.'

'Then let's go,' said Aletes, switching his attention to Anchises. 'Don't make my friend do something he doesn't have to,' he added, and as he lowered his sword, Melampus reinforced the warning by holding the point of his drawn dagger to the boy's ribs.

'Remember you are a prince of Troy,' Aeneas said sternly to his sobbing son, and with Aletes close behind him, he swept from the chamber.

Aeneas marched the length of the corridor to a small antechamber which in turn gave access to a large, crowded hall.

'Leave your blade here,' he said over his shoulder. 'No one will question you at my side if you are unarmed. They'll think you're a servant.'

Aletes glanced cautiously around the congested hall before reluctantly heeding Aeneas' advice. He hid his sword behind the marble plinth of a statue of Apollo standing in one corner of the antechamber. Without a sword, he stood no chance of defending himself. In addition to Aeneas, more than thirty armour-clad spearmen lined the hall's fresco painted walls. Yet more guarded the entrance to the nearby throne room, through which Aletes could just see the back of Odysseus. The Ithacan was lashed to a high-backed chair, bloodied head slumped forward, the floor around him wet with dark blood like a pool of oil. Clearly his audience with King Priam had not gone as smoothly as he predicted.

A tall dark-skinned man wearing the traditional robes of a Hittite noble stepped across Aeneas' path. Beads of amber, gold and cornelian were woven into his tightly curled hair and beard. He spoke with a heavy oriental accent.

'What news from the lower city?' he asked, eyeing Aletes curiously.

'The situation is confused,' Aeneas replied, evasively. 'A force of Argives has penetrated the lower city, but reports say their numbers are limited and they will be repulsed.'

'But what say you, my friend?' The emissary grasped Aeneas' forearm to prevent him moving on. Aletes saw the glassy sheen of fear in the oriental's slanted eyes, sweat on his forehead and shaved top lip. He had good reason to be afraid. There was no love lost between the Argive and Hittite people, and if he fell into Agamemnon's hands he would not be spared.

'You should return to your apartments with all haste and prepare to leave. If we can hold out until nightfall it might be possible to slip away through the North or Phrygian gates.'

'I am grateful, Lord Aeneas. May your gods be with you.'

'And yours with you, Mursilis.'

Stepping into blinding sunlight, the chaos of a falling city washed over Aletes' senses. Choking stench of smoke, screams of men, tormented cries of women, constant movement of people crossing and colliding. Inside the palace, the atmosphere was relatively orderly. The reality of their impending doom was concealed from the occupants by the king's optimistic pronouncements and the misleading comfort of the presence of so many royal guards. Beyond the citadel walls, the ash and acrid smoke of a hundred fires diseased the summer sky to grey. The Argives were swarming everywhere, their bright bladed swords and spears spreading indiscriminate slaughter.

True to his word, Aeneas reached the courtyard without Aletes' presence questioned. But once there, the sight that greeted the Argive intruder was crushing. Many more soldiers ringed the courtyard's extensive perimeter, each one facing the bedraggled, surprisingly numerous hostages sitting on the flagstones.

'I can't see him. I need to get closer.'

'Do what you have to,' Aeneas replied, following Aletes to within a few paces of the destitute band. 'But make it quick. Too long and you'll find yourself sitting with your former companions. Then we'll both rue the consequences.'

Aletes moved among the wretched captives, calling Orestes' name in a whisper. Out of the corner of one eye he saw a young Trojan guard with acne start to take an interest. With redoubled urgency he continued his search, grasping an emaciated shoulder, lifting a pitiful face.

'They didn't see your fear, I hope. These motherless jackals didn't break you?'

It was barely a voice. Aletes turned. For a moment he was frozen. Orestes looked like living death. He was afraid to touch him in case his bones would break into dust.

'What did Paris want you for?' The prince was slurring,

talking in circles.

'Where are we going?' Orestes was moaning, confused.

'We're going home, Prince.'

'Not me alone? Where are our friends?'

'For now, yes, Prince.'

'I won't go.' Orestes' words were punctuated by a hacking cough. 'I won't abandon my comrades. You of all people should understand that. They will be lost without me.'

'They're all dead,' Aletes said, unable to control his desperation.

'Then I shall die with them.'

Aletes looked up and saw the acne-scarred Trojan striding towards him. A few more paces and all would be lost, Aletes realised.

With no other course of action left to him, he punched Orestes on the point of the jaw, knocking him out. Dropping to one knee, he sucked in air, gathered all strength, and hoisted Orestes' limp frame over his shoulder.

'My lord, the hostages are not to be moved,' the acne-skinned guard called out, addressing Aeneas. 'Especially not that one. I'm told he's the most valuable of the lot.'

Aletes stepped past Aeneas without slowing, paces short and fast, breath sawing in his throat, legs losing sensation.

'It's alright, Lycaon,' Aeneas responded. 'He's carrying out my orders. Go back to your place in the shade.'

Lycaon was not convinced. He was about to speak again

when a huge boom erupted outside the citadel walls. A resounding crash followed, the unmistakable sound of two shield walls colliding. The palace was now under attack, and the attention of everyone in the courtyard, including Lycaon, was refocused.

Aletes reached the entrance to the hall and slumped against one of the fluted stone columns that supported the portico's decorative pediment. Arrows rained from the sky now, a few shafts at first, then hailing volleys dense and dark as a hissing storm powered by the gods. Lycaon was hit, a bronze-tipped shaft passing diagonally through his stub neck and rupturing his windpipe. By the time he wheezed his last, at least ten more Trojans and many hostages were dead or writhing in agony on the ground.

'Put me down, Zygouris,' Orestes said, recovering his senses. 'I have no desire to be slain by our own archers or slapped on the jaw again.'

Aletes stood Orestes on his feet. The prince's sarcastic comment served as encouragement his spirit had not been broken.

The scene that greeted them in the hall was foreign to that Aletes and Aeneas had left just minutes before. The fragile pretence of calm had been shattered by the first arrows. As Aletes helped Orestes across the wide expanse of checker patterned floor they were bumped and jostled by panic-stricken magistrates, attendants and court scribes, intent upon vacating the palace. Only the royal guards retained a semblance of composure, forming up behind bellowing officers to defend their doomed king. Aletes retrieved his sword from behind the statue of Apollo, and with one arm around the flagging prince, pushed on after Aeneas.

Melampus was waiting exactly where Aletes had left him in the chamber. His huge arm was clamped tightly yet carefully around Ascanius' little chest, the dagger kept out of sight in his other hand.

'I was beginning to think you'd forgotten me,' he grumbled.

He fell silent when he saw Orestes' emaciation. Aletes had looked frail after his escape, but Orestes was a dead man breathing.

Aletes helped the prince to sit on the comfortable bed before turning to face Aeneas.

'You don't have long. The Argive host is about to storm the citadel. Take your son and father and go.'

Released from Melampus' grasp, Ascanius sprung into his father's outstretched arms. Aeneas swung the spidery limbed boy onto his hip and braced him there, well away from the sweep of his sword arm. His vitriolic gaze remained locked on Aletes.

'You have great courage, Argive. And you have proved yourself a man of your word. It's a pity I'll have to kill you the next time we meet.'

'Let us hope we've seen the last of each other then.'

'Let us hope so,' agreed Aeneas, and with a curt nod, that of one lauded warrior to another, he opened the chamber door and glanced each way along the corridor beyond.

Anchises had remained quiet during Aeneas' absence from

the chamber, anxious not to do or say anything to endanger his grandson's life. Now his impassive demeanour changed.

He fixed his milky eyes on Melampus, hawked a thick glob of phlegm onto the rush-matted floor and rasped, contemptuously.

'If my son doesn't order you killed, I will arrange it. I served as polemarch of the royal guard until age dictated that I pass the honour to Aeneas. I still have influence in these matters.'

'And if your influence has waned, old man?' Melampus' spikey eyebrows arched in amusement. 'Will you bore me to death with more shameless boasting, or poison me with your rank breath?'

Anchises lurched forward, reaching under the folds of his chiton for the small dagger that had remained hidden there until this moment. Aeneas grabbed him by the neck and shoved him protesting from the chamber. He slammed the door shut behind them.

'What now?' Melampus asked.

Orestes had slipped into a sleep. Aletes watched his chest. Still breathing.

'For the time being, nothing.'

He bolted the chamber doors and opened the shutter of a window just enough to see what he already feared. The gardens. Trojan elite royal guards everywhere. No way out the way they came.

'The prince needs to rest. And we need to find him some water.'

Aletes was trying to create a plan.

'The kitchens,' he said. 'I went by them when I was summoned here to Helen. We'll find oil, lamps, anything else we need.'

'Need for what, a cosy night in around the fire?' Melampus grunted.

'No,' Aletes grinned, 'just the fire. We're going to set this place alight.'

21

The King in his Bath

Two days later, a wine-sotted Agamemnon stumbled into the ransacked hall of one of the few noble houses in Troy that had not been burned to the ground. He was plastered from head to foot in a thick paste of dry blood, sweat and soot, the severed head of a silver haired Trojan lord wearing a gold crown tucked under his arm. He almost tripped on a toppled plaster statue of Demeter, the household's patron goddess, before spotting the two Argive princes gorging themselves at small round tables.

He bellowed a delighted morning greeting, his piglike, hanging belly, rumbling at the succulent aroma of the family's roasted pet guard dog. The feasting men ate with their faces in roast dog, too ravenous to wait for their hands to reach their mouths. Outside, bodies lay at obscene angles, cut down as they ran or cut apart as they fought. The occasional scream. A clash of bronze. Always the smoke of smouldering timber from the fires.

The stench of decay as the newly dead quickly became long-stinking as the sun quickened their corruption.

Equally drunk, smears of dog grease in his matted beard, Orestes clambered to his feet and embraced his joyous father. They were still locked together, Agamemnon slapping the younger man's prominently knuckled spine, when the Argive king's noisy, battle-soiled entourage joined them in the once palatial home of Priam's eldest son, Hector.

'Where is he?' Agamemnon demanded.

He stepped away from Orestes, tore a strip of stringy flesh from what remained of the dog's carcass, and searching around the ruined hall with his eyes, devoured it ravenously.

'I've come out of my way to thank him and brought Priam to pay his respects.' He gestured to the head under his arm. 'The least Zygouris could do is to be here to greet me?'

'You've missed him,' Orestes said, sucking grease from his fingers. 'He begged the loan of my warship and sailed on this morning's tide.'

'He did *what*?'

'Nauplia, I believe. To begin a search for Iphigenia.'

'Agghhh.' Agamemnon rasped, dismissively. 'Searching for a corpse? Iphigenia was slain by corsairs on the shores of Locris. Your elder sister, Electra, was there to witness it. The warband I sent to punish her captors followed their spoor deep into Epirus but found no evidence to suggest your sister had been taken with them. You've both gone mad in that dungeon. It's played with your mind.'

'They did not find her b-body,' Neoptolemus, the second diner in the hall, chipped in.

'Which proves nothing. Only that she was carried off by the rabid wolves who seized her and, if the gods were merciful, died shortly after of her wounds. Either she was buried in an unmarked grave or her remains were devoured by scavengers.'

'Who says she was wounded?' Orestes asked, draining the sweet red Lyrnasson vintage from Hector's twin handled gold cup.

'Glaukos, son of Aegisthus, the only other reliable witness to survive the ambush.'

'Ah y-yes, Glaukos, the celebrated hero oth Trachis,' Neoptolemus lisped, his sardonic words further distorted by a mouthful of dog. 'Now there's a slippery s-serpent. After what I w-witnessed the other night I would not t-trust a word he utters.'

'What are you babbling about?'

'On the night our camp woth last attacked I heard him t-taunting Aletes. His w-words were not those oth s-someone who laments your daughter's death ath much ath he p-pretends to.'

'Are you saying he's been lying?'

'I believe s-so. When given the chance, he made no attempt to r-refute Alete's assertion that your daughter is still alive.'

Agamemnon placed King Priam's head on an unoccupied table. He looked around the debris-strewn hall again. A naked woman stood close by, her curvaceous body and noble bearing attracting the attention of the lustful Argive warlords. She was Andromache, Hector's widow. After being brutally beaten and raped by Neoptolemus, she had been forced to butcher the family's pet hound – the only meat to be found in the house – and spit roast the carcass over the hall's central hearth.

The broken body of her small boy, Hector's infant son, lay crumpled at the foot of the wall Neoptolemus had thrown him at to dash out his brains.

'I was told about the incident you speak of,' Agamemnon said at length, recalling what his loyal head servant had confided to him when they were alone in the royal compound the following afternoon. 'I'm sure there's a reasonable explanation, but to put your minds at rest I will speak to Glaukos again.'

'I want to be there when you do,' Orestes started before being distracted by a commotion.

At the far end of the hall, the bronze panelled doors flung open, a blonde-haired young woman appeared with the veteran Spartan hero, Amasis, close on her heels. Her pleated saffron pharos had been ripped open to reveal heavy, copper nippled breasts, blood flowed from her nose and mouth where Amasis had used his fist to stop her biting him. Slim and fleet of foot, she might have outrun her inebriated pursuer had not one of the watching warlords stuck out a greave-clad leg and sent her sprawling at Agamemnon's dusty feet.

'What have we here?' drooled Agamemnon, feasting his bloodshot eyes on her shapely legs and breasts. 'Polyxena by name, unless I'm mistaken, the youngest of Priam's legitimate brood.'

At the sight of her father's severed head, Polyxena uttered a cry of unbridled grief and revulsion. As she scrambled to her feet Amasis grabbed her by the hair and pinned her arms behind her back.

'I found her hiding in a laundry cupboard, King of Men,' explained Amasis, hopping from one foot to the other as the princess stamped on each of them in turn. 'With your leave, I will take her aside and teach her a little respect for her new masters.'

'You have my permission, Amasis, although it is hard to see who will be teaching who a lesson.'

Bawdy laughter and words of lewd advice reverberated around the hall as Polyxena sank her teeth into Amasis' thigh, drawing blood.

Agamemnon raised his voice to make himself heard.

'Before you drag her off somewhere, Amasis, and spend the rest of the day breaking her to the saddle, I have another task for you. I want you to find Glaukos and bring him here. If he has obeyed my last order, he'll be rounding up fugitives on the Phrygian road. Tell him there's an urgent matter that Orestes and I wish to discuss with him.'

Amasis looked dismayed, loath to let Polyxena out of his sight before he sated his depraved appetites. Emboldened by the prodigious quantity of wine he had consumed, he was about to protest when a cautionary voice inside his fuddled head reminded him who had given him the order.

'I shall return within the hour,' he said dutifully, and still

274

grasping a clump of Polyxena's silky, sand hair, he set about finding somewhere to hide his delectable prize from the envious warlords.

The sun was halfway to its zenith by the time Amasis reached the force of Argives Glaukos commanded outside the city's Phrygian gate. True to form, Glaukos had managed to turn the mundane task of guarding a less frequently used entrance to the city and dusty stretch of road, into a lucrative and highly entertaining opportunity.

The trickle of refugees attempting to escape Troy by that route had swollen to a flood once the city's western defences were breached. Men, women and children of all rank and age had fallen his way. With the help of Euthemus, who was still limping heavily due to the stab wound in his thigh inflicted by Aletes, he had filled a generous clothes chest with gold and silver pendants, bracelets, rings, jewelled necklaces, earrings, good luck charms and other priceless adornments.

He had also conducted a cull. No males of any age were spared. Same for infants not yet weaned and females deemed too old to work or bear children. A nearby olive grove was strewn with stinking piles of contorted corpses, while the holding pens of the city livestock market were crammed with several hundred women and adolescent girls. Frightened, thirsty, and traumatised by watching their loved ones die, they waited listlessly in the stifling heat to be loaded onto warships and transported to a new life of degradation and servitude.

'The king wants to see me?'

Glaukos eyed Pylades, who along with his younger brother, Nireus, Meleager of Thebes, and several other disgruntled warlords, had joined him the previous evening to drink wine and discuss the implications of Troy's sudden, unexpected collapse. Pylades glowered at him, making the hairs on his neck prickle with irritation.

He looked back at Amasis. 'Did the senile old goat say why?'

'I'm afraid he did not,' the Spartan replied, ignoring Glaukos' disrespectful reference to the Argive king.

Amasis was surprised to find so many senior warlords together in the same remote location. He was distracted by visions of Polyxena and chose not to dwell upon it.

'I wasn't present to hear what the three of them were talking about,' he replied.

'Three of them?'

'Orestes and Neoptolemus of the Myrmidons had the king's ear.'

'Tell the king I will report to him directly.'

'My lord, the king expects you to accompany me without delay.'

'He also expects me to ensure the fortune I have amassed on his behalf is secure. Go on ahead, Amasis, while I see to it. I'll follow.'

Amasis hesitated only briefly, the lure of Polyxena's curves overcoming his devotion to duty.

'Don't keep the king waiting,' he said curtly, turning on his heels. 'If you do, he will vent his ire on me.'

As soon as Amasis was out of earshot, Pylades cursed. He was holding the point of his sword to the throat of the blood-drenched Hittite emissary kneeling on the ground before him. Naked and viciously beaten, the tall satrap had been discovered that morning at the back of a crowded stock pen, disguised as a woman. He had been clubbed and kicked near to death, his carefully groomed hair and beard hacked off, or in places torn out by the root, to get at the beads of gold, amber and cornelian woven into it.

'I warned you this would happen,' Pylades rasped. 'I said your feud with Aletes would be our undoing.'

'We don't know he is the reason for my summons.'

'Why else would Amasis be sent to fetch you? I suggest you open your eyes and consider the facts. The king's been talking to Orestes and the dribbling Myrmidon. One of them was locked up with your bastard sibling, the other was present when you taunted him about Iphigenia. Neither of them has any great affection for you. If Agamemnon didn't already harbour doubts about the ambush, I'll wager he does now.'

'Why should he have doubts? I've said nothing to incriminate myself. All I did was lament the tragic slaying of his daughter.'

'In case you've forgotten, Neoptolemus questioned your sincerity and accused you of being up to something.'

'Neoptolemus is a drunken fool, a gibbering idiot no one takes seriously. The king believes his daughter was killed by pirates, and rest assured that will remain the case.'

'I'm not convinced. Nor I suspect is Atredes,' said Pylades, and as if to emphasise the point, he thumped his sword into the startled Hittite's throat.

As the tall emissary slumped forward suffocating on his own blood, a chorus of piercing wails emanated from the stock pen in which he had been discovered. It was there that his disconsolate wife and three tearful, repeatedly raped daughters clung to each other for comfort.

'That hostage was worth a lot of gold,' Meleager pointed out.

'What use is gold to us?' Pylades replied, cleaning the blade of his sword with a handful of sandy earth. 'Before nightfall we might all be dead. You'd be better advised plotting your survival, my friend, instead of filling the treasury at Thebes with a fortune you'll never spend.'

Glaukos had learned a lot about Pylades' volatile temperament during the moons they had lodged together. Much of what he discovered he disliked. That was why he had sought an understanding with Pylades' younger brother, Nireus.

As king of the largest contingent of rebels, Pylades had demanded to be appointed leader. Glaukos had agreed, pledging that Pylades would sit on the Argive throne when Agamemnon was overthrown. An agreement Glaukos had no intention of honouring. He would need the Phocian host if the citadel of Mycenae had to be taken and held by force. But once that objective was achieved, he would send Pylades, and anyone else who opposed him, to join the shades of their ancestors.

'I should get going,' Glaukos said. 'The sooner I find out what Agamemnon wants, the sooner I can return and put all your minds at rest.'

'I wouldn't hurry on my account,' Pylades replied. 'I have no intention of being here when you get back.'

'You're abandoning our cause?'

'For now. To avoid suspicion it would be wise to keep as far away from each other as possible.'

'Instead of running like a frightened rabbit, has it not occurred to you this may be the gods' way of telling us it's time to act? To cease talking, gird ourselves and slay the Atrean tyrant?'

Pylades snorted dismissively, ramming his sword into its silver engraved scabbard.

'Now I know you're hysterical,' Pylades laughed. 'Either that or last night's wine has curdled your wits. Not content with kidnapping his daughter, you'd have us march into Agamemnon's lair and kill him while he basks in the adulation of his loyal cohorts? I'm returning to the safety of my own host. I suggest you all do the same. The success of the wooden horse has set us back by a full turn of the seasons. The sooner we come to terms with that the better.'

The burning in his back made Pylades' legs collapse beneath him. Spine cut through. Blade sticking through his chest.

He clutched at the sword hilt he could not reach, falling forward onto the Hittite he had just slain, grunting, snorting like an ox.

Nireus removed the sword he had thrust into his brother's back. He smiled at the astonished warlords and calmly wiped his blade clean on Pylades' long braided mane of hair, leaving his paralysed brother to die in the dirt.

'I have the loyalty of the Phocian host,' Nireus announced. 'The polemarchs will declare for me as soon as they know my brother is dead.'

'I assume our agreement stands?' Nireus turned to Glaukos. 'In return for my support, you will consent to me marrying Electra once her period of mourning is over?'

'Providing Electra agrees.'

'She will.'

'Then our agreement stands.'

It was exhilarating what could be achieved with a keen-edged sword gripped in a willing hand, Glaukos mused. Pylades had become an irritation. A liability. With his main rival eliminated, there was no one among the rebel lords ambitious or powerful enough to challenge his hegemony over the disparate band. He was now their leader in all but name, and when the time came for action, they would follow his orders – or suffer the same fate as Pylades.

'Send word to your captains, Nireus, then follow me at a distance should I need your help. You too, Meleager. And you, Euthemus, assuming your leg can cope with another brisk walk.

The rest of you wait here until I send word or return.'

The sturdy cedar gates built to bar entry to Hector's luxurious town house had been smashed off their bronze hinges. Glaukos stepped over the splintered timber, his three discreetly armed companions close behind. He caught sight of Orestes asleep on a laurel shaded stone bench in the gardens, a wasted arm fallen limp and resting on the floor. His abused body had taken as much pillaged wine and meat as it could. The absurd Neoptolemus lay close with the soles of his upturned feet extending from under a neatly manicured border of bloom-covered shrubs.

'Let them sleep,' Glaukos ordered. 'Whatever Agamemnon intends to say to me is best said without his interfering son around.'

More of the king's inner circle of advisers were scattered in the ransacked house in various attitudes of drunken repose. All of them had a jug of wine close to hand and at least one unfortunate woman entwined in their muscular arms. Armed guards lounged everywhere, some of them as drunk as the warlords they were tasked with protecting. Others were nursing wounds or continuing to loot the house. Glaukos moved among them without attracting much attention, guided to Agamemnon's location by the king's unmistakable war horn voice.

'We will drive them back to their capital, then batter them into submission. They have never liked facing Argive bronze, and the sight of our battle-hardened host—ah, Glaukos!'

Swathed in clouds of steam, immersed to his shoulders in

piping hot water, Agamemnon reclined in a huge bronze bathtub with a cup of wine in one hand, a bowl of stuffed olives in the other, and a cluster of shapely female attendants surrounding him. One of these women was Hector's grieving widow, Andromache, whose duties had changed from pouring wine and roasting family pets to combing out and oiling the Argive king's long, matted hair and beard, almost grey now, and sponging clean his furred torso and feet.

Another was Polyxena who, much to the dismay of the watching Amasis, had been forced to perform oral sex on the king below the surface of the murky water. Every time she reared up gasping and spluttering for air, Agamemnon grabbed a clump of her sodden hair and pushed her under the water again.

There were two smaller tubs in the room, occupied by Argive warlords and their reluctant consorts. Odysseus, and Penelaos of Plataea, the former recovering from his brutal interrogation by the Trojans, the latter a long-standing member of the council of war.

Glaukos stood facing the king, the hot steam making the skin of his neck prickle uncomfortably. The chamber's terracotta tile floor was flooded, so that scummy, lukewarm water lapped over his dusty sandals.

'I was hard at work carrying out your orders when Amasis arrived. As soon as the plunder accumulated on your behalf was secure, I made my way straight here.'

'In which case give me the benefit of your opinion. I intend to return to Mysia next spring and lead a punitive expedition against the Hittites. I will deploy two columns, one driving north to their capital, Hattusas, the other south into the soft underbelly of their shrinking empire. If we set out after the last winter storm, can we sack Hattusas and force them to sue for peace before the grapes are ripe on the vine?'

Glaukos looked at the silent warlords. His contempt for the raving tyrant was mirrored on their perspiring faces. Although in terminal decline, the vast Hittite empire was still a force to be reckoned with. The ramparts of its ancient capital were nigh on impregnable, while any army it put in the field would be at least five times the size of the Argives. Man for man, their elite warriors, so-called Immortals, might not be a match for a bronze-clad hero, but many of the Argives' finest sons had perished in the struggle with Troy, and to seek another major conflict so soon would be an act of monumental folly. Unless he came to his senses, the deluded king would have to be dissuaded, but Glaukos had no intention of being the first to speak out.

Instead, he harnessed all the conviction he could muster.

'With you at its helm, warrior king, we'll take Hattusas in a single moon. We'll slaughter their Immortals and teach the Hittites a lesson for succouring our enemies. We'll destroy what is left of their decadent empire.'

The two other bathers glared at Glaukos, who responded with a mischievously arched brow and knowing smile. A delighted Agamemnon tossed aside the bowl of olives, sending the juicy appetisers rolling onto the watery floor. He drummed the heel of his fist on the rim of the bronze tub.

'There you have it, my lords,' he exclaimed. 'This bold young peacock agrees with me. Perhaps I should dismiss you from my council and appoint him in your stead?'

Legs splayed and naked, water streamed from the king's hulking, scar-latticed frame as he climbed to his feet like the dreaded Kraken rising from the ocean depths. He brushed aside the linen towel offered to him by one of his quailing attendants. His face darkened.

'What is this little thing I hear about my precious daughter being alive?'

Glaukos blinked three times and set his jaw straight. 'I fear my brother has let his mind run away with him again.'

'It is alleged you suggested she was alive. Why would you do that?'

'Brothers do odd things, lord. We scrap, we bicker, we misunderstand.'

Agamemnon's sorrowful smile was for Menelaus, just as Glaukos hoped his words would stir him.

'I am sure we both know my little brother was in awe of the princess. The little fool as we endearingly call him at home was speaking of saving her. After everything he's been through, I didn't have the heart to tell him there's no hope. I fear I am guilty of having encouraged his belief, where there is none. You will know from your son that so long in the Trojan dungeons has ravaged their senses.'

'So, you stand by your original testimony?'

Agamemnon swung a stocky leg over the side of the brim-full bath. A luxuriant bush of tight black curls crowned his pendulous testicles, a dark line of hair joining it to the pelt on his chest like a wiry umbilical cord.

'She was taken before your eyes?'

'She was, lord. I fought like a bear in a baiting pit to reach her in the waves, to recover her body for ritual purification and cremation, but Poseidon was too powerful.'

'That is strange,' said Agamemnon, lifting his other leg out of the oily water. 'Zygouris has sailed for Argolis this morning on a quest to find my daughter. He's convinced she is alive and imprisoned somewhere in Epirus.'

'May I offer my services to help him?'

'I think that would be unwise.'

'I know the location of the ambush better than anyone. My knowledge could be of great help to him.'

'It could also be a hindrance.'

Agamemnon's clipped smile was devoid of warmth, his words laced with insinuation. He drained the wine from Hector's gold cup and held it out to be refilled by the youngest of his naked attendants. The girl's tiny breasts were swollen brown rosebuds and she had yet to reach her first flowering, but that had not prevented her being raped like every other royal maiden.

'I think it best you return to the Phrygian gate and continue the good work you are doing there. Zygouris can manage well enough.'

'My work there is finished, king. Surely I can better serve you at my brother's side?'

'You will serve me how I tell you, not as you see fit,' rapped Agamemnon. 'Go back to the Phrygian gate and supervise the branding of slaves and safe transport of the bounty you have harvested. When I have spoken to Orestes and properly considered what you said this afternoon, he or I may wish to question you again. We cannot do that if you are on the other side of the Argive sea.'

Glaukos' body throbbed with fury. The king saw through him. Things were falling apart. Or the Fates had put him here in this bath chamber for a reason. Agamemnon was as vulnerable as he had ever been. Ever would be.

Glaukos plunged his sword to the hilt into the startled king's wine bloated gut. Viscid blood vomited over Glaukos' hand, making the hilt slip. He used his maimed hand as a lever, withdrawing the sucking blade. The king's black eyes were thunderstruck. Incredulous. Agamemnon gripped Glaukos' forearm, crushing it, but the king slipped on the scented oil slicked bathtub and Glaukos' follow up thrust sliced up under his ribcage, through a lung and his heart. The screaming eyes and hanging mouth, acknowledgment the king knew he was a dead man. A dead man not ready to die. Terrified captives ran screaming from the chamber, and voiding his bowels, the stricken king fell backwards into his bath.

Glaukos spun around to confront Amasis. The Spartan's sword remained sheathed. Holding up open palms, he rushed to help Polyxena from the blood and faeces soiled water. Dismissing him as a threat, Glaukos turned to defend an attack from the two bathing warlords. Odysseus and Penelaos were sat upright in their respective tubs. Their hands were raised, echoing Amasis. They remained mute, their silence loud. They felt little sympathy for Agamemnon. They did not wish to become involved.

A royal guard. In the open doorway. Glaukos dropped into a defensive crouch. The guard did not move. His bulging eyes glazed as a sword punched through the back of his neck under his helmet and out through his jaw like the bronze ram on a warship. The sword was withdrawn; he fell head-first onto his shattered jaw on the flooded tiles. Euthemus stood over him, ready to stab again if the guard showed any, unlikely, sign of life. Glaukos looked beyond his loyal henchman and saw the mangled shapes of more felled guards on the hall floor. Nireus and Meleager had cornered three more near the vestibule entrance, and with merciless efficiency, were busy ensuring no one fled to spread word of Agamemnon's assassination.

Euthemus limped towards the other two baths.

'Leave them. They're no threat to us,' Glaukos asserted as a warning.

He climbed into the fallen king's bathtub and pushed his head under the water with a sandalled foot.

'Let them live to tell their brother Argives how the bloated despot met his end.'

The warlords watched in silence as a last cluster of air

bubbles gurgled to the surface. Glaukos reached under the water and tried to pull the king's intaglio ring from his finger. Stuck. Drawing his dagger, Glaukos sawed off the whole finger. He stepped out of the bath, picked up an abandoned wine jar and drank his fill from it.

'Did you kill the prince?' he demanded when Nireus and Meleager joined him.

'You told us to leave them,' Nireus rapped. 'He and Neoptolemus have vanished.'

Glaukos did not risk antagonising his allies with his true thoughts.

'We go to sea then. Day and night until we reach Argolis. Your spears are still camped in the dunes by their beached ships? We must reach Mycenae before Orestes and we need to get to my father.'

'I thought we had the warden's support?' Meleager queried.

'My father won't cause us a problem. Now are you with me or do I go on alone?'

Nireus knew Glaukos was bluffing. He needed them as much as they needed him. If the warden proved difficult and barred Mycenae's gates, Glaukos would need the Phocian host to help storm the citadel and persuade Aegisthus to cooperate. On the other hand, for the rebellion to succeed, to prevent the Argive warlords flocking to Orestes' banners, they needed the legitimacy Glaukos' lofty bloodline provided. More so married to Iphigenia.

Nireus grasped Glaukos by the forearm. 'We are with you,

my friend. We have gone too far to back out now. Our fates bound together, the prize within our grasp.'

'We go on,' agreed Meleager. The King of Thebes leaned over the bronze tub and spat at the body floating face down in the water.

'From my brother, exiled without just cause,' he snarled.

Wiping a slug of phlegm from his bearded chin, Meleager turned and strode from the hall beside Nireus. Euthemus limped after them. Glaukos called him back.

'Cut off his head and bring it with us. It may prove useful if my father or his councillors need convincing the tyrant is dead. Wrap it in something. Our work here must not become known until we are ready.'

Glaukos followed Nireus and Meleager outside into the proud sun. Euthemus set off after them with the king's head tightly wrapped in Polyxena's pharos.

Around them, Troy lay like a warrior with a mortal wound in every part of its golden-skinned body. It had been glorious. Invincible. Rich. It had swallowed a blade and died from the inside out. The Argives could not allow Troy to stand. It must burn. Most of the citadel had been torched, once opulently draped in silks, furs, fashionable couches, carved tables, ivory vases, from the exotic Near East, wealthy Egypt and far-flung Scandinavia, the goods from so many merchants sailing in down the Hellespont strait. Vibrant frescoes had brightened the walls, of horses running free, of beautiful Aphrodite, gazed at by the equally brilliant eyes of

Helen of Troy. The seas of Troy had been full of fishermen and their nets, farmers ploughing fields of grain, forests busy with deer. Before the long war ravaged and drained the city. Troy's warriors had been highly skilled, fearlessly loyal to their wise king and beloved princes. To their city.

In defeat, the spacious plazas and elegant colonnades of the lower city had become stinking abattoirs. Bloated bodies blackened in the sun near the tables at which they would drink wine and lunch on octopus, oysters, mussels, clams, turtle, and exotic chicken, tasting rich desserts of fig, date, and honey. Taken by surprise. Hordes of captive women and children had been herded into open spaces, many of them beaten or violated by their brutal new masters. Tormented. Bereft of spirit. Thirsty. Starving. Defeated.

One day, when Zeus was ready to permit it, a new city would rise from the ashes of the old. For a long time, its people would be vassals of the new dominance of the Argives. They would produce wine, olive oil, cattle, and horses to pay the exorbitant taxes they owed. They would become prosperous despite this heavy burden, thriving for many generations after the Argives themselves were supplanted. The walls of their legendary city would be broad and strong, the columns of Poseidon's temple majestically tall. Yet for all her rediscovered glory, she would never be more than a shadow of Priam's fabled marble carved capital.

22

The Quest and the Pendant

After sailing into the harbour of Nauplia, Aletes rode northwest along the dust blown road to Mycenae, Melampus clinging to a mare chosen for her placid temperament with the elegance of a sack of vegetables.

'The gods are punishing me,' Melampus gasped, wincing as a spike of pain drove into his lower back. 'They've crushed my spine and sucked the strength and feeling from my legs.'

Aletes had told a reluctant Melampus there was nothing to it. The former herdsman had learned to ride while Glaukos and Aegisthus were regularly away in the city, his friend Kleonike teaching him to race the old master's stallions across the lush land of Zygouris.

After docking the warship in Nauplia's port, Aletes and Melampus had made their way through the town's sweltering, hustling agora. Dressed in short military tunics and high-laced sandals, on their backs were slung tight bundles of sword, helmet and rolled cloak. Aletes' sling and a small leather pouch of shot was attached to his wide studded belt. Market stalls filled the shady colonnades along each side of the otherwise unroofed space, a bustling throng of hawkers, farmers and craftsmen bartering everything from livestock, fresh fish and scraps of farm produce, to cooking tripods, kiln-fired pots, and new or second-hand clothing and footwear. At the far end of the agora, broad stone steps led up to the Temple of Zeus and an unimposing cluster of municipal buildings.

Aletes used a small clay tablet stamped with Orestes' seal to get past the guards outside the Nauplian council chamber. He presented the same tablet to Nausithous, the paunched, loose-necked leader of the council of elders. Once Nausithous read the words of introduction above Orestes' lion seal his attitude changed, and he became welcoming and effusive in his desire to help. After taking refreshment with the impatient travellers, he asked the master of the guard to accompany them to the royal stables where they were furnished with horses and provisions for their overnight journey.

When at last they halted for the night in a rocky gully screened by scrub oak and poplar trees, Melampus fell rather than dismounted.

Aletes was subdued as they ate their frugal ration of stonebaked bread, goat's cheese, and coarse red wine beside the fire. Melampus knew when to leave the younger man alone. Long after he settled down to sleep, his raucous snoring cutting through the peace like a shipwright's saw, Aletes sat cross-legged, staring into the dwindling flames. He stoked the fire with a forked stick, sending a comet trail of sparks spiralling into the starlit sky. Beside him, Melampus grunted like a contented hog and rolled onto his side, closer to the diminished heat of the flames.

The choice Aletes faced was a simple one. Either avoid Mycenae and press on without a guide or escort to Phocis and, if necessary, the Land of the Ironmen beyond, or trust Aegisthus to remain impartial and provide him with the provisions and seasoned spears needed to give his quest a chance of success. Aletes sat back and took the tiny, terracotta figurine of his mother from the kidskin pouch around his neck. He placed it on a smooth rock beside him, and after apologising to Danaea for neglecting her for more than a day, asked for her opinion.

'The warden is unpredictable, so be careful what you say,' Danaea cautioned. 'He does not know what became of Iphigenia and is not party to any mischief concerning her. He will do what he can to help you but is wary of his first born and will not say or do anything to incriminate him.'

'Will I find what I seek in Phocis?'

'I fear not. The young master is not a fool. You must go on to Epirus, the only region of Argolis where the dynasty of Atreus does not hold sway. Electra witnessed her sister being carried off into that wild and rugged domain, but if she was already dead, as Glaukos testified, why would the Ironmen bother? If their purpose was to honour their gods with her blood, why not conduct the ritual there on the beach? Find the Dorian chieftain who led that warband.'

'I will find him,' Aletes promised, placing the delicately painted figurine back in the kidskin pouch. 'I'm not sure how but I will persuade him to put aside the hatred between our people.'

He kissed the heron ring and with his eyelids drooping heavily, rested his head on his folded cloak. Exhaustion embraced him, and although he could still hear sounds coming from his mouth, he was unsure if he was speaking aloud or dreaming.

The sound of Melampus vacating his bowels at the far end of the shallow gully awoke Aletes with a start early the next morning. A fetid stench smote his nostrils.

'Never could shit over the side of a ship,' Melampus called out jovially, tuft of grass to hand. 'Riding the nag didn't help, but I've cleared the blockage now.'

'As it would seem,' Aletes replied, holding his breath as he rose stiffly to his feet.

The dawn chill made him shiver, yet once he started breaking camp he quickly warmed up. He shared a stale crust of bread from last night's supper with Melampus, washing it down with a mouthful of sour tasting wine. He put a saddle blanket and bridle on the patient sorrel and ignoring the stream of colourful invective that Melampus uttered, helped him mount up. Grasping a fistful of mane in his left hand, he swung onto his own spirited gelding, dug in his heels, and rode out of the gully.

For a long while that morning they had the road ahead to themselves, yet by the time Mycenae's gleaming white citadel merged out of the shimmering haze, a good many other travellers were moving each way along the hot highway. A peasant farmer pulled a cart loaded with more of his meagre harvest than he could spare to pay his overdue taxes, a shepherd boy carried a bleating lamb under each skinny arm, and a file of dour-faced spearmen set out on patrol.

Upon finally reaching the lower city, Aletes used the prince's seal to avoid joining the long queue outside the heavily guarded toll gate. They walked their tired horses past the colonnaded Temple of Zeus, where the relief force bound for Mount Oeta had mustered all those seasons ago. Then they remounted to climb the steep, winding ramp, tier by tier, to the citadel's monumental arch, the Gateway of Lions.

The senior of the two guards on duty at the citadel gates was an old friend of Melampus.

'Good to see you again,' the grizzled veteran said. He cast an eye over Orestes' seal before ordering his much younger colleague to open one of the sturdy gates. 'You look leaner, and you've collected a few new scars, but you're still as ugly as ever.'

'I've missed you too, Meriones,' Melampus called back.

Leaning on his spear, the grey-bearded veteran inclined his head towards Melampus. As Aletes handed the gelding's reins to the freckle-faced younger guard and strode through the open gate, he muttered: 'If you don't mind me asking, who is that?'

'I'm surprised you don't remember him.' Melampus slapped the sorrel's reins into the veteran's free hand, a hand shorn of the tips of its last two digits. 'He beat you onto your knees one morning when training with wooden swords. You would have lost more than the end of two fingers if I hadn't stopped him. Unless I'm mistaken, that was the last time you tried to make him look a fool.'

'The herdsman from Zygouris,' Meriones said, realisation dawning. Melampus grinned back at him.

'Take care of the nag, she means a lot to me,' Melampus said dryly.

He followed Aletes under the gate and across a small internal courtyard, flanked on one side by an ancient cemetery filled with the beehive-like royal tholos tombs, and on the other by an ornamental white marble fountain with sea nymphs and dolphins at play as its centre piece. Directly ahead stood the palace.

They waited in the cavernous vestibule, columns carved into stone paws of lions at the bases, vivid orange, red and gold frescoes of scenes of famous battles and hunts vibrantly decorating the walls. They were met by another guard who led them across the great feasting hall to the throne room.

'The warden is resting,' the gaunt scribe, Scedasus explained. 'He's not been the same man since his illness, and tires easily. I will wake him shortly, but he needs to rest during the hottest part of the day.'

'The warden is unwell?' Aletes asked, briefly distracted by

the imposing splendour of the gilded throne and impressive array of painted clay busts of long dead kings on name-inscribed plinths. It was not hard to imagine this opulently decorated chamber as the beating heart of a mighty empire; the room where Agamemnon and his warlike Atrean ancestors had taken momentous decisions which shook or shaped the Argive world and lands far beyond. An almost palpable aura of power emanated from the boldly frescoed walls, diffusing even the dust motes that danced in the beams of golden sunlight pouring through the small windows and the clerestory high above.

As he stood there waiting, sightless enamel eyes staring down at him from the distant past, he also felt close to Iphigenia, knowing this was where she ran chasing Orestes, as he had told him in the dungeons. Her feet on this ground. Her laugh within these walls.

'A seizure I'm afraid,' Scedasus was explaining. 'An affliction of the heart that cost him the use of an arm and control of the muscles on one side of his face. The demons that possessed him have been driven out, and he is slowly improving, yet the seers say much of the damage is permanent and he will never fully recover.'

'Which shows how little they know,' a voice from the past spoke from the doorway. 'I've already proved them wrong by learning to walk and talk again in a fraction of the time they estimated. With the help of Asclepius, god of healing, I mean to continue confounding them.'

If the voice had lost none of its vigour, the same could not be said for Aegisthus' appearance. The frail old man who shuffled slowly into the throne room was a pale shadow of the formidable warlord who had declared himself Aletes' father all those seasons ago. His hair had turned white and fallen like snow, his body withered, while the once hawk-sharp eyes were sunken and yellowed. He slumped heavily on the curule chair beside the gilded throne, and when he spoke, used a cloth to dab away the trail of saliva that dribbled from the rigid corner of his mouth into his limp beard.

'My lord, you should still be resting,' said a concerned Scedasus.

'Stop fussing, Scedasus, and have the servants fetch food and drink for our guests. They have travelled far and look ravenous.'

He switched his attention to Aletes, genuine affection radiating from the depths of his ravaged eyes.

'Welcome home, my son. It lifts my heart to see you again after so many long moons. We have a great deal to talk about, but first I must ask you to explain why you are here? I have not received a despatch from the king for several days, so I was not forewarned of your arrival. What is your purpose, and what news do you bring of the war?'

Aletes was silenced by hearing the warden address him as his son.

'The war is over, my lord,' Melampus spoke for his friend with typical directness. 'Troy has fallen, and our victorious host will soon be returning home. Our many dead have been avenged, our warships stuffed with booty and valuable slaves.'

'Fallen?' Aegisthus visibly stiffened. The knuckles of his ring-encrusted fingers blanched as he gripped the scroll-ended arms of the curule chair. He drew in a deep, ragged breath through pinched nostrils. 'How so, First Spear?'

'We built a wooden horse, filled it with tribute and hid Aletes in its hollow neck.'

Melampus paused to quench his thirst from the jug of wine mixed with chilled spring water delivered by a slave. He told the lord more of Aletes' exploits as the former herdsman wriggled in his seat, uncomfortable with the praise.

'Go on, First Spear,' Aegisthus urged when Melampus stopped again to cram his mouth full of the cold suckling pig that arrived on a heaped silver platter. 'Do not spare this fearsome titan's blushes.'

Melampus continued, washing the meat down with yet more wine. Aegisthus listened intently until Melampus finally fell silent, indicating his narrative was at an end with a satisfied belch.

'Nothing I have heard surprises me, Aletes. I watched you grow up and I never doubted you would fulfil the holy mother's prophesy. You taught yourself to survive at Zygouris, and when I sent you to Mycenae with Terpander you honed those skills to become the champion I see before me now. I could not be more proud, my son, and I know I speak for your mother, Danaea, when I say your exploits on the field of battle have far surpassed our

300

expectations.'

Speaking for his mother? Aletes was surprised at the anger he felt, yet the words seemed to unleash a resentment he had locked away. What had Aegisthus ever done for his mother? What had he done for his son? Aegisthus spoke of pride as if he played a part, yet he could have sent him to train with the palace guards at any time. The word son was empty. Hollow like the horse within he had hidden in the suffocating heat.

He realised something else. He did not trust him.

'You have made an old man very happy', Aegisthus continued. 'Yet I am not foolish enough to think that was your purpose in sojourning here. Where are you going, and what do you want from me?'

'We are bound for Phocis and the realm of the Ironmen beyond,' said Aletes, holding out the small clay tablet. 'We intend to find Iphigenia or settle what became her.'

'You think she is still alive?'

'Last time Glaukos tried to kill me he indicated as much.'

'What do you mean?'

'He lured me into an ambush, and when he believed me at his mercy, boasted about what he had done.'

Aegisthus handed back the clay tablet, his brow low.

'Are you saying Glaukos was involved?'

The warden rose unsteadily to his feet. He shuffled close enough to Aletes for the younger man to smell the decay on his shallow breath. Melampus shot Aletes a look.

'Be careful what you say Aletes,' Aegisthus said, still able to assert authority of iron. 'He is my son.'

And there it was. Aletes heard in those words the reason why all those years ago Aegisthus had not taken him in. It was not for *his* protection. It was to shield Glaukos. He feared the curse he spoke of three long years ago in the orchard for Glaukos' sake, not Aletes'. Without Aletes there was no rival brother. The line of their family was secure, unchallenged.

'Whatever childishness if going on between you and Glaukos, don't let it spill into politics. Our family name has been loyal to Atreus' line for generations.'

Aegisthus neglected to mention his plot to kill Agamemnon with Clytemnestra all those years ago. Theirs had been a reckless and passionate affair. An affair that ended when Clytemnestra found herself standing like a sleepwalker outside the door of her sotted husband's bedchamber with a dagger in her hand.

'Kill him while he sleeps, my petal, snoring like the drunken pig he is,' Aegisthus had told her. *'Erase the stain of his existence with one quick thrust.'*

The inebriated king had stirred. Waking with a grunt and resonant fart, he had risen to his feet and emptied his bladder into a clay chamber pot. Clytemnestra took it as a warning from the gods, hid the dagger in her robe and retreated to her own chamber where she bolted the door. Thanks be to Hera, Agamemnon had returned to his bed none the wiser. The next morning Aegisthus came looking for her, insisting the potion he had slipped into her wine was only intended to bolster her courage. Thereafter, Clytemnestra had refused to have anything to do with him. Until she came looking for his help to find Iphigenia when she was lost nearly three years ago now.

As if reading his mind, Aletes asked. 'I thought I might find the queen here?'

'The queen?' Aegisthus said, observing Aletes as if he were a spirit. 'The queen is long gone from here. She is a guest of her eldest daughter, Electra, at Phocis.'

'Scedasus will make sure you have what you need for your journey,' Aegisthus, added, wiping a fresh string of glistening saliva from his beard. 'He will also prepare a written order for the warship masters based at Sicyon to convey you with all haste across the Sea of Corinth. These are difficult times, Aletes, and the resources at my disposal are stretched thin. I must warn you the handful of novice spearmen I can spare for your escort will be no match for Glaukos' seasoned fighters should they catch up with you.'

'They will suffice,' said Aletes.

'I should also tell you that the court shaman will shortly be sacrificing a grain fed bull calf on my behalf. He will ask Zeus to hold his protective hands over you and my first-born. I make no apology. I hope your quest brings you the closure you seek, but for Glaukos' sake I hope it proves fruitless.'

Aletes considered his response carefully before replying.

'I am grateful for your honesty,' he said. 'For my mother's sake, I hope that whatever outcome the fates contrive we can still be friends. May Asclepius continue to watch over you, and may he restore you to full health before we next meet.'

With a curt nod, the eyes of long dead kings judging him, he turned and followed Scedasus from the throne room.

In the pounding heat of the port of Sicyon late the following morning, Aletes squinted down from a ridge as he tried to focus. A funeral. An unusual spectacle. The procession was making its way out of the octopus emblazoned gates, following a shroud-draped litter upon which lay the mortal remains of a peacock.

Fishermen and their families lined each side of the port's single dusty street, heads bowed respectfully as the prayer-chanting shaman went by, leading the solemn procession to where a small driftwood pyre had been prepared on the shingle beach. First among the mourners was a round shouldered, pot-bellied elder with a face contorted like a bellowing baby. He clutched a spiral conch to his food-stained breast, and held the hand of a diminutive, shrew-faced woman who walked beside him.

'This is unfortunate,' said Aletes, patting the big gelding's sweat-lathered withers and neck.

'Yes, very sad,' agreed Melampus, sitting awkwardly astride the winded sorrel as he had all night, a fistful of mane gripped tightly in his hand to help steady himself. 'It looks like they are going to cremate the fat elder's pet bird.'

'I wasn't talking about the funeral. How many warships can you see anchored in the harbour?'

'I can't see any.'

'Exactly. Which means we've ridden long and hard for nothing. Unless we leave the horses and mule behind, and cross to Phocis in fishing boats, we could be waiting days for a ship to return.'

Shading his eyes with one hand, Melampus scanned the expanse of diamond topped turquoise water under the polished blue sky. In the distance, floating like a mirage in the shimmering heat haze, he could just make out the rugged coastline of Phocis. It was no more than a dark smudge on the horizon, so far that the prospect of sailing there in a flimsy fishing boat filled him with more dread than this bloody horse. The sea looked calm now, yet Poseidon was notoriously fickle and much as he disliked riding, sitting astride the gentle sorrel seemed infinitely preferable to being caught in a sudden violent squall or sucked into a powerful whirlpool as Glaukos claimed to have been.

'Perhaps we should stay on dry land and follow the coast road north,' he suggested, glumly. 'It will take a day or two longer, but I'd rather crush my balls on this lumpy old mare than risk drowning.'

'We're not going to drown, and we don't have a day or two to spare.'

Aletes gave Melampus a sideways glance and pressed his heels into his mount's soft flanks. The big gelding snorted wearily, tossed its white blazed head, and with the unerring step of a dancing wood nymph, picked its way down the scrub-fringed ridge.

Liberally doused in olive oil, the pyre was burning fiercely by the time the last of Aletes' escort jogged onto the beach. A dark column of smoke rose high into the azure, the stench of burning feathers stung eyes and coated throats. A tense silence enveloped the sombre gathering as first the presiding shaman and then each of the mourners ceased chanting and switched their attention to the new arrivals.

'It's good of you to come,' Megapenthes called out, holding the conch to his preferred ear. 'I hoped the king would send someone to attend the funeral on his behalf and investigate Achilles' death. He was murdered. Shot full of arrows by those drunks over there. I will swear as much before the Altar of Zeus when their trial begins.'

As he spoke, Megapenthes levelled an accusing finger at the group of armed men who had approached to within a few paces of the mourners. Nine in number, they were led by a huge First Spear with a lazy eye, long oily hair, and an ugly piggish snout. He and seven others had the black hawk of Phocis painted on large oval shields they left stacked untidily on the harbour brothel's shady portico. With a stony-faced Orthagoras making up the ninth, they had been gulping mouthfuls of undiluted wine and hurling insults at Megapenthes and his steadfast wife as the funeral procession passed. Rising to his feet to urinate in the dusty street, it had been Pig Nose who first spotted Aletes' party atop the ridge. He had stopped scratching his itchy backside, dropped the front of his tunic, and led his companions to the funeral pyre.

Hermione smiled up at her husband, gently patting the back of his soft fleshy hand.

'We've spoken about this, my dear,' she said, as if speaking to a child. 'There isn't going to be a trial. We can't prove who drew the fateful arrow.'

'They should all be arrested. Questioned until one of them admits the truth,' Megapenthes insisted. 'You were there at my side, good wife, you saw for yourself. They were gathered around Achilles, watching his innocent blood seep into the ground. They openly mocked us with their laughter.'

'Which proves nothing, old man,' Pig Nose interrupted. 'Only that we were first to find the dead bird. You should listen to your fat little wife instead of running off at the mouth. Nobody's going to believe an old fool with ears so stuffed with wax he can't hear himself fart.'

'They will if he's telling the truth,' said Melampus, incensed by the Phocian's disrespect.

'And you are, friend?'

'He is First Spear Melampus. He speaks for me,' Aletes interrupted.

Aletes' attention was captured by the delicate, star shaped pendant Pig Nose wore around his unwashed neck. It was made of brightly polished, high grade Dorian iron. Far too valuable to belong to him.

'Now it's my turn to ask a question. What's a band of loud mouthed Phocians doing this side of the Sea of Corinth?'

'We were sent here by King Pylades,' said Pig Nose, lifting his bearded chin aggressively.

'For what purpose?'

'I suggest you ask him that. Who in Tartarus are you?'

'We travel on behalf of Prince Orestes to Epirus. My turn for a question. The pendant around your neck is Dorian unless I'm mistaken?'

Alarmed, Hermione silently cursed the swaggering Phocian's stupidity. He had been warned not to flaunt the star shaped pendant he had taken from Melissa as a trophy the first time he ravaged her, yet here he was standing before a stranger with it dangling around his neck.

She stepped in. 'My lord, the pendant is a mere trinket of no great importance. You have clearly travelled far and look sorely in need of rest and sustenance. Will you join us in the feasting hall? A funeral feast of sorts has been prepared to honour—'

Before she could finish there was a commotion at the rear of the mourners. It ended abruptly when Orthagoras' younger brother, Philocletes, was dumped unceremoniously on his backside. He scrambled to his feet cursing and lunged after the dark-haired woman who had upended him. He missed.

'The pendant is mine,' she gasped, her heart pounding wildly as she glanced round to see how close Philocletes was behind her. 'It was a naming day gift from my husband, Teucer, who is a great war chief among my people. It was taken from me—'

Philocletes' hand was around the woman's mouth. His arms around her in a rib hold. She scratched at his hands and tried to bite him.

The clay tablet struck him in the forehead, knocking him senseless.

Arching back on his tasselled saddle cloth, Aletes had hurled the clay tablet he had been about to show Hermione and her muttering husband. The muscles of his throwing arm were not as strong as in his fighting prime, yet his near-supernatural gift of throwing, remained. The sharp corner of the tablet struck Philocletes with a solid thud, drawing blood. His legs buckled beneath him, and as his spirited charge wrenched herself from his grasp and stumbled towards Aletes, Pig Nose's sword and those of his fellow Phocians rasped from their scabbards.

As if sensing the escalating tension, the chestnut gelding shied away and stamped the shifting shingle. Aletes shortened the reins in his hand to steady the nervous horse.

'Sheath your weapon, First Spear. I do not wish to kill you.'

Pig Nose hawked and spat on the ground. 'Bold words for a lightly armed man outnumbered seven to one. What say you, boys?'

Sniggers tailed off as Melampus brandished his sword, clutching a fistful of the sorrel's mane at the same time to avoid losing his balance and embarrassing himself.

'Learn to count,' he retorted.

'Stay out of this, old man. You're well past your prime and

those cubs behind you won't lift a finger to back you up. They might have the lion of Mycenae on their shields, but they'll piss themselves and run when I set these black hawks on them.'

'Thanks for the advice,' said Melampus, gaining the advantage as no one anticipated the speed he would dismount, draw his sword and charge like an enraged boar. He had a drunk Pig Nose staggering backwards trying to draw his blade. Melampus' kicking foot had already made impact with his balls causing his legs to bend in at the searing pain. The second kick connected with his windpipe, knocking Pig Nose choking onto his arse.

His pack of Phocians lowered their blades and backed off. Behind Melampus the yet to be blooded recruits of their escort stood with shields and spears braced, ready to enter the fray and prove the boastful Phocian wrong.

'Do I have your leave to open his throat?' snarled Melampus, breathing hard.

'No, let him live,' said Aletes, beckoning the dark-haired woman closer. 'He's a bad-mannered mongrel, but he doesn't deserve to die for that. Unless I am given cause to think again, the elders of Sicyon can decide his punishment.'

Aletes smiled at the feline-eyed woman, who was now standing close enough to reach out and touch the gelding's velvet soft muzzle.

'Tell me quickly, wife of Teucer, what is your name?'

'I am Melissa, daughter of Neoman, King of the Ironmen,'

said the woman, eyes on Philocletes as he knelt groggily to his feet and picked up the clay tablet that had felled him. He was joined by Pig Nose, who had been disarmed by Melampus before being permitted to rise off the pebbles.

'I was captured during an Argive raid on the village of Calydon and brought here in chains as a hostage.'

'By who?'

'A brute named Glaukos of Zygouris. He is the most foul—'

'What?'

'Yes, he coerced my husband Teucer into helping him abduct the Argive princess, Iphigenia of Mycenae. They sailed across the Sea of Corinth from here, I—'

Abduct? Then she could be alive. Aletes felt himself come back from the dead.

'You saw Iphigenia? Here?'

'Yes, she was here. With a Lydian priestess called Briseis. Glaukos falsified a pirate ambush to make it appear she was killed. They say she drowned, but that must be a lie too because as far as I know their deal stands. If not, I wouldn't still be alive, nor my boy.'

'If you agree to release me,' Melissa continued, 'to escort my son and I back to our homeland, Teucer will tell you what became of Iphigenia. I give you my word.'

'I am an Argive, sworn enemy of your people. If I venture into Epirus without a war band to protect me, I will not get out of there alive.'

'You will if you agree to help me. My father will be indebted at his grandson's safe return and will readily grant you safe passage.'

'Where is your son?'

'I have not seen him since we arrived here, a few days after we were seized at Calydon. He was taken from me as punishment for attempting to escape.'

Aletes measured the woman with his eyes. She could be lying. It could be a trap. Was Glaukos luring him into Epirus alone? By the looks of her she had suffered, her wrists were burned purple and she had old and fresh bruises on her arms. Straightening in the saddle, Aletes swept his angry gaze over all those watching.

'Who has this woman's son?' he demanded. 'Fetch him here!'

Silence. Just the rustling of the waves and crackle of the funeral pyre.

'No one leaves this beach till I am satisfied the boy has come to no harm.'

Nothing. Aletes had resolved to order a search of the port when the brothel owner Orthagoras stepped forward.

'The boy's not here. Glaukos took him, and his men said he's hidden him where no Ironman has ventured. As far as I know he's still alive, but no one here knows where he's been secreted.'

'This man is Master of the Watch,' hissed Melissa. 'Until the Phocians arrived, he and his brother were my worst tormentors. He has often lied to me and probably lies now. Give me your dagger

312

and I will cut out his deceitful black heart.'

'I am not lying, my lord,' said Orthagoras, more assertively. 'I had no part in the boy's removal and, for what it is worth, took no pleasure in his mother's treatment. Like several others here, I was simply obeying the orders of a man it's unwise to cross.'

Aletes' hand was clamped over the hilt of his dagger to prevent Melissa making a grab for it. He looked at Melampus, knowing the grouchy First Spear would be telling him not to trust the Dorian she-wolf.

'Ironmen have never ventured to Argolis,' Aletes said. 'I would wager Glaukos has taken your son there and I will search for him. But first, I am bound by oath to finish what is already started. I am leaving for the Realm of the Ironmen this day, so you must decide whether to come with me or remain here and wait for my return.'

Melissa spoke without hesitation.

'We will ride together through the gates of Tricca, and when I am reunited with my husband, I will tell him that despite being an Argive, you can be trusted to keep your word.'

'So be it then,' said Aletes, turning to Megapenthes and the huddle of elders behind him. 'I am sorry about what happened to your peacock. If you can prove that one or more of these Phocians fired the fateful arrows I will ask their queen to make sure you are properly compensated. In the meantime, I need to borrow two of your sturdiest fishing boats. I want boats with experienced crews who are familiar with these hazardous waters, including whirlpools along the coastline of Phocis.'

'Two boats won't be enough,' Melampus interjected. 'We'll need the whole fleet to ferry us all safely across.'

'We're not all going.' Aletes tossed Melampus the small leather pouch, now empty, that had contained the clay tablet Orestes had prepared for his mother. 'Wait here for our warships to return, then take this thug back to Phocis. While you're there, deliver Orestes' tablet lying over there, to the queen.'

'You can't trust her, Zygouris. You can't venture into Epirus alone.'

Melampus' words sounded like a father to a son. He knew his reservations made sense, but as so often, the son was about to disobey the father.

'If Teucer decides to kill me, you can't help me.'

Aletes stopped short of adding that the untested young guards supplied by Aegisthus would be useless.

'He commands several hundred Ironmen, every one eager to spill the blood of an Argive. But I will need your help if you'll stop bleating. When you leave Phocis, make your way north of Pharsalos to where the river Peneus flows out of Epirus. Wait there for my return. Before you leave, ask Electra to send a trusted polemarch here to Sicyon to instil some discipline into her subjects. If she offers to increase the size of your escort, be sure to decline. It won't help my cause if the Ironmen think you intend to raid farms and villages close to the border.'

'I don't like it,' Melampus said. 'But I am at your service,

Zygouris.'

The veteran kept it to himself, but he had a primal, gut feeling that Aletes had already fulfilled the prophesy and he was no longer under the protection of the gods. After all, he had stood shoulder to shoulder with the best among the Argives, he had saved the dynasty of Atreus by rescuing Orestes. Melampus' generous sized gut was never wrong. It had seen him through nearly thirty years as a military man. Yet he couldn't stop the boy. Even if he tried, he wouldn't listen. All he could do was take up his end of the job and do that right. He'd have to hope plain old luck would go his lad's way.

Melissa grabbed the star shaped pendant from around Pig Nose's grubby neck, snapping its cord with a sharp tug. She curled her lip, hawked, and spat in his ugly face, saying everything she wanted with her disgusted eyes. Clutching the pendant tightly, she grasped the hand Aletes offered her and swung up behind him on the gelding's silky broad back.

23

Among the Ironmen
Two and a half years ago

The shard felt comfortingly sharp as it dug into her skin. If Iphigenia's tormentor came for her as he promised, she was ready. She slumped against the wall adjacent to the flogging post, her movements hampered by her chained ankle, the dagger-like pottery shard hidden beneath her filthy tunic, biting into the soft flesh of her stomach. Her patron goddess, Hera, had forsaken her, consigning her to a twilight existence of despair and degradation, yet with or without the goddess' help she was ready to do what she had to.

She had Perimedes' words in her ears. All those moons ago when he had helped her escape through the night from Aulis on her brother's chariot and passed her the dagger.

'Take this', he had said as he drove the horses on. 'Stick it in the throat under the ear or go for the groin. Deep as you can.

Then twist. Don't let go till it sticks.'

Her stomach cramped from hunger, throat swollen, sore, and the nights were cold with snatched sleep. Many days had passed like this, fed rancid scraps of meat in watery gruel, toiling from dawn until dusk fell, emptying stinking chamber pots in the garden cesspool, removing ash from central hearth in the great hall, sweeping, scrubbing, fetching, carrying in the stifling heat of the day in the even hotter royal kitchens. She was constantly guarded by at least one Ironman or stick wielding Hillman, her only respite from the grinding drudgery Briseis' late night visits. The Dorians' honoured guest came as often as she could, bringing extra food and unguents for Iphigenia's blistered hands and the many injuries inflicted by her unsympathetic gaolers.

The sounds of lyre, flute and drink-fuelled gaiety beyond the barrack walls seemed to be coming from another world. It was the festival of Karnea, the Dorians' most important religious celebration, and the later it got, the more unbridled the revelry became. Even the guards on duty were drawn into participating, and recognising his chance, the lecherous hunchback had told Iphigenia to expect an overdue visit.

Iphigenia had risked a beating that morning by deliberately dropping a decorative storage jar. Fortunately for her, the hard-pressed master cook was far too busy preparing for that night's feast to worry about a smashed jar. As she cleared up the broken pot and its contents of dried figs, Iphigenia managed to conceal the shard without being noticed.

'This is folly, Naxos. If we're seen Teucer will have us both skinned alive.'

'Nobody's going to see us, Drago. I'll give the wench a tap on the head to keep her quiet and drag her round the back of the barracks.'

'Hit her with your axe and her skull will crack open like an egg. Let's go back to our own quarters, Naxos, before it's too late. Gaia, the beekeeper's daughter, will still be there. She likes you and will spread her legs if you ply her with enough beer.'

'Go back if you want, Drago. I'm staying here. I'm fond of Gaia, but tonight I've got my eye on a more gently bred prize.'

They were speaking in guttural whispers, yet such was her heightened state of awareness that Iphigenia heard every word. Naxos left his companion by the slightly open doors and crept towards her. She almost willed him forward now. Driven to a prepared attack by a manic state caused by sleeplessness, fear, and the innate human ability to inflict violence to survive.

She was sick of being afraid. She waited. Still. Naxos was unlocking the short length of chain that attached her manacled ankle to the heavier chain running the length of the barrack walkway. Still. He leaned over her. Stench. She retched. Still. Until the stone axe rose above her head.

For you Perimedes. She lunged at Naxos and stuck the shard as deep as she could into his throat, fury-fuelled for all who had hurt her and those she loved. She pushed with all her might, twisting like Perimedes told her. Naxos had thought she was

318

punching with her pathetic hands, it was too late when he realised, his eyes hugely round. The axe nearly hit Iphigenia as it clattered from his hand, grappling for this throat to desperately remove the shard. He ripped it out and panic-eyed, Iphigenia launched at the axe. Yet Naxos was already stumbling, blood spurting through his fingers. Iphigenia was breathing like a wild dog. Naxos' legs collapsed beneath him like a hiding spider. The slaves started screaming. By the time Drago knelt beside him he was already dead.

'Iphigenia!'

Briseis stood in the open doorway, bathed in flickering light from the olive oil lamp she held. A plain linen cloth covered the platter the kitchen maid behind her was carrying. Drago leapt to his feet and ran past them like a startled hare. He upended the platter and blundered into the waiting arms of a wiry young Dorian sentry named Guneus. Alerted by the commotion, Guneus had abandoned the farm labourer's daughter he was pleasuring in a nearby alley and hurried back to where he and another guard should have been patrolling.

'Keep hold of him, or I'll report you for abandoning your post,' Briseis snapped, with unconvincing severity.

She handed the lamp to the kitchen servant and told her to leave the platter of spit-roasted venison and honey-coated raisin slices on the floor where it was already being fought over by the slaves. A second, more experienced warrior arrived, and as he began restoring order she hurried to the side of Iphigenia, who was rattling like a snake, eyes manic around the red blood that had splashed on her face. Briseis took her palm, where the shard had dug a trench into the soft flesh. She helped her to her feet and escorted her from the barracks. Guneus followed, holding the struggling Hillman with his arms twisted behind his back.

There was no stone temple in Tricca, but on a grassy knoll overlooking the marketplace, where majestic marble columns would one day soar into the heavens, stood a grove of oak trees sacred to the Dorians' principle deity, Apollo. It was here Briseis brought the dazed Argive, her appearance interrupting a white bearded bard's recital of an epic poem about the brutal murder of a young seer named Karnus. It was the Dorians' slaying of the Argive raiders responsible for Karnus' death that had earned them the enduring gratitude of a grief-stricken Apollo. The grove was lit by resinous torches, mounted in iron gussets nailed to the surrounding trees, while all those present were seated upon a tiered circle of benches carved from huge oak logs. Their faces were gaudily painted and they wore elaborate costumes intended to represent beasts or heroes from mythical tales passed down through the ages. The severed head of a stag killed that morning had been placed at the feet of an imposing wooden statue of Apollo, the splayed tines of its antlers painted the same oxblood red as Apollo's benign features.

The stag hunt had been the focal point of that day's festivities, a symbolic re-enactment of the search for Karnus' butchers several generations ago. Set the challenge of running down a healthy stag in its prime before nightfall, without the help of hounds, the chosen hunters' success had ensured the continuing goodwill of Apollo during the forthcoming grape harvest and planting of next spring's crops.

Teucer had been first to spear the cornered stag, and as he rose from his elevated place of honour at the forefront of the gathering, an expectant hush settled over the grove, deepening until the hiss and splutter of torches was the only sound to be heard. Dressed as a satyr with long pointed ears, short horns and a cape fashioned from tufts of coarse grass, he listened patiently while Briseis explained what had transpired, his expression slowly darkening beneath the red ochre paste daubed upon his face.

'Your visit was timely, Priestess of Apollo,' he said. 'If you hadn't arrived when you did, Drago would have avenged his fallen companion and brought shame upon us. We are fortunate you decided to slip away and succour your friend.'

'Fortunate?' echoed Laodamia, rising from her seat beside a recumbent King Neoman on the far side of the log circle.

The queen was dressed in the flowing white pharos of a muse, her lips stained with berries, eyes outlined with kohl in a face that was otherwise covered in a thick layer of chalk white powder. Her naturally straight hair was a riot of loose curls, and in the crook of one arm she held a miniature tortoiseshell lyre. It rested against her distended belly, the size of which indicated the child growing in her womb had been there since before the hot summer moons.

'I doubt the shade of Naxos feels *fortunate* as it roams the dark abyss of Tartarus crying out to be avenged. The Argive witch is guilty of his murder, and soon the kinsmen of Naxos will make their way here seeking revenge. They will demand the witch's blood, so that Naxos can join the shades of his ancestors in the Underworld.'

'The hostage is not to be harmed,' asserted Teucer. 'Must I remind you that if she is slain, we will never see Melissa or little Neoman again? Naxos has only himself to blame. The Argive was defending herself, as any woman, hostage or otherwise, has the right.'

'I say she has no such right. She is guilty and should be handed over to Naxos' clansmen to do with as they see fit.'

Before Teucer could respond she held up a hand to silence him. 'No, I do not need reminding about the plight of your wife and son. I love them and think about them every day. It is more than two full moons since the Butcher of Calydon pledged to return here with them. Yet nothing.'

King Neoman peered bleary-eyed from the gaping mouth of the stylized lion head he was wearing over his own. It had been fashioned from embroidered linen stretched over a lightweight wooden frame, embellished with a mane of copper horsehair. Perched on one of his shoulders was the head of a bearded goat and on the other, the head of a serpent; to all who gazed upon him he was unmistakably the dreaded monster Chimera.

'Our sources tell us the Butcher of Calydon marched to

Trachis with the Myrmidon host,' the king said. 'We know he fought beside the Antmen yet whether he chose to or was forced, and why he then sailed with them to Troy, is far from clear. We must therefore be patient and wait until he sends further word. For the sake of the loved ones he has taken from us, whom I entreat our lord Apollo to keep alive, we must be steadfast and cleave to the terms he imposed upon us.'

'Naxos' kinsmen will not take kindly to being denied their traditional right to vengeance.'

'They are our guests, good wife, and they will obey our laws and abide by the decisions of their host.'

Neoman drained his horn cup and held it up for a wine mixer to refill. 'As a gesture of goodwill, they can have Drago back with his head still attached to his shoulders. It is the festival of Karnea after all, an opportunity for the King of the Ironmen to be generous and merciful. I will give them Drago, but not the Argive.'

'Sparing Drago won't be enough to assuage their anger. If you permit the witch to live, they will expect her to be ritually mutilated or severely punished in another way.'

'Then they will be disappointed. The Argive is the victim in this matter and she must not be harmed if we are to see Melissa and little Neoman again. I have made an error leaving her in your care, wife. Teucer, take her to your country estate at first light. Restore her to health before the Butcher returns for her.'

'Perhaps Briseis would care to accompany her?' Teucer said.

'I would be pleased to,' replied Briseis.

'So be it,' said Neoman, switching his attention to the young Dorian sentry struggling to restrain Drago. 'Release him and return to your post, Guneus. Your work here is done.'

As soon as Guneus complied, Drago dropped into a crouch, hawked, and spat at Iphigenia, then scurried away like a scorpion flushed from under a shady rock.

'Sit and calm yourself, wife, or you will bring on the birth of our son.'

Neoman waited until Laodamia sat beside him before raising his cup to the bard.

'Pray continue your recital, my learned friend. Apollo's eulogy at the funeral of Karnus and the Dorian king's vow to avenge his murder, are my favourite verses. Perhaps you could resume from there?'

After passing what remained of the night in Briseis' quarters, sharing the Lyrnasson's comfortable bed, Iphigenia no longer believed her patron goddess had forsaken her. She had much to thank Briseis for, yet it was Hera who had given her the courage to arm herself and confront her Hillman tormentor.

She could still feel the goddess' presence the next morning when they set off on foot to Teucer's nearby villa. Escorted by a brace of hungover guards, she and Briseis had started out shortly after dawn. They left the slumbering settlement through the smaller north portal, descending from the limestone plateau along a winding, much used dirt road. An hour later, they reached the swift-flowing River Peneus, and as the sun rose high like liquid gold, they turned east on a dusty track that followed its often steep, sometimes meandering bank.

The conversations of birds, soft drumming of insects in the trees, bushes and reedbeds along the margin of the river, infused into Iphigenia's body. Yes. She would escape here far more easily. She did not know where the river would take her, but if she could find a small boat or debris to cling to, she might reach a village whose inhabitants were not in thrall to the Ironmen. For a generous reward, they might be persuaded to escort her home to Argolis. Squinting into the distance, Iphigenia saw huge boulders strung across the river as if stepping-stones placed by a mighty titan. Turbulent, white capped water swirled and eddied around them with great ferocity, the current powerful enough to drown all but the strongest swimmer. It could not be worse than she had already suffered.

She bided her time, always preparing, planning. She quickly settled into her congenial surroundings, behaving well, keeping her head down. Her ever-present guards were more at ease away from Tricca, keeping their distance when she took her twice daily stroll around the estate's extensive gardens. These walks always took her by the wooden landing pier on the far side of an orchard of orange and pomegranate trees. There, she would linger as long as possible without arousing suspicion, observing the river and dark forests of its far bank.

She followed the same routine every day, until one morning she found a rowing boat moored unattended while its two occupants, a master tiler and his young apprentice, carried out repairs to the roof of the villa. Her guard that morning was Guneus, whose passion for a local farm labourer's daughter had not waned since the Festival of Karnea. Iphigenia saw them together in the long grass under a pomegranate tree.

Unsteady, she managed to step into the boat and balance herself. Now the rope and she would be away.

Poseidon.

The earth shaker struck the ground, his trident rousing a massive tremor deep in the earth's ancient bedrock. The water flipped upside down, turning the rowing boat on its back, the fish from the bottom of the river swam, stunned, on top. The ground ripped open, a cavernous fissure gaped up to the house across the landscaped gardens. It gulped the row of pomegranate trees down a throat of rock, Guneus was swallowed with the girl entwined in his arms. The house did not escape. An outside wall and most of the roof collapsed.

Iphigenia clung to the upturned boat. The river god's invisible tentacles were at her legs. Silence. Brief, unnatural. As if every living creature held its breath as they tried to comprehend the horror of what had happened. It lasted until the many trapped or injured began to find their voices, their pitiful cries for help carrying far on the strange, still air. Iphigenia's first concerns were for Briseis. She hauled herself up by the rope attached to the mooring post and clambered up the wreckage of the landing pier, her wet chiton dragging and tripping her.

At the same time, Guneus' head appeared over the edge of the opened ground, trying to pull himself up. He called upon Apollo to help him rescue the girl, before the root snapped and he slid back into the yawning chasm. Iphigenia scrambled to her feet and stumbled dripping wet towards him. She grasped his outstretched hand as it melted into the darkness, the Dorian's inert bulk and her own momentum almost pulling her down with him.

Too heavy. Hands slippery. Tearing every muscle, lungs sick with strain, she managed to help him onto solid ground before falling back exhausted. She grabbed at him again when he rolled onto his belly, refusing to let go of him as he crawled towards the rim of the fissure, calling the girl's name. Iphigenia peered down into the tomb of rock, finally seeing the girl's leg twisted the wrong way to her body, her neck obscenely angled.

'We need help!' she shouted after him, keeping considerations of the girl's chances to herself. 'She's too far down to reach. We need rope and more hands.'

'She'll die if I don't try to get her.'

'You'll die with her if you do. Come on.'

The villa greeted them in chaos. The number killed or injured was much higher than expected, while nothing had yet been done to organise a search for those lost under the rubble. In Teucer's absence the master steward was duty bound to take charge, yet instead of providing leadership he was sitting on the plinth of a toppled statue with an ugly gash on his hairless pate and vacant expression on his dust and blood daubed face.

Iphigenia ordered him to get up, raising brows with her manner. The battered steward got to his feet like a scolded child. She explained what Guneus needed. The girl's father and one of the gardeners were called over. Iphigenia left them.

She needed to find Briseis.

She was nowhere on the ground floor. In one doorway lay the master tiler and his apprentice whose boat she was going to steal, the tiler staring at her from the wrong side of his neck. The lintel of a doorway was across his back, debris crushing his apprentice's chest, buried beneath a grave of stone and wood. Iphigenia pressed on into the undamaged vestibule. There, to her great relief, she caught sight of Briseis standing in the front courtyard watching a speeding chariot approach the villa.

The sweat-lathered mare strained at the traces, snorted, and tossed its velvet-muzzled head. Soft, jet coloured eyes rolled nervously as it stamped a dusty hoof, ready to bolt at the slightest hint of a threat.

'The earth shaker's trident startled the horse,' said Phemios, the charioteer, thumping to the ground.

He tossed aside his whip and extended a hand to his royal passenger, the heavily pregnant and less than amused Laodamia.

'We were riding along sedately, enjoying the cool river breeze, when the mare took off like she'd been shot up the arse with an arrow. The queen was taken unawares and thrown to the ground. She's hurt her hip, and worse, the baby growing inside her has decided to make an early appearance. We were much nearer here than Tricca, so my mistress had no choice but to seek your help.'

'Bring her into the vestibule, we'll make her comfortable there.'

Briseis tried to sound calm and self-assured, despite feeling neither. The vestibule was hardly the best place for the Queen of the Ironmen to give birth, yet until she knew which other rooms were safe, it would have to suffice. Traumatised servants had begun to congregate in the gravel courtyard, well away from the gaping crack in the front wall of the villa. One of them nursed a crushed foot, another a broken collarbone, a third, like the master steward, had a bone-deep cut on the crown of her head. Briseis asked two of the men to fetch bed linen and a mattress from the nearest storeroom. She looked around for Teucer's former nursemaid, whom she knew to be a skilled midwife. There was no sign of the lore-steeped healer.

'Where is the nursemaid, priestess?' asked Laodamia, dismounting from the chariot.

'I have not seen her, queen. I fear she may be trapped somewhere under the rubble.'

'Then you must conduct an urgent search. I will shortly have great need of her services. If she can't be found, Phemios will have to return to the palace to fetch the royal midwife.'

'Should you consider going with him, queen? The

nursemaid is the only person here with the skill to deliver your baby.'

'No. My hip is too painful to ride any further, while the little warrior inside me is impatient to fill his lungs with air. Leave me and go. Phemios, the sooner you depart—'

Laodamia suddenly cried out, clutching her hugely swollen belly. Her legs almost buckled. Another agonising contraction cramped the muscles around her womb; she slumped against the slightly built charioteer. A fresh flow of blood soaked through the front and back of her pharos and ran down her legs. When Briseis saw how much blood there was, she knew it did not matter how fast Phemios rode. She rushed forward to help support Laodamia.

Iphigenia instinctively followed. The Dorian shrunk back, face contorted by loathing as much as pain.

'Keep your distance, witch. I'll not have your tainted hands on me or my unborn child.'

'Queen, we need her help. More so if the midwife is—

Briseis trailed off.

'Find someone else to assist you. I'd rather chew through the cord myself than let the Argive anywhere near me.'

The pain unabated, Laodamia shuffled slowly along until she could reach out and cling to one of the vestibule entrance columns. Bathed in sweat and too drained to go any further while the contraction lasted, she hung there breathing in laboured gasps.

'The kitchen cold store is at the back of the villa,' she said to Phemios. 'Shut the witch in there before you head for the palace.'

330

'Is that wise, mistress, given—'

'Do it, Phemios, or you'll be keeping her company. I have not forgotten how you lost control of the chariot when Poseidon struck the earth, causing me to fall and damage my hip.'

Phemios knew better than to try the queen's patience by speaking out of turn again. He shrugged apologetically to Briseis, took hold of Iphigenia by the top of her arm, and marched her away.

The cold store Laodamia referred to was one of a network of underground storage areas, everything from wine, flour, and olive oil, to smoked meats, fish, and animal fodder, all kept out of the spoiling heat of the sun. It was located down a short flight of narrow stone steps directly beneath the kitchen annex. It was dark, cramped, and cool inside, with shoulder-high racks of perishable foods in clay jugs, jars and bowls lined in ranks against each side wall. The low ceiling and walls were lined with yellow plaster, the iron-hinged door fashioned from thick planks of oak.

'Just obeying orders,' said Phemios, shoving Iphigenia back against the barely visible rear wall. He turned on his heels, and pulled the door shut behind him.

Poseidon slammed down his trident. A second, more powerful tremor. Iphigenia heard the charioteer cry out as the roof and walls of the kitchen annex collapsed. He disappeared under a storm of timber, tiles, rough dressed stone, as he scrambled to the top of the cold store steps.

The tremor seemed to last indefinitely, shaking the ground so violently that Iphigenia feared the rock beneath her flattened body would crack open and swallow her like it had the labourer's daughter. Choking dust filled the air, clogging her mouth, nostrils and laying in her hair and face. Chunks of plaster fell from the walls and ceiling, covering the jumble of broken pots and spilled produce that littered the tiled floor. The noise was as frightening as it was deafening, bludgeoning Iphigenia's ears.

As abruptly as it started, the rumbling earthquake came to an end. The ground stopped shifting like a raft on a storm-churned sea. Into the void the cataclysm left, rushed another eerie silence as crushing as the quake.

A storage rack had toppled into the one opposite as if held in prayer, leaving just enough room for Iphigenia to wrap her arms over her head in a ball and avoid being crushed. Trembling with shock, she muttered a prayer of thanks to Hera for saving her life, crawled from under the rack and wiped grit from her streaming eyes. She stepped over the remains of the door and found herself staring up at a steeply sloping mound of debris where the steps were. Picking each foothold carefully, she clambered up to ground level.

Her vision burst at the brightness from being in the gloom. She squeezed more grit and stinging from her eyes and the villa came into focus. A ruin. The vestibule where she had last seen Briseis was rubble. Not a single workshop, byre or hovel was standing; the handful of stupefied survivors who emerged into the open, stumbling aimlessly like apparitions of blood and ash. Iphigenia ran towards the vestibule, slumping breathlessly against the same fluted column that Laodamia had used to support herself. Shorn of its plain Doric capital, the truncated column was all that remained of the once impressive portico.

She clawed at timber and stone until her fingernails tore and bled, her shins bruised and chafed. Only then was she overwhelmed by the futility. She fell back. Pleaded to the sky. Was this her fault? The House of Atreus was cursed, she had heard the stories all her life. Everyone she touched, suffered. The princes she married who never became kings, her brother Orestes hacked down by Calchas' men to protect her, Perimedes butchered to help her get away, Aletes, kind brave Aletes, who could be lying in the dust of this cruel land. Her father, brother and mother were likely all dead by now at the hands of Glaukos who would wear her father's crown. Now, gentle Briseis. Her only friend.

A sound so faint she almost missed it. At first, she thought it was a finch in the bushes, except no birds were singing in that place of death. Iphigenia cocked her head and tried not to breathe. A baby. The cry seemed to come from a long way off. A tiny voice muffled by its stone tomb. She forced her way into the confined space under a creaking section of roof.

Laodamia was laying on a fleece stuffed mattress, piercing blue eyes open and horrified at the sight of Iphigenia. She was pinned down helplessly by Briseis. Not moving. Gripping every muscle in physical prayer to her gods, Iphigenia moved Briseis' beautiful wheat-gold curls from her face. No blood, no damage.

As if she were sleeping.

'Briseis?' Iphigenia whispered. Then louder. 'Briseis!' She was yelling now, tapping her face. 'Briseis!'

'She's dead!' came the voice. 'I'm sorry. She's dead. I know you hate me, but for Briseis' sake help my baby. Briseis saved his life. If the king's son dies, her sacrifice will be in vain.'

Iphigenia looked at the massive wooden joist that was pinning them, weighted with irregular chunks of wall and roof. If they were disrupted and plunged further, Laodamia and her baby were dead.

The newborn baby Briseis had given her life to protect was lying on the floor beside its mother. Still attached to the umbilical cord, perfectly formed, biscuit-hued body smeared with dry blood and birthing fluid.

Laodamia tried to lift her head, but a searing stab of agony from her badly broken leg and hip caused her to stop with a sharp intake of breath.

'You need to cut the cord. Tie it and cut it,' Laodamia instructed.

Iphigenia looked at the roof above them.

'You can do it. Just be careful. It will hold for now,' Laodamia said, wishing she knew that to be true.

Working as fast as she could, Iphigenia tied off the baby's umbilical cord with a thin leather strap from one of Laodamia's sandals. Then she cut through the cord using the serrated edge of a broken tile.

'It's not a little prince, you have a beautiful daughter.'

'Go!' Laodamia said, turning away from the baby. 'Get out of here now. You won't get us both out before the roof collapses. Go!'

The roof groaned, dust rained on Iphigenia's head. She flinched, drawing the baby into her. With a look into Laodamia's desperate blue eyes, she bent and curved out of the tower of stone and wood.

24

Fighting the Wild Boar

Damia's naming ceremony was held ten days after her birth in accordance with tradition. It was a brief ceremony by Dorian standards, conducted in the late afternoon when shafts of dazzling sunlight were piercing the canopies of trees that encircled the sacred grove of Apollo. After placing a loaf of freshly baked bread and bowl of rich mutton stew at the foot of the statue of Apollo, the presiding seer held the naked infant aloft, recited her name and the names of her illustrious ancestors, and asked the gods to formally accept her into the tribe. Satisfied by the appearance of a darting swift in the sky above, the name chanting seer carried Damia three times around the perimeter of the grove so the assembled people could, for the first time, get a good look at their new princess.

Laodamia's broken leg was not yet strong enough for her to join the rest of her family and the assembled ephors who followed the seer. She was forced to watch from her usual high-backed seat on the tiered wooden benches, having first given her place in the garlanded procession to the one person who did not want it. Her guest of honour. The guest who had defied the queen's order, returned for her with help, and refused to let her die.

The irony of finding herself walking alongside the King of the Ironmen, applauded by his adoring subjects, was not lost on Iphigenia. Only a short while ago she had spent her nights in the slaves' barracks, dreading the appearance of a savage bent on using her like a worthless piece of meat. A moon before that, she had watched the warlord behind her despatch a helpless Argive on a beach of death, his expression pitiless, the blood of his victim splattered on his greave-swathed legs and the star shaped buckles of his sandals. These horrific images served to remind her this respite was temporary. Glaukos would soon return, and when he did, another hideous nightmare would engulf her. Unless she could find a way to warn her father, all her loved ones would perish, if they had not already. Her vile captor would seize the throne of Mycenae, and she would live out her days like a brood mare in a gilded stable, rearing the usurper's progeny.

Yet Glaukos did not return. As days turned into moons, and moons to whole seasons, the threat he posed no longer cast a shadow over every moment. Her life among the Dorians assumed a degree of normality that almost made her forget she was not one of them. She was given comfortable quarters at the palace, and as a new city emerged from the rubble of the old, she learned the ways of the Ironmen.

She came to understand there was more to their ancient culture than their warlike reputation suggested. They shared the Argives' passion for music, dancing, epic poetry, and athletics, yet one special gift bestowed by Apollo set them apart from the people of Argolis. They alone knew where to mine the iron ore smelted in their hidden forges. Fashioning the metal they extracted into the weapons, earned them their name.

Iphigenia saw what these weapons could do to bronze. They gave the Ironmen a significant advantage on the field of battle, and as the number of hot-blooded young warriors in Epirus grew, so too did the clamour for conquest.

One renowned warlord championed the cause, calling to mount a largescale raid against the stretched Argives. Now was the time to attack, with their depleted host bleeding on the battlefields of Troy. Compared with rugged Epirus, Argolis was a land of plenty. Much of the land was fertile, crops flourished, herds of cattle and sheep grew plump, and now its cities and towns had been left poorly defended. There would be plunder enough for all, the warmonger promised. By the time he arrived at Tricca for the second spring gathering of Iphigenia's captivity, there was strong support for the bloody path he was carving with his iron blade.

Kynortas was clan chieftain of the northern black bears. He was a man of more than fifty summers, with a receding mane of thickly oiled grey hair, a sheen like the blade of his iron, a cropped beard and titan frame that had not yet started to run to seed. The entirety of the skin on his neck, chest and arms was marked with potent warrior symbols. Engraved iron bands, awarded for courage in battle or slaying an enemy in single combat, adorned his wrists and biceps.

As Kynortas rose to speak in the torch-lit hall of the palace midway through the feast to celebrate the gathering of clans, an expectant hush settled over the warlords seated around him, each one facing the dais upon which King Neoman, Laodamia, Teucer and the senior ephor, dined.

'I would know your answer, my lord king,' Kynortas pressed. 'Will you muster the clan war bands and lead them south to burn and pillage the land of the Argives? Or are your hands still tied, as they have been since the day your daughter and grandson were seized at Calydon?'

'My hands are not tied,' King Neoman hurled back, vexed by the hostility and absence of respect from his rival. 'It is true that Melissa and little Neoman are still held captive by the Butcher of Calydon, but I have never let my concern for them come before my duty to the Dorian people.'

'Then you will summon the clan war bands?'

'I will not.'

A growl of discontent grew through the hall as Kynortas' allies showed their displeasure by shaking bearded heads and gesturing heatedly. Heightened tension pervaded an atmosphere already thick with the odours of stale sweat, woodsmoke and spit-roasted mutton.

Neoman cast his gaze over warlords who remained silent

and wondered how many of them had the courage to remain loyal if Kynortas mounted a challenge to his leadership.

'Your ardour is commendable, Kynortas, yet I am not convinced plundering Argive towns and villages is a sensible path. They are like the black bear your clan is named after, and we are a wolf pack snapping at its heels. The bear is wounded and more vulnerable than it has ever been. Yet it is still dangerous. Bite too hard and it will turn on us with a ferocity few in Eprius have known, decimating our pack of brave young wolves.'

'We mean to slay the bear, not bait it,' Kynortas retorted.

Barking cheers and drunken table thumping followed his words.

'We have no reason to fear the Argives. We are many and we have iron. They are on their knees, ready to abandon their costly Trojan war and sail home with their tails between their legs. We will hit them hard, and if you don't have the stomach to lead us, I will be forced to demand a vote and replace you as King of the Ironmen.'

This time the cheering became a cacophony as even more warlords joined in. Laodamia leaned closer to her grim-faced husband and whispered.

'To Hades with them all. If they want a brute like Kynortas as king let them get on with it. They'll come crawling back to you when they've been beaten by the Argives' battle-seasoned heroes and chased back here to Epirus.'

Teucer spoke quietly beside the king.

'A disastrous outcome for all, our loved ones included. When Glaukos returns, it will be in the van of a marauding host, laying waste to everything in their path. He'll take back his hostage by force, without keeping his side of the bargain and returning Melissa and little Neoman. With hundreds of our bravest warriors already slain, their bones bleached white in Argolis, there will be nothing we can do about it.'

'Then we must hide Iphigenia so the Butcher cannot claim her,' said Laodamia.

Teucer drained his horn and silver cup and rapped on the long, cloth covered table. All eyes turned in his direction, and as he rose, the muscles of his jaw clenched, a respectful silence settled like a heavy winter cloak. Teucer was a warlord they revered above all, a warrior whose deeds always spoke louder than his words. He alone had the agility, strength, and skill with spear and sword to match the formidable Kynortas.

'Stand!' a voice yelled from the back of the hall. 'Put your own name forward.'

'Yes! We will vote for you,' added another close by, but as others took up the call, Teucer shook his head and gestured for silence.

'I will not so debase myself,' he told them, his tone one of admonishment. 'I have no wish to offend a man I love and respect as my king and adopted father. Are your memories so short? Have you forgotten how much we owe this virtuous potentate who has devoted his life to serving his people? Is this how you would thank him, by casting him aside like a soiled garment or the gnawed bones of a capon?'

Teucer paused to let his scathing words sink in. Several of the warlords studied the contents of their horn cups to avoid meeting his blazing eyes.

'I for one will not. If King Neoman says this talk of war is foolish, that is good enough for me. It is true the number of Dorians donning the loincloth of manhood and receiving an iron spear has steadily increased and will continue during the seasons to come. Yet it is also true the seers have consulted Apollo, and he has advised them that our sons will have grown sons of their own before we are strong enough to vanquish the hated Argives. We must be patient, my lords. We must return to our workshops and fields and bide our time. We must trust wise Apollo when he tells us that one day the Ironmen of Epirus will be masters of Argolis and many lands beyond.'

Kynortas sucked in his cheeks as if he had something bitter in his mouth. Teucer had a persuasive tongue, he grudgingly conceded, and the tumult of conflicting opinions he had stirred sounded like a wake of vultures squabbling over carrion. Most of the warlords were on their feet, bellowing at each other across the hall, their hirsute faces flushed with ire and the effects of too much beer and wine.

Kynortas could see he still had sufficient support to wrest control of the gathering from King Neoman, yet he dared not delay calling for a vote in case Teucer decided to speak out again.

'I am disappointed, my lord,' Kynortas said, forced to shout louder than the room until the ruckus died down. 'I had hoped to reconcile our differences and win your support. Yet you have spent too long in the company of old men, pining over your lost wife. I hope you are one day reunited, and that she forgives you for doing nothing to find her and her precious son.'

There was much Teucer could have spoken in reply. He might have pointed out that his wife and son were being held separately, his son in an unknown location. If he had succeeded in rescuing Melissa before her throat was cut, little Neoman would certainly have perished. His severed head would have been lobbed over the walls of Tricca a few nights later, and that, most assuredly, was something Melissa would never forgive him for. He could have mentioned this and more besides, but instead he hid the anger boiling his blood.

'They will be first to die when you cross the border into Argolis, as well you know.'

'In which case, you will have no further use for the Argive you are at pains to conceal from us,' barked another. 'Name your price and I will spare you the trouble of disposing of her.'

Eurotas. Chieftain of the wild boar clan. He was Kynortas' foremost ally, younger and more compactly built than the other, with a prominent broken nose that curled down to almost touch the wiry bush of sable hair that framed his mouth. One of his front teeth was snapped near the gum, while the distracting scar on his forehead stretched a short way across the crown of his head, giving his braided black hair a slightly skewed, unusually wide parting.

'The Argive king's daughter is not for sale. At any price.'

'Everything has a price,' grinned Eurotas, provocatively. 'Suppose I offer you a couple of nags, or a small herd of goats?'

'Like I said, she is not for sale.'

Eurotas shrugged. 'Perhaps I'll just take her when this gathering ends and you no longer have a king in the family to back you up. I'll use her like a whore until we reach Mycenae, then I'll offer her for ransom. I'm sure her father will pay a handsome price to get her back, soiled or otherwise.'

Until Eurotas uttered his sobering threat, Iphigenia had watched the feasting warlords with the detached interest of someone who has seen it all before. She had witnessed many similar events at Mycenae, so one group of drunken warlords gorging themselves with all the decorum of hogs at the trough, spitting food from their stuffed mouths when they guffawed at a joke or an amusing tale told at someone else's expense, looked much the same as any other.

Laodamia had warned her to stay out of sight while the gathering was in progress. There was no reason to suppose her unusual status as hostage and honoured guest would not be respected, yet uncouth men in their cups could be volatile. Iphigenia shrunk back into the shadows of the corridor linking the hall with the kitchen annex. She had been standing there for most of the evening, pressed close against the wall to avoid being seen or getting in the way of hardworking servants as they scurried back and forth.

If the wild boar chieftain held sway, he would march her south as part of his personal retinue. When he tired of her she would be ransomed, then she would be able to warn her father about Glaukos and the cabal of rebel warlords plotting his downfall. The price was high; sharing the Ironman's bed was no less abhorrent than marriage to Glaukos. Yet pay it she would, if the Fates permitted her to save the lives of the loved ones she missed so much.

She heard Kynortas demand a vote, and after the senior ephor called for a show of hands in support of each candidate, her ears were assaulted by the jubilant roar and landslide of stamping feet that greeted Kynortas' victory.

She had heard enough. She needed to leave now before she was spotted and paraded like a trophy by the gloating Eurotas. Kynortas spoke again. This time he did not have to shout to make himself heard, and his words were conciliatory.

'I do not seek to be your enemy, my lord Teucer. It would not please Apollo for me to be at odds with one he favours and held in such high esteem by the Dorian people. I therefore decree our war bands will muster here two moons hence, after the haymaking is finished and the crops harvested. I hope your wife and son will have returned safely by then. If not, I will be forced to let you and Eurotas settle who owns the Argive the traditional way.'

'Trial by single combat,' said Eurotas, satisfied. 'I trust we fight to the death?'

'It will be your death, Eurotas,' said Teucer. 'But if that is what you want, you are welcome to it.'

Many times in the days that followed, Iphigenia thought of what she had seen and heard that evening. She asked Hera to ensure Teucer's quiet confidence was not misplaced, that Laodamia was right when she said Eurotas was a fool to believe he could slay Teucer. Laodamia had told her that one of the apprentice seers had seen Troy burning in a drug induced trance. It was a prophesy discounted by his more senior colleagues until a lightly clad runner arrived a few days later bearing momentous tidings. The war with Troy was won. The Argives had snatched victory from the jaws of defeat and sacked mighty Troy.

Iphigenia's joy at the news was tempered by the prospect of what now lay in store for her. She started paying more frequent visits to Tricca's rebuilt ramparts, shadowed once again by watchful guards as she gazed apprehensively across the patchwork of cultivated fields and darkly wooded wilderness to the south. Every time she saw movement on the narrow dusty road her spirits plunged, for she was convinced Glaukos or men sent by him under a flag of truce would soon appear.

Yet still none came. When one full moon became two, it was the clan war bands who arrived with banners fluttering, horns braying, iron blades aflame in the sun. They pitched camp on the broad stretch of open ground at the foot of the wall-crested escarpment, and all day their numbers steadily grew like the heat of the late spring sun.

A small flock of sheep and several goats were slaughtered, and that night the most lavish feast in living memory was held outside under a canopy of stars. The drunken revelry continued until every campfire was reduced to a pile of smouldering ashes and only Sirius, the dog star, shone proud in the dawn twilight. Iphigenia remained in the palace, preparing herself for the clash of iron clad titans before the assembled clans in the morning. Late into the night she lay awake, mulling over the consequences of each potential outcome. Laodamia remained adamant Teucer would prevail, yet much as Iphigenia wanted the same, she could not shake off the nagging sense of foreboding that gnawed at her, slowly unpicking the frayed stitching of her confidence. It was almost dawn before she finally fell asleep, only to be awakened shortly afterwards by the appearance of a maid carrying a bowl of hot porridge and honey on a tray.

'The queen bids me tell you she'll be waiting in the vestibule,' she said holding out the tray. 'She would like you to join her there as soon as you are ready.'

Much as she liked honey sweetened porridge, Iphigenia was far too nervous to eat anything. She thanked the maid and sent her away, then quickly dressed in a white linen chiton and laced up her sandals. She poured water from a jug into an earthenware bowl on the small table beside the bed and washed and dried her face. She rubbed rose scented olive oil on her cheeks and nose and noticed how much darker her skin had become since her life changed two and a half years ago now, her face glistening in bronze painted on her by the sun's fingers.

From a pot that had been given to her by dear Briseis she tapped cherry infused oil onto her lips. She rubbed olive oil into her hands as she set off to meet Laodamia. As she crossed the cavernous, largely empty hall, she glanced up at the sparrows fluttering around the sunlit clerestory high above, chirping shrilly as they struggled to find their way out.

'I know how you feel,' she told them ruefully.

Laodamia was accompanied by two hard-bitten iron bearing guards as she stood in the vestibule holding Damia, who now had a full head of tousled hair.

'I've brought Damia to see you, in case this is farewell,' said Laodamia, looking shame-faced and saddened. 'Teucer is already on his way down to Kynortas' camp, so we don't have long. These guards have been sent to escort you.'

'Iphigenia smiled and extended her hands, her delight at seeing little Damia making Laodamia feel even more uncomfortable. She had the rank of a former queen, yet she was impotent, unable to influence events and help a friend who had done so much for her.

It was as if the whole population of Tricca, as well as the massed ranks of clan warriors, was waiting for her when Iphigenia was led across the cleared space to stand beside the imposing figure of Kynortas.

Teucer greeted her with a silent nod as she walked by,

quickly switching his attention back to his restlessly pacing opponent.

Eurotas was stripped to his loincloth and sandals, muscle stacked on muscle in his arms and legs, his tattooed torso liberally oiled, chest and abdomen protected by a scuffed leather cuirass. He wore a plain iron helmet and carried no shield, a shortsword sheathed on his hip. In his right hand he wielded a twin bladed axe. In his left, an equally formidable war hammer.

'You know why we are here,' said Kynortas. 'The Butcher of Calydon has failed to return, so today you fight to the death and pray Apollo's judgement favours you. Before we depart this field, one of you will be in Elysium greeting the shades of his ancestors, the other—'

'Enough of these tedious pleasantries, my lord king,' yapped Eurotas. 'Give the order and let us get on with it. I'm eager to send noble Teucer on his way to the ferryman and sheath my itching sword between the pretty Argive's legs.'

An eruption of sound. Support split evenly between the combatants as Eurotas lost patience and stalked towards Teucer without waiting for Kynortas' signal. Teucer hefted his shield and the long-handled spear Iphigenia had seen him use to deadly effect during the pirate ambush. He dropped into a defensive crouch, spear raised like a scorpion's tail, his warrior mass supremely balanced on the toes of his star buckled sandals.

Eurotas sprang at him with raw power and fluid grace. The axe sliced through the air. Teucer had to drop his spear and take

349

his shield in both hands, instinctive, invisible it was so fast. The axe head thumped through the oxhide and wood, and Teucer punched out with the impaled shield into Eurotas' hurtling body. Eurotas anticipated the move and spun to the right, the hammer already shifted to that hand, swinging as he moved, smashing into the side of Teucer's helmet with huge force. Brain knocked skull. Eyes flashed white. Teucer fell to one knee. Eurotas smelled his quick kill. Unexpectedly easy. He drew the blade from his hip, the iron hissing as it left its sheath. Teucer's hand was already in the dust, his spear gripped.

A horn brayed. A short insistent blast that silenced the mob.

'Hold!' Kynortas yelled.

Teucer was on his feet with his spear in hand, eyes on Eurotas, the two men sidestepping and circling.

A second blast. Urgent. Eurotas dropped his hammer to his side and stepped back, eyes still on Teucer. The mob turned to the lookout on the ramparts above Tricca's main gates, and then, a few at a time, in the direction that he was pointing. Two riders. Escorted on the windswept road by a Dorian polemarch and one of the warriors detailed to guard the approaches to Kynortas' camp.

They were still a long way off, yet Teucer discerned that one of the riders was a man, sitting astride a big chestnut gelding. The other was a woman with very dark hair, swathed in a cloak and mounted on a sway-backed sorrel. Teucer peered hard at her, his brown eyes, unfocused by the hit to his head, narrowed to slits. His heart started to pound harder than when Eurotas had stormed at him.

'Melissa,' he gasped, casting aside his spear and managing to get his dented helmet off.

He stumbled through the parting ranks of Ironmen, a coarse high-pitched note ringing in his head and right ear. He shouted thanks to Apollo and, barely able to constrain himself, waited to embrace his long absent wife.

Iphigenia shaded her eyes with one hand, her gaze fixed on Teucer. She recognised Melissa, but it took longer to realise who the second rider was. Could it be? He was too lean; it could not be him. Older. But then, so much time had passed. He sat upright on the big gelding, his chiselled features those of a seasoned veteran rather than the youth she had last seen standing before the Altar of Zeus at Mycenae three long summers ago. One of only two recruits awarded the honour of holding aloft the relief force's gilded, blood-anointed battle standard.

'A high-born lord in the guise of a humble herdsman,' he had been called, the words of the holy mother all that time ago moving on Iphigenia's lips. 'A hero destined to stand shoulder to shoulder with the best among the Argives and one day save the dynasty of Atreus.'

Iphigenia had prayed daily for his safe return, adding his name to a list that included Orestes and many other noble sons serving with the host at Troy. She made frequent, generous offerings, yet as summer became winter and then another summer, and the great war dragged on, she began to fear the prophesy was wrong and she would never see his wonderful face again. She certainly had not expected him to appear in the heart of Dorian Epirus, riding confidently into a hornet's nest of heavily armed, Argive hating Ironmen.

Aletes halted the gelding where the road met the open space encircled by Ironmen. He waited patiently while a tearful Melissa kissed and hugged her more reserved husband, hooking a stone out of the pouch of slingshot on his sword belt and wrapping it in his fist. One small stone was little use against a host of several thousand, yet holding it made him feel marginally less helpless. If the Ironmen decided to kill him, he would at least give one of them a headache to remember.

Teucer prised Melissa's hands from around his neck and held her at arm's length. 'Why is little Neoman not with you?'

'He will be soon,' Melissa assured him, but before she could explain the horseman's involvement, Kynortas addressed her husband.

'Now your wife has returned, I suggest you give up the Argive and depart this field with your honour untarnished. You have fought Eurotas bravely yet will lose if you insist upon fighting him to the death.'

'To the death?' said Melissa, sharply. 'I'm not sure what is going on here, but you are mistaken if you think Iphigenia is going anywhere other than with the Argive hero who brought me home. I have given him my word, on behalf of my father, King Neoman—'

'Your father is no longer king,' Kynortas pointed out. 'He has been deposed, which is why he is not here.'

'Deposed?' echoed Melissa, shaking her head.

'By Kynortas, clan chief of the northern black bears,' said Eurotas, nodding at the new king.

He grinned lecherously as he studied Melissa's shapely figure, his lips crawling back to reveal the blackened stump of a front tooth snapped off near the root.

'Your wife is an alluring creature, Teucer, the more so when roused to anger. Perhaps I could buy her from you instead of the skinny Argive. I've always preferred buxom women with big breasts and wide, child-bearing hips?'

Teucer's back stiffened. Exactly the reaction Eurotas wanted.

'We fight on,' Teucer rasped, pushing Melissa aside and starting to retrieve his helmet, spear, and shield.

'Is this wise?' Kynortas called after him. 'You've already suffered a heavy blow to the head. You cannot hope to give a good account of yourself until you have rested and steadied your legs.'

'Let me fight him,' Aletes said, dismounting. 'I have not ridden all this way to leave empty-handed.'

Iphigenia felt sick. The ranks of watching Ironmen grew loud again with anticipation they would be further entertained. She wanted to tell him to get back on his horse and ride while he still had the chance. She did not want to be fought over like a prize mare. But she did not have a say. She was voiceless again. She found herself furiously angry. Aletes was a fool. He was going to

353

die here in the Dorian dust.

Eurotas glanced at his king and shrugged. This Argive was skinny, young, hardly a champion. Eurotas would take him over Teucer any day. Swaggering, he returned to his previous position on one side of the wide clearing, thirty paces or more from the naive Argive. He stood legs wide, retrieved axe and hammer raised high above the extended parting on his head, glassy eyes bulging maniacally as he basked in the adulation of the Dorian horde. The tumult rose to a deafening crescendo then quickly fell away as Kynortas called for silence.

'What are you called?' Kynortas demanded. 'I would know the name and rank of a warrior bold enough to ride alone into our midst and challenge the undefeated champion of the wild boars?'

'My name is not important. I am only a servant, sent here by my royal master, Prince Orestes of Mycenae, to find his abducted sister and escort her home.'

'Servant or not, I would know your name,' insisted Kynortas. 'If you fight bravely and die well, as I suspect you will, we will give you a funeral worthy of the Argive king himself. We cannot honour you thus unless we know your name.'

'And if I prevail?' Aletes' gaze was locked on his posturing opponent. 'Will you permit me to leave unharmed with the daughter of the Argive king?'

'Only if I am told—'

With a blood curdling war cry, Eurotas launched himself at Aletes. The Dorian had already decided to cleave off his head. The lightweight Argive's neck was exposed, he had no shield, and his sword was still sheathed. He was dead where he stood.

So heightened were Aletes' senses that he saw every aspect of Eurotas' movement. The lines separating muscles as his thighs burst forward, the exploding tendons in his neck, the arcing of the axe. Still. Like the riverbed all those moons ago. Still. Melampus' grandfather's sword in his hand. He was still.

The axe cleaved the air, Aletes dodged, parried and swung his blade fast and hard against the back of Eurotas' knees where no warrior can wear armour. His legs went from under him. Face in the dirt, Aletes' sword was buried in the soft skin between his neck and collarbone down into his heart. Dead.

An angry growl rolled across the clearing like a rumble of thunder. Several thousand disgruntled Ironmen surged forward, intent on avenging their defeated comrade. Kynortas pulled Iphigenia closer to him by the arm, halting the advancing Dorians with a raised hand and bellowed warning.

'Harm the Argive and Apollo will punish us all. He has won the right to leave here in peace with his prize, so stand back and allow him to pass. The contest was fairly won by the better man.'

Satisfied the threat of retaliation had passed, Kynortas released Iphigenia. He watched the intensity drain from Aletes' expression as she approached him, a knowing smile flitting across his own rugged visage. When he spoke, the respect in his voice was that of one battle-hardened warrior for another.

'Assuming the omens are propitious, we Ironmen will shortly

break camp and march south to pillage your homeland. Make haste then Argive, because if one of my foraging parties comes across you along the way they will slice off your head. I will have it pickled and sent north to Eurotas' grieving kin, with a small plaque inscribed with your name. Eurotas' ancestors will shun him and refuse to acknowledge his death in honourable combat unless they know the identity of the hero who slew him. His shade will be exiled, forced to dwell in the purgatory of Tartarus until he is told what you are called.'

'He can have my name, but I intend to keep my head.'

Aletes helped Iphigenia mount the gentle sorrel, rejoicing at having her so near after praying for so long.

'Understandable,' said Kynortas.

Mounting the gelding, Aletes dragged his rapt gaze away from Iphigenia.

'My king calls me Aletes of Zygouris.'

'I shall make sure Eurotas' kin are told. Go then, Aletes of Zygouris, and for your sake let's hope next time I see your face it's not pickled in wine.'

Aletes shortened the gelding's reins, and as he swung its white blazed head around, spoke to Melissa.

'I have not forgotten my promise. If your son is still alive, I will find a way to return him to you.'

Melissa nodded, her feline eyes veiled with tears of gratitude. Beside her, Teucer's head lifted at the mention of his son. He blinked his own eyes into focus and tried to ignore the throbbing pain inside his skull.

'I must go with the Argive,' he said. 'After what has happened today, he can never again cross the border into Epirus. I will do that for him, and once little Neoman is safe in his mother's arms, return south to take my adopted father's place as war chief of the dog star clan.'

Kynortas considered Teucer's words carefully before responding. He would rather the boy was left to rot in Argolis. Rescued and brought home, he might one day become a rival to his own male progeny. It was a risk he had to take, because without old King Neoman or the greatly admired Teucer to lead them, the dog star clan would not be quite so keen to fight alongside his own black bears.

'You will find us easily enough,' he replied at length. 'Just follow the trail of rotting corpses and burned villages deep into the heart of Argolis. I expect you to join me as soon as you can.'

'As soon as I can,' Teucer confirmed.

He looked at Aletes: 'Like it or not, I'm coming with you.'

'It would appear so.' Aletes nudged the gelding's flanks with his heels and cantered after Iphigenia. She had already reached the dirt road and pulled up to wait for him.

'We're heading due south,' he said over his shoulder, loud enough for anyone listening to hear him. He did not expect Teucer or the expert trackers tasked with watching them from a distance to be fooled for long.

An hour or more from Tricca he intended to cut back along

a deer trail he had seen on his journey there. He hoped it would lead them to the River Peneus. From there, he could follow its course southeast, to where he had arranged to meet Melampus. They would be travelling in the opposite direction to the Dorian host, so if fortune allowed, Kynortas would decide he could not spare a band of warriors to hunt them down after the truce he had granted them expired.

'We'll be riding hard through the night, so you'll need a horse with wings and plenty of stamina if you're to catch up with us.'

'I will catch up with you before nightfall,' Teucer answered confidently, taking Melissa's hand and leading her in the direction of their riverside villa.

He was familiar with the deer trail that Aletes clearly intended to follow. He knew another shortcut and calculated he had time for a private, long-awaited reunion with his wife before his favourite horse was brought from the villa's rebuilt stables.

Aletes guessed what Teucer had on his mind and hoped Melissa's seductive charms would occupy her husband until at least the following morning. His time alone with Iphigenia was precious and would come to an end soon enough.

25

A Message from the Antmen

Agamemnon's stinking head lay on the tiled floor at Glaukos' feet. His sightless eyes were sunken and opaque, huge black flies crawled in and out of his gaping mouth and nostrils. Traces of the honey used to preserve it were still smeared on its pasty grey flesh. Glaukos stepped down from the podium at the front of the hall where he had been standing and prodded the obscenity with the toe of his sandal. It rolled onto its bearded, filth-encrusted cheek, leaving a smudge of brown, stew-like ooze on the tiles where its severed neck had stood.

'There lies your proof. The bane of countless Argives, returning to the formless slime from which he came. Those of you who mourn his passing would do well to reflect upon the contempt in which he held his subjects, and those who had the temerity to disagree with him. The gods opposed his war with Troy from the start, as they made clear at storm-lashed Aulis, yet still he pressed on, ignoring his council's advice, sacrificing thousands of fathers, sons and brothers on the altar of his hubris.'

Glaukos held up his undamaged hand, so all the warlords summoned to Mycenae so soon after sailing home could see the deposed king's heavy gold signet ring on his finger.

'*Agamemnon is dead,*' the herald sent to each of their citadels had announced. '*Gather at Mycenae three days hence to hear the new king of the Argives speak.*'

'No more,' Glaukos continued, his scarred face twitching as if one of the bloated flies was crawling across his cheek. 'All that is past. I stand before you today offering an alternative to tyranny. A new age of peace and prosperity governed by the rule of law. Any of you who are against me are free to leave this palace now. You have my word there will be no reprisals. I will simply form a new ruling council without you.'

Glaukos swept his eyes over the seated warlords like a raptor seeking out prey, looking for any sign of dissention. None. Not that he expected to while his conspirators were arrayed behind him in full brazen panoply, and grim-faced royal guards lined the four walls of the hall. They were meek as lambs, ready to swear the oath of allegiance and accept his hegemony over all the Argive people. To a man, they had seen enough bloodshed to last a lifetime. They craved peace and stability, to put away war-tarnished swords and armour, and immerse themselves in the husbandry of their vast estates. They wanted to hunt deer, stray wolves, and wild boar, and above all to spend long winter evenings around blazing hearths with their wives, children and invited friends.

Content he had the lords in the palm of his hand, Glaukos ordered the head shaman to press on with the oath taking ceremony. He was looking forward to the grand feast and debauched revelry that would follow when someone he did not think had the courage to speak out, rose to his feet.

Penelaos of Plataea had witnessed Agamemnon slain without lifting a finger. Hardly surprising; he was lying in a tub of steaming hot water at the time, praying his own life would be spared, the only weapon to hand his decidedly flaccid cock. He had felt little sympathy for the son of Atreus either then or later, yet the fate of Orestes was a different matter. The popular crown prince had not inherited his father's notorious quick temper or callous disposition. He did not deserve to be executed or exiled. Disgusted by the silence of those around him, Penelaos was determined to say what he knew less resolute warlords than he silently believed.

'What of Orestes? He is a man of courage and honour. He will not let his father's death go unavenged?'

'He is of no consequence. He would have died with the tyrant had he not slunk away like the craven cur he is. I am told he fled north to Pharsalos with Achilles' gibbering whelp. Meleager of Thebes is on his way there to demand King Peleus hand him over.'

'The Myrmidon king may refuse,' ventured Penelaos. 'He may not want to go against the wishes of his grandson.'

'He will do what is best for his people, not Neoptolemus. He is ever-pragmatic, and when Meleager convinces him Orestes' cause is lost, he will readily give him up. He will not be swayed by the council of a stammering jackass who spends more time on his back in a wine-addled stupor than sober on his feet.'

'Forgive me, but Prince Neo is not the drunken fool some mistake him for. I scaled the walls of Troy behind him and watched him cut down boastful Paris after Menelaus had fallen. There was nothing muddled or irresolute about his actions. With or without his grandfather's approval, he will stand by Orestes should the need arise.'

'I hope he does.' Out of the corner of one eye Glaukos spotted Euthemus entering the hall. 'It wouldn't be the first time he has stood in my way, but it will, I assure you, be the last. Now if you're done with your questions, I suggest we press on. The sooner we conclude the formalities, my lords, the sooner we can quench our thirsts with wine from Priam's personal store—served by his former courtesans—and feast on the spit-roasted bullock and suckling pig my senses tell me is being cooked to perfection.'

Coated in ochre dust, Euthemus limped along the side of the hall. Glaukos and Nireus had both seen him.

Hungry warlords rose from their seats, moved by their grumbling bellies to begin the oath taking.

'Well, spit it out,' Glaukos pressed. 'What news do you bring from Sicyon. Favourable, I trust?'

'I fear not,' Euthemus sighed wearily. 'The herdsman arrived there two days before me, seized Melissa, and set off at once into

362

Epirus.'

'So why are you here? My instructions were clear. If the Dorian vixen was gone when you got there you were to stay hidden in Sicyon and wait for the herdsman's return.'

'The octopus gates were barred, my lords, the ramparts manned by locals, their harpy wives and Phocians hostile to our cause. It would have taken a sizable war band with siege towers or scaling ladders to storm the place.'

'Phocians,' spat Nireus. 'By whose order?'

'Electra's, I imagine, at her mother's behest,' Glaukos explained.

Glaukos recalled the last, faint words of his dying father before he took pity on him and hastened his departure from this mortal world. He told him that Clytemnestra had journeyed to Phocis after the pirate ambush to help Electra organise a search for Iphigenia. Despite Aegisthus' many lovelorn entreaties, she had never returned to Mycenae.

Oh yes, his father was dead.

'It was not the queen,' Euthemus corrected, disturbing him from his recollections. 'Not according to Philocletes, who slipped out of Sicyon the night I arrived and paid a secret visit to our camp.'

'Why would he do that? The castellan loathes us. If I remember correctly, you beat him to within a foreskin's width of his life for bragging he had never lost a scrap?'

'I was wary at first, yet the explanation he gave was convincing. He wants his tavern back and hopes you will agree to

363

its return once the information he has provided proves reliable. I gave him another painful lesson in boxing to make sure he was telling the truth, then sent him back the way he came.'

'So, what did he tell you?'

'It was the herdsman who asked Electra to send a trustworthy polemarch and any warriors she could spare to help defend Sicyon. The request was delivered on his behalf by that First Spear who murdered Alcinous, the ugly one with a nose like a truffle. Instead of returning to Sicyon, that ugly First Spear made his way north to meet the herdsman where the River Peneus flows out of Epirus. When Electra heard who else he hoped to be meeting, she promptly invited herself and Clytemnestra along.'

'Then we must do the same,' Glaukos asserted.

'My lord, there's more to tell. Tidings of an alarming nature that did not spring from Philocletes' loose-tongued mouth.'

'Go on, Euthemus, before you exhaust my patience.'

'We were about to break camp when one of the warships patrolling the sea of Corinth rowed into harbour, its master spreading panic like a plague. He claimed a host of Ironmen marches on Argolis, their new king vowing to sack Mycenae and spread death and destruction as far south as the shores of Laconia.'

'How large a host?'

'Several thousand, according to the master. More than twice the number we have faced before.'

'He exaggerates, surely?' said Nireus, distracted by the

jarring percussion of stamping feet and fists thumping tables as ravenous warlords demanded to be fed. They had done what Glaukos asked of them and pledged their loyalty to the fledgling regime. Now they expected to be rewarded with a bounteous feast; their carnal appetites sated by the compliant company of exotic, scant clad Trojan concubines.

'Perhaps not.' Glaukos signalled for the palace servants to begin serving food and drink to his noisy guests. 'Teucer threatened as much when I told him what I wanted in return for his wife and son's release. The master was probably not far wide of the mark, but whatever the Dorian's true number, every warlord here should expect the worst and prepare for a long, hard fought campaign.'

'When will you break the news to them?'

'Not until they have gorged themselves and sampled the delights of Priam's extensive personal harem. I want this night of bonding and debauchery to stay long in the memory, for in the chill light of dawn they must all sally forth to do battle with an enemy every bit as formidable as the one they have just vanquished.'

Glaukos paused to acknowledge the first vassal king to lift his brim-filled cup in a respectful salute. Others followed the warlord's lead, until most were on their feet toasting their preoccupied host. Glaukos allowed himself to bask in their fickle adulation. Then one of the wine mixers placed a twin-handled gold cup in his undamaged hand, and after gulping down the contents, he raised it in a reciprocal gesture. Yet even as he did, his gaze rested inadvertently upon the dead king's head. Lipless, maggot-ridden, and obscene, it spoke to him.

'Remember the prophesy, son of Aegisthus. The hero I call Zygouris is destined to save the dynasty of Atreus. Destroy him soon or he will be your undoing. He will force you to flee into exile, and the new order that you spawned with treachery will be reduced to dust.'

'I suggest Euthemus accompanies me when I leave at first light,' Nireus was saying. 'I don't expect the Ironmen to linger long outside the walls of Phocis. My heroes have given them many a bloody nose, and there are softer targets further south. Once they've moved on, I'll send half the Phocian host here to assist in the defence of Argolis. Euthemus and I will then hasten north to apprehend the herdsman. Leave Electra to me, she won't be a problem.'

'Agreed. But move fast and make sure you take the maggot alive. I've waited a long time to be rid of him, so the pleasure of ending his miserable life is mine and mine alone. Understand? Euthemus? Defy me in this and a stab wound that refuses to heal will be the least of your concerns. I will castrate you with a war hammer and have you boiled in olive oil.'

'I hear you, my lord.'

Agamemnon's head laughed from across the hall.

'Dust, son of Aegisthus. All you dreamed reduced to windblown dust…'

366

Meanwhile, on a low rise a short gallop from Pharsalos, the Senior First Spear of the Theban host stepped onto the footplate of his absent king's chariot and again scanned the ramparts of the Myrmidon capital. The First Spear's name was Clambrotus, and he was becoming concerned.

Clambrotus had been left in command of Meleager's hundred strong escort while the King of Thebes strode into Pharsalos to demand Prince Orestes be given up. The charioteer escorting him had held aloft a symbol of peace: a crown woven from sprigs of olive.

That was several hours ago. Long before fiery Helios began his descent towards the distant rugged hills. Still there was no sign of Meleager's return. How long did it take to exchange pleasantries, hand over the brace of unspoiled Trojan maidens that Glaukos had sent as gifts for King Peleus, then depart with Orestes in leg chains and manacles? Something was amiss, Clambrotus decided, and dismounting from the chariot, he paced anxiously up and down.

'Movement on the ramparts,' said the Second Spear standing close behind him. 'Looks like they're loading two catapults.'

Clambrotus stopped pacing and cupped his wedge-bearded chin. Sure enough, a gang of ant-sized figures were milling around the giant catapults located on either side of the main gates.

'They're aiming them at us,' Second Spear Nicander said.

'Surely not,' muttered Clambrotus.

A cloth-wrapped bundle arced towards him from one of the

catapults. It landed on the flattened grass with a soft, wet thud and bounced towards his parted feet. Clambrotus stooped, peeled back one corner of the blood-soaked cloth, and with a grunt of disgust, recoiled. The cloth was Meleager's cloak, and it concealed his mutilated, barely recognisable head.

Hacked off with a sword, Meleager had been blinded with the same hot tongs that tore his tongue from his cleft-lipped mouth. The olive crown of truce had been rammed down over his protuberant ears, pressing them flat against the sides of his mangled head.

'Shield wall!' Clambrotus yelled, recovering his composure, yet before the spearmen behind him could react to the command, the second catapult's arm snapped upright, its shallow bucket spewing forth a flaming ball of oil-soaked rags and tightly bound grass. It hit one of the wheels of Meleager's chariot and burst, showering the terrified horses with fragments of orange-hot fire. Whinnying shrilly, their eyes rolling wildly, they reared up and flailed the smoky air with their hooves. Nicander tried to restrain them, but with their long manes and tails smouldering, they knocked him aside and surged into a headlong gallop. The empty chariot bucked along behind them like a blazing comet. Until it turned over and broke apart, much to the delight of the watching Myrmidons. Still in their traces, the horses galloped on across a field of stubble and away into the distance.

Clambrotus stamped out a puddle of fire and cursed. 'Change of plan. We're getting out of here while we still can.'

'Without Orestes?' asked Nicander, picking himself up off the ground. 'That won't please the usurper?'

'Never mind him. If he wants Orestes that badly, let him try negotiating with these raving Myrmidon wolves. We've done our best, and its cost our king his head. Line of march, Nicander. Quickly.'

The Thebans slung their shields on their backs and peeled away in pairs, Nicander leading them with Meleager's gory head tucked under his arm. Clambrotus waited until they reached the deeply shaded oak and beech wood that straddled the road north for hours, then he turned and jogged after them. The jeers and laughter of the Myrmidons who had loaded each catapult, cranking its twisted horsehair restraining rope to maximum torsion, speeding him on his way.

Inside Pharsalos, King Peleus watched his inebriated grandson cavorting on the battlements with a reproachful shake of the head. He was standing in the paved ceremonial courtyard of the lower city facing the towering main gates. A close order phalanx of veteran guards was arrayed behind and on either side of him.

The city's hushed population watched proceedings from every available vantage point. Like their silver-haired king, they were neither shocked nor surprised when their beloved prince suddenly turned on the overconfident Theban. Throughout Neoptolemus' short, pampered life they had witnessed many examples of his volatile behaviour. Even his most ardent supporters were forced to conclude that on this occasion he had gone too far.

Beside the king stood Orestes, his darkly handsome face slowly beginning to look as it did before the ravages of the dungeons. He felt no sympathy for the rebel Theban king, but he did not approve of his summary, messy execution. Meleager deserved to die for his part in his father's debasing murder, yet after a formal trial and once pronounced guilty in a manner decreed by the gods.

Orestes looked at Meleager's truncated corpse, the glowing brazier and the gelding tongs discarded on the blood-stained flagstones. All the same, he could not bring himself to condemn or stop the drunken prince's actions. Without Neoptolemus' help on the day the traitors struck, he too would have perished. Whatever the fates held in store for the dynasty of Atreus, he would never forget the great debt he owed the impetuous son of Achilles.

'They hath their answer, g-g-gwandfather,' said a jubilant Neoptolemus, descending from the ramparts two steps at a time. He was still brandishing the sword he had used to clumsily behead the protesting King of Thebes.

'Ores-thes ith our honoured guest and enjoys the protection oth this royal household. He will not be g-given up to those who hath the b-blood of hith father on their mutinous hands.'

'You realise this means war?' replied Peleus, lugubriously.

'It ith unavoidable. If Ores-thes ith to win back hith throne he must wrest it from the scar faced mongrel who presently hath his bony arse upon it. The task ith a daunting one, but he doth not face it alone. I will be at hith side and will not sheath this fabled bronze until hith kingdom ith restored. I hath sworn this before the Altar oth Zeus and the shade oth my own slain father.'

Manic-eyed, Neoptolemus switched his attention to the cringing charioteer. Fearing his end was upon him, the Theban sunk to his knees and pleaded for mercy. His terror was infectious, for it caused the doe-eyed Trojan captives with him to cling to each other for comfort and weep piteously. Orestes recognised one of them as King Priam's youngest daughter, Polyxena. He had last seen her on the day his father was murdered, shortly after bidding farewell to another loyal friend to whom he owed a very great deal.

Not for the first time he wondered what had become of Aletes, and if his quest to find Iphigenia had been successful. It occurred to Orestes that if Aletes' search had taken him into the wilds of Epirus, he might not be aware of what had transpired at Troy so soon after his departure. Unless warned, he would return to Mycenae and unwittingly deliver his sister, whom he prayed he had rescued, back into the usurper's clutches.

'On your f-f-feet,' spluttered Neoptolemus, prodding the charioteer with the point of the Reaper of Shades.

'I hath no desire to kill you but will do so un-leth you get up at once and cease your puerile b-b-bleating. You're free to go. You must tell the u-therper everything you hath seen and heard here. Prince Ores-thes ith returning to Mycenae, girded for war and accompanied by a host oth Myrmidons.'

With a curt nod to the polemarch of the watch, Neoptolemus

indicated that one of the creaking main gates should be opened. He jabbed the Theban again for good measure, swaying.

'Be gone! Report my words accurately and take these two mewling innocents with you. War, I say. War!'

The charioteer feared a trick. He scrambled to his feet in the flick of a whip and fled from the city like a hare pursued by a pack of dogs. Polyxena followed him at a more sedate pace, hand in hand with her somewhat older, yet equally comely fellow captive.

King Peleus watched them go with another slow shake of the head, howls of derision and cries of delight reverberating around the windswept courtyard. He deplored his grandson's gratuitous violence yet did not condemn the sentiment behind it. Agamemnon had been his lifelong friend and ally. They had been guest of honour at each other's wedding and the naming day ceremony for their firstborn sons. Senile or not, if Neoptolemus hadn't pledged his sword to Orestes, he would have dusted off his own armour and done so himself.

'We must send forth heralds,' he said. 'The longer we delay, the more time the usurper has to prepare the defence of Mycenae. Our heroes must depart from here before the new moon rises.'

'I cannot wait until then,' Orestes said, his troubled gaze locked on the fleeing charioteer as he and the women behind him reached the soughing canopy of trees. 'I must beg the loan of a chariot and ride south to Sicyon as soon as possible.'

'To warn Aletes oth Zygouris,' Neoptolemus added for him.

'Yes. I have to find him before he leads my sister into a trap.'

'I understand why you are concerned,' said King Peleus. 'Yet I fear it would be unwise to leave alone before the host is mustered.'

'Not ith I and a band oth war-tempered veterans go with him.'

Lifting his wine-stained tunic, Neoptolemus directed a pungent stream of urine over Meleager's headless corpse.

'Cousin Thaos will command the h-host in my absence. Ith we reach Mycenae before him, we'll conceal ourselves close by until he arrives.'

Thaos, the grizzled commander of the palace guard, stood spread legged between King Peleus and the rank of spearmen behind him. He turned to the nearest First Spear.

'You heard the prince', he barked. 'Chariots from the royal stables and provisions for a long journey.'

The First Spear saluted crisply and ordered two guards to accompany him. He marched at a brisk pace, his heavy oval shield decorated with a giant black ant, slung over his broad back.

'You three, clean up this mess. Carry the Theban's body outside the city and burn it before it starts to ripen.'

The trio of Myrmidons allocated the unpalatable task stacked their spears and shields as they would in a temporary camp while on campaign and set about carrying out Thaos' terse command.

'My throat ith as dry ath a desert. Will you join me for a horn oth wine, my friend, to quench our thirsts before we depart? We've a long ride ahead, and I d-doubt we'll be visiting many s-staging post taverns until after we've found Aletes?'

'We won't be visiting any. We'll eat while we rest the men and horses, then press on, night or day.'

'Ath I f-feared!' exclaimed Neoptolemus, feigning horror. 'I am to be denied the pleasure oth drinking fermented grape or b-barley for the duration oth this expedition. Reason enough, I s-suggest, to consume a last jug oth wine together before I am t-turned into a r-root eating anchorite?'

Reluctantly, Orestes nodded in agreement.

'Forgive me, but I hath another b-boon to ask. Gwandfather wants uth to join him at the temple after our brief s-sojourn at the palace. He will instruct the s-seers to pour a libation and entreat Zeus to hold hith hands over uth, over your sister Iphigenia, and Aletes oth Zygouris.'

Orestes pursed his lips and nodded again. His own mouth was dry, but the cause was not lack of refreshment. Acute foreboding gripped the muscles of his stomach as his sight was filled with visions of the fetid dungeon at Troy where he had languished so long. Without Aletes he would not have survived.

He had an opportunity now to repay him. Orestes' expression hardened as his gaze was drawn back along the deserted road to the south. He watched a funnel of golden dust and shrivelled leaves swirl into the air a stone's throw from him. Gyrating, it swept the road clean where it hovered and spat out specks of stinging grit before darting away snarling on the stiffening

374

wind like a demented wraith. It seemed to show him the way to go, urging him to grasp the bronze and follow the path of his destiny without delay.

His enemies would not have to wait long to hear the tramp of seven thousand approaching Myrmidons. Their voices would rise as one in the song of war, their feet would drum the dirt, horns split the ears and nerves of their foe. Orestes vowed to turn the earth red with rebel blood. He would not rest until every Argive who debased and defiled his father in the plot against him lay dead in return. No mercy. He would slice off their treacherous heads at the neck, rip each limb from their body, pull out their guts.

If he reached Sicyon too late to prevent Iphigenia being recaptured or Aletes put to death, the bloodletting would not end there. Orestes would avenge a man who could not be replaced, as Achilles, god of men, had when Patroklos was slain. Achilles would have understood the loss of a friend from his world that would make the sun turn to stone, wine tasteless, hands lose their touch. Orestes would seek out and butcher the wives and children of every conspirator. He would lay waste to whole communities, slaughtering anything that breathed. He would not desist until his vengeful wrath was sated, until he was ready at last to put down his bright blade and take his rightful place on the gilded throne of Mycenae.

He was coming. The usurper could be sure of that. Before the shades of his all-conquering ancestors, he, Prince Orestes, son of warrior-king Agamemnon, son of the son of mighty Atreus, had sworn it.

26

Counting to Three

A day's ride by chariot to the north, in a cottonwood glade close to the gorge through which the River Peneus flowed as it left Epirus, First Spear Melampus hung by his tightly bound ankles from the bough of a tree. Naked and bleeding from a dozen flesh wounds, he had been strung upside down for hours until he passed out, was taken down, then restrung each time he woke, since the previous evening when Electra's welcoming party had been ambushed.

As his many injuries attested, Melampus had not been easily overcome. He had fought like a cornered lion, but Nireus' war band had outnumbered Electra's escort ten to one, so he and the small party of Argives with him stood no chance. He would have died in the fighting had not Euthemus of all people, intervened at the last moment. He had prevented Pig Nose, who had been restored to the rank of First Spear in Nireus' force, from plunging a sword into Melampus' exposed belly and scattering his steaming entrails like tangled yarn. He had not forgotten Melampus kicking him onto his arse at the port of Sicyon.

'I want him alive,' growled red-bearded Euthemus, pushing aside Pig Nose—or Hippacoon, as Nireus better knew him. 'He *will* die, slowly and painfully, but not until he's no more use to us.'

'What use is he dangling from a tree?' demanded Pig Nose.

'When the herdsman gets here, you'll see. Having the life of this raging bull to bargain with could prevent the loss of several good men, spearmen I'm sure lord Nireus would prefer not to lose.'

'He's right, First Spear,' Nireus interjected, 'for now the ugly pig is to live.'

Nireus stood with his fingers entwined affectionately in Electra's long auburn hair. She was taller than her younger sister, athletic and could handle a sword. She was more curvaceous and looked like her fair-skinned mother.

Melampus cursed and snorted blood and snot from his blocked nostrils to help him breathe. The weight of downward force on his lungs made opening and closing the organs tortuous, exhausting. Most of the clotted mucus he ejected splattered his dirt, sweat and blood-coated forehead. His hands were lashed together behind his back, making any lateral movement difficult and excruciatingly painful. Clenching his broken teeth behind bruised and swollen lips, he swivelled his barely recognisable head left and right to try to see what was going on.

Clytemnestra had been taken a short distance from the glade, and after being roughly bound and gagged to silence her threats and protests, was forced to sit against the bole of a tree with her legs folded under her on a prickly carpet of grass, twigs, and leaves. Nearby, the stripped and mutilated bodies of Melampus' reduced escort had been dumped unceremoniously in a shallow, brambled defile, overlooked by a neat row of more reverently handled Phocian corpses.

Nireus and Electra were somewhere behind him, out of sight yet close enough for him to detect the warmth and unexpected familiarity in the hushed tones of their conversation. Melampus guessed they were alone, for the near one hundred unscathed Phocians of Nireus' handpicked war band were hidden beyond the screen of rustling cottonwoods and pockets of dense undergrowth that marked the perimeter of the glade.

Euthemus was with them, moving stealthily from warrior to warrior, group to group, checking their disposition and readiness to move when their quarry came into view. The big henchman was limping badly, Melampus noted with grim satisfaction, no doubt due to the stab wound in his thigh that Aletes had inflicted more than a moon ago. Despite his own debilitating injuries, Melampus managed a rattling laugh, the resulting spasm of agonised coughing racking his inverted frame as he implored Apollo, 'Turn your back on him, lord of the bow. He is a black hearted mongrel and doesn't deserve to feel your healing hands.'

The day grew warmer. Then hotter. Biting insects added to his torment by sucking blood from his wounds. Melampus drifted into darkness again. Fearing he might not reawaken, he flipped like a hooked fish on the end of the stout rope. It was a deliberately violent motion that smeared the remaining skin from his ankles and thrust a blade of searing agony into all his straining joints. Hot stinging urine dribbled from his weakened bladder, and as it trickled over his belly and chest, he wept tearlessly on his contorted face with the shame of it. But then anger returned and with it came the binding cement of stiffening resolve.

He knew he was going to die. Yet he would not allow it to happen until after he warned Aletes. To distract himself, he remembered happier times, recalling the heat-drenched summer day at Zygouris when he had first met the humble, quietly spoken herdsman. While Aletes was taken to the great hall, where he learned that he had been sired by a high lord and favoured by the gods, Melampus had made the acquaintance of a flirtatious young peasant wench. After impressing her with the latticework of battle scars on his forehead, arms, and shoulders, he had enticed her into a musty tool and tack store where they made the beast with two backs over a cluttered work bench.

His amorous exploits had been the source of considerable amusement to all the men under his command. Some of them, emboldened by a generous ration of sweet red Zygourian wine, had called out to him as he marched Aletes across the twilit compound to meet the tightknit group of veterans who would be his constant companions from that day. Melampus had readily joined in the good-natured banter, and for a wistful wingbeat, his own ribald comments and those of long dead, sorely missed comrades echoed back to him across the dark void of distance and time.

'Is it true, First Spear? After lying dormant for longer than I've been alive, the bearded heifer managed to rouse the greasy serpent between your legs?'

'She did, Maron, I'm pleased to say.'

'What potion or magic did she use to achieve that?'

'No potion or magic, Maron. Just lips as soft as your sister's. She wasn't as experienced as your sibling, I'll admit, but I enjoyed her all the same. We're meeting again later in the same tack store, after she's shaved and polished her horns.'

Bawdy laughter and hoots of derision reached out to Melampus from the past. He smiled, and as he stared down at the dark stain of his blood on the flattened grass, he ached to be back there with his friends. He longed to share a wineskin with Pytho, who he had known most of his adult life, or with Echetus and Chersicrates, who were so easy to fleece in a game of flipping the marked stones. He missed them all so much, and he was still immersed in his reverie when their laughter became strident yells, and a shrill neighing of horses was accompanied by the scrape of swords urgently drawn from scabbards.

Melampus blinked the sweat and piss from his eyes and roundly cursed his lack of vigilance. While he daydreamed, three riders had entered the glade: he knew even though his vision was blurred and slow, it was Aletes, a female rider, a thick limbed warrior on the other side. As soon as they rode into the open, the Phocians attacked, pouring out of the trees. Melampus' croaked warning came too late as a whooping swarm surrounded them.

Aletes' sword flashed in the bright sunlight, slashing and hacking at every Phocian rash enough to venture close to him. Hampered by the gelding's instinct to bolt, he struggled to keep the rearing, plunging animal between Iphigenia and the bristling hedge of spears. On the opposite side of the hunched over Iphigenia, Teucer was attempting to do the same. They both fought on tenaciously, and soon the ground around them was littered with dead or maimed Phocians. The chastened attackers drew back to regroup and lick their wounds, ignoring Pig Nose's exhortations to press home their overwhelming advantage. They were still deliberating, peering warily over battered shields emblazoned with the stylised Phocian raven, when Euthemus limped up to Melampus and held a dagger to his exposed throat.

'Throw down your swords or he dies.'

Aletes cursed his idiocy. Melampus could not die. He could not watch him die. He loved him like a father. How he guessed the love from a son was meant to be.

But he could not get to him, he could not fight his way to him before his throat was cut. Even if Apollo was still guiding his sword arm. He still had his sling, and the longer the standoff persisted, the more irresistible a target the lame henchman's forehead became. He had nothing to lose, he told himself, and if asked, Melampus would tell him to stop dithering and take the shot. He carefully released the whickering gelding's reins and slid his freed hand towards the kidskin pouch on his hip.

'Touch that infernal sling and his life ends,' Euthemus warned. 'You have to the count of three to disarm. One.'

'Don't listen to this piece of horseshit,' gasped Melampus, ignoring the blade at his throat. 'We both know I'm finished whatever happens. Crack his skull for me and—'

Euthemus silenced him with an elbow jabbed viciously into already-broken ribs, Melampus crying out, losing control of the pain, sagging unconscious.

'Two.'

It was Iphigenia who hollered over the chaotic voices of men. None of the Phocians had lunged to maim or kill her, they were avoiding her. One of the Phocians had edged close enough to run her through with his spear, yet he had retreated without striking a blow.

'My father will hear of this! The Argive under your knife is well known to him, and does not deserve—'

'Your father rots in Tartarus!'

Nireus cut the air with his words. 'I saw his fat body float face down in a bath of blood not two moons ago. Slain by your future husband, Glaukos, who sits on the Mycenaean throne.'

Iphigenia recoiled in pain as if one of the Phocian blades had been buried in her chest. Her heart hurt, her lungs struggled to function. She gaped, too shocked to speak. Her father had been invincible to her, a king, a giant made of bronze. Despite the nightmare of Aulis, she had come to understand him. To be king is to be made of stone, even if it meant killing your daughter to save your people. She could not imagine life without him.

Iphigenia looked at Electra, assuming her escort had been overpowered and she was forced to be there. Electra refused to meet her eyes. Iphigenia turned to her mother, bound and gagged. In her eyes she received the truth. Clytemnestra knew above all how close the bond between father and his youngest daughter had been. She tilted her head to one side, nodded compassionately, and reached out with her pain-filled eyes.

'Three,' said Euthemus, with grim finality.

Teucer tossed his sword on the ground in front of him and raised his hands in the air.

'I'm sorry,' he said to Aletes, 'I have to put my son first.'

'I would do the same,' Aletes replied.

Rough hands wasted no time dragging Teucer from his horse. They forced him to kneel on the ground, ordering Aletes to follow.

Nireus was satisfied his warriors had the situation under control.

'Bind them and make ready to depart. I want to be far from here before nightfall. Iphigenia rides with her mother and sister. These two can eat dust at the back of the column.'

'Why don't we kill them all and be done with it?' Pig Nose asked.

'Glaukos wants Zygouris alive and unharmed, he made that clear. The Dorian isn't supposed to be here, but we'll take him along in case he is to be spared.'

384

'And this one?' asked Euthemus.

'He has served his purpose. Dispose of him as you see fit.'

With sadistic relish, Euthemus sliced open half-conscious Melampus' throat from ear to ear. His eyes flew open and found Aletes. Aletes looked back, silver eyes wet with tears. Melampus died gargling blood, and once he stopped twitching on the end of the rope, Euthemus cut him down and dumped his body.

Iphigenia looked at Aletes and again knew his suffering. Yet at least she had been spared watching her father killed in front of her eyes. It was as if she saw something die in Aletes in that moment, a look she had never seen on anyone before. She could only watch from a distance as he and Teucer were stripped to their loincloths and bound by the hands at the end of separate lengths of rope.

They were kept apart during the long trek south to Mycenae. Iphigenia rode beside her mother near the front of the tramping column, while the captives were choked by dust at the rear. When they halted for the night after a gruelling day's march, the women were made comfortable close to a blazing campfire. Aletes and Teucer remained lashed to a tree beyond the warmth of the fire without food or water.

Until they fell into the trap, the journey from Tricca had been a time of great relief and renewed optimism. It took a while for Iphigenia to accept she was finally free and returning home. Travelling at a measured pace, she and Aletes followed the River

Peneus to the border of Epirus. Aletes had gone from youth to man in the years that had passed. He was leaner than the thickly muscled warrior he had become on leaving Mycenae three years ago, yet sturdier now than the boy who had carried her in the riverbed and spoken shyly to her in the moonlit orchard.

'Were you not scared?' she had asked him when they rode away from Tricca after his single combat with Eurotas.

'No,' Aletes said with a grin.

'Liar,' she grinned back.

He met her eyes, and she met his. Silver on black. He broke his eyes away first. Truth was, she scared him more than that warrior did. Right there, in that moment. Whenever he was around her, he was terrified.

They spoke for hours. He told her of Orestes' rescue from the dungeons of Troy, assured her that her brother was being cared for and would recover, he played down his part in the rescue and gave Melampus most of the credit. He spoke of battles against Troy, leaving out the carnage of blood shooting from the artery in a man's neck, tasting his blood on your lips as you buried your sword in his body. He left out the seizing panic of having your blade kicked from your hand on the battlefield, those hands your last weapon, around his neck, his around yours, in a grotesque contest of strength, of who could squeeze the hardest, the fastest, to win the chance to live.

He spoke of Troy, of her glory and her downfall, of the wooden horse and how he hid within it. Of her father, his success at Troy and the joy of the Argives to finally return home. He did not speak, however, of how visions of her face, her voice, her conversation, kept him alive in the darkest of all times.

They spoke as they rode. They spoke as they rested. They spoke as they ate the rabbit Aletes had tracked and killed, before the crackling fire.

'You speak fondly of Melampus,' she had said, pronouncing his name slightly incorrectly.

'Melampus? Yes', he said, laughing fondly. 'I would never be able to tell the hairy oaf, but he's like my father, really.'

'And Lord Aegisthus? Could he ever be a father to you?'

Aletes met her eyes and she understood him. Regret. Disappointment.

'I believe he cares only for one son,' he said. 'The son you and I both care very little for.'

Eventually, he plucked up the courage to hold up the heron ring and tell her how it had saved his life more than once. How it hung in a pouch around his neck, with his other most treasured possession, the terracotta figurine of his late mother, Danaea. The expression of pride and pleasure on his boyishly grinning face as he showed it to her, had melted her heart. So much so that later, when she recalled that magical, starlit incident on the first evening after their departure, she realised she had fallen in love with him.

From that dream to this nightmare was unfathomable. Iphigenia's mother's words brought her back to the present. Clytemnestra's gag had been removed before they left the cottonwood glade and she had finally found a moment they were not being observed or overheard.

'See how she fawns over him?' Clytemnestra was saying quietly. 'She is his paramour and cannot be trusted. She carries his child and is devoted to him. Be careful what you say when she is listening.'

Electra and Nireus rode side by side at the front of the creaking, jangling column.

'Are you sure?'

Iphigenia was appalled. Despite the evidence in front of her, and her mother's words, the suggestion her much-loved elder sister was now an enemy was beyond comprehension.

'When the chance comes, I'll speak to her alone,' she said. 'She is merely being cautious and will help us when she can.'

'She will refuse you, as she did me. She and the Phocian king-slayer were lovers long before I journeyed north to help search for you. Electra will not have a word said against him.'

Later that day, when Nireus called a halt beside a gurgling rill to rest and water the men and horses, Iphigenia got the chance she needed to test her sister's loyalty. While Nireus conferred with pig-nosed Hippacoon, she approached Electra and asked what fate would befall Aletes.

'You will find out soon enough,' Electra told her, as if a stranger. 'I can do nothing for him. He is friend and ally to Orestes, so he can expect no mercy. Do not presume to ask me again.'

'Orestes is our *brother*. I understand it is dangerous to say aloud, but surely you can give me a sign that you still support him?'

'I do not. In my opinion, it would have been better for all if Orestes had perished with our father.'

'What has become of you, sister? Is this really you speaking? How can you share the bed of a traitor who has our father's blood on his hands?'

'The blood of a tyrant, who deserved to die.'

Electra hesitated. For a moment she softened, as if appalled by her own words. She seemed about to add something but stopped herself as others around them took an interest.

'Listen to me,' she went on, tersely. 'You are destined to be cousin Glaukos' bride. He and Orestes are enemies now. For your own safety, and our mother's, you must abandon our brother.'

'I will never forsake Orestes or agree to marry Glaukos. I would rather be strung up and tortured like First Spear Melampus.'

'You are young and headstrong, sister. Trust me, Orestes is a lost cause, he would not want you to risk your life for him. You will soon get used to the idea of being a queen. It is a role you've spent your whole life preparing for.'

Iphigenia returned to where her mother was sitting in the grass with disgust on her sun-reddened face. Electra's defection was almost as sickening as the news of her father's death. Yet she refused to accept the inevitable. She would not betray her brother. The nearer they got to the Argive capital the more desperate she became however, until she was forced to accept the gods left her no choice. She would use her marriage to Glaukos to win Aletes' freedom. She would plot and plan until she found a way to help Orestes.

Tormented by thirst, Teucer tried to reach the sparkling, crystal water of the rill. He shoved the guards who had turned their backs and dropped to his knees at the edge, bending forward so his mouth met the water. The butt of a spear struck him, knocking him senseless. Aletes looked on impassively as Teucer was dragged towards him by his ankles.

In his hand, Aletes clutched something small and hard. He was determined never to weaken and give his captors a similar opportunity to beat him. He helped the dazed Ironman sit up beside him, and with his bearded jaw clenched, his swollen tongue stuck to the roof of his mouth of sand, he drew upon the deep well of strength that had sustained him season after season in the depravation of the Trojan dungeon.

It was his fault Melampus was dead. He had arranged that meeting place, and ordered him, selfishly, to keep the number of men in his escort small. Why did he not find a way to save him if he was such an undefeatable warrior? Where was he at the shoulder of Melampus? Was Melampus not glorious enough to be saved by the gods? The guilt ravaged him with nausea. It was only after an angry Danaea accused him of forsaking Iphigenia that he began to crawl out of his abyss of despair as he jogged beside Teucer.

In the night, he had scratched at a piece of rock until his

fingernails turned to blood, prising a sharp piece of rock from the earth. Undetected, even by Teucer, he started to saw through the rope binding his hands behind his back. He kept going until after the first light of dawn. By the time the column set out on the last stage of the journey, his wrists were lacerated and bruised, yet he had deliberately left enough strands to keep him bound, and few enough to break free.

Aletes was ready to wreak havoc, to seize a weapon when the chance came, free Iphigenia and make good their escape. The odds on him succeeding were low, but he would rather die trying than continue to do nothing. With Apollo's help he would avenge Melampus; his old friend's shade could find peace in the underworld.

He had repeated his plan. Over. Over. First, he would slash Euthemus' throat. Nireus next. Pig Nose would die after them. Anyone else who tried to fight him would die too. He would cut off the serpent's head by killing the leaders and hope that in the confusion, the remaining men would mount horses and run. They would take Teucer with them, but when he reached Mycenae, Aletes would honour the promise he had made to Melissa. He would find and release her hostage son – if he was still alive. Last, he would confront Glaukos. They would fight to the death. He would kill him. Whether the gods willed it or not. Whether a prophesy declared it or not. He would kill him.

'He has been marked for greatness, to stand shoulder to shoulder with the best among the Argives. A hero in the guise of a

391

humble herdsman who will one day save the dynasty of Atreus.'

The words rang in his ears, yet he felt himself turning from the gods and their games. This was brother against brother. The curse of the House of Atreus had come full circle. Brother would kill brother.

All morning Aletes waited. Cautious as a prowling fox. When eventually they halted beside the rill, he had seen his chance. He rose onto one knee and was about to free his hands and launch himself at the distracted Phocians when Teucer, maddened by thirst, lunged past him. As sudden as it presented itself, the opportunity to strike was gone. Again, the gods threw obstacles in his path. Again, he was too late. Aletes did what he could to make the battered Dorian comfortable after being knocked unconscious by the guards. Then he resumed his patient watch. Noon came and went, and he was still waiting, sweating in the overwhelming heat, when the distant cacophony of a large-scale battle carried to them on the warm breeze.

An hour from Mycenae. Yet the sound was from there. Undoubtedly. The ground reverberated from the drums and clashing of shield walls.

Nireus gave the order to halt beneath the wooded slopes of the foothills to the north of the Argive plain.

'The clans have arrived before us,' said Teucer, as he and Aletes managed to get into the shade.

'So, it would seem,' agreed Aletes, straining his ears to make sense of the muffled sounds of conflict.

'I thought Kynortas would be more cautious. I expected him to spend the autumn plundering Elis, winter at home in Epirus, then raid further south next spring once his younger warriors have been bloodied.'

'This is no cattle or slave taking raid,' observed Aletes. 'Your kinsmen are trying to storm the city.'

'They've no chance. Kynortas is no fool. He knows we don't have the numbers to mount a lengthy siege. I'd say he means to give you Argives a bloody nose, then negotiate terms for a peaceful withdrawal from a position of strength.

'Glaukos won't pay him off. He doesn't like being dictated to, and he won't avoid a fight he knows he can win.'

'Then I pray to the gods his confidence is misplaced. My son and I will not leave here alive if the Butcher of Calydon prevails.'

Teucer's prayer was not answered. The gods did not favour his kinsmen that morning, as Nireus was to find out when he climbed to the hill's summit with Euthemus and Hippacoon. From the lofty vantage point the vast Argive plain was laid out below them. It stretched away into hazy distance towards the lesser city of Argos and the shiny mirror of sapphire ocean beyond. The citadel of Mycenae, rising into the sky, stood without damage, only the lower parts of the city were on fire. They had been bombarded by flaming catapult-hurled missiles, black plumes of smoke spiralling upwards.

The Dorian clans and their less numerous Hillman allies had failed to overrun the outer city. The cyclopes had done their job well, the giant walls were thick arms protecting the city in an embrace of stone. Much of the early fighting had been done just outside the walls, where from up high, warriors looked like rag dolls discarded by the gods in the middle of a game. Now their catapults had been withdrawn and the ranks of men sent in, the smaller, outflanked Dorian host had been forced to pull back.

A single combat. Upon its outcome rested the fate of many who had yet to face death. Nireus observed from the safety of the high ridge as all fighting on the plains below ceased. Men of all rank waited to see which of the warrior kings would keep their head, let alone their crown.

Kynortas' iron sword ate into the softer bronze skin of Glaukos' shield. Breathing hard, Glaukos crabbed sideways to keep the blinding sun in Kynortas' eyes. Glaukos swung low with his sword, aiming to take Kynortas' legs off at the ankles while the sun masked his sight. The Dorian King anticipated the move. Obvious. They crept around each other like spiders.

Kynortas had his eyes back. He used his height advantage, and charged, sword raised ready to thrust down into Glaukos' collarbone, into his heart and lungs. Unable to use his shield offensively because of his hand, Glaukos slipped his forearm out of the shield's adapted grip, turned it sideways like a discus and spun it into Kynortas' head. It slammed into his face, dazing him, knocking him off balance.

Glaukos looked for the gaps between Kynortas' armour, the necessary spaces for body and limbs to bend. Blade jabbed between Kynortas' iron cuirass and his leather belt. Scraped his hip bone. Kynortas staggered backwards with a grunt of pain, blood crying down his leg.

Glaukos was too exhausted to pursue him. He watched with relief as Kynortas was helped onto his chariot and swiftly conveyed towards the Dorian shield wall, which parted to let him through. A resounding cheer rose from the Argive ranks. Clarions sounded the Dorian retreat. One by one the clans marched. Orderly. Not north to Epirus and the rugged land that spawned them. South. South along the road to Laconia to the gold-rich cities and fertile pastures that awaited them.

'Get the men on their feet,' Nireus said to Pig Nose. 'Make sure the black raven on their shields can be seen clearly. We don't want archers on the ramparts mistaking us for Dorian stragglers.'

Hippacoon saluted and strode ahead, leaving Nireus and Euthemus to linger. The men kept their thoughts to themselves, watching in silence as Glaukos mounted his chariot. He raced back and forth along the Argive battle line, basking in the warriors' fickle adulation. Head tipped back, breeze tugging at the plume of his helmet, he pumped the air with his fist just as Achilles had done the day Paris slew him with an arrow before the walls of Troy.

27

The Brazen Bull

'Welcome.'

Glaukos grinned as he addressed the weary band of new arrivals huddled in the open space between the dais and the press of battle-soiled Argive warlords.

'You have joined us at a most opportune moment.'

Although physically drained, Glaukos felt exultant. The fates could not have been kinder if he had sacrificed more than one of his Trojan concubines or a whole herd of grain-fed bullocks to the gods that morning. He had achieved so much in the short time since he slew the tyrant, he told himself contentedly. He had vanquished the mightiest host of Ironmen to set foot in Argolis, and by so doing cemented his alliance with all but one of the leading Argive potentates. Not even the legendary Atreus could boast so auspicious a start to his reign.

'We have much to celebrate, my lords,' he continued, looking up and raising his voice so it carried to everyone gathered in Mycenae's great hall.

'This evening we feast and give thanks to the gods for our victory over the Ironmen. Then, on the morrow, you are invited to join me at the Temple of Zeus, where I intend to wed the tyrant's long-lost daughter. She has been found by my good friend, King Nireus, and stands here ready to do her duty to the Argive people.'

The assembled warlords approved of the match. They ignored Iphigenia's lack of enthusiasm. That was usual in marriages of politics. They clapped, cheered, stamped their hobnailed feet on the tiled floor.

Not all of them were overjoyed at the prospect of delaying their departure for a wedding. Glaukos saw Nicostratus, the bastard son of Menelaus and recently crowned as the King of Sparta, shake his head and exchange troubled looks with each of his fellow Laconians. The Dorian host had last been seen marching south towards his homeland, and Nicostratus was understandably anxious to drive them out before they pillaged too many farms or villages.

Go if you must, Glaukos said to himself, feasting his eyes on the rounded peaks and shallow clefts of Iphigenia's tunic clad body. I will not stand in your way, nor will I weep when you are soundly thrashed by the larger Ironman host and your surviving heroes scurry back here like scalded dogs with their tails between their legs. I have more pressing matters to attend to and will not leave Mycenae until Aletes dies pleading for mercy, and I have planted my seed in Iphigenia's ripe belly.

'I know some of you are impatient to return to your homelands. I urge caution.' Glaukos focused eyes on Nicostratus. 'It would be a mistake to divide our forces. The enemy we face is stronger than we anticipated. Divided, this is not a fight any of us can win. We must stand together. Two days hence, when our heroes are rested and I am wed, we will march forth as one indestructible host. A little hungover perhaps yet bonded as brothers in arms. Bide your time, lords, and I swear before thundering Zeus we will teach these iron-bladed raiders to keep their filthy feet off Argive land.'

Animated applause. Glaukos congratulated himself on a most rousing performance. He was becoming a skilled orator, he told himself. A great king whose name would eclipse Agamemnon.

'Come, little cousin,' he said, his eyes hungry. 'Stand up here beside me and give these lords a smile to melt their hearts.'

Iphigenia remained unmoved.

'Look who has come to greet you. See how he smiles at the prospect of becoming a grandfather.'

Glaukos gestured to the back of the dais. Iphigenia looked and took a step. Agamemnon's putrefying head rested on a fluted alabaster secluded at the back of the dais.

Agamemnon's eyes and lips had rotted, his cheekbones protruded beneath grey, parchment-thin skin. His equine teeth and mouth gaped in an eternal scream, preserving his final hideous mortal expression.

Iphigenia recoiled at the obscenity. She tried in vain to stop herself retching, tears unbeckoned, filled her eyes.

'You're are a monster! I want nothing to do with you,' she hurled at him.

'I didn't ask what you want.'

Glaukos was no longer smiling and he had lowered his voice. 'You will do as I say, or it will go badly for your mother. I will have Euthemus take you both from here, to somewhere secluded where you cannot be seen or heard, and there he will strangle the witch in front of you.'

'Don't listen to him, daughter,' said Clytemnestra, scornfully. 'He means me harm whether you cooperate or not.'

The foremost rank of warlords had overheard the vitriolic exchange, and a murmur of disquiet spread from them to the lesser kings standing at the rear of the hall. Glaukos acted quickly to dispel it.

'Silence the crone', he said in a low voice to Euthemus, who along with Pig Nose was guarding the group of prisoners. He stepped off the dais, and as Euthemus grabbed the protesting queen and gagged her with one hand, he lifted Iphigenia onto the dais with the other.

'Take your hands off her,' Iphigenia cried out, held fast in Glaukos' unyielding grasp so she could not turn her head far enough to see what the henchman was doing to her mother.

'Behave and she will come to no harm. Our guests are watching, my sweet. One or two are starting to look concerned, so smile and let them see how happy you really are.'

Aletes had endured enough. He could not bear to see Iphigenia roughly handled or listen to Glaukos threatening violence against her mother. His guards had been lax and not checked his bindings since Teucer was knocked unconscious beside the rill.

He wrenched apart the last fibres of rope, and leaping on the dais, pulled Iphigenia behind him before grabbing Glaukos by the throat. By the time Euthemus and Pig Nose reacted, Glaukos' overlarge head had turned a mottled purple. He punched at Aletes, but his half-brother was stronger. Aletes was expecting to be knocked out by the men behind, but he was seized by the arms and dragged onto the floor.

Glaukos rammed his foot hard into Aletes' windpipe. It was worth it, Aletes thought.

'I could end you, you piece of shit but a swift death is too easy. Strip him, Euthemus. Spread his legs. See how much of the warrior remains after I cut off his manhood at the root.'

'He is high-born!' Iphigenia blurted. 'He is entitled to be tried by his peers for any wrongdoing you deem him guilty of. It will offend the gods if you defile him like this.'

'He's a cave dweller, a herdsman. He's nothing.'

'The daughter of Agamemnon is right,' Nicostratus interjected, his firm yet respectful voice cutting through the silence that had enveloped the hall. 'Zygouris is the son of high Lord

Aegisthus just as surely as Menelaus sired me.'

It was well known the Spartan king was Menelaus' bastard son, and his mother had once been a palace slave.

'If accused of a crime,' Nicostratus continued, 'in this case an attempt on your life, only the gods or his fellow lords can sit in judgement. I would add that after what he did at Troy, gaining the ramparts single-handed and lowering a rope to my father's waiting warband, a trial is the very least your sibling deserves.'

'The very least,' echoed a Laconian, prompting others around him to nod their scalp-knotted heads and mutter agreement.

Glaukos slowly, reluctantly, stepped back, sheathed his dagger and held up his empty hands in a placatory gesture. The mood in the hall had soured, and he was determined to reassert his authority before he lost control of proceedings.

'As you wish,' he said, his tone anything but conciliatory. 'He will have a trial, and it will be the gods who decide his fate. Tomorrow, in the forecourt of the Temple of Zeus, before all who gather there to celebrate my wedding, he will fight the Ironman to the death. If he prevails, he will be permitted to live out his life in exile, far beyond the borders of Argolis. If he loses – and know that the Dorian will have ample reason to defeat him – the gods will have demonstrated his guilt. Bring in the brazen bull.'

Hollow, like the wooden horse Aletes had hidden inside at Troy, the cumbersome bull was almost twice the size of a live bull and fashioned out of gleaming bronze. A rarely used device for inflicting the most heinous form of torture. The roasting alive of incarcerated victims. It had not seen the light of day since before the reign of Atreus.

Bronze wheels screeched as the bull was hauled into the hall, huge, polished head, sightless eyes, long curved horns, glittering diabolically in the lambent glow of recently lit torches. None of the warlords had seen its like before. Along with Iphigenia, Clytemnestra, even Electra, they watched in stunned silence as it was positioned over the fire in the central circular hearth.

All were waiting for Glaukos to reveal its purpose when the first muffled screams emanated from within its rapidly heated belly.

The screams were those of a child. Unmistakably. Shrill with terror. All could hear the clawing from inside as the child frantically tried the locked hatch in the creature's metal flank.

Teucer knew at once who it was. He cried out in horror. He struggled against the two burly Argives assigned to guard him after Aletes' attempt to throttle Glaukos.

'My son is in there! Release him, I beg you! I will fight anyone you ask!'

'To the death?'

Glaukos seemed oblivious to the effect the nerve-shredding sounds inside the bull were having on those outside it. Only Nireus looked like he was enjoying the spectacle. Electra was calling for the boy to be shown mercy and released.

Glaukos lifted his palm to the hall for silence.

'Let me be clear. You will fight to the death. If you lose or fail to give a good account of yourself, I will have the whelp roasted like a plucked capon. Do you understand?'

'Yes, I understand,' gasped Teucer helplessly, his son's piercing shrieks fast eroding his sanity.

'On the other hand, if you fight bravely and defeat this peasant, I will permit you to leave with your mewling son.'

'Yes, yes, I understand. Please, his skin will be blistering!'

'You might be right. It doesn't take long for bronze to heat up in a good fire, does it. Is that the runt's piss I can hear bubbling away like a pot of rabbit stew on a camp tripod?'

'Enough, I beseech you!' Iphigenia did not expect to be heeded but could not stay silent any longer and watch Teucer being tormented. 'On behalf of the boy's mother, I implore you to release him.'

'It's a shame she isn't here. If she was, and her husband disappoints me, I could roast the whole family.'

'I will not disappoint you. I shall fight this Argive and earn my son's freedom. I want him back unblemished, not shrivelled to a husk by fire.'

'He has not been harmed, nor will he be if you fight half as well as you bleat.'

With a casual flick of his maimed hand, Glaukos signalled for the bull to be pulled away from the hissing flames.

'The bull is not yet hot enough to cook the boy. I tested it yesterday on a scribe who has long irritated me.'

The hatch in the bull's flank opened, and out of its stifling

403

interior tumbled a boy of eight summers with a shock of black hair and a freckled face that mirrored his mother's. Covered in sweat, tears streaming down his cheeks, he stumbled sobbing towards his father and clamped trembling arms around his waist.

Glaukos laughed as if it were entertainment. Nireus and a handful of other rebel lords joined in. They were quickly silenced by the groundswell of uneasy muttering that issued from everyone else in the hall.

'Take our guests to the temple, Euthemus, and make sure they're properly guarded. The seers are to feed and water them, and in case you're tempted to exact revenge for your pricked thigh, don't. The herdsman is not to be mistreated. Hear me? If he's unable to play his part tomorrow, *you* will fight in his stead wearing a blindfold, armed with a blunt sword. The runt stays here with me. I want him lashed to the bull, so he can be tossed back inside should his father displease me.'

The inner sanctum of the Temple of Zeus was one of the few buildings in Mycenae secure enough to hold prisoners. It was the chamber where the brightly painted statue of Zeus resided with the city treasury, and in addition to having a sloping tile roof that extended over the open sided porch, it was always locked when seers were not in attendance.

The two captives were kept apart by chaining them by the ankles to the broad girthed stone columns supporting the front corners of the porch roof. They were brought soft white bread, cheese, and olives by the shaven headed seers, and later, when a squally wind and driving rain swept the temple compound, they kept dry by sheltering behind the sturdy columns.

'You should eat what they give us,' Teucer advised, when he saw Aletes picking at the food in front of him. 'You need to build up your strength for tomorrow when we fight on these flagstones. I am in your debt, Aletes of Zygouris, and do not want to kill you. But for the sake of my son, I am going to try. If the gods favour me, I will give you as swift and clean a death as possible.'

'The gods.' Aletes echoed.

He had done all the gods asked of him. He had left his home, saved the daughter of the king, the son of the king, saved the dynasty. Yet the gods had left him with nothing.

He would not kill Teucer. He would make the contest look convincing, by fighting him to a standstill and spilling a quantity of Ironman blood for good effect. In this way, he hoped Glaukos would be sufficiently entertained to grant father and son their freedom. If he was not, and he demanded Teucer's death, Aletes would refuse to carry out the order and turn his blade on the royal guards protecting Glaukos.

They would be many, and he would be overwhelmed swiftly. His conscience would be clear, and he would join his ancestors in Elysium without the blood of an innocent man on his hands.

'Glaukos will flay you alive for defying him,' said a scornful Danaea when Aletes explained his intentions to the terracotta figurine of his mother.

He had waited until a sated Teucer slipped into a fitful sleep before taking the precious, thumb-sized effigy from the kidskin pouch around his neck. He stood it on the weathered stone between his legs, where Teucer could not see it if he woke up unexpectedly. Satisfied no one was watching or listening, he spoke to Danaea in a whisper, his voice further muted by the swirling wind.

'I gave Melissa my word. In return for her help at Tricca, I promised to find and release her son.'

'You agreed to search for him in Argolis after escorting Iphigenia home, but you are mistaken if you think Melissa has your word. She has not, and where her son is concerned you have nothing to reproach yourself for. You did not know Glaukos had seized power, or that Euthemus and the Phocian king would be waiting to arrest you at the border of Epirus. Your quest to rescue Iphigenia has failed, my son, and unless the gods intervene on your behalf, she is destined to become Glaukos' wife before the sun sets tomorrow. I'm sorry, I know how painful this outcome is for you, but I will not allow you to use it as an excuse to give up hope and throw away your life for a Dorian boy who cannot be saved.'

'I will not do Glaukos' bidding and kill the Ironman. If Teucer dies, his son will never be reunited with Melissa. He will be disposed of in the brazen bull. I would not wish that gruesome fate on anyone, even Glaukos.'

'And yet after he's peeled your skin, Glaukos will amuse himself by slowly roasting you in the bronze bull.'

'If that is Apollo's wish. I have played my part in the gods' games. If it amuses them to boil me alive, so be it. I have let Iphigenia down by walking into a trap. I became arrogant, believing myself invulnerable to mortal hands, protected by the gods. I delivered her to Glaukos. Melampus—'

He trailed off. 'I do not expect her forgiveness. Or his.'

'There is nothing for them to forgive. Iphigenia is your friend, and she has few of those in this world. You cannot abandon her when she needs your help more than ever.'

'She is better off without me.'

'Horseshit!'

The voice was instantly familiar and came uninvited out of the formless ether like a violent gust of wind.

'I'm the one who walked into an ambush, not you. That's why you found me hanging upside down in a tree, pissing over my own face. Danaea is right, you have nothing to reproach yourself for where the boy and his mother are concerned. It is Iphigenia you should be thinking of now. She still has faith in you, even if you don't. So stop feeling sorry for yourself and explain to me how you're going to spare her the indignity of sharing Glaukos' bed?'

'My legs are chained in case you haven't noticed.'

Aletes realised he had spoken aloud, almost waking Teucer. Quelling his anger, he waited until the Ironman settled down again.

'Glaukos is a cautious man, so I don't expect them to be removed before I swap blows with Teucer. This will slow me and restrict my movement to the lumbering shuffle of a hobbled bear. I

407

will be mocked, a source of bloody amusement for Glaukos and his guests, exactly as he intends. Being chained will ensure the palace guards can easily overpower me should the need arise. My life will end tomorrow, either inside the bull or on these flagstones, so unless you've something useful to add I suggest you stop interfering, go back to your gardening, or wine making, and leave me in peace.'

Melampus snorted explosively, a sound like a cornered bull bursting from cover and charging its tormentors.

'More self-pitying horseshit,' he retorted. 'Listen to me, my miserable excuse for a friend. Your fate is far from decided. Glaukos will put a sword in your hand, on that much we're agreed, so shackled or not you can do what I've seen you do better than any man I served with. You can fight. Fight like you did on the streets of Troy, or in the shadow of Mount Oeta, where you were first to step up beside me and face the charging Amazons. Silence the mocking laughter of Glaukos' fawning followers and stay alive as long as you can. It may have escaped your attention, but Glaukos isn't the most popular Argive lord to plant his hairy arse on Mycenae's throne. There are others here still loyal to the old regime.'

As Melampus fell silent, a last eddy of wind hurled spite into Aletes' downcast face. The rain had finally stopped, overhead the scudding blanket of cloud had broken into jagged streamers. Quicksilver moonlight illuminated shimmering puddles.

'Who knows what might come about if others are inspired by

408

your courage and defiance?'

Melampus' gravelly voice was softer, more distant, as if speaking over his shoulder as he walked away.

And with that, Melampus was gone. Aletes felt a profound sense of loss as his presence departed, and for some while afterwards, as rain dripped off the temple roof and gurgled along run-off channels, he reflected upon what the irascible First Spear had said.

'Mother, are you still here?'

'I am, my son. I will stay as long as you want me to. Your friend spoke well. Now eat your supper, every morsel, and try to get some rest. You've a long, testing day ahead.'

Aletes kissed the smiling figurine, tears of gratitude and affection blurring his vision, his jaw clenched. He placed it back in the kidskin pouch. He did the same with the heron ring and then, his appetite restored, devoured his rain-dampened supper.

On the moonlit balcony of what was formerly Clytemnestra's bedchamber in the Palace of Mycenae, within the towering walls of the citadel, tears of another nature, stained Iphigenia's eyes. She gripped the balustrade's ornamental coping and scanned the rain-glazed rooftops of the lower city. She had upset her mother and deeply regretted it.

'What if I was always fated to die at Aulis? If I were already dead, Glaukos could not secure his claim to the throne, he may not have been able to bargain with those warlords. Father would still be alive, you would still be queen. Orestes would still be heir to the Argive throne. Electra would not have betrayed us. I could jump and defeat Glaukos in a heartbeat.'

Clytemnestra had grabbed her daughter's arms so tightly the flow of blood to her hands was almost cut off.

'I know I should speak to Hera and seek her permission first, but time is pressing if I'm to thwart Glaukos.'

'Hera would refuse your request.'

Clytemnestra swung her daughter round so she was no longer staring into the abyss. A wash of golden lamplight from beyond the open balcony doors illuminated the expression of horror on the old queen's face.

'She would scold you for being selfish and remind you how precious your life is. It pains me to hear you talk like this, daughter. After enduring so much, it would be cowardly to hurl yourself to your death.'

'No one said Chryseis of Lyrnessus was a coward for slashing her throat. Even Achilles acknowledged her bravery.'

'Chryseis' situation was different. She was a hostage taken in war. Her people were our enemies, and it was her misfortune to fall into the hands of Achilles, who presented her in turn to your father. Rather than live out her days as his concubine, she did what was deemed honourable under the circumstances and killed herself.'

'Am I not also a hostage?'

'You are in your own home, among people who adore you.

In the eyes of many, your words could not be further from the truth. You are about to become queen of all the Argives, and after two ill-fated marriages, and the tragic death of Achilles in battle, you should perhaps be a little more grateful. Women of our rank do not marry for love, daughter. We are pawns in the game of alliances, given away to cement old and new friendships, or to breathe life into failing dynasties. I did not love your father when I was brought here from Sparta, but I did as my mother had taught me and made the best of the situation. I played the part of a devoted wife, and in time I was rewarded with three beautiful, healthy children. You must do the same. You must do your duty. You are Iphigenia. Daughter of King Agamemnon. Daughter of the son of Atreus. History will say you lived. Live.'

Her mother would have made a great ruler, Iphigenia considered. She held her tongue, imprisoning the words she wanted to say, putting on a false face she knew she would have to wear now. She inhaled a deep, steadying breath and squeezed Clytemnestra's blue-veined hands.

'Let's go back inside and warm up. We'll ask one of the maids to fetch mulled wine from the kitchen.'

Arms linked, they walked back into the bedchamber, heated by charcoal burning braziers. Clytemnestra sat on a comfortable, low-backed couch, the same she had lain upon exhausted all those years ago after riding from Aulis to seek the help of Lord Aegisthus. She had sought him out, as he conducted legal duties at the palace, and urged him to help find Iphigenia. All that had happened since, and here they were back where it had all begun.

A series of knocks on the chamber doors. Mother and daughter's eyes met in silent concern. A cloak-swathed Electra swept into the room. She threw back the hood of her cloak, ordering her escort of Phocians to wait outside in the corridor. She had the look of her mother, amber eyes, a fine-boned face, the same auburn hair of Clytemnestra before hers was stroked with grey.

'What is your purpose here, traitor?' Clytemnestra demanded.

'I have words for my sister's ears if she would hear them,' Electra said.

'Who else knows where you are?'

'Only the guards escorting me.' Electra looked past the bristling queen and spoke directly to Iphigenia. 'I am here of my own volition, to seek your forgiveness for my earlier indifference to your misfortune. I love you dearly, sister, although my recent conduct has clearly persuaded you otherwise. I give you my word that from this moment, whatever the fates hold in store for us, I will be here at your side.'

'Why come now, at this late hour?' a bemused Iphigenia asked. 'We have been travelling the same road for many days, always in sight of each other, yet not a single kind word has passed your lips. What has happened to bring about this welcome change of heart?'

'The Dorian boy's screams brought me to my senses.'

Electra stepped closer to Iphigenia and lowered her voice

412

so the Phocians waiting in the corridor could not overhear. A whisper.

'It turned my stomach to watch Nireus drool with pleasure as he listened to the Ironman's son begging to be released from the brazen bull. Given the chance I would gladly send him to the dungeon of Tartarus, to suffer there with the Titans for all eternity, for he does not deserve to dwell in the realm of civilised men.'

'Something we agree on at last,' Clytemnestra muttered.

Electra glanced warily over her shoulder, back towards the corridor.

'I have not spoken of this to anyone, but I have vowed before the altar of Athena at Phocis never to forgive Nireus for his part in our father's murder. I want to see him and every traitor with blood on his hands pay for what he has done. We are not alone in opposing Glaukos, sister. There are many beyond this citadel's walls – men like Nicostratus of Sparta – who secretly revile him and will rally to our banners when they hear the call to arms. You must remain strong, submit to your husband's demands and bide your time. One day, I promise you, Hera will answer our prayers. Good men will rise up and justice will be done.'

Iphigenia was cautious. She had been played the fool before. She stood stiffly and took her mother's arm.

'Let us see,' she said, so unlike the young girl Electra had known in Mycenae. 'You can prove your loyalty with your actions. Until then, sister, we bid you goodnight.'

413

28

The Wedding Speech

At the appointed hour late the next morning, Iphigenia walked towards the Temple of Zeus, which stood imperial in white marble, the thirteen columns on each side of its body supporting a vast flat, rectangular roof leading to a triangular frontal pediment that sat high above the tallest rows of poplar trees. Steps led up to each of the four sides, allowing access between the towering columns, above which were brilliant gold orbs with black lions in each, interspersed with majestic lapis lazuli blue stone.

To reach the temple, Iphigenia left the palace and passed under the citadel's imposing Gateway of the Lions, descending the broad circuitous stone causeway into the lower city. Her arm was entwined with that of her mother. Glaukos had sent his flower garlanded hunting chariot to convey his bride to the wedding ceremony. Iphigenia had chosen to continue afoot. It was a small gesture of defiance that quickened her blood.

Iphigenia had been bathed and massaged with exotic, sweet-scented oils. Glaukos had sent guards with masters in the art of hair and dress, not as a gift of goodwill, but to ensure she did not rebel by refusing to look the part. They had styled her in the image of Aphrodite, the most beautiful of the gods, her black curls weaved around a diadem of solid gold, the rest of her hair spiralling down and around her neck, with tightly coiled strands falling down each temple. Her pharos was white, the colour of the gods, secured with gold and sapphire clasps and adorned with gold foil geometric circles. Around her neck, Aphrodite's favoured seashells and ivory, with armlets of gold and rings of emerald, the goddess of love's stone, and diamond. Pendant gold earrings, inlaid with small pearls and garnets, hung glittering from the lobes of her ears. A procession of white-robed priests and priestesses followed, chanting prayers to the accompaniment of finger cymbals and seed filled rattles. Behind them came a line of musicians playing a variety of wind, string, and percussion instruments, while bringing up the rear was Electra and her escort of Phocian guards.

A vast, highly animated crowd waited for the royal party at the bottom of the causeway despite the rising heat. It was strange for a wedding to be held in the day, the tradition being torchlit night. Yet, Agamemnon's daughter and the former queen were popular figures from an ancient line of warrior kings and the crowd cheered, clapped, and threw handfuls of petals at the procession as it passed.

Some of the men were already drunk, quenching their thirsts

from goatskin flagons of mead and wine. They were hardworking men with weathered faces and calloused hands and were enjoying themselves on a rare day of leisure away from toiling in fields. Along with their loved ones, they stood five deep on either side of the paved thoroughfare leading to the Temple of Zeus. There, many more waited, their number swollen by a steady stream of late arrivals. They pressed against an unyielding cordon of royal guards, positioned a few paces inside the expansive outer courtyard to prevent the enthused crowd getting too close to the proceedings.

'Have you ever seen the people so happy?' Iphigenia asked her mother, stunned by the deluge of sound produced by the multitude's rejoicing.

'In truth I have not,' Clytemnestra admitted, squeezing her daughter's arm reassuringly. 'There were as many gathered here to welcome me the day I wed your father, but they had only one reason to celebrate. On this occasion, the people of Mycenae have two. They have a beautiful new queen to feast their eyes upon, and a hard-fought victory over the Ironmen to write songs about. I am sure every person here feared for their life when they beheld the size of the Dorian host. Yet thanks to Tyche, the bestower of good fortune, they are still alive and free to tell the tale.'

'Not the outcome I had hoped for,' Electra said, acerbically. 'I wanted the Dorians to be routed of course, that goes without saying, yet not before their bear of a king decapitated Glaukos. Another day in the field like yesterday and the unwashed rabble will

417

forget that Glaukos is a bloodthirsty, backstabbing coward and hail him as Atreus reincarnated.'

As Electra fell silent, Iphigenia's gaze fastened upon the odious creature she had been speaking about. Glaukos was standing in front of the horn shaped Altar of Zeus in the middle of the compact inner enclosure, Nireus and the residing shaman alongside him. Behind them was the entrance to the deeply shaded inner sanctum, where the seated, laurel-crowned statue of Zeus could be seen through an open doorway festooned with swags of flowers. Before them, a short distance from the ramp that led down to the much larger outer courtyard, stood the gleaming bulk of the brazen bull. To the left and right of that, the kings of every major Argive city stood shoulder to shoulder with thrice as many lesser warlords, magistrates, and visiting foreign emissaries.

Glaukos hooked the thumb of his intact hand over his studded sword belt and watched his reluctant bride take her place beside the altar. A look of supreme triumph. He wore a gold trimmed red tunic, and upon his feet, tasselled calfskin boots. Serpentine armbands, awarded to himself for bravery in battle, adorned his biceps. His overly oiled hair had been gathered into a hero's top knot on the crown of his head, while his wispy beard was neatly pared and oiled.

He greeted Iphigenia with exaggerated courtesy, the lustful gleam in his too-close eyes causing a shudder to run down her spine. Legs spread confidently, he raised his unmaimed fist aloft in demand for silence. A partial hush slowly settled over the sunlit courtyard, and as it did, a horrified Iphigenia heard a forlorn sobbing coming from the dark interior of the nearby bull.

'Lords of Argolis, citizens of Mycenae. Behold you my betrothed as few of you have ever seen her before. Does her beauty not compare with that of flawless Aphrodite? Is there a man here who would not proceed at once to the ceremonial bedding, if convention would allow?'

Bawdy laughter filled the ceremony like flocks of geese flushed from their roosts. Warlord and peasant alike took up the customary chant of 'Bed her, bed her, bed her!'

'Worry not, friends. Tempted though I am to dispense with these tedious formalities, I have promised to lavishly entertain you. A day of unrivalled spectacle and revelry is about to begin, starting with the trial by single combat of the peasant you call Aletes of Zygouris. Instead of a sacrificial bullock or ram, Zeus will be honoured with a libation of human blood. Before the seer conducts the wedding ritual, and I accept the dead tyrant's daughter into my household, one of the two men you see standing before you will lay dead on these flagstones. Euthemus, arm them with sword. I am impatient to be rid of at least one of them.'

Approval rose from thousands of rustic throats, but closer to hand the less animated kings exchanged uneasy glances. Glaukos was aware and was determined to press on before he was reminded about what had been agreed the previous day. He had no intention of keeping his word if Aletes prevailed. The herdsman would die before nightfall, and nothing Nicostratus of Sparta or any

419

other interfering potentate said, would change that.

'Get on with it, Euthemus. Give the Ironman a weapon first and tell him to make good use of it.'

Grinding his teeth, Aletes picked up the dull bladed sword Euthemus belatedly tossed at his feet. It was true that Iphigenia looked heart-meltingly lovely, but to hear that from Glaukos' lecherous mouth, and to watch how he drooled over her as if she were a painted harlot plying her trade, made him believe he could tear free from his chains and kill Glaukos with his bare hands.

Though still chained, wearing no more than a grubby loincloth and sandals, Aletes was ready to do what Melampus' shade had urged him to. Throw caution to the gods of the four winds and scrap like the war tempered hero he had been moulded into. He would deal with the lame henchman first, then fight his way past the guards surrounding the inner compound and leave Glaukos with a parting gift to remember him by. Danaea would scold him for throwing his life away, yet better to die this way than cross swords with someone who was not his enemy.

Aletes ducked into a defensive crouch, anticipating Teucer seizing the advantage he had been handed by being armed first with a sharp sword to his blunt one.

The Dorian did not move. His sword lay untouched on the ground. Ignoring Euthemus' exhortations to fight, he was staring in the same direction as everyone else in the courtyard. Aletes followed his gaze and sighted two men in a chariot travelling at speed along the causeway from the citadel. As the charioteer drove on the galloping horses with a whip, his passenger, the Captain of the City Watch, blew on a clarion to warn the throng below to make way for them to pass. The chariot swung into the outer courtyard, the horses brought to a snorting, prancing halt.

Polemarch Argalus dismounted and jogged up to the ramp leading to the inner compound. He saluted stiffly, the plume of his helmet as black as the expression on Glaukos' twitching face.

'King, another host approaches the city.'

At once, his words were relayed from one mouth to the next among the assembled warlords and guests, until far beyond the reach of his confident voice, like a fire spreading out of control through the driest of grass.

'They march behind Myrmidon banners. As I speak they are deploying in order of battle.'

'Sooner than expected,' muttered Glaukos, his scarred face convulsed by another violent spasm. He was clearly vexed by Argalus' announcement, yet not surprised or unduly perturbed.

'Prince Orestes leads them. The son of Achilles rides at his side.'

Uproar ensued. A commotion that could not have been more chaotic than if volleys of fire arrows and flaming catapult-hurled missiles were raining down on the city. The name of Agamemnon's admired son, whom most had mourned as dead, moved on the 30,000 lips of Mycenae.

'Prince Orestes is alive!' the voices came. 'He means to take back the Argive throne!'

The crowd evaporated, barring doors of their homes, preparing to wait out the looming confrontation. The temple enclosure reverberated with desertion, leaving the macabre wedding party and increasingly alarmed guests, the two combatants, and a large contingent of royal guards.

On the arid plain to the south, seven thousand Myrmidons. Coalesced into a chanting, shield-thumping phalanx that stretched so far, they faded into a line of ants in each direction. Two chariot-mounted figures clattered across the rocky terrain before them as the force marched, as if one giant who was bodied of black and bronze. Its metal limbs clapped like thunderbolts from Zeus, it took breaths of sweeping leather, growled in drum and hobnailed feet, and jangled with flute.

Polemarch Thaos, Neoptolemus' grizzled cousin, held the centre, elite veterans of the renowned Myrmidon military making up the front rank with him, leather-armoured irregular mercenaries of farmers and labourers followed, shieldless archers bringing up the rear ranks, battle standards aloft like hawks, emblazoned with the huge black ant of the Myrmidons. In its wake, a cloak of dust swept behind the advancing war giant.

In the columned Temple of Zeus, warlords' eyes thrust into Glaukos. They awaited his reaction, his order, his leadership.

None of the kings knew about Meleager's head arriving from Pharsalos two nights earlier in a blood-stained reed basket. Only Nireus. Glaukos had deliberately kept it from them, swearing

Clambrotus to secrecy before sending him and his depleted war band home to Thebes to recuperate. He was determined to let nothing interfere with the union that would secure his claim to the throne. He had planned to convene a council of war the next morning, but Orestes' early arrival had preempted that.

He was left with one unpalatable course of action: confront the dead tyrant's son before his fickle allies started to desert. Unless he moved swiftly, they would slip away one by one to their distant halls, or worse, defect to the enemy.

'It's hard to tell from here,' Nireus said, squinting across the hazed plain. 'But I'd say Orestes looks pissed off. Perhaps it was a mistake not to invite him to his little sister's wedding?'

'Spare me your banter. There'll be enough time for that when I remove Orestes' head and leave it to rot beside his father's.'

'You mean to give battle?'

'What choice do we have? Look around you, Nireus. Our allies are spineless.'

Glaukos drew his sword and held it aloft as he turned to address the vacillating warlords.

'My friends, we must cast off our fine dress and gird ourselves for war! Before we feast tonight, we must go forth together and vanquish this scourge of reiving Myrmidons. If we stand united, and you are true to the oath of loyalty you swore to me, we will soon have another glorious victory to celebrate along with the one I gave you yesterday.'

'This is your fight, Clawhand, not ours,' Nicostratus called out. 'Penelaos warned you Orestes wouldn't rest until he avenged his father. He was right, and you were a fool not to heed his words. The warrior of Atreus has returned, and I'll not draw my blade against him.'

'Nor I,' said the fat, fork-bearded King of Pylos, who always supported his Spartan neighbour.

'Go then, oathbreakers,' Glaukos hurled back at them.

An abrupt quiet. An indication the Myrmidons had halted beyond the range of Glaukos' archers and his force was awaiting the order to launch an assault.

'Run back to Laconia and skulk behind your city walls!' Glaukos exploded. 'Know this, that when the Ironmen descend upon your homeland and your outnumbered heroes are swept aside, your pleas for help will fall on deaf ears. Mycenae will not march south to your rescue.'

This was no idle threat, for the Mycenaean host was more powerful than any other in Argolis. At full strength, it was more than capable of defeating any Myrmidon, Dorian or combined force ranged against it. Denied this protection, many of the smaller city states were vulnerable to attack from raiders or avaricious neighbours. The lesser potentates understood this. When Nicostratus eyed around to see how many of them were with him, all but one looked the other way.

Glaukos was gratified to see the reaction. Without support, the outspoken Spartan posed no threat.

'The time for discussion has passed, my friends. Go with the war bands that escorted you here and take your places on Mycenae's flanks.'

'My armour!' he demanded to Argalus. 'Call to arms has been sounded in the guards' barracks and the training camp on the Field of War?'

'Yes, lord, on both counts,' confirmed the Captain of the Watch.

'Where are my ranks of heroes? They need to be here now.'

His face was twitching now, both eyes as manic as the one stretched wide with the old scar. A long column of highly disciplined Mycenaeans marched into view from the west of the city and formed up behind bellowing First Spears. By the time the dust settled, an impenetrable shield wall confronted the watching Myrmidons, and Glaukos' mood had improved.

Spear points and bronze helms gleamed like gold in the warm autumn sun like a field of barley. The plumes of the First Spears' helmets were as black as raven feathers, while overhead banners adorned with the maned head of a lion, snapped and fluttered in the light wind.

'This may yet prove enjoyable,' Glaukos said, his murine eyes flitting to and fro, absorbing every detail of the scene before him. 'I'm taking your chariot, Argalus. I'll have need of it if I'm to lead our host from the front and rout these presumptuous Myrmidons. Escort my bride and her family back to the citadel. Ensure they're kept out of danger. Euthemus, disarm the prisoners. Secure them until its their turn to fight.'

Breathless, a trio of youths entered the outer courtyard at a run. They were carrying Glaukos' enormous oval shield and bronze armour, all carefully cleaned and polished after his hard-fought victory over the clan chieftain of the northern black bears.

'By the stars, I said he looked peeved,' Nireus was saying. 'Seems I was right, and he means to have it out with you.'

'What?'

The son of Agamemnon. Deposed Prince of the Argives. He charged at the Mycenaean line in a chariot that roared with flame. Orestes was the sun god, bronze of the chariot burning as an inferno in the golden hands of the sun, muscled breastplate and arm guards ablaze, dazzling as if his skin belonged to Helios. The olive crown he held aloft inexplicably shone, as if he had set it on fire.

Glaukos felt fear. It was a trick. Orestes had men positioned with mirrors to shoot the sun at him or similar deception. A ruse like the wooden horse to trick the Mycenaean warriors into believing Orestes was a god.

Glaukos dragged a swallow down his narrow throat.

'Why should we give him more respect than he showed Meleager when he took off his head?'

'He holds aloft the crown of truce,' Nireus pointed out.

'Meleager went in peace. Who here is our most accomplished bowman?'

'I have that reputation, King,' smirked Pig Nose.

'Stand ready behind your lord with your arrow set. When I

give the word, take out his eye.'

Even Pig Nose looked at Glaukos like he was a madman, but he did as he was ordered.

Orestes could have been Agamemnon in his youth as his charioteer halted close enough for the prince to be heard. Warrior king to warrior king, Orestes spoke with his father's power. Agamemnon had never had a hand of help from the gods, unlike Achilles, Hector, Paris, Priam. His son would show what a mortal man could do.

'Old comrades, fellow Argives,' Orestes boomed. 'You know me, you know I do not possess my slain father's power of voice to rouse the ardour of warriors. I am no great orator. I have no poetry or clever words. Some of you remember the last speech I gave was long and as painful as a lanced boil.'

Rueful laughter. Just as intended. Nodding. Recognition. Remembrance.

Glaukos' stomach decayed with concern. Words could win a war. He needed to silence him. Fast.

'My quarrel is not with you, warriors of Argolis! I stand before you under the crown of truce. You are my blood. My home. My people. If you bleed, I bleed. I desire only to draw the blood of the men who murdered my father. The coward who slay my father naked and defenceless in his bath. What the son of Aegisthus did was an affront to the gods, and in the name of the gods I will avenge my father! I claim only what is mine. My cause is just. I urge you to stand aside or stand with me!'

The whisper of the arrow leaving Pig Nose's bow was lost in the wave of support for Orestes. Growing. Orestes recoiled. Buried. A hideous, pitying shriek of unbearable pain as the arrow entered under the charioteer's chin and into his brain, a collapse of bronze and body into Orestes, knocking him off his feet.

The warriors in the Mycenaean ranks turned like a roused dragon. Flaming fury at the cowardice, a storm of outrage blackened and swirled from both armies. United.

The stallions of Orestes' chariot had reared up and he was forced to push his charioteer out of the back and clamber to the reins, fighting to control the horses as they spun and turned the chariot.

'Against my orders!' Glaukos yelled to Pig Nose, lying.

He pivoted on one leg to give himself more space, then swung his sword in a shoulder high arc. A blur of movement. Pig Nose's head remained by threads of muscle and skin. Balanced on his neck. Hot blood spurted, drenching Nireus. The head held in place by its own weight now like the boulders of Mycenae's great walls.

The Phocian's bulging eyes blinked once, glazed over and slowly closed. His head tipped forward, the strip of skin holding it tearing like wet parchment and hit the flagstones with a wet thud.

Gradually at first, like the grains of dirt beneath their feet, men of all ranks stepped out of the Mycenaean formation and strode towards Orestes. Nicostratus and his Spartans led the way, followed by the Pylians, and as Glaukos looked on with rage, the whole phalanx began to disintegrate. Chanting the returning prince's name, they lifted him off the footplate of his chariot and carried him shoulder high around it.

'Avenge my father!' Orestes cried, his sword held aloft.

The crown of truce lay trampled in the dust under warriors' feet. More and more Argives took up the call.

Neoptolemus gave the signal and a stampeding herd of chanting, cheering Myrmidons surged to join them.

'Vengeance!' they cried. 'Vengeance, vengeance!'

Nireus wiped blood from his face. 'We should get to the citadel?'

'Too late,' said Glaukos.

His brief reign over the Argive people was coming to an end. Unless he wanted to lose his head like Pig Nose and the tyrant before him, it was time to take his leave. He would depart on the watch master's chariot, before all the roads out of Mycenae were blocked by soldiers loyal to Orestes.

First, he would make Orestes pay.

'Vengeance!' came the united Myrmidon and Mycenaean voice. 'Vengeance, vengeance!'

'Recall your war band, Nireus, and return to Phocis. When I join you there we'll decide our next move.'

'We must surrender,' said Nireus. 'We have no choice. Orestes has the lower city, he'll soon have us surrounded. We must lay down our arms, prostrate ourselves, entreat him for clemency.'

'Don't be a fool! You think Orestes is going to forgive when he sees his father's rotting head on a pedestal in the throne room?'

'Who's the fool who put it there?' Nireus fired back, spit erupting from his mouth.

For Melampus! Aletes' heart cried out the name. The scrape of Aletes' blunt sword against the sharp bronze of Euthemus' blade echoed in a hideous shriek around the stone of the temple. Euthemus had let his guard down, gawping gormlessly at the pandemonium across the plain.

He had strayed too close to the man in chains who wanted him dead. The red giant who had slain Melampus was caught off guard, off balance, stumbling backwards against the offensive strikes of Aletes' blade. Rapid swipes. High. Low. High. Aletes thrust for the groin, Euthemus dodged, returned with a swipe that nearly took Aletes' head off. He crouched, Euthemus came at him leaping and thrusting downwards.

The thigh wound that would not heal. Aletes dodged to the right, anchored his body parallel to the ground with his left arm and kicked at the wound. Euthemus collapsed in on himself in agony, a moment enough for Aletes to take his blade, blunt as it was, and ram it up into Euhemus' armpit with every muscle in his body. Arterial blood rushed, Euthemus grappled for the wound. Aletes left him to bleed out.

'Vengeance, vengeance, vengeance!' The united force was coming.

Aletes heard Iphigenia cry out. Glaukos thrust with his blade held flat, Clytemnestra pushed her daughter aside and the sword slid between the former queen's ribs. She gasped but a force inside her awakened a ferocious dying energy, the final blood pumping around her body and brain allowing her to grip hold of Glaukos' hair with her nails, sinking them in, buying precious time, as Glaukos withdrew his blade and plunged again into her lung. Iphigenia obeyed the silent, ardent order in her mother's eyes to run. Run!

'Mother!' Iphigenia cried out as she turned, grabbing her long pharos, her legs restricted, wrapping around her legs like tree roots trying to trip her.

At the same time, Nireus grabbed Electra by the forearm.

'We have to go,' he told her.

Electra smiled.

She snatched the dagger from his sword belt and plunged it into the soft flesh under his bearded chin.

'No. *You* go! To Tartarus!'

She shoved him into Glaukos with all her might, her arms strong, her body tall. She knocked him back, and Nireus grabbed at Glaukos, desperately, begging him for help.

Electra hauled Iphigenia towards the temple, through the pillared porch entrance, where royal guards were running to intercept them. The guards swallowed them in their numbers and heaved the Argive princesses into the temple's inner sanctum, shutting the towering bronze doors behind them, those at the fore ready to fight off Glaukos if he came any closer.

'Vengeance, vengeance, vengeance!'

Aletes' hand dropped instinctively to his waist, feeling for the kidskin pouch that usually hung there. He needed to get Glaukos away from Iphigenia. His sling and shot had been taken from him. Howling at the top of his voice like a tormented, caged lion, he hacked futilely at his chains with his blunt sword, skinning his shins and ankles.

'Brother!' His mouth ripped at the force of the cry. 'Brother!'

Glaukos stopped, the distraction Aletes wanted.

'Come and end it, it's what you want!'

Hurling the expiring Nireus out of his way, he rushed at Aletes with his sword held high in both hands, ready to cleave the skull of his detested sibling.

'You are not my brother!' he was screaming.

Aletes tried to adjust his footing but tripped over his manacled feet. He sprawled backwards, raising his weapon in time to deflect Glaukos' sword. The force of the blow sheared Aletes' rusted blade, the muscles in his arms scorching with strain. Flat on his back, with no other way of defending himself, he looked on helplessly as Glaukos' sword rose in the air again.

'It ends at last,' rasped Glaukos, breathing hard through clenched teeth and distended nostrils. The twin-edged blade carved the air, hissing as it sliced towards Aletes.

Teucer held his sword in both hands to survive the downward power of Glaukos' slicing blade.

'Vengeance, vengeance, vengeance!'

Like ants from a disturbed nest, the streets of the lower city were filling with jubilant, ululating warriors and crudely armed citizens. As they surged towards the temple enclosure, Orestes and Neoptolemus rode chariots at their head along separate, converging streets. They were little more than a spear cast away.

Glaukos kicked Teucer in the face, and slashed his sword away, racing for where Argalus' chariot still stood. Sheathing his sword on the run, he snatched the reins and whip from the charioteer before pushing him headfirst onto the flagstones. He rode out of the courtyard as Orestes and his warriors flooded into it. Galloping north out of the city, he sped past the causeway leading up to the high-walled citadel, laying on the whip as he swung right, along the well-trodden road to Corinth.

Teucer helped Aletes to his feet. He used the point of Euthemus' dagger to prise the locking bar from the grateful Argive's manacles, waiting impatiently as Aletes did the same for him. His anxious eyes were on the brazen bull, his ears tuned to the increasingly shrill, nerve-shredding sounds escaping from it. Even without fire, the inside of the bronze behemoth had become stiflingly hot long before the bright autumn sun rose to its zenith and the boy was fast running out of air.

Teucer sprinted to the brazen bull and threw open the hatch in its metal flank. He reached inside, lifting his panting, hysterical son from its airless interior as Orestes, and then Neoptolemus, came to a halt facing Aletes.

With a creak of bronze hinges, the temple's inner sanctum doors were heaved open by milling guards. Arm in arm, Iphigenia and Electra emerged cautiously into the dazzling sunlight. Orestes clamped his eyes shut in relief.

He ran to them. 'Mother? Where's mother?'

Iphigenia was crying. Shaking her head. Orestes wrapped his arms around her and they wept. Electra took them both in her long arms.

Finally, Orestes turned. Aware of Aletes' presence. Aletes looked at Iphigenia, wanting to embrace her and take away her pain. But who was he to her? Nothing. No one.

'You kept your word, Zygouris,' Orestes said, tears for his mother in his dark eyes.

'You said you would find my sister. I owe you much and will reward you. But first I must go after the creature even Hades does not want. I will hunt him down and rip every part of his body.'

Aletes put an arm across his king and met his angry brown eyes.

'I know you have more reason than even I do, to sink your blade into Glaukos' flesh. But if you mean to reward me, let this be it. King, you are needed here. You must sit on your throne and claim it as yours. Let me go after Glaukos.'

Orestes clenched his jaw.

'It is what the gods always intended. Apollo will hold his hands over me until Glaukos' shade is imprisoned in Tartarus and he begs forgiveness for his crimes.'

Aletes could see the physical pain the decision caused Orestes. But he could not deny Aletes. Not after what he had done. The king was in his warrior's debt. He nodded an almost invisible acceptance.

'I cannot let you do this alone.'

'No! Do not listen to him brother,' Iphigenia called out, pushing through the tight press of warriors surrounding the two chariots. 'You are King of all the Argives. Surely you have some say?'

Aletes walked towards Iphigenia. His words were low and only for her.

'I would obey you anything,' he said, telling himself to have the courage to say what needed to be said. 'If you understand me at all, do not ask me to stay.'

Iphigenia looked into those eyes of silver and waited for him to change his mind. Yet she saw the eyes set from flaming rage to cool revenge and she knew she could not order him to stay. She reached out and put her palm over his hand, the hand on the hilt of his sword.

'Go!' she said, knowing with every part of her she was sending him to his death.

He took his free hand and layered it on top of hers, in turn upon his sword hand. For more than a moment, he feared he might stay.

'W-w-wide with me, Zygourith!' Neoptolemus stammered, ordering his charioteer to dismount, undress from his tunic and leather cuirass, and give them to Aletes. 'These s-stallions oth grandfather's are the s-swiftest beasts ever harnessed to an Antman's chariot. They will s-soon catch Glaukoth's plodding nags,

435

and when they d-do he will hath no choice but to s-stand and f-fight you.'

'I have your word you won't interfere?'

Aletes looked back at Iphigenia before scanning the dust blown road to Corinth. A handful of farmers and merchants travelled each way. Glaukos' chariot was long gone.

'You hath my w-word.' Neoptolemus tapped the hilt of his dead father's overly large sword, which hung awkwardly at his side. 'The Weeper oth Thades will remain sheathed, unless oth course Glaukoth looks to be getting the b-better oth you, in which case I'll be f-forced to intervene, ath I did once b-before.'

'I won't need rescuing again.'

Neoptolemus whipped the stallions' muscular haunches, causing them to snort indignantly, toss their white-blazed chestnut heads and surge into a gallop. Hour after hour, he drove them on. The rushing wind tugged at the bronze bangled top knot in his long mane, as golden as his father's was. Sweat coated the horses' rippling flanks, and flecks of foaming spittle flew from their broad muzzles. Still, they raced on, proving more than worthy of the praise Neoptolemus had lavished upon them. Eventually, they slowed to a weary trot, and when at last they came to a halt by the undulating track branching east to Zygouris and the Nemean wilderness beyond, their breathing was laboured and harsh.

It was almost dark, and the unnatural glow of a huge fire emerged on the horizon. Glaukos was sending Aletes an invitation.

'He hath lost hith wits.'

'It's a beacon, and he's lit it for me.'

'Then we go no f-further until s-sunrise. We'll camp here and when Helioth returns I'll s-scout ahead and find out what awaits uth.'

'No, we go on now. I have friends at Zygouris, they need my help.'

The familiar oak gates of Zygouris stood open and unguarded. The expansive Court of Honour was bathed in crimson from the inferno engulfing the villa. A contorting wall of flame reached up through a skeleton of smoke-blackened roof timbers like the fiery breath of the Chimera. High overhead, a billowing column of choking smoke blotted out the stars. The same infernal red glow illuminated the face of everyone watching. Powerless.

The body of the holy mother, who had spoken the words that had come to shape Aletes' life, lay in a pool of blood. Elissa, who had cared for Iphigenia, had her throat cut with two other servants. They had tried to stop Glaukos kicking Kleonike, his head pulped on one side, his eye likely to be blind.

Aletes' boyhood friend, the one who had told him about the lion, given him a stone to bring down a Trojan, shared a thousand lonely campfires. The dazed Kleonike had regained consciousness to find himself tightly bound and gagged on the ground. He could not open his left eye, his head boomed, his face pulsated as it swelled and was pomegranate red. The skin on his forehead had split at the repeated impact of Glaukos' boot and soaked into his dark curls. He instinctively reached up to feel the wound, his available eye bulging in panic when he realised his arms were stretched taut and bound with rope.

Aletes' eyes followed the rope. It was looped around the slabs of stones of the central well. A second rope ran from his bound legs to Glaukos' chariot.

Glaukos stood beside the chariot, sword in one arm, his crushed hand grasping the tail of the nearest stallion. It meant Aletes could not fight him without Glaukos first punching the unsuspecting animal where it hurt so the horse harnessed to the chariot would bolt. The chariot would hurtle forward, pulling Kleonike's body apart. His limbs would dislocate. Then with a wet, tearing sound, they would be ripped from his torso.

Neoptolemus bristled. He held the hilt of the Reaper of Shades with a spluttered curse. His celebrated father's sword was halfway from its scabbard when Aletes stopped him, clamping a restraining hand around his slender forearm.

'This fight is between us,' Aletes said to Glaukos, dismounting and drawing his own weapon. 'The prince will not interfere. Leave Kleonike out of this too.'

'Pity. I would have enjoyed plucking out his eyes on the point of my dagger and peeling the skin off his scrawny carcass.'

Neoptolemus squirmed with indignation, gripping the hide-covered frame of his chariot with a strangled cry.

'Why do you hate me?' Aletes cried, unable to stop himself from asking the question, bereft of any course of action.

Glaukos laughed. A manic, long laugh.

'I don't *hate* you. I never have. I just don't want you to exist. And you're *always* there. Always in the way.'

'I didn't ask for any of this.'

'That's right Ratshit.' The voice grated like bronze tyres on gravel. Unmistakably his. 'Keep him talking. We'll find a way.'

'Ah yes, the prophesy,' Glaukos was mocking. 'You really believe that? Any man who trains with the royal guard is going to come out a warrior, it's got nothing to do with the gods. You didn't do much to save the dynasty of Atreus today standing in your shackles.'

'Let's find out then. Man to man. Sword to sword. This is between us.'

Glaukos had left little to chance; ensuring the inferno blew into Aletes' direction. He was struggling to see, red-hot embers gusting his way. Soot stung his eyes. Thick smoke crawled down his throat and clung there, choking him.

'Horseshit!' Melampus' voice blew like a horn. Suddenly it seemed as if he were there, standing bandy legged in the dirt behind Glaukos.

'Into the horseshit!' Melampus' shade cried.

Aletes swung his sword, slicing off Glaukos' maimed hand. His incredulous eyes registered what had happened before his brain reasoned it, blinking stupefied, numb, painless, at his amputated hand in the horseshit on the stone ground.

Glaukos reacted as if under water. Slow. Heavy. Then manic

pain. Hot blood spat from the truncated limb, he staggered backwards, desperately fending off Aletes' follow up hacking sword, forcing him away from the horse and towards the blazing villa.

Aletes arced his sword across Kleonike's bonds to his legs. Yet neither horse pulled against its harness as Kleonike fumbled with the ropes to free his feet.

Glaukos was unsteady, weakened by the loss of blood, the hideous pain. Dizzy. Eyes blinking black and yellow. He had to run if he was going to live. The lead stallion snickered, flicked its tail and lifted its drooping head.

Aletes was wild now. Savage. This had to end.

'Finish him Ratshit!' Melampus bellowed. 'Finish this!'

Aletes charged at Glaukos, driving him back towards the house of flame. Part of the roof came to life like a phantom, lunging at Glaukos and setting his back on fire. He screamed out.

Aletes plunged his sword into the hollow behind Glaukos' collarbone. The whetted blade pierced his heart, he fell to his knees, and as his head dropped forward, the hatred at last melted from his defeated face.

Aletes looked for Melampus in the darkness but there was no one there.

The inhabitants of Zygouris surged around Aletes and Kleonike. Kleonike wrapped his friend in a grateful, joyous embrace, but fell to his knees in wailing suffering when he saw the body of his sister, Elissa. Aletes tried, he knew in vain, to console him, before forcing himself to break away and organise water and manpower to put out the flames.

Meanwhile, Neoptolemus had begun dragging Glaukos' corpse towards his chariot, a dark slick of blood on the stones marking his laboured progress. Aletes helped him carry the heavy body the last paces, and together they lashed it feet first behind the chariot, using one of the ropes that had restrained Kleonike.

'We s-should leave at first light. Once the horseth are r-rested and before this rat's turd starts to r-ripen.'

'I agree, we should. But I won't be going with you. I grew up among these people, I cannot abandon them while so many are grieving. I will stay to help them honour their dead, and while I am here there are others to whom I must pay my respects.'

'Oresth-esth, will be unhappy ith I go back w-without you.'

Aletes placed his hand, shaking with adrenaline, on his shoulder. 'He will understand. I trust you to speak of both our parts in what happened here.'

'You f-flatter me, Zygour-ith. My p-part in this is oth little consequence. This victory ith yours alone. All Mycenae shall learn of it and rejoice when I return.'

Neoptolemus departed shortly before dawn. Only embers burned now. Small flames sparked up from their deaths and were swiftly sent back to their tombs. As the day woke, the extent of the destruction could be seen. The main hall, where the dramatic events had unfolded and sent Aletes on his new path, was covered in a mask of black where the vivid frescos and bright tiles had once brought cheer and life into the room.

The bedchambers on the first floor had burned away and sat open to the elements where the roof had caved in. The kitchens too were all gone. The temple's tile roof had collapsed onto the Altar of Zeus when the supporting wooden columns burned through, but the flames had been prevented from spreading to the adjacent workshops and stores by continually soaking them with water.

Soot-blackened and exhausted, the people of Zygouris halted at last to rest and eat a frugal repast. Aletes joined them, and with the morning sun drying the sweat upon his back, the stench of burning coating his throat and nostrils, he helped them build a funeral pyre for each of the dead.

A bull calf was slaughtered and roasted whole over an open fire, close to the smouldering ruins of the kitchen annex. With the holy mother dead, and no other seer present to officiate, Aletes was pressed into taking the role. He poured a libation of wine and calf's blood on each pyre, placing payment for the ferryman in the mouth of the washed and shrouded corpse upon it. Prayers and tearful eulogies followed, and flaming brands were used to light the pyres. Wood and flesh burned swiftly, and with the formal proceedings over, a variety of rustic musical instruments appeared, and the singing, dancing, and feasting commenced. Aletes ate and drank his fill, dancing a little stiffly with the mothers and daughters of Zygouris' artisans. Afternoon became early evening, and satisfied no one would miss him, he slipped away.

The riverbed looked exactly as he remembered it. The undergrowth along either bank was somewhat greener perhaps, due to the recent rain. Aletes had no trouble finding the mound of earth and rocks where Argus was buried. He unfolded the scrap of cloth he carried and placed succulent cuts of beef on the flattened mound. With a hard lump constricting his throat he sat cross-legged on the ground, apologised for his long absence, and thanked Argus again for what he had done, speaking aloud.

'Without you my friend, I could not have helped Iphigenia. I will never forget that.'

Bright daylight had faded to gloaming by the time Aletes climbed reluctantly to his feet and loped from the ancient riverbed. He followed a little-used path that took him past the high rocks and secluded pool where, long ago, Glaukos and his henchmen had brutally beaten him. For a moment, he felt the familiar regret of a life of brothers that could have been. Swimming together in that pool, play-fighting, bantering, bonded with unbreakable love. A life that never was.

He stroked the kink in the bridge of his nose as he clambered up a rugged, wooded hillside, coming at last to the hidden cave where Danaea's shrine was located. The undisturbed screen of brush across its narrow entrance told Aletes no one had been there during his absence. He lit a small fire to keep the darkness and night chill at bay. He took the terracotta figurine from the pouch around his neck, swept away the cobwebs and dust, and placed it on the shrine.

Much later, the happy flow of conversation was interrupted by an owl hooting in the trees outside the cave. The sound transported him back to the moonlit orchard at Zygouris all those years ago. Aletes fell silent, and as his thoughts drifted back to that short yet blissful meeting with Iphigenia, his spirits plunged. Soon he would return to Mycenae and take his leave of her for the last time.

'I would rather stay here. I could find somewhere to live and help Kleonike tend the new master's herds. I was happy in the old days.'

'You are deluding yourself,' Danaea replied. '*You* are the new master of Zygouris, and tomorrow you must return to Mycenae and take your rightful place among your fellow lords. We cannot hide from our lives. You must stand tall, unbowed, and trust Apollo to ensure you are justly rewarded.'

'There is only one reward I covet but I would lose my tongue if I were to ask for it.'

Glaukos' bloated head had replaced Agamemnon's in the Palace of Mycenae. It sat on the fluted alabaster pedestal on the dais at the front of the congested audience hall. The Greek kings had assembled to pledge allegiance to the new King of Mycenae, joining his council of advisers. A day earlier they had honoured the beloved former queen at her cremation, feasting into the night to celebrate her life.

444

Aletes scanned the hall for Iphigenia. The only women present were palace servants, pouring wine from slim-necked jars into the drinking horns and silver cups of thirsty, bleary-eyed warlords. As soon as King Orestes disbanded this conclave of kings, Iphigenia was certain to depart with the important ally he had united her with to secure the Argive coalition.

'Brother!'

The new King of the Argives glowed with renewed health and optimism as he descended the marble steps of the platform and walked towards Aletes with arms outstretched.

Orestes wore a plain white chiton, unarmed but for the gold hilted dagger displayed on his leather belt. His dark beard had been neatly trimmed and shaped into a wedge of perfect circular hairs, and upon his washed and sweet-scented locks of hair he wore the gold crown of the Argives. He had risen from the centre of a row of ornate, high-backed chairs, a drunk Neoptolemus and several other rugged, hard drinking warlords to his left. To his right, the first chair was unoccupied. Next to that, his guests of honour, Teucer, and his bright-eyed young son. Beyond them, more high-ranking warlords.

Orestes wrapped his arms around his friend and slapped his back.

'Take your place on this dais beside me knowing you are as much a part of my flesh as my sisters. This seat is traditionally reserved for the champion of Mycenae and all the Argives. It is now your seat, Aletes of Zygouris. The Dorians will return and when they do, I will be in need of a champion. The many kings you see around you considered your appointment this morning, and when they voted, their decision was unanimous. There will of course be a formal ceremony at the Temple of Zeus, to seek approval of all the gods. But after everything you have done for me, my sister, and the people of this city, no one could doubt the wisdom of the decision we have made.'

Aletes did not trust himself to speak. He did as Orestes urged and stepped onto the dais.

He looked for Iphigenia again. The kings of Argolis rose to their feet as one. Clapping. Cheering. Chanting his name. Stalwart, armour-clad royal guards joined in, pounding lion-emblazoned shields, or the butts of their long spears on the tiled floor.

'Zygouris, Zygouris, Zygouris!'

Orestes raised his arms aloft and gestured for silence. Once order was restored, he clamped his hand on Aletes' shoulder and drew him in for a conversation for his ears alone.

'I have asked my sister if she will agree to marry you.'

Aletes legs almost buckled. His mother was right, it was his destiny to return. Happiness awaited—

'I am sorry to say she does not wish the marriage,' Orestes continued.

It was a cruel ploy, but a necessary one. Orestes was watching for Aletes' face. Confirmed. He had believed in the dungeon that Aletes loved her. He had been unsure of Iphigenia's feelings until he had seen the same look on her face before it transformed to sadness. She had her reasons.

'Unlike my father,' Orestes continued, 'I will not arrange her marriage. She has been through too much. She has chosen to join the Daughters of Artemis at the goddess' temple in Tauris. Perhaps in time—'

'No,' Aletes interrupted. 'No, she must do as she wills. I would not want it any other way.'

'She believes the House of Atreus is cursed. I am not sure if you know that two of her husbands died. The people of Mycenae began to talk. She had already decided to go to Tauris. Then she was promised to Achilles and he too perished.'

Aletes nodded. His ears had stopped registering.

'Aletes?' The prince spoke as he sat beside him. 'Know this. You are my brother.'

29

Destiny

Iphigenia knelt alone in the Temple of Zeus watching the candles glow. Her mother's flame stood tall and proud. Her father's light drew the shadow of a giant, burning broad and strong as if his name would never be extinguished. She lit another candle for all the warriors who had died in the struggle with Troy. One flame, else the temple would have been set alight like a funeral pyre for so many thousands of souls. One war was over. Another had begun. The Dorians had been driven away for now. They would return.

Her brother was a good man; he would make a great king. She considered his words again. The offer of marriage to his new champion. Iphigenia loved Aletes, that was true. That was why she must never marry him. She did not want to be a pawn in another ill-fated marriage. Liodes, Neleus, Achilles. It was clear the curse of the House of Atreus would see Aletes dead if they were to be married. It was better for all if she joined the Daughters of Artemis at the goddess' temple in Tauris.

Aletes stepped into the inner sanctum, Zeus on his golden throne as tall and wide as the entire wall of the temple.

Iphigenia turned. She wore a pleated black pharos, which brushed the top of her silver filigreed slippers. Her eyes had been rimmed with kohl, making them shine brilliantly, her lips were stained with red berries.

What need for warriors and wars, Aletes realised in that moment. Just send in denied love and watch it slay a man without a blade.

Aletes held out the silver heron ring in the palm of his hand.

'You were right, it did protect me, and it did bring me good fortune. I return it in the hope it will bring you some comfort now, as you told me it once belonged to your mother. I am so sorry for your loss.'

Iphigenia looked at the ring and into those grey eyes. For five beats of each of their hearts they remained there, listening to each other's unspoken words.

Aletes nodded, throat dry, nausea rising from the pit of his stomach. He believed he had spoken farewell, but no words had left his mouth. He turned and stepped away from the altar, into the dazzling light of the aisle. He moved forward on numb legs.

'You just going to let her go, Ratshit?'

Aletes walked on, ignoring Melampus' voice in his ears.

Now the bandy legs were in front of him. Scratching a deep line in the stone with his spear.

'This is as far as you go, Ratshit.'

Aletes knew he could not really be there, that it was only his shade, but he seemed as real as if he breathed the same air. Aletes looked down past the familiar hairless head, to the stubborn brown eyes of the only father he had ever known. How he missed Melampus.

'Why are you always right?' he said in a low voice. 'It's irritating.'

Aletes turned and strode back to Iphigenia. Courage like he had never known before. Fear threatening to take his legs from beneath him.

'What if *you* are my destiny? What if I am yours?'

He spoke as he walked, he walked as he swung his arms up at the at the mammoth throned statue of Zeus.

'Even the mighty Zeus cannot change fate. He can weigh us on his golden scales, but he cannot step between us.'

Aletes was speaking loudly now, almost a shout, almost a cry from the heart.

'Zeus cannot interfere. None of the gods can. Our paths have been weaved as one by the Fates. Our lives have always led to each other. They led me to you in the riverbed, they led me to you in depths of Ironmen lands, they led me to you here. Do not believe I deem myself worthy of you, I do not. Do not be fooled by my brave words, I fear your rejection. But I know I would rather be denied by your words than risk not saying mine.'

Iphigenia looked up at the towering statue of Zeus as if she were seeking an answer. She placed her hand over her eyes to shield them from the brilliant sun. A fork of light struck the silver heron ring she had placed on her finger, speared back to the glorious statue, and rebounded onto Aletes' face. Illuminating. Showing her the way.

Silver light. Silver eyes. The eyes of the man she loved.

Aletes stepped towards her. A single combat. Defenceless. At her mercy.

A smile swept across her face like the sun across the sky. Aletes kissed her and drew her to him.

'What took you so long, Ratshit?' growled Melampus' shade. 'I was losing my hair watching that performance.'

'I had a stone in my sandal,' Aletes said, taking Iphigenia's hand.

Iphigenia looked to where he was speaking, but did not ask to whom he was talking, as she believed she knew.

She tipped her head to the side and lent on Aletes' shoulder, into his wrapped arms. She held out her hand and the silver of the heron ring caught the light again, shooting into Zeus' sceptre like lightning.

'At least I have a ring,' she said.

*

EPILOGUE

I was Iphigenia. Daughter of Queen Clytemnestra.

Another power is coming, greater than the mighty Argives. The men of other kings.

They will take my written words, erase them one by one. A language defeated and buried.

The kingdom of Mycenae will blow on the dust.

New kings will tell stories of the ruthless Agamemnon, who killed his daughter on the Altar of Zeus to sail with his warships to Troy.

If you read these words, know this.

This was my story.

For I lived. I lived.

Printed in Great Britain
by Amazon